I0633948

*Canaan's Secret's suspense and intriguing plot made for a great read. It was so good I read it twice, and it was even better the second time.*
Wanda Snow Porter

*I love the mysticism and characters in these books. Always a hypnotic page turner and can't put it down. Gamble is a great story-teller. I can't wait for the next one in the series. One of my favorite authors.*
Amazon Reviewer

*Give me a book that opens with what looks like a religious ritual killing ...and an author who knows how to keep readers dangling, and you've got me from the first page. That's what R. Lawson Gamble gives us in Canaan's Secret. Sound like a good read? It definitely is...*
Readers' Favorite Five Star Review

Also By R Lawson Gamble

Zack Tolliver, FBI

The Other
Mestaclocan
Zaca
Cat
Under Desert Sand

Other Books

Payu's Journey (YA)

Los Alamos Valley
(Arcadia Press)

**All Available AT Amazon.com**

# CANAAN'S SECRET

## A Novel

Zack Tolliver, FBI Series, Book Six

## R LAWSON GAMBLE

This is a work of fiction. Although the author describes many actual locations, events, organizations, and historical figures, any resemblance to other persons living or dead is entirely coincidental.

CANAAN'S SECRET Copyright © 2018
R Lawson Gamble
All Rights Reserved

R Lawson Gamble Books
Cover by Kristallynn Designs
ISBN 9780692167755 Rich Gamble Associates

No part of this book may be used or reproduced in any manner whatsoever without written permission from the author except in the case of brief quotations embodied in critical articles and reviews

For My Mother
as she approaches her 98th Birthday

Special Thanks to my wife Ann, for reading, encouraging, and praising (whether deserved or not), friend Craig Snell and fellow authors Wanda Snow Porter and Barbara Hodges for reading and contributing constructive observations.

# CHAPTER ONE

It was as foretold. He was making a delivery to the Quality Inn in Kanab when he saw the boy lounging by the pool, shirtless, feet dangling in the water, leaning back on his elbows to catch the meager rays of the early spring sun. The boy's age, gender, hair, eyes, and black skin all matched the description given him by the Voice.

He prayed that night and waited patiently for a sign. It came with the first hint of dawn, a red flaming cross projected on the wall—and then the Voice. It told him what must be done.

He made casual inquiries and learned the boy was sixteen years old, the son of the innkeeper. The boy attended the local high school, walked there and back, was on the school wrestling team. His athleticism might be a concern, but the element of surprise should overcome it.

The next week he spent watching the boy from his car. He parked near the Inn, at a different place each time, even switched vehicles occasionally. He followed the boy when he walked to school and when he walked home after practice, looking for any variance in routine. There never was.

His best chance would come during the walk home. Dusk would shroud detail and obscure activity just enough to leave doubt—until it was all over. Midweek would be best, when townspeople went about their set routines in mesmerized lockstep, like a column of ants. He decided it should be Wednesday.

Tuesday night he gathered his tools and walked through his procedures in minute detail, considering every possibility. He would not sleep until every doubt was vanquished, every conceivable mishap anticipated.

Wednesday dawn broke to dark clouds and occasional rain. From this he knew his mission was blessed. Although filled with restless eagerness through the long day he remained resolute, disciplined, kept his routine. No one must suspect this day was different from any other. At five p.m. he entered the dark security of the barn, removed the rear seats from the Travelall, and put his tools in place. He drove slowly toward Kanab, maintaining his speed just as he'd practiced so as to reach the selected section of sidewalk at the perfect time. There was no traffic. When he arrived, the boy was right where he needed him to be. It should have been perfect.

But there was a problem. Someone was with the boy.

He accelerated, drove on, cursing his luck. How could this be? The boy had always been alone. Who was this person? Why today? He drove on to the next intersection, made a U-turn and approached again from the opposite side. The boy's companion was a girl. He saw the short plaid skirt beneath the raincoat, the long hair under the cap. He crawled by. They never glanced up. He slammed his fist on the steering wheel in frustration. It should have been this boy, on this day.

He glanced in the rearview mirror and his eyes widened. The girl had turned away, was walking up a sidewalk to a house. She was home. The boy was alone now. He breathed out, felt his excitement renew. His faith had been tested and was vindicated. He steered the Travelall into a wide turn and crept back. The boy looked up as the vehicle came alongside.

It all went according to plan—the request for directions, the soaked rag over the boy's face, catching him as his legs collapsed, lifting him into the back seat.

No one was watching, no one had noticed. He drove home, observing every traffic law. Back in the barn, he closed the large sliding door and began preparations for the next step. His actions were efficient, every move had been rehearsed. His timing at this phase was critical. The boy must be completely ready while still unconscious.

Everything was going as planned, which was not surprising, really, since it had all been foretold.

# CHAPTER TWO

Canaan Mountain rose as a sheer wall, towering three thousand feet above the arid plain, its red tinted cliffs glowing like heaven's gateway in the early morning sun. Below, the tiny buildings in the twin towns of Hildale, Utah, and Colorado City, Arizona were still nestled in shadow.

On this morning, two men rested on a sandstone ledge high on the mountain near its wide summit plateau, rifles across their knees. In front of them the fortress-like cliffs fell away, behind them the mesa top broke into a wonderland of domes, pinnacles, hoodoos and canyons. Isolated groves of stunted pine poked up here and there like a bad haircut, partially obscuring the view across this unnatural wonderland that stretched all the way north to the summits of the East and West Temples and the Watchman in Zion National Park. Against a slowly bluing sky it looked like a land with its skin turned inside out, the crusted barren undersurface now on top, the stiff gnarly pines resembling the roots of submerged trees.

The men who rested there were hunters, professional guides on a busman's holiday with special permits to explore the extent of proliferation of Bighorn sheep in the Canaan Mountain Wilderness Study Area. The sheep had been reintroduced to nearby Zion National Park back in 1977; the guides hoped to establish that there was an increase in the sheep population sufficient to support occasional hunting, with a view to bringing in clients on a limited, but extremely well paid basis. The men had risen long before the sun to ascend the nine-mile Water Canyon trail. Now they paused to share a thermos of hot tea.

Despite the sun, the air was chill and the stone slab beneath them cold. White vapor columned up from the thermos mouth. The sweet incense smell of Juniper brush around them enhanced their enjoyment of the spiced tea. They looked out over a stunning vista, all the way across the

Uinkaret Plateau, mile upon mile of flat and seemingly uninhabited land stretching all the way to the rugged Virgin River Valley of Arizona.

"What do you reckon those vultures are after, Tubs?" asked one of the hunters.

Tubs glanced at the birds. The nickname ill-suited Jack LeBaron, a tall, lean man with Lincolnesque gaunt cheeks and outsized arms and hands. With typical satirical humor his fellow woodsmen had awarded him the moniker Tubby; it stuck and was now shortened to Tubs. His skin was weathered and brown, his blue eyes shimmered against the dark background of his face.

"Must be something big to attract so many of 'em. A range heifer, mebbe, or an elk." He shrugged. "On the other hand, it might be nothin' more than a nice warm updraft they're enjoying."

His companion, whose name was Randy Musser, removed his flat brimmed hat and absently studied the sweat in the headliner. He was a robust man and as fair as his companion was dark, with hair the color of straw and green eyes that tended toward hazel in this early morning light. He replaced the hat and tapped it into place.

"You know this mountain, Tubs. Where are we going to find some sheep?"

Tubs grinned, stood, and stretched his arms high above his head. "Follow me, Pilgrim," he said, putting on his best John Wayne accent and led the way up the slope.

Randy kept pace. Both men were in good physical shape, their movements efficient. The trail they followed angled away from the precipice and gained more elevation before it ventured back toward the cliff edge again. They emerged into a meadow of bristle-topped Indian grass waving in the breeze like ripples in a pond.

In the center of the meadow, partially hidden by the tall grass, was a strange wooden structure much like a huge barrel, derelict, slats falling askew, its metal rings rusted. A six-foot spindle-like shaft extended from it to another wooden device, even more decayed, apparently the remains of a similar but smaller cylinder. Beyond the machines, a large groove had been carved through the sandstone cliff edge as wide as two men shoulder to shoulder.

"This the Windlass, is it?" Randy stared, fascinated. "I've heard about it, how in the early days the pioneers used it to lower timber down the cliff to build their houses."

Tubs shook his head in wonder. "Them Mormons never shirked work."

"God shows the way so man can make it happen," Randy said, a certain ring of pride in his tone. "The settlements didn't get built by themselves."

"Reckon not." Tub's eye went back to the movement of the birds, more visible now. The circling scavengers seemed more frantic and their numbers had increased. The black mounds of sitting vultures studded the lower tree branches.

Tubs nudged Randy and pointed. "Them birds is just over there. I'm gonna go take a look since we're this close."

A flash of annoyance crossed Randy's face.

"Don't fret," Tubs said. "It's right along our way." He started off without waiting for a reply.

They worked their way north, away from the cliff edge. Tubs led the way through a thick stand of dwarf pines and almost stepped over the edge of an abrupt canyon wall that slashed across their path. It fell away two hundred feet or more. Tubs peered over. He could see the tops of trees in a narrow canyon far below. Across from him, the far canyon wall was less than a hundred feet distant, but was considerably higher with tall pines where vultures roosted and others wheeled above against the cloudless blue sky. At the appearance of the men, wings fluttered and red eyes glared. Even from this distance, the foul reek of the birds came to them.

"Whatever they're after, it's down there." Tubs craned his neck, trying to see beyond the curvature of the cliff face. "It'd be easy for some critter to fall down there. I damn near did."

"If you had fallen there, by the time I got down to you, there'd be nothing but bones." Randy covered his nose. "Are we about done here? This place stinks."

Tubs glanced at Randy and stepped back from the edge. "Sure, okay." He looked ahead where the ground rose beyond the canyon. "We should be able to skirt around it up that way."

They resumed their northerly path, staying on the shoulder of the canyon where smooth sandstone made hiking easier.

Tub's eyes flicked here and there in constant inspection as he walked, his brain assessing unconsciously, an old woodsman habit. Now something caused him to stop and stare down into the canyon.

"You see that?" He pointed.

"What?"

"That light, that reflection. Somethin' down there is reflecting the sunlight."

"Must be a piece of glass or a beer can."

"No, it reflects like metal, a shiny metal surface."

Randy stared, looked at Tubs. "Okay...so...?"

"So we got to go down and see what it is."

"Why on earth do we need to do that?"

"Think about it," Tubs said. "We're here because of the vultures. They're here because something big and dead is down there. That reflection could be polished metal of some kind. Could be anythin'—belt buckle, rifle, one a' them mountain bikes, who knows? But whatever it is, it most likely was brought down there by a human. An' that human could still be down there." He looked at Randy, shook his head. "We can't walk away now."

6

# CHAPTER THREE

Deputy Marshal Jeffrey Danes Harlow tilted his Stetson hat back on curly salt and pepper hair and stared at the scene with a mixture of fascination and horror. He stood in a natural bower at the very bottom of a slot canyon. Intertwining branches of short but thick Pinyon pine formed a barrier behind him, in fact so concealed this opening he wondered how the hunters had found it in the first place. The small meadow backed against the smooth surface of the cliff face—smooth except for the gash where a twenty-foot high slab had broken away and fallen forward, eons ago, leaving a cavity behind it. It lay there like an open Murphy bed, protruding forward on the canyon floor.

Suspended above the platform was the body of a young boy pierced through by a two-foot long wooden stake fixed in the stone slab beneath him. Blood, black as tar from the sun, dried in rivulets and rubbery pools on the rough sandstone surface and ran over the edge of the slab and down the sides in congealed drips like icing on a cake. The boy was no more than fifteen years old, dressed in a white toga-like garment that contrasted with his dark skin. Dried blood surrounded gashes in the sheet where the buzzards had worked. The boy's face was contorted, his mouth open as if screaming the moment the stake pierced his body. Bluebottle flies buzzed a constant background noise; the smell of dried blood and bowel contents stewing in the high-altitude sun suffused the area.

Tubs stood with the stock of his rifle resting on the ground and gestured with his other hand. "You ever see somethin' like this before?"

Harlow breathed out. "Hell, no," he said. He put his sleeve over his nose.

Randy Musser sat on a rock, hunched over. He'd lost the contents of his stomach earlier when they'd first discovered the scene. His innards were still in turmoil.

"What will you do now?"

Harlow glanced at Tubs, and back at the body. "First thing, I'm calling for help." He pulled his eyes away. "Where'd you go to get a cell signal to call me?"

Tubs pointed with his rifle barrel. "Just up this arroyo a hundred yards or so."

The deputy hurried off.

Tubs stepped closer to the slab and inspected it closely. "Who you reckon could've done this?"

Randy angled his head toward him without looking up. "Some sick nut, obviously."

Tubs let his long fingers play along the surface of the stone. He glanced up at the smooth cliff face above the cave opening. "There's somethin' etched up there. Kinda like petroglyphs. I bet this was some kind of sacred site for the Indians." He peered at the body. "Maybe some Indians done this."

There was no response from Randy who remained bent over, eyes to the ground.

"You don't look so good, partner," Tubs said with a shake of his head.

Tree branches moved. The deputy entered the clearing. "You didn't touch anything, did you?" he said, eyeing Tubs.

"Nope. Jus' lookin' around."

Randy glanced up at Harlow. "You got help coming?"

Harlow nodded. "The other boys are on their way up, should be here soon. Just now I called the Washington County Sheriff's office. We're gonna need all the help we can get."

Tubs eyed Harlow. "Aren't you the deputy marshal who can't work in the State of Arizona, only in Utah?"

"We're not in Arizona now," Harlow said, an edge to his voice. He wore the standard police uniform for the Colorado City Marshal's Office, the black-billed cap with 'Marshal' in white letters, black undershirt peeking from beneath a gray uniform shirt with black epaulets. The colorful

'Marshal's Office' badge on his right shoulder showed a sunrise over rust-colored cliffs. He wore a glistening silver badge over his left shirt pocket.

"Thet why you here all alone?" Tubs asked. A duty team from the Colorado City Marshal's Office usually meant two deputies.

Harlow stared at the cave mouth. "Is somebody in there?"

"In there? Nobody's in there," Tubs said. "It's only us here."

Harlow stared at Tubs with raised eyebrows. "I just saw something move in there." He turned and worked his way around the slab. With another glance back at Tubs, he started up the heaped rubble toward the dark entrance. At the cave mouth, he unlatched his gun in its holster.

"You in there, come out now."

There was no response. Harlow pulled his gun and removed his flashlight from his duty belt. With the light poised over his pointed gun, he disappeared into the cave.

The hunters watched the flashlight's beam move here and there in the darkness. There was a muffled exclamation. Soon after Deputy Harlow emerged and climbed quickly down to them.

Tubs started toward the cave.

"You're fine. Just stay where you are," the deputy said. His radio came to life. "Harlow, where the hell are you? Are you in that slot canyon?"

"Oh, thank God," Harlow said. He pushed the button. "Yeah, I'm down here. You got to walk north along the rim about a hundred yards. You'll come to a rock fall. You can come down that. At the bottom, head south along the east wall. You'll find me."

Randy peered up at Harlow. "Can we go now?"

Tubs grinned. "An' miss all the fun?"

Harlow shook his head. "Sorry. I can't let you two go until the officers have a chance to talk to you."

Tubs studied him with curious eyes. "What'd you see in the cave?"

Harlow didn't meet his gaze. "Nothing. Just lots of bones."

The two hunters stared at him.

"What kind of bones?" Tubs asked.

Harlow said nothing.

"You mean human bones?"

Harlow nodded. "Looks like it."

"Christ," Randy murmured.

"Mebbe this is some kind of a cult," Tubs said.

Harlow shrugged.

Tubs nodded toward the body. "You know this guy?"

"Never seen him before." Harlow leveled his gaze at Tubs. "Have you?"

Tubs shook his head.

"I know him."

They turned and looked at Randy, who was standing now, although not too steady.

"I saw him once in Kanab at the Quality Inn," Randy said. "I think he's the Innkeeper's boy."

"George Wilson's boy?" Harlow took out his notebook.

Randy shrugged. "Maybe."

They heard voices beyond the trees.

"Over here," Harlow yelled.

After considerable crashing and hollering, two men in deputy marshal uniforms identical to Harlow's burst out of the brush into the clearing. The men were bookends, both very fair with round faces and thick necks, and wearing identical rimless dark glasses.

"Here you are, Harlow, you scoundrel. What the devil did you..." The man's voice trailed off as he saw the body on the slab for the first time.

The other deputy stared and whistled. "Holy...!"

"Did he fall off the cliff or somethin'?" the first deputy asked.

Tubs gave a dry chuckle. "Yeah, took off his clothes, wrapped himself in that there white sheet, and dove right onto that stake."

The second officer glared at Tubs. "Who's this wise ass?"

"These are the two men who found the body. They're the ones called me."

The second officer, whose nametag read Stanley Taylor, eyed the two hunters. "You guys hunting? You follow a deer down here?"

"We saw the buzzards," Randy explained, gesturing toward the trees and the circling birds.

"You know what I think, Stan?" LeRoy Taylor, the first deputy, said.

"Uh-uh."

"I think this is some kind of sacrifice, like maybe some Indians from hereabouts up to somethin'."

"Maybe it's a Blood Atonement," Stanley said.

Harlow gave a grim smile. "If it's Blood Atonement, the killer had a long list." He pointed at the cave. "There are enough bones in there for a whole lot of people."

# CHAPTER FOUR

"Zack, I have to go to Kanab tomorrow." Libby was at the sink, her eyes on the soapy dish in her hands, her back to the breakfast table where Zack savored his last sips of coffee.

"Kanab, Utah?" Zack's blue eyes were lazy with sleep. He always succumbed to torpor when the smell of fried eggs in butter blended with the acrid scent of coffee in this room of a morning, when the sun beamed warm through the southeast window, and Libby stood busy at the stove or sink, tall and striking, chatting about whatever was on her mind.

"Is there another Kanab I don't know about?"

Still sleepy, Zack missed the barb. "Your sister?"

Libby rinsed the plate, carefully wiped it, placed it in the drying rack and turned to face her husband. "Yes, Emma."

"Just a visit, or is something wrong?" Zack propped his eyes open a bit wider.

"She's worried about something to do with Pru." Libby wiped her hands on her apron, came and sat at the table. "She wasn't clear what it's about, tried to laugh it off, but I can tell it bothers her."

Zack smiled. "It's not easy raising a teenage girl by yourself."

"I keep thinking how Emma's voice sounded on the phone last night, the way she kept drifting off the subject, the underlying tone of, well, fear, almost. It might have been fear." Her earnest eyes engaged Zack. "It's more than that, Zack. Something is going on, but I couldn't get her to tell me what it is."

Zack hesitated. "It's a long drive up there. Did she actually say something was wrong? You know how Emma can be, well—"

"Dramatic. Yes, I know. I thought that at first right after I hung up. That's why I didn't say anything to you then. But I thought about it last night and again this morning. I'm convinced something's wrong, and she's not going to tell me, not over the phone, anyway." Libby took it up a notch. "I have to do this, Zack."

Zack reached over and put his hand on Libby's arm. "Then you'd better go, I guess. What's your plan?"

"I'll spend today getting everything ready for you and Bernie and drive up there early tomorrow morning. I'll stay the night, at least. You and Bernie will be okay, won't you?" She stood and smiled. "I'll probably end up driving home the very next day."

Libby went back to the sink, picked up a sponge and wiped down the counter. "Everything is probably fine; I just have to know for sure."

Zack knew Libby had always felt more than a sister's usual sense of responsibility for Emma—for all her younger siblings, for that matter. After her father died, all too soon, she'd taken over running the ranch and the household. Her mother was grief-stricken and no help. Libby was the oldest child by a number of years, the result of her parents' whirlwind love affair. Reality came later, her father needed all his strength and focus to revive a foundering cattle operation. The next child didn't arrive for another five years. After her father's death, Libby found herself feeding three youngsters and bundling them off to school every morning as well as feeding and caring for her mother, all before her daily meeting with the foreman who always waited patiently in the parlor for his instructions of the day. Although the children were now adults and had their own lives, they still did not hesitate to call Libby when anything went wrong. Libby always responded. Zack learned long ago not to intervene.

* * * * *

The two-hour drive to Kanab in the early morning light provided Libby with a lot of time to think. Despite her worries, her first thoughts were of the magnificent scenery around her, the massive red rock formations and rising buttes sharp against the dawn sky, views she had seen all her life yet always awoke in her a sense of wonder. She understood in a general way the geology of this land. She knew her home, south of the Little Colorado River Gorge, represented one period in geological time, the area beyond the North Rim of the Grand Canyon another and the abruptly rising lands of the Grand Staircase an even more recent epoch, all of it a crazy geological-chronological pattern. Libby sighed and just contented herself with admiring the steel blue sky behind red-rock buttes.

The trip would bring her almost to Page, Arizona, very close to Zack's old ranch, his home when they first met. She was drawn to him right away by his intense blue eyes and earnest manner. Later she grew to admire the love and respect he showed the Navajo people, and sympathized with his wholehearted, if sometimes flawed attempts to understand everything about the Dine culture. His complete acceptance of the people and their traditions assured success in a role most FBI agents would not have wanted in the first place. She smiled, thinking about it. It was not a choice assignment, but he had turned it into one.

Their marriage became a partnership as well as a love match; both had been in their early thirties, Libby was a widow. Each had lives, careers, and respected each other's need to continue them. The rough patch in the road came with the birth of little Bernie. Libby cut back on her work, hired a man to help train the dogs and look after the horses. Zack continued as an FBI agent, consultant and lecturer, a very full schedule, leaving little time for family. Left on her own more and more, Libby grew increasingly resentful.

It came to a head one awful day when Zack's work followed him home, quite literally, in the form of a Navajo Witch intent upon murder and mayhem. Libby and Bernie barely escaped with their lives. Later, Libby gave Zack an ultimatum: quit his job, stay home and be a father—or move out. Zack reluctantly moved out.

She could smile about it now. The separation had been short, just six months. Zack decided to retire from the FBI following a narrow escape of his own and the realization he might never see his son grow to manhood. He continued his consulting work and his lecturing, which took far less time. They were once again a family.

Libby saw the sign for the turnoff to Route 89 A. She steered toward Lees Ferry, and accelerated the Subaru down the empty highway. Her thoughts now drifted to her sister.

Although a widow, Emma was young and attractive and men of the Mormon Church in Kanab took notice. But she was not a member of the faith and therefore could not marry in the temple, an obstacle to her suitors. She confided to Libby she was feeling subtle but consistent pressure to convert to Mormonism. Meanwhile, her daughter Pru had grown into a young woman every bit as attractive as her mother. It wasn't long before she too caught the attention of the Mormon men.

Libby snorted to herself. Whatever was bothering her sister likely had to do with all the attention the men of the Latter-day Saints were showering upon mother and daughter.

# CHAPTER FIVE

Zack put his mug of coffee on the kitchen table and sat down. Little Bernie was fed, Libby had seen to that, and she'd guided him through his bathroom maneuvers before she left. The boy was now engaged in his own imaginative world with some small action figures in a pool of sunshine in his bedroom.

Zack reached for the paper, the Saturday afternoon edition of the Arizona Daily Sun. Talking to Libby, helping her get away, he never got the chance to read it. He flipped it open and stared at the bold headline: "Deranged Killer in Utah Mountains." The article described a gruesome discovery made by a pair of hunting guides drawn by vultures to an isolated gulch in the Canaan Mountain Wilderness Study Area. "Descending into the gulch, they found a deceased young male. Marshals responding to the scene speculated he might have fallen from the cliff above, a distance of several hundred feet. The possibility of murder has also been raised. Some bones found in a cavity in the cliff face nearby are being analyzed. The victim has not yet been identified. Colorado City Marshals are cooperating with the County Sheriff's Department and the BLM to determine, etc., etc."

He skipped through the article hunting for factual information. There wasn't much. A marshal from Colorado City, Utah had been the first to respond. He was soon joined by more marshals, members of the Sheriff's Department of Washington County, and a representative of the Bureau of Land Management.

Zack put the paper down, went to his study and Googled the Canaan Mountain Wilderness. He found it had been established in a bill presented to the 110th Congress 2nd Session on April 8, 2008 setting aside 44,295 acres on Canaan Mountain to be administrated by the Secretary of the Interior. In many particulars, including tribal Indian rights, the normal practices of the state in regard to the land would continue. Access, however, was under the authority of the BLM.

Shaking his head, he put the computer to sleep and walked back to his coffee, aware of the administrative mess about to occur up there in terms of law enforcement, with no one sure who was actually in charge. He had just experienced a similar situation; his last case before retiring from the FBI, in fact. He'd been lucky with the cooperation and assistance given him, but this? Throw a bunch of fundamentalist town marshals into the fray and no telling what would happen.

Zack's thoughts turned to Libby. She was headed to Kanab, Utah, no more than twenty-five miles from the crime scene as the crow flies, probably forty miles by road; entirely too close to the uproar, in Zack's estimation. He decided he needed more information. He thought about people he knew who might help and called the number of a BLM acquaintance for whom he'd once done a favor.

"Hello, Butch? Zack Tolliver here. Sorry to bother you at home."

"Well, hey, Zack. How are you?"

"I'm just fine. How is everything in Needles?"

"After you left, it all slowed down to a crawl," Butch said with a chuckle. "You tend to stir things up."

Zack laughed. "Not anymore, Butch. I retired from the FBI. I'm a stay-at-home dad now."

There was a pause. "Well, now, I'd heard you were contemplating doing that, just never thought you really would. How's it going?"

"So far, I love it. I've learned it's one thing to have a family, it's another to actually be part of it." Zack paused. "But I didn't call you to describe my familial bliss. I called to see what you know about the killing they are reporting up in Utah."

"The Canaan Mountain thing? What's your interest?"

"Not so much an interest as a concern. Libby, my wife, is visiting her sister in Kanab. Maybe I'm being overprotective, but I'd like to know how much of a mess this thing could turn into."

"Hmmm, yes, I've been hearing bits and pieces. It's most likely being handled out of the Kanab BLM office. I don't know anybody there, but I do know somebody in St. George. They share that area; he might know something. Why don't I give him a call, get back to you."

After that, Zack peeked in on Bernie, still occupied with his little soldiers defending a fort made from Popsicle sticks. Zack stretched, yawned, and walked out on the front porch. He'd have to head down to the barn soon to care the horses and dogs, but he didn't want to get involved in something else until he heard back from Butch—just a feeling he had.

It was still early in the year. The sun mingled in the tops of the pines projecting bars of light and shadow across the front lawn and driveway. The smell of them was in the air. He breathed it in and gazed at the tops of the trees marching up to the ridge summit like an army of green soldiers. Beyond the ridge, he knew the land sloped down to meet the sudden edge of a deep gorge carved out by the Little Colorado River, winding its way to join its big brother and the spectacle of the Grand Canyon a few miles west. The land was beautiful; Zack never tired of it.

His phone vibrated.

"Zack Tolliver."

"Hey, Zack, I was just talking to Dirk Waldo in St. George. He's a BLM investigator assigned to the office there."

"Anything I should be worried about?"

"Well, they don't know much just yet. They don't think it was an accident. They also found a whole lot of bones in a cave near the crime scene."

"What kind of bones?"

"They looked human, he says. Might be an old burial or something, but no one knows for sure. They plan to get an anthropologist to help their forensics guy sort out which is what."

"What about the dead boy?"

"Yeah, well, they have identified the boy already. Seems one of the hunters knew him. Local boy."

"Local where?"

"Kanab. Young kid, adopted son of the innkeeper at the Quality Inn there. Dirk's seen him around, says he's a real nice kid, athlete, hard worker, like that."

"How'd he end up on that mountain top?"

"They don't know that yet. He was last seen leaving the high school to walk home, no more than eight or nine blocks along the main drag. He never made it there."

"Abducted right off the street?"

"Maybe." There was a pause. "Zack, I wouldn't worry much about Libby being up there. Whoever did this will be lying low or has already run. If you're worried about a serial killer, it's probably young boys he's after. And if it's not serial, well, then it's probably done with."

Zack sighed. "Yeah, you're right. Thanks, Butch. I really appreciate this."

He clutched his phone absently after the call. A sudden well of cold air made him shudder. Despite Butch's assurances, he had a bad feeling.

* * * * *

"So what's going on?" Libby set down her cup of tea and reached for another cookie from the plate. "I saw camera crews and media trucks all over town when I drove in last night."

They sat in her sister's small but comfortable kitchen. When Emma's husband Tom died suddenly of an air embolism in his brain during what should have been a routine procedure, life for Emma and five-year-old Pru changed dramatically. They had to sell their home and purchase something smaller, less expensive. Emma could not find work in Kanab. Then the Latter-day Saints Church reached out and arranged a contingency fund for her, despite being a non-member. While no leverage was applied to Emma to join the LDS, there was a tacit expectation she would remain open-minded about the possibility.

Emma interrupted Libby's thoughts. "There are always camera crews around town. Kanab is often used for a movie setting, although today I expect some of them are news people." Worry creased her face. "They started showing up after they learned the identity of the poor boy who was killed on Canaan Mountain down near Hildale. Turns out he lives—or lived—right here in Kanab, just a few blocks away."

"I heard something about that on the radio driving up here. The boy fell off a cliff or something? How did that happen?"

"They're not saying whether he fell or someone pushed him."

"Why was the boy there in the first place? Was he a hiker?"

Emma reached for the pot, held it up. "More tea?" Libby shook her head. Emma poured herself a cup. "Nobody seems to know how he ended up there. The cops aren't saying much, still too early, I guess."

Emma replaced the pot in the center of the table. She stared at it, lost in thought. She looked up at Libby. "My Pru knew that boy. I think she knows something."

Libby raised her eyebrows. "How well did she know him?"

"Not well, at least I don't think so. She started talking about a certain boy a few days before this happened." Emma tightened her lips, shook her head. "Pru had a hard time of it when Tom died. Even before that, she hadn't really adapted to the change—the new town, new classmates, all that. I was glad when she started talking about this boy, it seemed like things were on the mend. I guess the boy was a quiet kid like

Pru, shy but sweet. From what she told me, she actually made the first overture, started to walk home with him." Emma gave a shy smile. "They had always walked the same way to and from school, but never together—you know how kids are. Then one day I got home and Pru was bubbling over, talking about how she'd just gone up to the boy that day and started walking along with him, and they'd talked, and so on. She was all excited. Couldn't wait to see him the next day. And now this."

"You mean it's the same kid, the boy who was murdered?"

Emma paused, almost whispered. "Yes."

"My God! And Pru? How is she dealing with it?" Libby glanced around. "Where is she?"

"She's visiting a friend. She's okay, at least physically. But she's real upset as you can imagine. I've arranged for her to see a counselor. The school provides them."

Libby stared at her sister. "You poor thing. Poor Pru. As if things haven't been tough enough."

Emma gave a brief, tired smile, stood, went to the sink and absently rinsed her teacup. "Maybe we're tougher for all our trials. We'll get through this." She glanced at Libby. "I never asked. How's Zack? He must be walking around nervous as a cat now he's not with the Bureau anymore."

Libby smiled. "I haven't seen that yet, he seems completely content to be home. He even turned Professor Apgar down the last time she asked him to help with a lecture. Not so long ago, he'd have jumped at that."

Emma cocked her head and grinned at Libby. "It won't last."

Libby laughed. "No. It won't last. But I'm enjoying it as long as it does."

# CHAPTER SIX

Jeffrey Danes Harlow bunched his fingertips and studied his immaculately groomed fingernails before glancing up at his friend's questioning smile.

"You know I can't talk about these things, Dan."

Dan Fogelberry picked up his cup of coffee and regarded the marshal over its rim, took a sip, and returned cup to saucer. "J.B., you are much too loyal to a police department not so loyal to you."

"It's not about the department and before you say anything else, it's not about the Fundamentalist Latter-day Saints Church. It's about personal work ethics."

Dan shook his head slowly. "I admire you, man. I don't know how you managed to acquire your code of ethics with your upbringing—your blind loyalty, yes. But ethics...?"

Harlow raised an eyebrow. "I could say I don't know how you managed to avoid a code of ethics with your upbringing, yet here you are."

The banter between these two friends was lighthearted, but illuminated a world of hidden truth for those who possessed the key. Here in the Merry Wives Cafe in Hildale, Utah, most folks at nearby tables would have found this discussion intimately familiar, for everyone but the obvious tourists were likely to be members of the FLDS, and so share a similar background with the marshal.

Jeffrey Danes Harlow's father, Darwin Danes Harlow, had raised him within a large compound enclosed by a wall tall enough to impede the curious, enveloping the buildings that housed his father and mother, his nine stepmothers and his thirty siblings. In such a communal setting procedures were necessary and rigorously enforced; the rules of the FLDS Church were first and foremost, the rules imposed by his father for the safety and wellbeing of his family a close second. Among the unspoken rules (which were enforced just as rigorously, if not more so) was the assumption any ethical equation that did not serve the church was de facto not ethical, and those rules or purposes not serving the family did not serve the church. This tended to leave a very narrow path for moral navigation.

For Dan, raised in the bosom of a traditional Mormon family with one father and one mother and limited siblings, the median separating "true ethics" and "FLDS ethics" was wide. Yet he shared much in common with his childhood friend since the essential tenets of the Latter-day Saints Church and its runaway branch were universal, even if the essential differences were repugnant to both church hierarchies and condemned by them.

To Jeffrey Harlow's mind, his friend's career choice of journalist—even for a news agency corporation owned and operated by the LDS Church—opened a quagmire of ethical choices no less imponderable, constituting an extremely unstable bridge over a seething sea of Hell-Fire. Yet to all appearances, Dan negotiated it quite happily.

"In truth, it is more a matter of knowledge than of ethics," Jeffrey said in response to his friend's original question. "We just don't have answers yet. We don't know how many victims were involved. We don't know how long this has been going on. We don't even know if some of the bones in that cave are actually ancient burials of some sort."

Dan's eyebrows rose. "Bones? Ancient burials?"

Jeffrey glanced around the room. "This is strictly off the record." His gaze came back to Dan. "Seriously, Dan, if word gets back I told you any of this, my chances of getting my Arizona badge back are nil."

Marshal Jeffrey Harlow had recently experienced a most unusual situation, one that pitted his fundamentalist upbringing against the outside social norm and threatened his job, his religion, and even his life.

"I didn't think you had a chance to get it back."

"If I can prove, or at least get the Arizona Commissioner's Board to believe my first priority is to uphold the laws of the State of Arizona as well as the State of Utah, they might reverse their decision."

"You would put the FLDS Church second?"

Jeffrey stared without speaking for a moment. "If I could get them to believe it..."

Dan nodded. The US Department of Justice and the State of Arizona were determined to prosecute members of the combined Marshal's Department of Colorado City, Arizona, and Hildale, Utah, for blatantly misusing their authority to protect ranking members of the FLDS Church. When a FLDS Elder elects to take a twelve or thirteen-year-old girl as his multiple bride, it is a violation of state law in both Arizona and Utah, but the marshals had always turned a blind eye.

Now the State of Arizona was scrutinizing the credentials of the individual marshals and Jeffrey Harlow's record contained several minor felonies, all from looking the other way. This could no longer be tolerated and his Arizona badge had been revoked.

"So in other words, you want to make them believe you are putting the state law first whether you actually are or not," Dan said.

"What can I do? This is my chosen career. I was encouraged toward law enforcement by my father and even by the Prophet himself. And I love it. So now I have to make a choice?" Jeffrey raised both arms. "It's not fair. What about my family? I have two wives. How could I support them? Should I give one up? Is that what the outside world demands? Which one? I love them both. And which of my children should I deprive of a mother?"

Jeffrey's voice was rising. People in the small cafe began to glance their way.

Dan laid a hand on his arm. "Okay, okay, I understand your frustration. I don't think this is about your own plural wives—it's about bending the law for the sake of the church."

Jeffrey let his arms drop. He peered around, now conscious of the glances of the other customers.

Dan leaned in toward him. "Look, Jeffrey, you're a good man. You simply want to do right by your family, your religion, and your job. But, unfortunately, circumstances have made that impossible. So maybe you will have to make some choices soon, maybe you need to start adjusting your mindset toward that."

Jeffrey stared at his plate. "I know, I know. You're right. I have a little time, maybe even a year, before the Department of so-called Justice brings its case forward and our department is disbanded. The church won't let me down, they'll find some sort of work for me."

He set his jaw. "Right now, there are too few of us in the Marshal's Office—just me, the town marshal, who is caught up in this legal briar patch himself, and the Taylor twins. They get to partner together because they can patrol both sides of the border, but because I can't operate in Arizona, the boss has to take those calls when I'm on duty or someone does double-time. When there's a call on the Utah side, I usually respond all by myself as I did on Canaan Mountain." Jeffrey twirled his juice glass, stared at Dan. "I was way up on that mountain top where I couldn't even get a cell phone signal, stuck with two backwoods yahoos and a boy with a stake through his middle. It was pretty scary, I can tell you. For all I knew, those two hunters were the murderers. It took half an hour for anyone else to get up there once I finally got a call through. I spent half my time watching to be sure the tall weird guy didn't disappear, or worse, slip around behind me." Jeffrey leaned forward now, dropped his voice. "And there was something else."

"Yeah?"

"You know me, you know I don't imagine things." Jeffrey paused.

"Go on."

"There was someone, or something, in that cave behind that rock slab."

"What are you talking about?"

"I don't know." Jeffrey gave a slow shake of his head. "I saw movement in the cave while I was talking to those two hunters, just a glimpse of something. I thought maybe they had a third friend hiding in there. So I made them stay and went for a look. As I'm walking toward the cave, I swear someone peered out at me, turned away and disappeared. He's in the shadow, it's just a flash, but I get this impression of someone with real mean eyes and lots of dark hair."

Jeffrey glanced at Dan, saw his eyes glued to him.

"I had to climb a rocky slope to get to the cave. The closer I got, the stranger I felt. By the time I got there, got my flashlight out and shone it around, no one was there."

"Was the cave deep?"

"Deeper than I expected. I figured it would be the size of the rock slab that fell out of the wall. It was deeper than that, but narrowing toward the rear."

"No place for anyone to hide?"

Jeffrey shook his head. "Not that I could see."

"No other way out?"

"Nothing."

Dan stared, silent.

Jeffrey shrugged, defensive. "I saw what I saw, but no one was there when I got inside, just this big bunch of bones."

"Bones? What kind of bones?"

"Human bones. And a really bad smell."

"Do you think this person you saw in the cave might be responsible for killing the kid?"

Jeffrey leaned toward his friend. "I think someone, or something, has been making shish kabobs out of people up there for a long time."

# CHAPTER SEVEN

Three men stood on the narrow strip of green grass just off the concrete sidewalk outside the main door of the Grand Staircase Escalante National Monument Bureau of Land Management office in Kanab, careful not to hinder passage of employees or clients. Their arms were folded across their chests, their long hair braided in Native American fashion, their broad faces expressionless. Each wore a sign hanging below his folded arms that read, variously: "Leave Our Ancestors in Peace" or "Burial Sites Are Sacred" or "Not All Bones Are Just Bones."

Agent Greg Stone first saw the men when he glanced out the window around eight that morning. He'd walked out to see what they wanted but received no response to his questions. With a shrug of his shoulders he'd gone back into his office and tried to concentrate on his work. Around ten a.m. he saw they were still there in exactly the same position. This time when he went out he brought a thermos of coffee and three cups. When he received no response for the second time, not the twitch of an eye, he placed the thermos and three cups on the sidewalk.

"If you want milk or sugar, you'll have to come on inside," he said and went back to work.

By noon, they still hadn't moved. He made one more effort. "I am happy to meet with you any time you want. Just come inside." When no answer came, not even a look his way, he went back and called his supervisor in St. George to explain the situation.

"No, they're not causing any trouble at all. They're not blocking ingress or egress, they're not even moving, for Christ's sake—haven't moved a muscle all morning, so far as I can tell. No, I'm not concerned about a crowd gathering, certainly not in this location." Indeed, the Kanab office of the BLM was located on a side street at the far edge of town with nothing but arid brush and steep-side mesa beyond it.

Stone listened. "Yeah, I got a pretty good idea what it's about. It's because we took several bones away from the Canaan Mountain crime site to sort the old from more recent ones. No doubt they're upset thinking we are disturbing an ancient burial."

He paused. "Well, yes, sir, we've had to remove the bones to age test them, but we only took a few from the top of the stack. We're trying to be careful."

He listened again. "Yes, I've invited them in. They'll come when they're ready, I suppose...okay, sir, thank you, sir."

Stone hung up the phone and swiveled his chair to stare out the window. The three Indians stared back. The bones the investigators had "borrowed" from the cave behind the slab had all been right femurs; the FBI sent them to the BYU Paleontology Department in Salt Lake City. There were so many bones at the site it had been difficult to know where to start. Worse, someone had been digging around in the cave and mixed up everything. So they'd taken the same leg bone from three different individuals off the top of the pile, bones that to the naked eye appeared to vary in age.

Stone occupied himself with trying to figure out which Indian tribe the protesters represented. The crime scene on Canaan Mountain was in Utah, just across the border from the Arizona Strip. It was not in the current Kaibab Paiute Reservation, but Stone knew those boundaries had moved many times. After some thought, he decided the bones must belong to the Kaibab band. Historically, their people would have claimed the entire area, as best he recalled.

There was movement outside. Stone swiveled his chair. He glimpsed another figure in native dress striding toward the door. Maybe the big honcho was here, ready to talk. Stone went to the door to welcome the new arrival. To his surprise, he faced an attractive woman with a pleasant smile on her face.

"Hello, I am Shana Bows, Tribal Council Chair Person of the Southern Paiute Band of Indians. Can we talk?"

Nodding toward the three statue-like Indians outside, Stone said, "You have a novel way of presenting yourselves."

She smiled. "We have found it is best to gain the full attention of administrators before speaking to US officials."

"Sorry, I'm Greg Stone, the BLM Agent representative for this area. Please, come this way."

Once they were seated and the offer of coffee was made and accepted, Stone leveled his gaze at Shana Bows.

"No doubt you are here because law enforcement removed bones from the Canaan Mountain site. Is that a burial site of your people?"

"Very good, Mr. Stone, you come right to the point. What do you know about my people?"

Stone shook his head. "Less than I should, I'm afraid."

Shana nodded. "Allow me to give you some background to give our conversation perspective. Today, many small bands of the Southern Paiute exist but once we were all one people, simply the Utes, and the territory we hunted extended from the front range of the Rockies to beyond the Great Salt Lake and from northern Utah and Colorado south to the New Mexican Pueblos. We have long been seen as three Peoples according to where we lived: the Utes, the Goshutes, and the Southern Paiutes. The Southern Paiutes have seen many divisions into separate bands as well, some before the Europeans arrived, but most later, particularly when my people were placed on reservations. In this area of Utah and Arizona we are five bands on five reservations: the Cedar Band, the Indian Peaks Band, the Kanosh Band, the Koosharem Band, and the Shivwits Band. It is important to remember that the locations of the reservations were designated for us, not by us."

Shana sipped her coffee, peered at Stone and smiled. "Do you see what I'm driving at? Our ancestors were buried in locations ascribed by the particular band to which they belonged. After all the relocations my people have experienced, it is impossible to identify those burial locations. Mr. Stone, until you stumbled upon the Canaan Mountain burial site, we had no idea it even existed."

"Then how do you know it's your people or that it's even a burial site for that matter?"

"We don't," Shana said. She held up a palm. "But it is likely. Until we know for sure, we don't want the remains disturbed or removed."

Stone leaned toward her. "It is impossible to learn the answer without removing a few bones for study. You must know that."

Shana nodded. "I do. Our concern is about protecting the site. We want to be involved in administrative decisions concerning the site once it is no longer a crime scene."

Stone swiveled his chair to stare out the window. The three Indians were now seated on the sidewalk, enjoying his coffee. He turned back to Shana.

"There are two federal bureaus and three law enforcement agencies from two states involved in this investigation already. I'd be surprised if I was asked to become involved in any administrative decisions. However, I can, and will make my personal promise to request that you are kept informed. But beyond that?" He held up his palms.

Shana stood. "I accept that."

Stone rose with her.

She extended her hand. "I'll leave you with this. While I must act for my people to potentially protect our ancestors, I have strong doubts the site on Canaan Mountain has anything to do with us. We are a people who have always lived as families and would want to keep our ancestors close, not far off on a mountaintop. You may need to find some other explanation for all those bones."

# CHAPTER EIGHT

"Aunt Libby! What a great surprise!" Prucilla bounded down the set of concrete steps from the gym toward Libby's car. The post-sports crowd of students trickling along the sidewalk toward the parking lot was dwarfed by the enormous Aztec-pyramid shaped gymnasium, its wall emblazoned with huge red letters around the picture of a bronco rider proclaiming, "Cowboy Country."

Pru rushed up to the passenger side of the white Subaru Impreza and stepped in, flipping her book bag into the back seat. She stretched long arms across to Libby and gave her a hug. "What brings you here?"

Libby was amazed at Pru's appearance. How could the girl possibly have grown so much in just a few months? She smiled at her niece.

"Your mom and I got to talking on the phone a couple of days ago, and I realized it's just been too long since we've seen each other. Looking at you, I see how right I was. How you've grown!"

Pru smiled. "That's my job at the moment."

Libby navigated the car away from the curb and along the drive toward the street. She flashed a glance at Pru.

"How are you doing? Are your classes good?"

Pru shrugged. "They're good enough. Are Uncle Zack and Bernie here?"

"They couldn't come this time. We thought we'd keep it just a girl thing."

Pru giggled. "Uh-oh, things could get a little crazy."

Libby laughed. "Your mom and I promise to be on our best behavior." She steered the car into E 400 Street. As she did, she heard a gasp from Pru. At the same moment, she noticed another vehicle disappear into a side street just beyond her sister's house. Her impression was of an oversize SUV covered in mud. She glanced at Pru. The girl was no longer smiling.

"Something the matter?"

Pru shook her head, didn't speak.

At the house, Libby pulled up along the curb and turned off the ignition. "I think we need to talk."

Pru stared down at her clasped hands in her lap, glanced sideways at Libby. "About what?"

"Well, about the effect that vehicle we saw just now had on you for one thing. And maybe about why your mother seems scared on your behalf. She hasn't said anything, but I know her pretty well."

Pru faced the window, said nothing.

Libby touched her arm. "You know me, Pru. You know I won't let go, I'll figure it out. I know this boy you cared about was killed, and that's got to be very upsetting." She studied her niece's face. "But I think there is something more to this you're not telling anyone, am I right?"

Pru gave a slow nod, lowered her head.

"Okay, then, young lady. I think it's time we go to Wendy's and grab a burger and have a nice picnic. What do you say?"

After another somewhat brisker nod from Pru, Libby pulled away from the curb and drove over to the fast food store. They did the drive-thru lane, purchased burgers and shakes, then drove east on Rt. 89 until Libby found a turnoff with a scenic view, a photo stop for tourists.

By now the car was filled with the enticing aroma of freshly-cooked burgers. They made the sandwiches their priority. As they ate, Libby feasted her eyes on the red rising buttes of the Grand Staircase Escalante National Monument, like a huge wall marching along the highway into the far distance.

Libby finished, wiped her mouth. It was time. "Okay, give!"

Pru turned to her, still chewing. "His name is...was Luke. We walked home the same way every day after sports, but never together. He was in several of my classes." She glanced sidewise at Libby. "He was such a nice boy, but

32

everyone kind of ignored him. He was part Indian, part Black and the kids here seemed to have trouble with that. They were nice enough to him, but kind of standoffish, you know? Anyway, I thought maybe I was acting just like them, walking the same way home but ignoring him. So last Wednesday, I caught up with him and started talking to him and he was really nice. I think he was really, really lonely. We talked a blue streak all the way to my house." She looked out the window. "He lives over at the Quality Inn, you know." She paused. "That's the last I ever saw him. He wasn't in school on Thursday. I didn't think anything of it, figured maybe he was sick."

Libby turned toward her niece. "You only spoke to him that one time? Your mom said you'd been talking about him for a while."

"Oh, I spoke with him at school, you know, during classes and in the corridors. No one makes anything of that. But when you walk home with somebody, well, that's..."

"That shows more purpose?"

Pru gave a wan smile. "Yeah, I guess so." She sipped her shake.

Libby watched her. "There's something else, though, isn't there."

Pru took the straw from her mouth. "The thing is, that car we just saw on my street? It's the same one I saw that day when we were walking together. I remembered it because it went by us so slow. Then it came back again going the other way. I looked up just as it passed. The driver, a man, was staring right at us with anger in his face, almost as if he was mad at us for some reason. I didn't say anything to Luke. I didn't want to stop our conversation, and besides, there are plenty of weirdoes around here. But I thought about it later."

"After you heard what happened to Luke?"

"Yeah. I just wondered if that guy had something to do with it."

"Did you ever see that car again, before today?"

Pru nodded. "This is the third day in a row. I noticed the car last Sunday when I happened to glance out the window. It drove by the house slow. Then yesterday I saw it pass as I was walking home. And then today..."

Libby reached over and touched Pru's hand. "Did it always appear as filthy as it was today? I don't think I could even say what color it was."

"Yeah, it did. I even tried to read the license plate once, but it was too dirty."

"So all this time you've been thinking the man driving that car had something to do with the boy's murder, and now he's got his eye on you."

"Yeah." Pru's response was almost inaudible.

Libby gave her hand a squeeze. "Okay, I want you to stop worrying about that right now. I'm going to call Uncle Zack and he will call the right people to be on the lookout for that car. Meanwhile, we'll see that you are protected. I will stay with you and your mom until it's all set, and I'll drive you to and from school. How's that?"

Pru gave a smile. This one was a bit brighter. Libby could tell a weight was lifted from the girl.

"I couldn't tell my mom," Pru said. "You know her, she'd go right into a panic and probably keep me home from school."

On the drive back, Libby thought the girl was probably right, her mom would've panicked. But would keeping Pru home be such a bad call after all? What if this creep really was the killer? What if he considered Pru to be a witness and planned to eliminate her? How do you protect a lively girl like Pru twenty-four-seven from a determined killer?

# CHAPTER NINE

Once the victim of the "Skewer Murder" (as the media labeled it) was identified as an inhabitant of Kanab, it became clear to law enforcement officials the kidnapper must have transported his victim across the state line into Arizona in order to get to Hildale, Utah, and thence up the mountain. It was an obvious call, therefore, to involve the FBI.

Zack figured that would happen even before the decision was made. After Libby called with her alarming news, he contacted a former colleague and explained the apparent threat to Pru, the possible connection to the murder and was able to arrange protection for her and the household. He passed along the general description of the vehicle possibly involved in the kidnapping.

His former colleague had laughed at that. "Even after you leave the Bureau you're able to turn up more evidence than the rest of us."

Zack slept better that night, confident in the net of protection now surrounding Libby and her sister's family. The next morning before rising he lay still and let his brain whirr, trying to fit pieces of the puzzle together as he always had done as an agent. He found the calm of early morning a fertile time for thought.

But he had little to go on. He could no longer expect the FBI to share information with him; all he had was Libby's account from Pru and the story put out by the media. His situation was strange. No longer was it his job to solve the crime, it was to protect his own family. But to do that he needed to understand the killer's motive and purpose. In effect, he needed to do what he would have done as an agent, but with one hand tied behind him.

Zack sighed and swung his legs to the floor. He sat on the edge of the bed next to the end table, littered with his keys, phone, wallet and watch, and thought about it. If he must work with one hand tied behind him, he decided, he needed someone else's hand to help out. He reached for his phone. He would call Eagle Feather, his friend and unofficial partner.

Eagle Feather, born to a Navajo mother and Jewish father, lived several miles east of the tiny town of Elk Wells, several miles east of Tuba City, Arizona, in the far western reaches of the huge Navajo Reservation. His mother, Lucie Yazzie, died when he was very young and he'd used his father's surname until given the nickname Eagle Feather by hunting clients. Now, no one knew him by any other name.

Ordinarily it would take Eagle Feather an hour and a half in his old Ford truck to reach Zack's home, but today he was at Julia's Diner in Tuba City for an early breakfast. Julia kept her restaurant open twenty-four hours a day so you could at least get coffee and some donuts, which was a boon to hunters and guides like Eagle Feather who rose early and returned late.

When Zack's call came, Eagle Feather had just started in on a stack of pancakes, a fact he carefully explained to Zack between bites. "You are not FBI anymore, White Man. Does that not mean you can no longer call me whenever you need my help?"

"I'm not calling you to help me, I'm calling you to help Libby."

"Well, that is different. I will be there in an hour."

About an hour later, a loud knock sounded on the front door. Zack knew it was Eagle Feather; no one else knocked in that particular way. Little Bernie knew it too and beat Zack to the door. Eagle Feather was like an uncle to him. Although stiffly erect and unsmiling, always wearing his leather pants, black deerskin vest, and black reservation hat with a lone eagle feather, this man who appeared formidable to most, to Bernie was a loved figure. After extended greetings and much tickling, Bernie drifted back to his play. Zack and Eagle Feather settled at the kitchen table.

"Why does Libby need help?"

Zack described the recent events. "I no longer have access to the crime scene or to any evidence. I need to get a handle on the situation, but I can't leave home to go there because of Bernie."

"Can you not leave the boy with someone here?"

Zack shook his head. "That's not an option in my mind, nor would Libby agree. He's been through enough."

Eagle Feather looked at Zack, no hint of a smile on his rugged features, but his dark brown eyes danced. "Out with it. You wish me to go to Kanab, White Man."

Zack gave a sheepish grin, nodded. "I need someone to be my eyes and ears up there. Someone I can trust."

Eagle Feather watched Zack without responding.

"I have a bad feeling in my gut about this," Zack said. He leaned toward Eagle Feather. "It's Libby we're talking about here."

"Whoa, White man, I did not say I would not go. I was simply reflecting on the fact that you have quit the FBI, but for me nothing has changed."

Zack leaned back, sighed. "Kind of seems that way, doesn't it?"

Eagle Feather stood and walked to the kitchen counter. "Coffee hot?"

"Help yourself."

Zack watched absently as his friend found a clean cup and filled it with a stream of the hot black liquid. His mind went back to the early days, when he was a rookie FBI agent fresh out of the academy assigned to the remote outpost of Tuba City in Navajo Land, trying to find his way in an empty land among people he did not understand. To this day, he didn't know what stroke of fortune brought Eagle Feather to his side, to smooth his path, to teach him skills, to become a bridge between the White world and the Navajo. Perhaps the guide had seen his earnestness, his desire to assimilate the culture, his desire to help—or maybe he just felt sorry for him. Either way, their friendship blossomed. Nowhere else could he have found a more loyal and trusted companion.

Eagle Feather turned to face Zack. "What have you got in mind?"

"I'd like you to go up there, keep a low profile, see what you can learn."

"Check in with Libby?"

Zack shook his head. "No, I don't want anyone up there to suspect your connection to her. That's our ace in the hole. I'll call her, let her know you're around, tell her not to react if she sees you."

"What exactly do you wish me to learn?"

Zack sighed. "It's hard to say. I just have this ominous feeling. Of course, I'd like to know who is following Emma in the muddy vehicle, the driver's connection, if any, to the boy's kidnapping. I need to know how to safeguard Libby and her sister's family. I have to know if I can rely on the people up there to keep her safe or if more drastic action is required." He gave Eagle Feather a grin. "I know—that's pretty vague."

Eagle Feather brought his coffee back to the table and sat down. "You want me to assess the situation."

"Yes."

"Not hunt down the killer?"

Zack grinned. "Let's give the local Marshals, County Sheriff's Department, BLM investigators and FBI a chance at some glory before you solve it."

Eagle Feather sipped his coffee, gazing at Zack over the rim. "Is there anyone I should connect with up there?"

Zack shook his head. "You will have to go completely rogue this time, find your own resources. I have no real relationship with any law enforcement in the area. I do not even know the FBI agents on the site."

The Navajo nodded, finished his coffee, put down the cup and rose from the table. "I will not waste time. I will leave now."

Zack stood with him. "I am grateful. Be careful up there. The people who live on the Arizona Strip tend to take matters into their own hands."

Eagle Feather turned toward the door.
"So do I, White Man. So do I."

# CHAPTER TEN

The needle on the temperature gauge of the '63 Ford pickup was hovering just over the red line after the steep climb up and over the Kaibab Plateau when Eagle Feather arrived at the intersection of Routes 89A and 389 in Fredonia, Arizona. Kanab lay straight ahead, just across the border into Utah, four miles down the road. But he was not going that way; he planned to head west toward Hildale and the crime scene.

He drove up to a mom and pop market with ancient pumps to allow the engine to cool and buy some gas. He had to hand crank the pump to start it up and saw he'd have to go into the market to pre-pay for the gas. There seemed to be a resistance to modernization around here.

From what he had seen so far, Fredonia was a wide spot in the road; just a few houses, a small, weed infested park, and one or two curio type shops that appeared to be closed and didn't seem to care about outsider business. Eagle Feather had read of the town's polygamist roots, settled by Mormons in 1865 after escaping south to avoid a federal law intended to strip them of multiple wives. The town was named by Apostle Erastus Snow, from a combination of the word "free" and the Spanish word for woman, "donia."

The screen door screeched like a wounded animal and the wood plank floor groaned underfoot. Inside the market was dark and smelled of oil. An overweight woman turned to stare at him, abruptly halting her conversation with a female clerk behind the counter. Both woman were conservatively dressed, not in traditional plain dress, but comfortable with long sleeves and tight collars, without jewelry or makeup. They appeared surprised and startled by Eagle Feather in his customary attire of black leather pants, purple satin shirt, black leather vest and reservation hat with its single feather. From their gaping stares, he knew he was going to have trouble blending in around here. He also guessed word of his presence would spread the moment he walked out the door.

As he drove west on Route 89A, the truck full of gas, he knew he had to change his plans. The idea he could slip into the Fundamentalist LDS community of Hildale unnoticed was clearly folly. When he came to the entrance to Pipe Spring National Monument and the Kaibab-Paiute Indian Reservation, he turned in there and pulled up to a Chevron market to rethink. He noticed a sign in the window saying people who wished to camp at the tribal campground should register there. He went in and paid his twenty dollars per night fee for five nights, bought a can of corned beef, a dozen eggs, some firewood, and drove to the campground.

It was a barren place with just a few newly planted trees and flat wide-open spaces with water and electric hook-ups. Eagle Feather chose the only tent spot with a tree. He climbed out of the truck and stood a moment, letting the scent of pinyon and sage greet his nostrils. Before him spread the enormous vista of the Kanab and Uinkaret Plateau painted in pastel strips by the lowering sun. Behind him loomed the face of the Vermillion Cliffs. He grunted in satisfaction; this was the place for him.

Although Eagle Feather had not expected to camp, he always carried minimal supplies behind the seats of the truck, including a one-man tent, a couple of blankets and a fry pan. He set up the tent, organized the blankets, set out the newly purchased wood and walked to the restroom and shower facility. It was brand new. He saw no other campers. Two small trailers were near the entrance road, but they had a lonely permanent look. For now, at least, he had the sparkling clean bathroom all to himself.

With plenty of time left in the afternoon, Eagle Feather decided to do some exploring and drove farther along Pipe Spring Road toward the Indian communities of Paiute and Moccasin. Paiute appeared to be solely residential. Moccasin was a cluster of buildings, but small; by far the largest edifice in the town was the Church of the Latter-day Saints. With little else to see, he returned to the campground.

He recalled passing the Paiute Tribal Office when he first turned off the highway and made a mental note to stop there in the morning to see what he could learn.

Eagle Feather got a small fire going, water boiling, and was about to open the can of corned beef when a white Datsun pickup pulled up in front of his campsite. The logo on the door was an eagle with letters spelling Paiute Indian Tribe of Utah. A tall, barrel-chested man squeezed out of the small cab and stretched. He wore a uniform shirt, his hair was in braids, his nose and cheekbones prominent on a broad face. His large hands held a clipboard.

"Afternoon."

"Ya'eeh te'h."

"You are Navajo."

Eagle Feather nodded.

The man glanced at his clipboard. "I see you are registered as Eagle Feather from Elk Springs, Arizona. Where is that?"

"It is just east of Tuba City."

The man nodded. "Yes, I do know the area. Are you sightseeing?"

"You might say so." Eagle Feather nodded toward the picnic bench. "Have a seat. It does not appear you have a lot to do here tonight."

"It is true, people have not yet discovered our beautiful campground." He sat down. With a wave of his arm, he said, "This is a tribal enterprise. There is growing tourism in this region and we hope to tap into it."

"You don't have a casino?"

The attendant grinned, shook his head. "We could not get a permit. We do what we can." He waved in a westerly direction. "We sell some handcrafts at the little store at Pipe Spring National Monument. And we farm." He reached out his hand to Eagle Feather. "I am Sam Wall. I take care of this place."

Eagle Feather shook it. "I heard about a killing near here recently."

Sam's manner changed. "Is that why you are here?"

Eagle Feather made an instant decision to risk all with this man and come clean. "Not about the murder, for the killer. My friend has relatives in Kanab, and he is worried. The boy who was killed came from there, the family knew him."

Sam eyed him. "Your friend thinks his family could be in danger?"

"Just a precaution."

"Why are you here and not your friend?"

"I am going to fry up some corned beef and eggs. Would you like some?"

"No, no, got to get home." Sam watched, still waiting for his answer.

Eagle Feather opened the can with his knife and dropped the contents into the skillet, and carefully cut the meat into even slices. He wiped the knife on his pants and put it away before he looked up at Sam. "My friend's wife is visiting in Kanab. My friend is home alone with a two-year-old boy."

Sam watched Eagle Feather drop a couple of eggs in the pan with the corned beef. They began to sizzle.

"Kanab is a long way from the top of Canaan Mountain," he said. "The boy was snatched off the street there. It seems strange."

Eagle Feather nodded. "That is what we thought."

"What is your plan?"

"I will look around and see what I can learn."

"I thought you might have come to see the cave."

Eagle feather peered up from the pan. "What cave?"

Sam's eyes were opaque. "The killing happened at a cave in an arroyo up on Canaan Mountain. The cave was full of bones. The FBI took some bones away to study them.

They did not consult the tribe. We staged a protest at the BML Office in Kanab."

"Does anyone think the killer had something to do with the bones?"

"We think they may be ancient bones."

Eagle Feather jerked the pan, gave the eggs and meat a flip. "How did they get up the mountain? Is there a trail?"

"There are several. One can be driven by four-wheel drive vehicles." He studied Eagle Feather. "Do you plan to go up there? They will not let you enter the crime site."

"Maybe, to get a sense of the place."

Sam paused, his face unreadable. "Yes, I think you will get a sense of the place." He glanced at his watch and rose from the bench. "It is time for me to go home." He stood and looked down at Eagle Feather. "Tomorrow morning, I will come back with a trail map for you."

Eagle Feather stood. "Thank you."

Later that night the moon rose full and bright. A soft breeze ruffled through the solitary tree. An owl hooted. Tucked in his blanket, Eagle Feather felt a shiver. To his mind, the presence of the owl was not a good sign.

# CHAPTER ELEVEN

She lay at the side of the road, a rag doll discarded like an unwanted toy. The motorist who found her was parked along the shoulder several yards away. Now he stood next to his car, answering questions put to him by a highway patrolman who scribbled the answers in a notebook. A second patrolman stood in the northbound lane next to a patrol car with flashing lights waving traffic around the scene.

They were three miles north of Kanab on Route 89 where a dirt road turned off toward the White Cliffs region. Abrupt coral cliffs along the highway here gave way for a gateway side road to the valley beyond. Pinyon forest covered everything that wasn't vertical.

A Kane County Sheriff vehicle roared up and pulled in behind the witness car, leaving its lights flashing. Two policemen climbed out, one began to direct traffic coming north while the other approached the highway patrolman and the witness.

"Hi, Clem."

"Will."

The policeman produced an identity card, flashed it toward the witness. "Chief Deputy William Brown." His eyes flicked to the patrolman. "What have we got here?"

Clem checked his notes. "This man, George Fields, was driving south when he noticed the girl alongside the road. She was on the shoulder downslope, as she is now, almost out of sight. Mr. Fields happened to notice something and pulled over. As soon as he saw her body, he called it in on his cell."

Brown regarded Mr. Fields and nodded. "I'll go take a look." He walked up the dirt shoulder to within a few feet of the girl. Her back was to him. Long brown hair matted with dirt and blood covered her face. She wore a bright colored dress, a light springy type. One arm was beneath her, the other lay along her body; her dress hem was at her knees, one leg twisted under her.

Clem came up behind Brown. "Seems like she hit her head."

Brown grunted. "Or had it hit for her." He glanced at Clem. "Who have you alerted?"

"Just the sheriff's office."

Brown pulled down his walkie-talkie. "Brown to dispatch. We've got a possible homicide. We'll need Sergio and his evidence kit. Alert Sheriff Rafferty and see if he wants to alert the FBI; might be some connection to the other killing."

After the static response, Brown walked around the girl to see her other side, slowly shaking his head. She was young—very young—maybe fourteen or fifteen: attractive, athletic and apparently healthy.

"Know her?" Clem asked.

Brown shook his head. "No. She looks like a high school kid. The way she's dressed, she might have just left school."

They could hear sirens approaching from the direction of Kanab.

"Do me a favor, Clem. Tape off a perimeter. I'll meet the team when they get here."

\* \* \* \* \*

Zack got a call from his FBI colleague telling him a young girl had been murdered and dumped along the highway. As the agent described the girl, Zack felt rising anxiety. He called Libby.

"Do you know where Pru is right now?"

"Why, she's at school, she stayed to speak with her counselor. Why, Zack, what's the matter?"

"Look, it may be nothing, but please call the school right now to be sure, then let me know."

46

Libby called back five minutes later. "She's not there, Zack. The counselor isn't there either. The school says she already left. Please tell me what this is about."

Zack paused, reluctant. "There's been another murder." He told Libby what he knew. "The description of the girl sounds like Pru—same age, general description, same hair color. I'm expecting more information any minute. The body has been removed to the Mortal Mortuary in town under the supervision of the sheriff's office." Zack paused again. "Libby, maybe you should go down there to see her. There is no point upsetting Emma for no reason."

\* \* \* \* \*

Libby found the Mortal Mortuary on the same road as the high school, just a block beyond. In the parlor, she identified herself to the attendant, a tall stooped man with a hooked nose and hands clasped in front of him, vulture like.

"I'm sorry, ma'am, the remains are in the custody of the police. It is an active criminal investigation."

"But I am the girl's aunt, her mother sent me to identify her."

The mortician studied her for a moment, then nodded. "One moment, ma'am. I will check with the police officer in charge."

He returned shortly with a sheriff's deputy, a rotund man in full uniform. He escorted her into a back room. "We are trying to establish the girl's identity," he said. "It's fortunate you have come."

The room was cool, a table in the middle held a figure covered by a sheet. The deputy stepped to the table, grasped the sheet, and stared at Libby.

She nodded.

He slid the sheet gently down to disclose the head and torso. The girl lay on her back, her long brown hair matted to the side of her head and neck.

Libby gave a gasp. It was Pru...it looked like Pru. The hair color was the same, the profile of her face and whiteness of her skin, even the dress was familiar. Libby felt her heart turn over, a sudden emptiness. She steadied herself against the doorsill.

"Is this your niece, ma'am?"

Libby forced herself to walk closer to the table. She stood a moment, hands clasped at her chest before looking down. At once her depression turned to unreasonable joy, gladness she should not feel in the presence of a young life snuffed out so early. It was not Pru.

"I'm sorry, Deputy, I can't help you after all. I do not know this child."

\* \* \* \* \*

An FBI agent arrived in Kanab an hour later. Pete Conley called Zack and told him what they had learned from the sheriff's department, which was not a lot. The girl had been literally dumped along the roadway, but she was dead before that happened, the cause of death a blow with a blunt instrument to the back of the head.

They did have an identity. The parents had been found, informed and brought to the morgue to verify the girl was their daughter. By then it was just a formality. She was a local girl, a high school student. They guessed she'd been walking home from school; the estimated time of death was about right.

Zack called Libby just as she was about to call him. Pru had called home from a hamburger joint where she'd gone with friends. Libby had picked her up. Pru had already heard about the murder from a friend whose father worked in the sheriff's department.

"Zack, it's all over town. Pru knows the girl, she's a grade behind her. Emma's in a panic now." There was a pause. "Zack, Pru says this girl often walks home the same way she does, along the same streets." Libby's voice became a whisper. "She has the same color hair, worn the same way, even tied with a ribbon. Zack, Pru thinks the murderer might have mistaken that girl for her. I think she might be right."

Zack's brain raced. Time was pivotal. He worked through his thinking out loud to Libby.

"We think from what Pru told you the killer followed Pru to her home, probably more than once. He knows where she lives, knows vaguely what she looks like, but apparently doesn't know her appearance well enough not to make this mistake, assuming Pru's fears are correct." He thought some more. "He'll see the newspaper articles, but hopefully the papers won't include a home address, at least not right away. We need him to believe he succeeded. That means we can't let him see Pru again until this is all over. She must stay hidden."

"We'll keep her home, Zack, keep her inside."

"No, that's not good enough. It's too easy to make a mistake, he might even spot her through a window." Zack paused, thinking. "Libby, she's got to come here to our house. That's the only answer. Wait until tonight, tell Emma and Pru to get in the car while it's in the garage, have Pru duck down behind the seat. You stay in the house, make the place appear lived in, lights on at night, TV going, all that. Don't go out. Leave your car parked on the street. If he's been scouting the place, we want him to think nothing has changed in terms of your visit. You will need to handle interviews with cops and the press yourself. What do you say?"

"Okay, Zack. I'll tell Emma and Pru to get ready."

"Tell Emma I'll be here to meet her. And Libby, when you talk to cops, journalists, anybody—just tell them neither woman is able to talk, they are too upset. Under no circumstances tell anyone, including the FBI, that they are gone."

"Not even the FBI?"

"That's right. Nobody. I'll handle the FBI from this end."

"Okay, Zack. I'll be careful."

Zack paused. "One more thing; get the .22 pistol I asked you to keep in the glove compartment and bring it into the house, keep it with you. Be careful. The killer might try to see for himself."

# CHAPTER TWELVE

The approach to the trailhead through Hildale was complicated, not helped by the predawn darkness. It had been necessary to pull to the side of the road more than once to check the directions Sam had scribbled on the trail map. Now Eagle Feather sat in the parking lot and stared at the trail sign, hoping the trail itself didn't prove as hard to follow.

Sam Wall had appeared at Eagle Feather's camp with the rising of the sun and the men had gone over the trail map together. There were three possible routes to Canaan Mountain summit. The first, Eagle Crags Trail, they dismissed because it was longer, less well maintained, and circuitous. Squirrel Canyon Trail was the most direct to the summit, and likely approached closest to the crime scene, but it was also the quad trail the investigators would likely use to gain access. Eagle Feather did not wish to chance an encounter and have to explain his presence. That left the Water Canyon Trail, now in front of him.

On the way here, he had passed several very large homes. His mind had cast back to something he'd heard about the Fundamentalist LDS families, how they progressed from house to house. It seemed as each practitioner of polygamy accumulated more wives and children, a hand-me-down home sequence was made possible for them through extremely low sale prices. At the top rung were the compounds owned by elders whose large income from church businesses enabled their purchases.

Eagle Feather locked the truck and reached in the back for his small pack. Once it was properly adjusted, he trotted past the sign and along the red dirt path. Within a short distance cliffs closed in and the trail followed a slot canyon where water sometimes trickled, sometimes rushed below him. Gray-brown granite enclosed him, retaining the chill of the early morning. At times the trail perched high above the streambed and narrowed to ten yards, at other times it neared the canyon floor among wavy sandstone shelf formations carved by floodwaters. When it seemed the trail could progress no farther, a switchback would appear and take him steeply up the slickrock. Eagle Feather stopped for breath several times, chiding himself for being out of shape.

The switchbacks eventually surfaced on the canyon rim. Here he found a wash. With no clear trail, he worked his way up it toward a group of white hoodoos shaped like hornets' nests. The wash led all the way to the summit plateau where he found a dirt path and resumed his jog. His practiced eye noted an abundance of footprints along the trail, most several days old, traffic from the prior weekend, he guessed.

He came to a huge cleft through the sandstone framing a view of the valley far below. Not until then did Eagle Feather realize the altitude he had gained. Despite his single-minded pursuit of his mission, he paused here, took water, and marveled at the vista. He passed the Windlass, appearing just as Sam had described it, and continued on without pause.

Eagle Feather studied the terrain ahead, a strange mix of stone terraces, clumps of pinyon pine, clefts and formations. He followed a discernable upward gradient headed west. Fifteen minutes later, the terrain began a gradual descent. He realized he must have missed the arroyo and turned back.

Reclaiming the high ground, he stopped to study the terrain once again. There was nothing to suggest an arroyo of any kind, so with no other options he went north, where he had not yet been. His path took him over slickrock mounds, in and out of juniper groves, down into clefts. Nothing remained as it appeared from a distance; a large ravine could be twenty yards away and he might never know it. He made several forays to the east and west of his path as he progressed. One of these diversions paid off. He broke through a thicket of brush and pinyon to an abrupt cliff edge—the arroyo.

The same terrain continued beyond the ravine as if never interrupted. Eagle Feather saw how a canyon could remain undiscovered for so many years. He followed its rim north to where the pinyon treetops below marched up the sloping ground. Here was the way.

Eagle Feather moved quietly now. The crime scene was near, the feds would protect it until they were done with it. He had no intention of trying to explain his presence to an FBI agent. He moved slowly down the slope into the arroyo, using trees for cover, pausing to listen from time to time. The breeze rustled through the branches above, an occasional bird called. He studied the sheer wall rising beside him as he descended, searching for any blemish that might suggest the presence of a cave.

A sudden stir in the underbrush took him to a knee. He waited. A tall man came into view, moving cautiously. He approached Eagle Feather's position with silent practiced steps, paused thirty yards away, blue eyes searching. The man wore clothing suited to the terrain. Everything he did spoke of long experience in the woods.

In a single motion, Eagle Feather rose to his feet. The man stared, then gave a thin smile. "I knew yuh was somewhere around here. I could smell yuh." The voice was pleasant, but the face gave nothing away.

"By whose authority are you at this crime scene?"

The stranger cocked an eyebrow. "Yuh don't look like one of them FBI fellas to me."

"I am a special consultant to the FBI."

"What do you consult about?"

"I will have to report finding you here."

The man kept his smile. "How do I know you are who you say you are?"

Eagle Feather reached into his shirt pocket and brought out a folded piece of paper, handed it to him."

53

The man studied it, returned it. "I am one of the fellows first discovered the body." He grinned. "Says there your name is Eagle Feather."

Eagle Feather nodded.

"They call me Tubs."

"Why have you come back?"

Tubs hunkered down, like a man with all the time in the world. He rummaged in a carry bag and brought out a tobacco pouch and pipe and went through the motions of filling it, tamping it, finding his matches and preparing to light it. He kept talking while he did these things. "Nothin' but curiosity. What I saw there made no sense to me. I went tuh take another look. Yuh been down there yet?"

Eagle Feather shook his head.

His pipe fired up, Tubs puffed several times. "The boy's body ain't there anymore. Yuh'll see a big slab of sandstone, flat as my palm that come out of the cliff behind it. There's a cave where the slab come out. You look around, yuh can see pictographs here and there. People been using that cave for a long time." He gave a thin smile. "Now I know yuh can go down there and figger all that out for yuh own self. The stake the young fella was stuck on is gone, so yuh won't see that. I can tell yuh it was just a stick carved from a tree branch set in a hole in the middle of the slab in somethin' like a metate for a mano to grind grains. You know what I'm sayin'?"

"I am Navajo," Eagle Feather said.

"Sure enough." Tubs eyed him. "Somebody fixed the hole so the stake would fit tight. It must of taken a bit of work."

"Do you think the killer did that for just one victim?"

Tubs shrugged.

"I heard they found bones in the cave," Eagle Feather said.

Tubs nodded. Taking his time, he smacked the pipe into his palm until it was empty. He stood. "Who do yuh suppose would leave a stack of human bones lying around?"

"Is anyone there?"

"Nah, nobody there. I expect the FBI moved out everything they thought was important. I doubt any of them wanted to stay there overnight by himself." Tubs chuckled. "There is somethin' a bit strange about that place."    With that, Tubs turned and walked away.

Eagle Feather watched him work his way up the slope, a tall man, lanky, but with deceptive strength. Was it enough to lift a boy high up onto a pointed stake?"

Moving down the slope, Eagle Feather's mind went to Tub's last words. Was he saying there was something going on in this place beyond the murder of the boy? Why had Tubs really come up here today? Was it simple curiosity, like he said? Or was he here to cover up something he didn't want anyone else to see? The man had been clever in deflecting questions.

Eagle Feather followed the trampled grass through a tight cluster of pinyon to a sudden clearing. With the trees surrounding it, no one would guess a cave was here.

The slab was in front of him, the cave directly behind it like an oversized ravenous mouth. The cliff wall was sheer, over one hundred feet high. Yellow incident tape was draped like a string of Christmas lights along the slab. A sign proclaimed the site under the protection of the federal government.

Eagle Feather stood at the edge of the trees and studied the scene. He saw how the slab would fit nicely into the opening in the cliff behind it. Desert varnish painted the outer roof of the cave suggesting the slab must have come out centuries ago. Blood was pooled on the flat stone, sticky and tar-like, partially obscuring an unnatural reddish tint to the surface. Eagle Feather guessed many deaths had occurred on this slab over time.

The Navajo found his eye drawn toward the cave. He felt a strong mystic sense here. Something of the presence of the Ancients still resided among the centuries old pinyon and in the eternal sandstone. The shadowy recess of the cave called to him in a way similar to Anasazi ruins. The feeling was strong now, but with it came a sense of evil. Eagle Feather pushed his feelings aside and walked to the cave.

# CHAPTER THIRTEEN

Something moved. Eagle Feather sensed rather than saw the motion in the blackness of the cave. Something was in the deeper darkness toward the rear.

Sometimes the eye plays tricks; sometimes light seen obliquely can suggest movement, or a fast turn of the head can cause stationary objects to appear to move. Eagle Feather knew all that, but dismissed it. Something large had moved in the rear of the cave, but his eyes could not penetrate the shadow. He stood against to the cool sandstone wall and listened.

The cave roof loomed high above him, at least twenty feet. The far wall was thirty feet away, he guessed. As his adjusting eyes delivered more detail, he realized the interior was larger and deeper than he had thought. The well-published pile of bones was in the center of the cavern floor, others were scattered here and there. A bone at his feet glowed ghostly white. He picked it up. It looked like a human femur.

Eagle Feather wanted to inspect the bones in more detail, but not until he identified whoever or whatever shared the cave with him. The movement had appeared to come from the side opposite where he now stood and toward the rear. He could see nothing but darkness with pockets of even deeper shadow. He would have to move a lot closer.

Eagle Feather had no flashlight. He would have to rely upon his ears to work his way toward the rear of the cave. His only weapon was his knife. He took a cautious step.

The moment he moved, there was a mosquito buzz by his ear and a crack against the sandstone where he had just been, followed by the whine of a ricochet. He heard the delayed report of a rifle, dropped to the cave floor and flattened his body against the dank hard surface, hoping his black pants and black vest would camouflage him in the darkness. As he lay still, he heard a slight rustle in the rear of the cave. Great, he thought, now I'm surrounded.

The sniper was his first concern; the rifleman would be watching, waiting for the slightest move. But the shooter's view must be limited, peering as he would be from bright sunshine into darkness. Eagle Feather decided to test it. He inched out a hand, searched, found the femur. With a flick of his wrist, he sent it flying toward the far wall. Instantly, there was another smack and whine of a bullet and the delayed rifle report. He used that distraction to worm his way into deeper shadow. Back here it was dark, he was certain the sniper could not see him. To kill him now, the attacker would have to come into the cave after him. If he did, the playing field would be leveled.

It was time to worry about who or what else was in the cave with him. During his maneuver to avoid the rifleman, Eagle Feather had thrust himself closer to the unseen presence. He drew his knife from its sheath and waited.

He waited a long time. No sound came from the darkness behind him.

Then he heard voices, men calling to each other beyond the cave mouth. "Do you see him, LeRoy?"

"I can't see anything in there. It's too dark."

Eagle Feather heard the scuff of feet approach the cave mouth.

"You go on that side, Stan," a voice said. "I'll stay on this side."

Eagle Feather pictured the men in his mind's eye, one on each side of the slab, approaching the slope. I have nowhere to go, he thought, nothing to do but wait.

"What did you see in there, Stan?"

"It looked like some Indian. There was a feather on his head."

The clunk of stone on stone, the sound of heavy breathing came to his ear. They were close now. The sounds came from both sides of the cave mouth.

"Did he have a gun, Stan?" The voice was now a whisper, tense.

"I don't know, man. I didn't see one. I just got a quick glimpse."

"I ain't goin' in there, Stan. He might have a gun."

"Just wait. Hang on." The second voice became loud now, authoritative. "You in there. We are deputy marshals. Come out slow with your hands in the air and we won't shoot."

"Yeah, come on out or we'll fill this place with bullets."

Eagle Feather thought about that. The threat was real. Any rifle bullet fired into this cave could rebound anywhere. There would be no safe place. The two turkeys outside could be hit just as easily, but they might be too dumb know that.

Almost as if in answer to his thought, the first voice called out again. "We're gonna count to three. If we don't see you standing with your hands in the air by three, we start shooting."

Yeah, they're that dumb, he decided. He put his knife back in its sheath and prepared to rise and give himself up. At that moment, he became aware of something stirring in the cave depth, now moving forward with incredible quickness along the far wall, a vague form, large, on two legs, just a blur of motion, a shadow flying along. It arrived at the cave mouth, was outlined there for a millisecond, and was gone.

Then came shouts, shots.

"What was that?"

"Did you get it?"

"I missed it."

'Where'd it go?"

"This way. C'mon, quick!" The sound of boots on rock, shadows flitting across the cave mouth, a thrashing in the underbrush, more shouting that gradually faded.

Eagle Feather walked out of the cave, blinking in the brightness. He could hear Stan and LeRoy calling to each other, deep in the arroyo somewhere. Whatever it was had saved him, it would keep the deputies busy for a while.

He turned back into the cave. His eyes adapted quickly this time. He went to see the bones. There was just enough ambient light to tell they seemed to be human. Some were clean, others had debris clinging to them, some appeared fresher than others. There were many bones spread about the cave floor.

The cave itself was bone dry, a perfect environment for preserving bones, and bodies for that matter, but he saw none. Just bones. He picked one up from the earthen floor and carried it to the cave mouth to study in better light. It looked smooth and bare, but after rubbing his palm along it he felt small gouges, little imprints. Birds might have helped remove the flesh. That would not have happened inside the cave. The bone must have been placed here later.

He reentered the cave and replaced the bone where he had found it, and stared again at the bone heap. There were no whole skeletons as far as he could tell, not even partial ones. Had all of these bones come from somewhere else, after all the flesh and sinew had been removed? If so, why?

Had the cave creature had something to do with it? The thing could not be human, he thought, it was too fast, but it was upright—maybe a bear. He shook his head. What he had glimpsed in silhouette at the cave mouth was not a bear.

Eagle Feather moved farther to the rear of the cave. With each step, the little light that there was diminished. He felt the cave closing in, funnel-like. The scent of it was musty, a smell of decay mingled with mold. Ahead was deep

60

blackness. Were there more creatures? His heart raced despite himself.

The hard earth softened beneath his feet. He reached down, felt loose soil. It felt as if someone had been digging here. The smell of decayed flesh was strong.

Eagle Feather turned back. Without light, he could learn nothing. He left the cave, slid past the slab and into the cover of the trees. He needed to be cautious. The deputies might still be around, ready to shoot at anything that moved. He hoped the cave creature had led the two lawmen far away.

Eagle Feather exited the arroyo and began the long hike back. His thoughts were troubled. His findings in the cave suggested great evil, whether from man or monster—or both.

# CHAPTER FOURTEEN

The voice was harsh, cruel. "Why did you kill the girl?"

The response was querulous, submissive. "I had to kill her. She was there when I took the boy. She must have seen me. I could not leave a witness."

"Now you killed the wrong girl."

"I thought she was the right girl. I followed her many times, I knew what she looked like."

"No, you killed the wrong one. You saw where the girl lived; you learned her name, yet you killed the wrong one. The papers gave the name of the girl you killed. It was the wrong girl."

There was indistinct mumbling. "Yes, I know it was the wrong girl. They were so much alike, she was walking on the same street at the right time. She even wore the same color ribbon in her hair." A pause. "It shouldn't have happened that way."

"No, it should not."

There were more mumbles, incoherent words. "I'll fix it."

"How will you fix it?"

"I will kill the right girl."

"If you mess up again, our work can not be done." The voice was harsher now. "Can you find her?"

The response contrite, "I think so. I have watched her house, she has not left it."

"The school is closed. There are no children on the streets now. Everyone is afraid. How will you reach her?"

"I will find a way. I will do what I have to do. I will find a way."

"There may be others."

"Others?"

"Other enemies who must be punished. You can not waste your time on one—small—girl."

"I know, I know."

"Perhaps if you find a way to kill the girl, we can forgive you."

Incoherent mumbling. "Yes, yes, I have a plan. I will succeed this time."

# CHAPTER FIFTEEN

It was nearly midnight when Zack heard the dogs bark and saw the flicker of headlights through the trees where the long driveway approached the house. Moments later, Emma's car pulled up in front. Mother and daughter climbed out, anxiety etched on their faces. Zack wrapped each of them with an arm and walked them up the steps into the house. Bernie was long since asleep and wouldn't wake up even if the earth moved.

Zack brought them to the kitchen, to seats at the table, and poured out hot chocolate he'd kept in a thermos.

"You probably haven't eaten, am I right?"

Emma gave him a haggard look. "No, we drove right through. We didn't dare stop. Every set of headlights behind us frightened me."

Emma's appearance always surprised Zack. She was as blonde as Libby was raven-haired, as plump and rounded as Libby was slim and tall. He never would have guessed them for sisters.

Pru had grown since Zack saw her last. With her long brown hair, she was a slender version of her aunt.

"When was the last time you saw anyone behind you?" Zack asked.

It was Pru who answered.

"We haven't seen anyone since we turned off Route 89 onto 64 at Cameron."

Zack nodded, smiled. "Well, in that case we can breathe a little easier. No stranger could know how to find us here unless they followed you." He opened a cupboard door and brought down some plates. With oven mitts, he opened the oven door and brought out a large steaming casserole dish. "We have here a three-cheese ravioli made specially by Chef Tolliver. I thought you might be hungry."

The women served themselves at the counter while Zack called Libby to let her know they had arrived safely.

Everyone sat down at the table. Emma's portion was small; fatigue and nervousness had taken their toll on her appetite, but did not appear to hinder Pru, who gobbled hers down and went back for more.

"No one knows you are here," Zack said. He smiled at them. "Your ruse will be a well-kept secret."

"What about my job?" Emma asked. "And Pru's classes? Won't there be questions?"

"Libby will handle all that." He looked at Pru. "Your school may be on lockdown by tomorrow anyway. The county sheriff's office doesn't want more potential victims walking to and from the high school."

It wasn't long before the food and warmth of the kitchen had its effect. Zack saw eyelids flutter and went for the suitcase in the car.

"We didn't bring much," Emma said when he returned. "We packed in a hurry."

Zack nodded. "I think we can take care of most of your needs right here for a little while, anyway. If necessary, we'll order whatever else we need. We'll just have to see how the case progresses."

The following morning, Zack was awakened by the unfamiliar feeling of warmth on his cheek and opened his eyes to bright sun shining through the living room window. It took him a moment to remember why he was on the couch. He glanced at his watch—7:30 a.m. He'd slept long. He climbed out from under the blanket and walked in his shorts to the kitchen. Emma drank her coffee black as he remembered, but he couldn't remember about Pru. Well, he'd just make a big pot.

All was quiet in the master bedroom, no surprise there. Bernie was chatting quietly to himself in his room as he usually did. Zack took the opportunity to jump into the shower and throw on jeans. When he emerged, Pru was in the living room staring out the picture window. She turned when she heard Zack.

"I always loved coming here as a child," she said. "These woods—it's so different from the landscape around our house."

"You don't enjoy the red rock and mesas?"

"Oh, yes, I do, but in a different way, you know?" She struggled for words. "The rock cliffs are exciting, almost dangerous feeling, but here is so relaxing."

Zack smiled. "I suspect you could use some of that right now."

She grinned back. "Can I go see Bernie? I think he is awake."

Zack laughed. "Of course. That will be his great surprise for the day. I've got coffee going; you can help yourself. There's juice in the fridge. I'll cook up some breakfast once I see to the animals."

But that didn't happen. When Zack came back to the house a half hour later, he was greeted by the smell of bacon and found Emma busy in the kitchen. She turned when she heard Zack. "Go wash up. We have scrambled eggs, bacon, and toast ready to go."

Zack smiled and did as he was told.

Breakfast chatter was lively, especially with Bernie drawing attention to himself constantly. Watching him, Zack wondered if the two-year-old was a lonely child. He certainly was making up for any lack of socialization at the moment.

Zack's phone buzzed while they were still at the table. It was FBI Agent Pete Conley, Zack's former colleague. He excused himself and walked into the living room.

"We've got some new information regarding the victim," Conley said without preamble. "We wondered how the killer managed to subdue a strong, athletic boy and convey him all the way up Canaan Mountain. I think we have our answer."

"I'm all ears," Zack said.

"The coroner's team found a puncture wound in the boy's neck. He was darted. A toxicology report shows the presence of Telazol and ketamine. They performed a gas chromatography-mass spectrometry to analyze quantities of tiletamine and zolazepam, which in equal measure constitute Telazol, which..."

"Whoa, slow down. Too much information."

"Bear with me, Zack. I'll give you just the pieces you need to know. First, understand that Telazol can take up to twelve minutes to produce an anesthetic effect. After darting the boy, the killer would have needed another agent, probably chloroform—they found very low traces present—to get the boy into the vehicle. The darting would have shocked the boy, allowing time to administer the chloroform."

"Who would know about these drugs, or possess them, for that matter?"

"Interesting, right? A veterinarian would be most likely, an anesthesiologist possibly, even a zookeeper might have access to the anesthetic and dart gun."

"How potent is this stuff?"

"Very potent. They've shipped a sample off to Behring Diagnostic, Inc., in Cupertino, California to determine concentrations, but results won't be available for a while. However, we think it very likely the boy was dead before he was impaled."

"That, at least, is a relief. But how did the killer get the boy up the mountain? Do you think there are more than one killers out there?"

"Well, that's possible, of course, but we think it unlikely. There is a well-used quad trail up the mountain that approaches to within a hundred yards or so of the arroyo. Getting the body from the quad down into the arroyo would have been the hardest part."

"Could the drug dosage have been such that the boy could walk? Maybe with help from the killer?"

"Again, it's possible, but would have required an intimate knowledge of the drugs and accurate assumptions of the boy's biology. The killer's planning was extremely detailed. Biological reactions to this anesthetic are variable, dependent on size, health, even the temperature outside. We doubt he would have left anything to chance."

"So we're looking for a large, strong man who owns a quad and works in a zoo."

Conley laughed. "Yeah, something like that. We've already begun checking connections to the anesthetic. It does narrow the field."

Zack paused, speaking in a quieter tone. "What have you learned about the death of the girl?"

Conley let out an audible sigh. "That's another matter entirely. According to the sheriff, this was not a well thought out murder. The girl died from blunt force trauma to the back of her head, crushing the skull. Must have died instantly. She was killed, transported to the scene, and dumped."

Zack thought about it. "But he had to get her into a vehicle first, right? I mean, he wouldn't have climbed out, whacked her on the head, and dragged her body into his truck on a town street in broad daylight. There was no trace of drugs?"

"There was chloroform, according to the sheriff. That does not significantly narrow the field." Conley interrupted himself. "Say, Zack, I've got another call. I'll get back to you when I have more."

The call ended.

Zack stared at his phone, feeling like a bride left at the altar. He wasn't used to depending upon other people for information about a case and found it frustrating.

While he had his phone out, he called Libby. She answered right away. He asked how her night had been.

"Well, it was a bit nerve-racking," she said. "I watched some TV, ate a microwave dinner all by myself, and spent time peeking out the window from behind the curtain. Don't worry. I didn't give myself away. At one point, I saw a man in a car parked down the street a ways. He was there for a long time. I guess he was my protection."

Zack felt a lurch in his stomach. "Libby, we didn't arrange protection."

# CHAPTER SIXTEEN

It took several moments for the impact of Zack's words to sink in. Libby's heart began to pound. "If he wasn't my protection—?"

"What did the car look like?" Zack asked. "Have you ever seen it before?"

"I don't think so. It was a dark sedan, but it glistened in the streetlight, very clean and shiny." Libby clenched the phone hard to her ear.

"Hmmm. I've got no idea who that could be. I suppose a local cop could have taken it on himself to watch the house. Or it could be something else entirely and nothing to do with us."

"Who else knows about Pru's situation?" Libby asked.

"All law enforcement personnel know Pru was with the boy the day he was kidnapped. She became a material witness because of that. Only a limited number of FBI agents know she left the house and is here with me."

"So I shouldn't worry?"

"Not yet. But let me know if you notice anything else unusual."

After Zack ended the call, Libby went to the window and pulled back the curtain. The car was gone. She peered up and down the street. Nothing seemed out of place, although it appeared unusually quiet out there.
She grunted to herself. With a mad killer on the loose, everyone would be keeping to their homes.

She stood in the center of her sister's living room and thought about her situation. The little sounds a house makes—
—a warming roof board creaking, the quiet whir of the refrigerator starting up, an occasional drip from the bathroom—now came to her consciousness one by one, contributing to a sense of isolation. Libby had spent months alone in the ranch house near Cameron, an old building originally built by her grandfather with rooms added on over

the decades. That house made a whole symphony of noises, but she was used to them and knew the origin of each sound. This house was strange to her, its small noises more mysterious.

Libby decided to tour the house and make herself more familiar. Comfortable in pajamas and slippers, she began upstairs in the master bedroom. Last night, she had slept on the foldout couch in the living room, despite her sister's protestations. She should move into the bedroom, Emma had said; after all, who knew how long this might take? Libby had refused. Now as she looked at the king bed and saw how inviting it was, she decided to accept Emma's suggestion after all. There were three windows in this room, two that faced the street and one the side yard. She checked the locks on all three, saw that the window alarms were set, and drew the curtains. Her sister had an office of sorts in the rear of the upstairs, a small desk and a file cabinet. One window was completely blocked, the other faced the side yard. She checked that window and drew the curtains.

Libby progressed in like manner around the remaining upstairs rooms: Pru's bedroom, Pru's study/playroom and the bathroom. Downstairs, she made her rounds through the kitchen, dining room, living room, and parlor. She checked the rear hall and saw that the back door was bolted and latched.

There was another door in the rear hall, also latched. She opened it. Steps led down to a cellar. Even in her slippers, the wooden steps rang hollow and creaked as she descended. The concrete floor of the cellar was spotless. Libby was not surprised; her sister was a notorious neat freak. The windows were high in the wall, small and rectangular, difficult for even a child to slip through, she imagined, and all were securely latched. Various chairs and tables were stored near a central gas burning furnace and the hot water heater, both of which hummed and murmured in their own way.

Satisfied, Libby climbed back up the cellar stairs and latched the door behind her. As an additional precaution, she found a wooden door wedge and jammed it under the cellar door. In the kitchen, her cup of tea sat forlornly on the stovetop. She hooked a finger in the handle on the way by and went upstairs for a shower.

Libby felt her tension melt away in the deluge of hot water. When she finally forced herself to emerge, she toweled off in front of a foggy mirror. The loud little fan above her head didn't accomplish much beyond making a racket so she reached for the wall switch and put it out of its misery. In the sudden silence the various house noises came alive again, but there was a new sound, a persistent scraping sound, like a chicken scratching at the wood floor of a barn.

Libby wrapped the towel close around her and tread silently on bare feet into the bedroom and threw on jeans and a shirt. She stopped to listen again; the noise continued, downstairs somewhere, toward the back of the house. Still in bare feet, she crept as silently as the stair boards would allow down to the living room. She took the small pistol from the side table drawer and made a mental note to keep it with her at all times from now on.

She paused again to listen. The sound had stopped. The noisy stairs must have given her away. She remained still and waited. After several long minutes, the scratching came again. She knew where the sound was now—the cellar door. Libby picked up her cell phone from the side table. She crept down the hallway, her phone in one hand, the gun in the other. Four feet from the door, she stopped, stood still and listened. The scraping was coming from the bottom edge of the cellar door.

A mouse. It had to be a mouse.
She felt relief until she saw the door wedge push back incrementally. This was no mouse. Someone was behind the door on the cellar step trying to reach the wedge. Her eye

72

went to the latch—it dangled uselessly. The scraping sound was louder, the wedge moved. Panic swept over her.

Libby aimed the pistol at the space under the door right next to the wedge, which by now had wiggled free. "You son of a bitch." Her words and the roar of her pistol came together. The gunshot was followed by a muffled curse and the sound of something heavy thudding down the steps.

Libby did not intend to wait for the outcome. She pulled open the door and fired into the darkness at the bottom of the stairs. There was more swearing and scrambling. She threw the switch for the cellar light and a ceiling bulb somewhere below shone on bare concrete at the foot of the stairs for a second before the light went out with a pop and tinkling of glass.

Libby flew down the stairs, firing into the darkness. The reaching flare of the pistol revealed a fragmentary vision of a shape wiggling through the tiny cellar window. She fired again as the blackness returned and was rewarded with another brief cry. She stood, waiting, listening. As her sight improved she saw the rectangular shape of the window, aglow with filtering sunlight. Shards of glass adhered to the corners. The space it outlined was empty.

Hands shaking, Libby fumbled for her phone and called Zack.

\* \* \* \* \*

Zack was on his way. After he heard Libby's story, he had not hesitated. Emma and Pru could look after Bernie in his absence. He sounded relieved to know the intruder never got far enough to realize Pru was not in the house.

"Should I call 911?" Libby had asked.

"No. We can't risk an investigation by the local cops, we need to preserve the idea that Pru is still there," Zack had replied. "I'll suggest the FBI send someone to take a sample of the intruder's fingerprints and blood, if there is any. Don't allow anyone in until he arrives. He'll call you first from the porch. Meanwhile, I'll get someone to keep an eye on the place."

The FBI man came within a half hour, in appearance a local deputy responding to a home intrusion. He set to work, finished in another half hour, and left.

Libby, still shaking and anxious, did not plan to simply sit and wait for Zack to make the two-hour plus trip from Cameron. She planned to take her own steps. First was to fortify the house.

Among the furniture stacked near the furnace Libby found shelf units. She removed the shelves, located Emma's toolbox and boarded up the broken window, then boarded up the other three as well. She stacked up furniture to block each boarded window.

Libby next turned her attention to the cellar door. She repaired the latch, using extra screws. The wedge served its purpose; she would use it again. As a final defense, she removed a cellar step, sawed it three quarters through, and replaced it.

The rear door, reached by the same hallway as the cellar door, was the next greatest vulnerability, to her mind. She searched the upstairs rooms and found another wedge. The door's windows were too small for entry, but when smashed a hand could reach in and unlock the door. Libby found duct tape, set razor blades into it, and wrapped the tape around the doorknob. She fortified the door latch with extra screws.

By now it was close to noon, and Libby was ready for another shower. The only other door to the outside was the front door. It had the best locks of all the doors and had a screen door that also locked. It was alarmed, and, of course, visible from the street. Libby decided not to spend time on it.

Slipping the pistol in her pocket, she went outside and walked around the house studying it from every angle. The second story was high above the ground and the siding offered no purchase for climbing. The only possible way to access the second floor was the drainpipe. She pondered it a few moments, went back inside and found the claw hammer. From the rear bedroom, she leaned out the window and pried the clamp loose and pushed the drainpipe away from the wall until it hung precariously. Let him try to climb that, she thought to herself.

Libby felt almost safe now. She returned to the bathroom to shower and begin her day all over again.

# CHAPTER SEVENTEEN

Zack's phone buzzed on the seat next to him near Lee's Ferry. He saw the FBI ID and pulled over.

"Zack Tolliver."

"Zack, it's Pete. Just a couple of things; first, I wanted you to know our man's been in and out of the Baker house. Libby seemed fine to him, and he was able to get blood samples, a partial footprint and maybe fingerprints—we'll see. Second, we heard back from the anthropology lab on the bones from the cave. Of the three femurs we sent them, two are recent, which is to say within the last decade. The third was one hundred thirty to one hundred fifty years old."

Zack pondered that. "So two deaths could be recent murders, the older one from the late 1800s?"

"Right. We're treating the recent femurs as suspicious deaths. That's enough to allow us to go back and dig deeper into the bone pile. Guys who saw the bones thought some were old enough to be fossilized. We may have a whole range of time periods represented in there."

"What's next for you?"

"We've got a meeting set up with Chairwoman Shana Bows of the Paiute Tribe along with Maurice Folkes from the BLM to try to get everyone on the same page and get the Indians to go along with this." Conley paused. "To tell the truth, Zack, these bones may have nothing to do with the local Native Americans."

"Is your expert able to get a reading on whether the older bone is White or Indian?"

Conley chuckled. "Not so much. She would like us to find a skull so she can determine craniofacial dimensions to help determine that. Which means, back to the bone pile—if we can get everyone's permission. But more important to us at this time is to determine where the two modern bones came from and how those two people died."

"That's not going to be easy."

"Not at all." Conley gave a short humorless laugh. "Once again, we need to go back to the bone pile and try to find the skeletons to match, then see what we can learn. It will take a while."

"But the boy who was just killed?"

"He is priority number one, of course. We'll proceed with that investigation regardless. Later, we'll see if the other bones connect to this case or not." He paused. "What are your plans, Zack?" He sounded concerned.

"I'm on my way to Kanab. I'm worried about Libby, I just want to be sure she is okay."

"Can you go there without giving things away? Won't the perp become suspicious?"

Zack grunted. "Emma is my sister-in-law, my wife Libby is there now. There would be nothing unusual in me showing up if the guy's done his homework. And hopefully my presence will prevent another break-in."

"Then what? I know you, Zack. You're not simply going to sit on your hands and hang around with Libby in that house."

"I just want to be sure Libby is okay. I'm not thinking beyond that right now," Zack insisted.

"Promise me you'll get in touch before you do anything else."

"Don't worry, Pete. I'll be a good boy." He ended the call.

Zack was at 400 Street shortly after 2 p.m. and parked directly in front of the Baker house, his bright red Jeep an unmistakable sign of his presence. He called Libby from the vehicle to identify himself before he knocked on the door.

Libby let him in, secured the door behind him, and gave him a bear hug.

Zack grinned. "Glad to see me, huh?"

Libby gave a mock pout. "Don't get carried away with yourself, it's been pretty lonely here. I'd of hugged Big Blue just as hard if he was at the door."

Zack's grin broadened as he imagined the scene. Their bloodhound Big Blue would likely have been the one doing the hugging.

Libby dragged Zack into the kitchen where coffee and two-day-old donuts waited.

A gnawing stomach drove him to a seat and a massive chocolate-covered concoction. Between bites, he encouraged Libby to tell the full story of her defense of the house. As he listened, he felt a wave of admiration and respect for her courage and ingenuity.

"How many shots did you fire?' he asked, his mouth full of donut.

"Three, I think...yes, three; once through the door, once into the dark at the bottom of the stairs, once in the direction of the window."

"Do you have the gun?"

Libby removed the gun from her pocket, slid it to Zack, who opened the chamber and examined it.

"How many hits, do you think?"

"I think two bullets hit him. At least, he yelped twice. But neither could have been serious, the way he scrambled through the window and ran."

Zack wrote the details in a small notebook he carried. He slid the gun back to Libby, nodded toward the hall. "Can you show me the basement?" He scooped up his coffee and followed Libby. At the cellar door he inspected the eruption of wood in the doorsill from the bullet. He found spots of blood. "You must have got a hand or an arm," he said.

They went down the cellar stairs, carefully avoiding the trap step.

Zack studied the window. "We're not looking for a fat man, are we?"

"My impression was a slender, active person, not all that tall," Libby said. "It's just an impression though, it was too dark for more than that."

Zack removed the shelf slats and scrutinized the basement wall under the window, then the window itself. "There are spots of blood here and on some broken window shards. It's hard to tell if you hit him a second time or if he cut himself in his haste to get out." He glanced at Libby. "Did the FBI man get blood samples?"

She nodded. "He said he got a partial print from the sill and some tissue also."

"That's good, real good. By now they're checking their database. If this guy is in it, they'll have his name and last known address. If Conley doesn't call me soon, I'll call him."

Zack restacked the furniture and followed Libby up the cellar steps. She inserted the wedge.

Back in the kitchen, Zack poured a coffee and had another donut. "This man must be quite desperate to attempt a daytime attack like this. He must be very concerned about Pru and what she may know."

"Is she safe at our house?"

"She couldn't be safer. Jimmy Chaparral will keep an eye on them." Jimmy was chief of the Navajo Police unit at Elk Wells and an old friend of the family.

Libby poured a coffee and sat down across from Zack. "What's next, Zack? Emma and Pru can't hide out forever, and soon the killer will figure out they aren't here just by the fact they never leave."

Zack stared down at his mug. "Yes, it is frustrating. We have to wait for others to resolve the murders. We need to wait for Conley to check in, and hopefully Eagle Feather will learn something." Zack shrugged. "So we wait."

Libby was startled when Zack's phone began to buzz on the wooden table. He saw how tense she was and laid a hand on her arm. He picked up his phone with the other. It was Eagle Feather.

"Are you okay?" Zack asked.

"Are you worried about me, White Man?"

"Well, yes, actually."

He heard Eagle Feather's quiet chuckle. "Maybe you should be."

The response was not what Zack wanted to hear. "What are you up to?"

"Where are you?" Eagle Feather asked.

Zack caught Libby's eye, raised an eyebrow. "I'm in Emma's kitchen in Kanab with Libby."

"You could not stay away from here, could you?"

Zack grunted. "It's a long story."

"I have a long story also, White Man. We should meet."

Zack paused, thought about it, and agreed. "Okay, where? We should not be seen together, not yet anyway."

"I have a campsite at a campground in the Paiute Indian Reservation near Pipe Spring National Monument. There is no one else here." Eagle Feather gave the directions.

"I'll be there in an hour."

It was late afternoon when Zack's red Jeep rolled into the Paiute Campground and parked near Eagle Feather's rusty red truck. The man himself sat on the rough-hewn bench of the picnic table, a coffee mug at hand.

Zack walked over, shook hands. "You look beat."

Eagle Feather ignored the comment, nodded toward another cup on the table. "There's coffee in the pot by the fire."

Zack picked up the mug. On it was a picture of a mule hitched to a covered wagon. A woman sat in the front of the wagon in a long plain dress and bonnet holding the reigns while a man in a wide-brimmed hat stood with a short whip in one hand and the mule's bridle in the other. The words above the picture read "Pipe Spring National Monument."

Zack raised an eyebrow, peered at Eagle Feather.

"I only had one mug. I stopped at the souvenir store."

Zack smiled. "You can put it on my expense account." He poured some coffee and brought it back to the table.

"You don't have an expense account anymore."

"True enough." Zack's smile widened. "Oh, well." He turned and gazed up at the red rock escarpment behind him, then out across the flatland of the Uinkaret Plateau. "Quite the view from your little home."

"It settles my soul."

The two men sat side by side absorbed in the play of shadow and light on the flatland all the way to the far horizon.

"Someone tried to break into Emma's house in Kanab," Zack said after a few moments. "Libby fought him off."

Eagle Feather jerked his head around. "Is she okay?"

"Just a little shook up." Zack grinned, shaking his head. "She put at least one bullet into the intruder. Not a serious wound, unfortunately."

"What about Emma and Pru?"

"They weren't there. We arranged for them to slip away to my house. That's where they are now." He began to sip his coffee, pulled his lips away. "Damn, that's hot." He blew on it. "Fortunately, the intruder never got beyond the basement, so he doesn't know they aren't there."

"The shell game." Eagle Feather chuckled. "Very good. Do you know who this guy is?"

"I'd guess he is the man driving the Travelall who's been following Pru. At the moment, it seems plausible to assume he is the killer."

"Are the cops looking for him?"

"No one got the number or state of the license plate. Not much to go on."

"How many times did he follow her?"

"Several." Zack tried his coffee again. "We think he thinks she saw him or at least saw his vehicle the day of the kidnapping. He wants to eliminate her as a witness."

"So he breaks in, Libby discourages him before he can learn if the girl is actually there, you learn about it and drive up to protect Libby."

"That's about the size of it."

"You'll stay there openly now?"

Zack grinned. "A flaming red Jeep parked right in front of the house is hard to miss." He shifted his seat. "In other news, the forensic bone analysis of the three femurs turned up two bones from within the decade and another from the mid 1800s."

Eagle Feather considered that. "They came from three different people?"

Zack nodded.

"There are many more bones to investigate in that cave."

Zack raised his eyebrows. "You were up there?"

"I was there today. I have only just returned."

Zack sipped, watched his friends face and waited.

"It is a long way up there and back," Eagle Feather said. "It took time to find the arroyo. The rock slab and the hollow behind it are just like the newspapers described it." He gazed out over the plateau. "I ran into the man who discovered the crime, a big man, a hunter. He said he went back there for another look because something did not feel right to him."

"What kind of man was he?"

Eagle Feather shrugged. "He is a white man. Who can tell?"

"Big and strong enough to impale the boy by himself?"

"Yes."

Zack stretched, resettled his butt on the hard bench. "Did you go into the cave?"

"I thought you would never ask."

"I just did."

"No one was at the crime scene, but I felt that someone or something was already inside the cave."

"Something?"

"I went into the cave. I had no flashlight, but there was enough light to see the bones. Some were scattered on the floor of the cave, but most were in a big pile in the middle. The bones were clean, all flesh gone, like you would see in a mountain lion's den. There were some fragments of sinew and cloth." He glanced at Zack. "Something was in there with me in the back of the cave. I sensed it, smelled it. But before I could do more some men claiming to be marshals saw me and shot at me with rifles."

Zack was startled. "Just like that? No warning?"

Eagle Feather told him about something erupting from the cave, leading the riflemen away, thus allowing Eagle Feather the opportunity to escape. "It was too dark to see in the rear of the cave. There was a place where the earth was soft, as if it had been disturbed recently. I smelled a mix of decayed flesh, blood, and very bad breath."

Zack studied his friend's face. "What do you think it was?"

"I do not know. It evoked a memory, but I can not place it."

Zack thought about it, then nodded. "Okay, I will call Conley and suggest he get some men deeper into that cave with lights and shovels. Anything else?"

Eagle Feather stared out into the growing dusk. When he spoke again, his voice was pitched low. "The cave reminded me of a predator's den, bones scattered around, that hair and hide smell." He looked at Zack, his dark eyes somber. "But on a much larger scale."

# CHAPTER EIGHTEEN

Jeffrey Danes Harlow shifted his weight from his right butt cheek to his left. He was in growing discomfort seated on a hard wooden bench at the long trestle table in President Brown's exceedingly hot kitchen, waiting for one of the humorless white-bearded faces around him to speak. This was not his first time in, or on, the hot spot. And his other meetings had not gone well.

President Josiah Brown was Head of the Priesthood Council out of which seven were now in attendance. Brown selected the title president for himself and liked to hold his meetings in his kitchen because it was convenient for him, inconvenient for everyone else, and usually hotter than blazes, which led to shorter, less oppositional meetings. The kitchen was very large, and the women always had food ready.

Jeffrey was summoned to describe in depth what he had seen when first dispatched to the top of Canaan Mountain to the scene of the murder. The Council had all the initial reports from the Marshal's Department in hand; they now wanted intimate details.

Josiah Brown had a large oval face with eyes set close together, a nose bent a tad to the right, and a tight smile that sent waves of increasingly large grooves like great parentheses across the broad seascape of his cheeks. To Jeffrey, it was not a smile of pleasantness but one of artifice, hung in place like an ornament to create a particular image. It was there now as President Brown regarded him from the head of the table.

"Brother Jeffrey, we understand the tribulation you have undergone, why it was you were sent to respond to the call on Canaan Mountain without a partner. Your so-called prior felonies committed to protect your brothers are regrettable in that they cost you the position of marshal in the state of Arizona. But we have spoken of that already.

"The question the Council wishes to take up today is specifically in regard to the crime scene and what you saw there." President Brown glanced at the men assembled. "Who would like to begin the questions?"

The man seated across from Jeffrey spoke up immediately. His full white beard was cut in an Old Dutch style that reminded Jeffrey of a Pharaoh. "Deputy Marshall Harlow, I'll get to the heart of the matter. You have given the impression that this crime might well have been Blood Atonement. The altar-like stone, the way the body lay upon it pierced by the single stake suggests this. Would you agree?"

Jeffrey nodded. "It could be many things, but it certainly could be a Blood Atonement."

Another Elder, his cheeks puffy and red from the heat, spoke. "Yet the boy was not from Short Creek and was not a member of the church. He was a black gentile, who as such in any case could never in this life have held church office and therefore could not have been an apostate. To become an apostate, and thus subject to Blood Atonement, one must be a member of the church and then renounce it. The Apostle Brigham Young teaches us God has marked the descendants of Cain with dark skin and restricted them from partaking of Temple ordinances. The Book of Mormon tells us of the conflict between Nephites and Lamanites and how the people led by Laman, cursed by God with their black skins, never accepted the teachings of Jesus when he visited the New World."

"Elder Owen, thank you for this history lesson," President Brown said with heavy irony. "However, regardless of the boy's skin color, the FLDS does not sanction the practice of Blood Atonement as you know. While both Joseph Smith and Brigham Young spoke of the righteousness of such a doctrine, they never actually legislated it, although we are aware certain counselors of the Prophets in the past utilized the doctrine as a punitive measure."

He peered around the table. "I believe I can speak for our absent brothers when I say neither they, nor I, nor none of us here practice the doctrine. As Elder Taylor has said, this cannot be true Blood Atonement, since a Lamanite could never be an apostate. Yet it has been carried out ritualistically and in a manner to suggest it." He grimaced and stared at Jeffrey. "The concern here is that outsiders, particularly outside law enforcement, will conclude this was Blood Atonement and persecute us accordingly. These people need only the smallest excuse to vilify us, and this will be more than enough."

"What shall we do, then?" Elder Owen asked.

President Brown studied Jeffery. "Indeed, what shall we do?"

Jeffrey Danes Harlow squirmed as the silence became prolonged, with all eyes on him. The president waited for full effect before continuing. "This is why we have summoned you, Jeffrey. You were first to respond and first to witness the scene; therefore, what you saw and how you describe it even to the very inflection you use while doing so will influence the way outsiders view this crime. You have stated publicly it suggests Blood Atonement." He planted a rigid index finger on the table to emphasize his words. "You will never use that term again. If you are asked about your use of that phrase, you must recant it. If a reporter or investigator or anyone else asks your opinion of the crime, you will suggest another, completely different scenario." He stared at Jeffrey. "Am I clear?"

Jeffrey swallowed, nodded.

Elder Owen studied him. "Tell us about the two hunters who were at the scene when you arrived. Could they have committed the crime? Shouldn't they be the first suspects?"

"They have been questioned and remain suspects," Jeffrey said. "But there is no physical evidence—no blood, no prints, nothing at all to connect them to the murder. The murder occurred long before they arrived, which begs the question why they would return to it and call attention to it if they are guilty."

"Have they been taken into custody?" another Elder asked.

Jeffrey shook his head.

"Does the FBI have a theory? A suspect?" Elder Taylor asked.

"The FBI hopes to establish from an examination of the bones whether other, similar murders might have been committed in that place. If so, this may be the work of a serial killer. That would shed an entirely different light on the crime."

"My two sons, Stan and LeRoy, believe the killer must be from Kanab as was the victim. They believe it to be a private dispute, perhaps a gang or something of that sort," Elder Taylor said.

"That sounds reasonable to me." President Brown leveled his eyes at Jeffrey. "Perhaps, Deputy Harlow, you could agree with your fellow marshals."

"Yes, sir."

Elder Taylor studied Jeffrey. "Might I suggest the security of the crime scene on Canaan Mountain be left to my two sons? Given your unfortunate remarks about Blood Atonement, it might be best if the press see you are no longer attached to that duty and therefore not a source of information." He looked toward the president for affirmation.

President Brown nodded. "An excellent thought. It would save Brother Jeffrey a good deal of trouble." He stood with great dignity and faced Jeffrey. "Deputy Marshal Harlow, we all thank you for your service." The Head's nod was one of dismissal.

Jeffrey stood, bowed and turned toward the door of the kitchen. He was met there by one of President Brown's two personal bodyguards, a man named Anson. Wiry and

weasel-like, the man's tight thin mouth and deep-set black
button eyes betrayed no recognition as he held the door to
usher Jeffrey into the living room and shut the door firmly
behind him. Jeffrey smiled at Mrs. Lucy Brown, who was
engaged in crocheting on the sofa, and thanked Mrs. Dina
Brown when she opened the outer door for him.

Outside, he breathed deeply of the smell of sage and
let the air depart his lungs slowly. He felt pulled in many
directions by a spider web of demands; from his church, the
Town Marshal's Office, the FBI, his journalist friend, and not
least of all his own conscience. And, of course, there was his
family to consider.

He walked through the formal gardens, past the wild
animal confinement where President Brown kept the exotic
animals he liked to collect, to the wide white marble circular
driveway, climbed into the truck and drove out of the
president's compound. All he wanted now was the comfort of
his own home and wives. He drove past other walled
compounds, the homes of respected Elders, and turned right
at a cross street. Here the compounds were smaller, the
houses constructed for smaller families, fewer wives. The
walls were less severe along this street, not so tall, less
commanding, and there were attempts at green lawns and
even flowers outside the barriers. Jeffrey drove through a gate
and into the driveway of a dwelling in the middle of the
block. The structure was a two-story square house,
unadorned, as most were, one or two window boxes
containing herbs the only ornamental features. Two
outbuildings stood toward the rear of the compound, one
housed utilities and the other was a small home mirroring the
architecture of the main house and was used for guests.
Jeffrey's second wife Cynthia's grandfather, a man of seventy-
odd years, had occupied this guesthouse for almost a year
now.

Jeffrey stepped inside his home with the comforting
smell of cooking and furniture polish, closed the door, and

called a greeting. Instantly, there was a pounding of feet on the stairs, thumping across the living room floor, and children flung themselves at him from every direction. Behind them came his first wife Patti, wiping flour from her hands onto her apron, reaching out for a hug. Cynthia peered out from the dining room where she was setting the table and smiled and waved.

Jeffrey felt his concerns melt away and contentment settle in. This, after all, was what life was all about.

# CHAPTER NINETEEN

Jeffrey headed toward the kitchen, surrounded by a cloud of children. He stood in the doorway watching Cynthia set the table, no small chore considering the number of diners and the size of the tabletop.

"Has Jedediah returned yet?" he asked.

Cynthia didn't look up from the silver she was placing. "Not yet."

Jeffrey walked over to his wife and put a hand on each shoulder from behind. "Don't worry about him. He's probably out at the old place imagining things as they used to be. He'll be back."

Cynthia nodded and spoke without turning around. "I hope so. It's been four days now. He usually returns after a day or so."

Jeffrey turned her around to face him by her shoulders. He had taken Cynthia as his wife after she approached him at the Meeting Hall one evening, introduced herself and said God had called upon her in a vision to marry him. Jeffrey had been surprised. He knew the power of God's revelations, but it was unusual for God to reveal his commands to a woman. He had dragged his feet, believing his brothers in faith might not understand, but Cynthia was earnest, persistent, and not unattractive, and eventually Jeffrey's resistance faltered. He prayed over it and then took Patti, his first wife, into his confidence. To his surprise, she had no objections. Having a sister wife, she explained, would make things easier around the place and less lonely when Jeffrey was away. Theirs had been a marriage of love, and she did not think sharing her husband would change that. She had been raised in a true Fundamentalist family; therefore, the arrangement did not strike her as unusual.

Neither Cynthia nor God had mentioned Cynthia's grandfather, however. He was the patriarch of Cynthia's family, five generations of luckless farmers. Their history had been filled with fatal accidents, ill health, and uncommonly early deaths. The only ones left on the family farm had been Cynthia and her peppery old grandfather, Jedediah. The old man had more than a trace of senility and could not be left on his own. Jeffrey would have to accept Jedediah along with Cynthia. He did.

Jedediah moved into the guesthouse, but proved restive and unhappy when away from the farm. From time to time he disappeared and was later found two miles away at the old place. Someone would drive out to retrieve him, find him either on the front steps wondering how he got there or in the family cemetery out back, lost in his own thoughts. Sometimes he was not ready to be found, and the emissary would return empty-handed. This had been the case these last four days.

As far as Jeffrey was concerned, he could not bring himself to worry about Jedediah. The man was a tough old buzzard, apparently the sole member of his family with the ability to survive. He'd be back eventually.

Jeffrey gave Cynthia a hug and went to his study. This one room was his sanctuary, off bounds to children and wives alike. Right now, he needed to sit in his leather desk chair, rock back and contemplate the words of the president. Clearly the church wanted Jeffrey to assume the position expressed by the two Taylor boys, that the killer or killers were from Kanab, either acting out as gang members or from some private dispute.

Jeffrey did not believe this.

First, in his opinion, the Taylor twins were idiots. Second, it made no sense to him for killers from Kanab to carry their victim all the way up Canaan Mountain and perform some sort of sacrificial murder for a grudge. Why would they do that?

Jeffrey stared beyond the tidy surface of his mahogany desktop and out the large window to the backyard where the grass was scuffed bare from the running feet of active children and beyond it to the twelve foot high white board fence that surrounded his property and obscured his home from the view of the curious. Despite efforts by the FLDS Church to remain under the radar, the town of Hildale had become a tourist attraction. Lawsuits and legal action against a society that condoned plural marriage was headline news and a magnet. Travelers on their way to or from Zion National Monument and Grand Staircase Escalante National Monument saw the fundamentalist community in Hildale as one more attraction on their schedule. Most fundamentalist families felt the need to surround their homes with walls like Jeffrey's to protect their children from rude or inconsiderate remarks and questions.

Jeffrey understood why the president wished to deflect blame away from the FLDS Church and direct it toward Kanab instead. He sympathized. But Jeffrey was guilelessly honest. He found it difficult to bend the truth, even for a good cause. This compulsion toward truth had put his job in jeopardy; there had been opportunities to destroy his criminal record, or at the very least obscure it, an act that might have preserved his Arizona badge. He knew for a fact the Taylor twins had done just that, but Jeffrey simply could not bring himself to do the same.

The tenuous relationship between job and religion had caused Jeffrey to walk similar tightropes many times. He knew in his heart the time must come when he would have to pick a side. He had always thought the choice easy; the church must come first. Yet as his family had grown, his decisions had become more difficult; the need to keep his family fed and sheltered now came first. The simple choices he faced as a single man had grown exponentially more complicated now that he was a family man.

Jeffrey sighed and sorted through the stack of bills on his desk. The church had always helped him in his time of need; he must see what he could do in return. But he would not, could not do so with lies and deceit. He would not propagate a story so perceptibly false.

His thoughts went back to the cave, the impaled boy on the slab, all the bones. The president was correct about one thing—the impression of ritual sacrifice surrounding the murder was like a huge finger pointed at the FLDS Church, despite the fact the church had never in its history engaged in human sacrifice or anything close to it.

A thought crossed his mind. Was it possible some other person or agency constructed the scene for precisely such a purpose? The judicial arm of the federal government and its law enforcement agencies were in the midst of renewed efforts to prosecute the FLDS Church. The popular view across the country already supported such an action; this murder scene, this imagery could serve to bring any remaining doubters into line. Would any arm of the US Government actually stoop to such a despicable ploy?

He remembered a chance remark from the twins, who returned to check on the crime scene after the FBI had taken possession—how they were surprised not to find any agents at the site. No one had been there to safeguard the evidence, the bones, the bloody slab, almost as if the FBI was not as concerned about the murder as the imagery it represented. Jeffrey did not really think the FBI was responsible for murder but thought the agency was certainly capable of taking full advantage of it. Then who was responsible for the killing?

Jeffrey now saw a path, a way to help the church without resorting to lies. He would solve the crime himself. If he could find evidence implicating someone else, the pressure would be off the church and off him. He shook his head—easier said than done. Although trained as a police officer, Jeffrey had not pursued investigative skills, nor did he have the tools and information that were available to the county sheriff's department or the FBI.

There was one thing, though. The FLDS Church doctrine had taught Jeffrey that God could and would speak directly to any member of the faith, not just a chosen messenger. Jeffrey Danes Harlow believed this with all his heart; after all, such a revelation was how he came to marry Cynthia. He smiled to himself. Maybe he did have a tool not available to the gentiles; he had the ear of God. God would help him to solve the murder.

Jeffrey went to his knees next to his chair right then and prayed.

"Dear Heavenly Father, I am grateful for thy hand which guides me. Please lead me to know the perpetrator of this ghastly murder that I might bring him to justice. In the name of Jesus Christ, Amen."

The bell sounded for the noon meal. He climbed up off his knees and walked to the kitchen. His family stood behind their chairs around the large table, waiting for him. He took his place at the head.

As he offered thanks for the meal, Jeffrey noticed Jedediah's empty chair. Cynthia said it had been more than four days now; the last time had been a period of five days with just two days in between. When everyone was seated and the meal had begun, Jeffrey turned to Cynthia.

"No word from your father, then?"

"No," she said, her face creased with concern.

"Well, don't worry," he said. "I'm sure he's fine." He helped himself to sliced turkey and passed the platter along. "However, these absences are becoming a distraction. I think he must decide where he will live, here or there, and make up his mind to it."

Cynthia glanced around the table at the other family members who were hardly able to conceal their interest. She looked at Jeffrey. "I don't think he is able to care for himself at the farm. He has those memory lapses and could come to harm during them. He truly does need to be here with us."

Jeffrey smiled. "It is settled, then. I will go and bring him back right after the meal. I will make it clear to him he must stay here with us as his only option."

Cynthia smiled at him, her face relaxing with relief. "Thank you, Jeffrey."

Kaylee, Patti's oldest daughter, scrunched up her face. "That old man gives me the creeps."

"Young lady, your opinion was not sought," Jeffrey said and led the family discussion toward the subject of tolerance and understanding.

Jeffrey decided to take the patrol car to go to the farm, intending it as a symbol to help underscore his demand of the old man. He doubted Jedediah ever took him seriously. The man seemed to exist in another time altogether, a time from the old days when the souls of the Saints had been tested, and God had called upon them to stand and deliver. He seemed to view Jeffrey as a product of a generation that had grown lazy and unequal to such challenges.

It was two miles to the farm, nestled under the protective cliffs of Canaan Mountain, the old family cemetery behind it edged up against the red bluffs. The land around the farm rose in a gradual manner, like seats in an amphitheater, exposing a long view out over the Uinkaret Plateau. The property provided one of the best views in Hildale, to Jeffrey's thinking, but Jedediah's pioneering ancestors had chosen the location for more practical reasons—the bluffs served as a rear guard from marauding Indians, and the vertical proximity to the mountain summit offered a supply of the wood needed for home building.

The main road beyond the town was unpaved, and the farm driveway overgrown and full of potholes. The patrol car bounced on its springs, trailing a stream of dust. Jeffrey pulled up to the white frame house and climbed out. He stood for a moment, studying the place. Signs of neglect were everywhere, visible on the house exterior long before Jeffrey and Cynthia were married; the property was far beyond the capacity of one old man and his granddaughter to keep up. Now roof shingles checkered the weed infested lawn, shutters dangled, peeled paint draped in strips, broken windows were patched with cardboard and tape. The property still had value, could be restored and sold for a profit if the old man would only let go.

Jeffrey hallooed the house, heard no response which was no surprise. He followed the old drive around to the back, his boots crunching gravel beneath the overgrown grass. He approached the steps to a small porch and a back door, now hanging open. He hallooed again. No response.

The drive wound beyond the house into a nest of trees to the great old barn. The old structure had always been the heartbeat of farm life, where the plow horses had been kept, the hay stored, feral cats moused, chickens wandered. Later a tractor replaced the draft horses, machinery filled the stalls, motor oil and grease coated the old floorboards instead of dung and hay. But now the tractor too was gone, sold to pay debts. But Jedediah still kept his tools here. He loved to tinker with things, kept the old car running somehow. Lord knows what else he found to do here.

Jeffrey stepped through the great open entrance, large enough for two side-by-side draft horses and a wagon. His boots thudded hollow on the ancient plank floor. A mixture of scents surrounded him—stale hay, oil, gasoline, mold, the usual smells. But there was something else too, something herb-like or medicinal he couldn't quite identify. His eyes adjusted to the shadowy interior. Haylofts perched high above on either side, a full twenty feet above the ground. The old horse stalls lined one side, still smelled of their occupants from half a century before. On his right there was open space, interrupted only by the huge roof support beams rising from the floor and here and there various bits of farm equipment, some of which he could identify, some not. Canvas draped a couple of vehicles; he could see the tires beneath the covering. Nothing seemed disturbed.

The barn was like a large tunnel, its massive sliding door at the far end open, the cobwebbed, rusty chain dangling. Where the stalls left off, Jedediah had a work and storage area. Old leather halters and wide leather straps still hung on the walls. Beneath them was a large plank workbench with two wood vises and various tools scattered on the surface. Jeffrey noticed signs of recent activity. Jedediah must spend time here. But he was not here now.

On through and beyond the barn he followed the stone-lined worn path up a gentle slope to the old cemetery. Gravestones rose from the ground, leaning this way or that, most so weathered the surfaces were rounded, the inscriptions worn away. The newest graves were in the rear, highly-glossed shiny marble with black-highlighted inscriptions. There were many of them. Jeffrey wondered how many of the expensive markers the tractor had financed. Cynthia's parents, brothers and sisters were all beneath these stones, a hard luck lot.

Jedediah was not here, either.

# CHAPTER TWENTY

Dan Fogelberry sat relaxed in his chair, legs crossed, notebook in hand. He smiled across the wide desk at Sheriff Rafferty. The sheriff's workspace was littered with files, the rectangular white labels of the top folders visible but the hand scrawled ink writing on them not quite decipherable from where Dan sat.

The sheriff was a large man, ruddy cheeked and balding. His large square hands were folded together on the desktop and he wore a what-can-I-do-for-you expression on his face.

"Thank you for seeing me, Sheriff. As I said, I report for the Deseret News. My readers want to know more about the bizarre murder that occurred up on Canaan Mountain. What can you tell me?"

Sheriff Rafferty maintained an amiable expression. "Very little, I'm afraid. The FBI took jurisdiction of the case almost immediately."

"Yet you must have some information, some communication with the FBI?"

"Very little, I'm afraid."

Dan smiled. "Let's try this. I'll tell you what I have heard, and you tell me what you can about it. Fair enough?"

"I'm afraid you'll be disappointed."

Dan kept his smile. "Let's try anyway. For instance, I'm told stacks of human bones were found in a cave behind the murder site. Is it true some of the bones are from recently deceased?"

The sheriff's expression turned from placid to annoyed in an instant. "Who told you that?"

"I'm afraid I can't reveal my source."

The sheriff grunted. "That is a wild assertion, and I won't comment on it."

"Okay, let's try this. The killing appeared to have been done on an altar of sorts. Do you believe it was a sacrifice or blood atonement?"

"That is absurd. Where are you coming up with these wild ideas?"

Dan leaned forward. "My source was quite specific about the appearance of the crime scene."

The sheriff eyed Dan, a hard look on his face. "No one knows the appearance of the crime scene other than the attending officers and the FBI. You are on a fishing trip, and you are wasting my time."

"What about the anthropologists at the site? What do they make of the scene?"

The sheriff's face moved from ruddy to red. "I know nothing of anthropologists. Your questions are becoming increasingly ridiculous." He half stood. "I must refer you to the official release concerning this death, which I'm sure you have read."

Dan's relaxed manner never changed. "The release states a young boy died under suspicious circumstances while hiking on Canaan Mountain. Police are investigating. That's more absurd than my questions."

The sheriff was standing. "That is all I have. I must ask you to leave."

Dan leafed through his notebook. "A pity. I had hoped to verify the connection between the murder of the young girl here in Kanab and the Canaan Mountain murder."

"There is none that I am aware of."

"And the fact that the young girl and the Canaan murder victim were both residents of Kanab? As sheriff of Kane County, you must be aware of that?"

"As I said, the FBI—"

"And that they attended the same high school and had the same school-assigned counselor?"

The sheriff paused. Still staring at Dan, he turned back and sat down. "I need to know your source."

"I told you, I can't reveal the name."

"Have you been to the FBI?"

"Not yet."

"You should."

Dan raised an eyebrow. "Why is that?"

The sheriff leaned back in his chair, the springs creaking in protest. "Because if any of the information you just asked me to verify is true, and I'm not saying it is, and you go to print, you may well jeopardize their investigation. The FBI is inclined to treat such things harshly."

Dan smiled. "Sounds like a threat."

Sheriff Rafferty spread his hands wide. "You wanted some information. I just gave you some."

Dan inclined his head in acknowledgement. "I think we both know how the FBI will respond to my questions. I also think I have all the verification I need from your hypothetical concern. How about this? I won't go to print listing you as my unofficial source if you will feed me something I can use."

The sheriff's complexion went from red to purple. "How about this? If you aren't out of my office in ten seconds I will arrest you." As Dan started to reply, the sheriff roared, "And don't ask me on what grounds, that won't be a problem."

The sheriff was apoplectic. Dan grinned, put away his notebook, bowed, and left the office. He was quite satisfied his information was accurate.

# CHAPTER TWENTY-ONE

"Zack, it's just a matter of resources. The FBI can't spare agents to stand guard over a cave filled with bones nine miles up a remote mountain." Pete Conley sighed. "Besides that, the Colorado City Marshal's Office said they would send a couple of men up there from time to time. However, the point will soon be mute; we've sent a team from the Anthropology Department at BYU up there. They hope to get to the bottom of the bones." He chuckled. "Quite literally."

Zack switched his phone to the other ear. "Pete, you might want to get one of your agents up there with a shovel. There could be a fresh burial toward the rear of that cave your guys missed."

There was silence at the other end. "Zack, how do you know this? In fact, how did you know the cave was unguarded? Were you up there?"

"No. I told you, Pete, I'm interested in keeping Libby and her family safe. That's all. But I've got my ear to the ground, and I'm learning things, and as I do, I'm passing it along to you."

"So you know someone who was up at the cave snooping around. I see you're not passing along that bit."

Zack chuckled. "Believe me, that's the smallest piece in a big picture."

Conley let out a long breath. "Okay, Zack. I'm gonna pass this along to the guys. Don't get me wrong, we do appreciate the information, but I'm the one who's gonna get grilled to supply the name of the informant."

Zack put his phone away, caught Eagle Feather's eye. "He's going to forward the information and let me know what they find. He was a little pissed to learn someone was mucking around up there and that no one was guarding the place. Seems the local marshals were supposed to be there."

"They were. Shooting at me."

"I wonder where they were when that fellow you spoke to was satisfying his curiosity. What was his name?"

"Tubs. He called himself Tubs."

Zack moved along the picnic bench chasing the shade of a newly planted puny tree. "What about this man Tubs? Is his appearance up there suspicious to you?"

Eagle Feather pondered this. He was seated cross-legged on the packed dirt, disdaining the bench for the coolness of the shaded earth. "As one of two men who first discovered the murder, he must stay at the top of the list. But would a murderer take people directly to the scene of his crime? Unless you know where to look you would never find this cave."

Zack nodded. "That's a powerful argument." He paused, then asked, "Would you say he is physically capable of hauling that boy up the mountain and spearing him on the stake?"

"Yes. As I said, the man was lean and strong. He moved easily saving his energy, something I have tried to teach you many times, White Man."

Zack grinned. "I could save my energy and not talk to you, but I do it anyway."

Eagle Feather glanced at the road where a truck had entered the campground. "It is Sam."

"Sam?"

"Sam is the caretaker of this campground. He is Paiute. He showed me how to find the trail up the mountain."

They watched the truck pull up. A rawboned man with sharp features extricated himself from the cab. He nodded at Eagle Feather, then his gaze lingered on Zack.

"Sam, meet Zack. He is the friend I told you about yesterday."

Zack stood. Sam extended a large calloused hand.

Sam looked at Eagle Feather. "Did you find your way up the mountain today?"

102

Eagle Feather nodded.

"Back again already? You travel swiftly."

Sam walked to the rear of his truck where he had an Igloo container, poured a bottle of water, and passed it to Eagle Feather. "Cold water with lime. Refreshing." He watched the Navajo take a long swallow.

Eagle Feather wiped his mouth. "I found the cave and I found the bones."

Zack studied Sam. "Do all native people know about this cave?"

Sam shook his head. "The Kaibab Band did not know of it. I can not speak for the other Paiute tribes."

"Yet I am told the chairperson of the Kaibab Band protested the removal of bones from there, saying the bones might belong to tribal ancestors."

Sam gave a ghost of a smile. "They must protest each time old burials are uncovered. Who can say where every Paiute burial is located? Protest first, learn later. That is how we protect our ancestors."

"Do your people have any legends of cave dwelling spirits?" Zack asked. Eagle Feather sent a glance at Zack.

Sam held Zack's eyes, as if to explore their depths. "I sense your friend saw something in that cave."

"What do you know about it?" Eagle Feather said.

"What did you see?" Sam countered.

Eagle Feather told Sam about the unknown being in the cave and how it had saved him from the marshals.

Sam did not seem surprised.

"Do you know of this creature?" Zack asked.

Sam shrugged. "Perhaps you have heard about Nimerigars, the evil little people." He looked at Eagle Feather. "Do the Navajo know of the Little People?"

"I have not heard of them."

"This surprises me. The Shoshone, Crow, Arapaho, Cheyenne, Sioux, and all the Paiute tribes know of Nimerigar."

"What is it?" Zack asked.

"The name Nimerigar means roughly "people eaters." Another name for them is Nunumbi, which means "little people." They are enemies of mankind and very dangerous. They shoot poisoned arrows with tiny bows and are cruel to others and to themselves."

"What do they look like?" Zack asked.

"They are somewhat like what your people call goblins, but dark-skinned. They are between a foot and two feet tall, have sharp teeth and squat necks. They are said to be great thieves and mischievous tricksters, but they can also mutilate animals and even steal children to eat. Some say they have the ability to become invisible, others say they are hard to see because they move so fast. They are very aggressive and warlike and do not fear death because they believe they must die in battle to reach their afterworld. It is said they died out long ago after long wars with humans." Sam shrugged. "You saw a creature that moved with great swiftness in a cave with many bones. Perhaps it was a Nimerigar."

Zack smiled. "Do you believe in these creatures?"

Sam shrugged again. "My people have many stories of the old times. We preserve these oral narratives from generation to generation. They include stories of our origin and of the great flood and other stories similar to those white people have preserved on paper. No one scoffs at those. I do not disbelieve the stories of my ancestors. So many have proven true." His eyes went back to Eagle Feather. "When I consider that the same story may be found among many peoples—the Crow, Shoshoni, Arapaho, even the Wampanoag of the lands to the East—I do not discard it lightly." Sam grinned. "Even the tribes of Europe have tales of the goblins."

"It's true. But we believe them to be just that—tales," Zack said.

Sam lowered his eyes to the fire pit. "Have you heard of the San Pedro Mountains Mummy?"

"The mummified body found by two prospectors back in the 1930s near Casper, Wyoming," Eagle Feather said.

Sam glanced at Eagle Feather. "Ah, you know of it." He turned to Zack. "In 1932 two prospectors found the mummy of a tiny person, its head crushed in, sealed in a cave in Wyoming. It was sitting with its legs crossed. They estimated it would be seventeen inches tall when standing. It was examined by several prestigious institutions, including Harvard University, where they estimated it was a full-grown adult of about sixty-five years of age."

Zack did not comment.

"Believe what you want," Sam said. "But according to the stories the Nimerigar were known to crush in the heads of their old or infirm before abandoning them as they followed their food sources."

"That was a standard practice for nomadic Indians in the past who had no way to carry their elders along with them. It was a mercy killing," Eagle Feather pointed out.

Sam looked from one man to the other with a slight smile. "I've shown you my Nimerigar—now show me your goblin."

* * * * *

Jeffrey Danes Harlow returned along the worn dirt path from the cemetery and entered the barn. He waited just a moment for his eyes to adjust to the dark interior. Again, his nose brought him the moldy hay and oil scent tinged with that medicinal something. His eye caught something he hadn't noticed before, canvas crumpled on the straw strewn floor near the covered vehicles. A car or truck was gone. The medicinal scent grew stronger at his approach.

It had been his belief the old man had sold most of the farm vehicles to pay debts. Yet at least two remained. He lifted the edge of the cover on the nearest one. It was an old

Dodge pickup truck, apparently in good condition, although clearly an antique. The next vehicle was larger. This one proved to be a truck, an International Harvester, one of the early SUVs. It too appeared to be in running condition.

Musing, Jeffrey walked back to the canvas on the floor. There were tire impressions in the dust. They seemed recent. So the old man still kept a car. With his absences not necessarily limited to the farm, he could be anywhere.

This was good news, bad news for Jeffrey. He would tell Cynthia there was no sign the old man had come to harm. On the other hand, the old man had apparently motored off chasing his own caprice, whatever it might be. Still, there was no reason to think the worst.

Jeffrey strode toward the barn door, his mind still puzzling over the identity of the medicinal smell. Did the old man have a condition he was treating, like poison oak? But it didn't smell like calamine lotion really, it was stronger, more like something one might smell in a hospital corridor.

He shrugged, gave it up. He'd ask Cynthia if Jedediah had a condition for which he was being treated with topical medication.

# CHAPTER TWENTY-TWO

"We have a suspect."

Zack was still numb from sleep. The bedside clock said 5:30 a.m. He swung his legs over the side of the bed, gently, not to wake Libby. Neither had slept well; the possibility of another home invasion hovered in their minds. Every natural creak and snap the house made took on greater meaning.

"The FBI has a suspect?"

"We do. His name is David Patterson." Conley's voice had an edge of triumph to it.

"Who is he?"

"Briefly, he is an itinerant school counselor. He works with kids at Kanab High School and other schools in the district."

Zack tried to make sense of this, but his brain was fuzzy. He felt a crushing need for coffee. "What's this counselor got to do with it?"

"I don't have a lot of detail for you, it comes to me second hand. Everything that they decide is need to know, I don't know."

Zack grimaced. "What do you know?"

Conley coughed somewhere away from the receiver, came back. "Okay, it seems this Patterson has spent many hours with the victim in after-hours counseling there at the high school, knew his life and habits inside and out. He has no alibi for the hours of the kidnapping and the approximate time of death. He is a hiker. He invites kids along on his hikes." Conley paused. "One place he likes to take them is Canaan Mountain."

"That's not much to go on."

"Wait, there's more. It seems another kid went missing five years ago, not from the high school, from the Middle School. He was on an overnight camping trip in the backcountry in an area called the Cottonwood Point Wilderness. Do you know the area?"

"Not really." Zack stifled a yawn.

"The Wilderness surrounds Cottonwood Canyon, which is just east of Canaan Mountain. The boy became separated from his group somehow, was lost and never found. It was chalked up as an unfortunate accident."

"Okay, so?"

"So the kid was a little troubled, it seems, and was seeing a counselor on a regular basis."

Zack sat up straight. "Patterson."

"You got it. And Patterson has no alibi for that timeframe because he was doing what he loves best—"

"Hiking?"

"Yep. Up on Canaan Mountain."

Zack's brain was stirring to life as these facts sifted in. "Still, it's circumstantial."

Conley chuckled. "Yeah, it is. And so is the fact he was fired from a private boarding school on the east coast prior to the Kanab job. One of our guys had to go pay a visit to the headmaster of that school to learn the cause. Those schools keep their secrets. Seems he was let go because he was suspected of playing with the little boys. He'd take them hiking in the Adirondacks. There were complaints."

Zack let his breath out slowly. "What kind of car does he drive?"

"That's all I got, Zack. I don't know any more detail. Easy enough to find out about the car, I suspect." When he resumed, his voice was brisk. "Look, Zack, I got to go. I have actual work to do. We're not arresting this guy—we're bringing him in for questioning. I'll keep you posted." Conley rang off.

Zack sat still, sorting through this new information. He knew Pru had been seeing a counselor at the high school recently. Was it the same one? He needed to talk to Emma.

When he returned his phone to the bedside table, he saw Libby sit up.

"What is it, Zack?"

Zack had returned to the house late the prior afternoon following his meeting with Eagle Feather and Sam. He'd told Libby about their conversation. Her day, fortunately, had been uneventful.

Now she stared at Zack, eyebrows raised.

"Conley says they have a suspect, a man named David Patterson. He's a counselor at the high school."

"Oh, my God. Pru was seeing a counselor at the high school. But I don't know the person's name."

Zack turned back to the night table to pick up his phone. "That is exactly the question I want to put to Emma. It's time we caught her up anyway."

Libby put a restraining hand on Zack's arm. "I'll call her, Zack. She'll likely panic if you call. Let's give her another hour to wake up."

Zack put his phone back, his mind still chewing at this new information. "There's still a part that doesn't fit. How could this guy know about that cave? From Eagle Feather's description, you wouldn't just stumble upon it. This Davidson apparently likes to hike up on Canaan Mountain, I get that, but he's a fairly recent transplant from the East Coast. There are people who have lived here all their lives, hiked all over that mountain and still never found that cave."

"It's not impossible, right?"

"No, it's not, but it's improbable," Zack said. "How about the murdered girl? I wonder if Patterson counseled her. "

Libby yawned, threw back the covers to climb out of bed. "I'll ask Pru that as well. She may know." She shuffled into the master bath, her voice floating out to him. "How long do you expect us to keep up this ruse, Zack? I don't want to be too long away from Bernie."

Zack was pulling on his trousers. "That's why it's important to resolve the guilt of this Patterson guy quickly. If he's not the murderer, we need to continue to protect Pru." When Libby reemerged, he said, "That doesn't mean you can't leave, but if you do, we'll have to assume someone is watching the house. We'll have to figure a way to conceal your departure."

Libby started to smile.

"What?"

"Well, it's the irony. You quit the FBI to spend more time at home with Bernie and me. Now here we are entangled in an FBI murder investigation with both of us away from home. We're more involved than before you quit."

"Like old times, back when we first met," Zack said, trying to keep it light.

"I'm not feeling waves of nostalgia at the moment."

Zack grinned. "I will take this opportunity to remind you who got us involved in this." He walked over to the window and peered out. "I don't see any FBI presence out there. They were here yesterday when I pulled in. Maybe they dropped us, thinking they've got the culprit."

"Maybe they're having breakfast, which is something we should do." Libby started down the stairs.

"Wait!" Zack took another look out through the curtains.

"What?" Libby stopped, turned back.

"The car you saw before I came up to Kanab, the one you thought was the FBI. Can you describe it?"

Libby approached the window. "Well, it was an old model sedan, shiny, dark blue or maybe black. It was dark, so it was hard to tell. I think blue."

Zack leaned away from the window. "Peek out around the curtain, look down the street to the right. Do you see it anywhere?"

Libby peered around the curtain fold, studied the street. She pulled back from the window with a sharp intake of breath. "Yes, I do see it. That's the one, I'm quite sure. It's just behind the white truck." She stared at Zack, her brown eyes wide. "What does this mean?"

Zack was grim. "It means either the FBI have the wrong guy or the killer has a partner."

# CHAPTER TWENTY-THREE

The call came as a surprise to Fogelberry. He was assigned to report to the editor in charge of news in St. George and southern Utah, a modest cog in the large machine that was the Deseret News. The man was responsible to guide and manage Dan, challenge his premises, evaluate his sources. It was certainly not usual for the manager of the entire newsroom to call him directly, yet here he was on the phone.

"Dan, you should know the governor has filed an injunction against the federal government to prevent them from removing bones from the cave on Canaan Mountain."

"What? Why? How can he do that?"

"I can answer only part of your question. He can do it based upon the Utah Transfer of Public Land Act of 2012."

"But—"

"You were going to say despite its passage in the State of Utah, it has not been and will not soon be accepted by the federal government, so how can the governor do this? And the answer is the Utah Enabling Act of 1894 in which the federal government promised to transfer these lands but never did. The governor's injunction states the ownership of the land is unresolved, hence no one may remove resources and physical attributes of the land: not the FBI, the BLM, or any other federal group. Of course, this injunction also restricts state and private parties. Since the ownership question is not likely to be resolved in our lifetimes, the bones must stay where they are."

Fogelberry's mind raced to assimilate this. "But the bones did not originate on the land, they were brought there. How can they be said to be resources or physical attributes?"

The editor gave a short laugh. "Who can actually prove the bones were brought there? If a creature was born on the land, lived and died there, are not its bones physical attributes of the land? As I see it, to prove otherwise the FBI needs to remove them and study them in a laboratory. But they can't do that now. It's a perfect Catch 22."

"Why would the governor want to stop this investigation?"

"You're the reporter—that's for you to figure out. To my mind, it's got to be pressure from either the Indians or the FLDS Church."

"But—?"

"That's all I've got. Go figure it out."

The line went dead. Dan stood staring at his phone. This news would turn the entire FBI investigation on its ear—essentially cause it to grind to a halt. How could they catch the kidnapper/murderer without the evidence of the bones?"

His mind went down another avenue. Who was behind this? Whose best interests lay in halting the investigation? Did the Paiute have something to hide up there? Was the Fundamentalist LDS Church concealing something?

To Dan's mind this case had been interesting before——now it was intriguing.

\* \* \* \* \*

"Zack, have you heard? The governor has filed an injunction to prevent us from removing bones from the cave."

It was Conley.

Zack pushed the phone tighter to his ear. "What? Why?"

"Well, obviously, someone doesn't want us poking any deeper into that bone pile for some reason."

"You don't know who is behind this?"

"No." Agent Conley harrumphed. "But I can make an educated guess."

"What about your suspect?"

"Yeah. That's part of the problem. Unless we can find evidence to link him directly to the bones, all we have on him is circumstantial. We'll have to let him go."

Zack eyed Libby across the breakfast table as he spoke. "Where is the suspect right now?"

"He's still tucked away in a holding cell."

Zack had a thought. "Pete, does this guy you're holding have any fresh wounds?"

"Only to his ego."

"So I guess he wasn't the one who tried to break in." Zack told Conley the latest news about the watcher in the car outside the house.

"Well, Zack, as you say, he's not one of ours—maybe local law enforcement. But we'll make sure; I'm gonna check around."

Zack smiled toward Libby. "Thanks, Pete, that will be a great relief to us. What about your investigation, though? Without the bones..."

Conley laughed. "The injunction prevents us from removing the bones to the lab. It does not prevent us from taking the lab to the bones. A forensic team is up there as I speak, along with the anthropologists. We'll truck generators and lab machines up there to them." He changed his voice to sound like Efrem Zimbalist, Jr. "The FBI always gets its man." He promised to keep Zack posted and ended the call.

Zack peered at Libby as he put down his phone. "Whoever is outside right now, it's not this Patterson fellow. Nor is Patterson the one you shot unless his wounds are so superficial he can hide them easily."

Libby shook her head. "I hit him twice. If they did any kind of body search, they'd find the wounds."

Zack nodded. His mind was on the governor's injunction. "I'll give Eagle Feather a call. Maybe he can get a line on the reason for the governor's action."

\* \* \* \* \*

The Paiute Tribal office was a rather plain two-story building on a freshly macadamized side street near the entrance road to Pipe Spring National Monument. Eagle Feather pushed through the pneumatic door into a hallway. Beyond was a second door leading to a recreation hall. He turned left instead and found a door marked Tribal Council and knocked. A female voice called to him to enter.

A young woman sat at a desk, pen poised over paper, a friendly smile matching crinkled eyes. In response to her polite questioning glance, Eagle Feather introduced himself. "Sam Wall sent me here. I am looking for Shana Bows."

"I am Shana. How can I help you?"

"My interest is the bones discovered in a cave on Canaan Mountain." He tried his most pleasant expression. "I am Dine. Although my people historically occupied the territory east of here, it is possible the bones could be our ancestors."

Shana smiled. "Whether that is true, I believe it is important for all tribes to raise their voices to draw attention to the bones. The worst response is silence, which would allow fortune seekers to sell or otherwise defame and insult the ancestors, whoever they are." She studied Eagle Feather where he stood framed in the doorway. "Do you represent a particular group of Navajo?"

He shook his head. "I represent only myself. I was in the area, and learned of the bones. If it proves needful, I would contact the leaders of my people." He smiled. "I am from the Tuba City region."

Shana waved him to a chair and rising to her feet stepped around the cluttered desk and took a seat opposite him. He noticed her natural grace of movement.

"So, Mr. Dine, what is your name?"

"I am called Eagle Feather."

"How romantic." Her eyes danced with humor.

Eagle Feather flicked his gaze around the small room, took in the pictures tacked to the wall of Indians in formal dress lined up as if for ceremonies, others in tribal costume dancing. His focus came back to Shana. "Not as romantic as it sounds. It comes from the white hunters I guide and refers to this." He pointed at the hat on his head with the single feather.

"Who are your family?"

"My mother was a Yazzie, born of Feather People, born to Salt People."

"And your father?"

Eagle Feather's eyes creased with humor. "Jewish."

Shana chuckled at that. "An interesting heritage. The bones up there are least likely to be of Jewish origin, I think."

"Do the Paiute claim them?"

"No more than any other tribe. We have no direct knowledge of that location as a burial site."

Eagle Feather cocked his head to one side. "Then you have no reason to block the removal of bones from the site."

Shana grimaced. "I said no direct knowledge, not a certainty."

Eagle Feather kept his gaze leveled on her face. "You are aware of the governor's injunction?"

Her eyebrows arched in surprise. "I am, but how did you come to learn of it. It just happened."

Eagle Feather shifted his weight in the chair. "I'll be straight with you. I am here to investigate the murder of the boy. A friend is close to the situation."

Shana studied his face. "I see." She paused. "What do you hope to learn from me about the murder?"

"Was it pressure from the Paiute that influenced the governor's action?"

"Short answer? No. But we are pleased, nonetheless."

Eagle Feather decided Shana was quite pleasant in appearance, attractive, actually. Her facial features were broad, indicative of her heritage, her body slender. Now as

116

she grinned at him her face took on an impish quality he found intriguing. He enjoyed talking to her.

As if in answer to his thoughts, she said, "May I offer you a cup of coffee?"

Eagle Feather followed her from the office to a small kitchenette where a glass coffee pot stewed on a hot plate. She pointed to paper cups, a sugar bowl, and a small can. "With enough sugar and a touch of that sweetened condensed milk this coffee can sometimes be made palatable. Help yourself."

Shana demonstrated the procedure and fixed a cup for herself. As Eagle Feather followed her example, she continued the conversation. "We did enact a small demonstration in front of the Kanab BLM office, simply to put our views on record. But we knew at the outset the man had little say in the situation."

Eagle Feather sipped his concoction, tried not to make a face when he tasted it. He leaned against the wall, stirring the mix with a stir stick, and gave her a long look. "What do you know of Nimerigars?" he asked.

# CHAPTER TWENTY-FOUR

As Shana's brown eyes widened, Eagle Feather noticed they were flecked with gold. "Nimerigars? Where is that coming from, out of the blue?"

"You know what they are?"

"Well, of course; the little people of the old days. Why?"

"Sam and I talked about them. When I visited the murder site I went into the cave. But even before I did, I knew someone or something was in there. When I was at the mouth of the cave, I was fired upon—I later learned the shooter was a marshal. I might have been trapped in the cave, possibly killed, but someone or something ran out the mouth of it and drew their attention. It moved extremely fast. Sam suggested a Nimerigar."

Shana's eyes glistened, excited. "I have not heard talk of Nimerigars since I was a child. I had a mean old aunt who scared me with stories of them."

Eagle Feather watched her face come alive. "There, I have piqued your interest."

"Perhaps. What else have you got?"

Eagle Feather set his coffee down on the table. "Have you been to the murder site?"

She shook her head.

"The slab, altar, table top, whatever you choose to call it, has been there for hundreds of years, probably been used by various people for centuries. There are petroglyphs, quite faded along the side. There are pictographs, also very faded, on the smooth sandstone just inside the cave mouth. On top of the slab is a deeply worn metate, which held the stake the boy was pinned on."

"It sounds like an Aztec temple."

"That is not a bad description. The opening to the cave behind the slab is above the floor level of the arroyo with tumbled rocks in front. Once I was beyond the mouth of the cave it was very dim. I had no light to see by. Even without light I could see a pile of bones and others scattered across the cave floor. The ones I could see appeared to be human. Some looked very old."

"So the cave has been used for some purpose or other for a long time."

Eagle Feather nodded. "That is what I think. Perhaps not always the same people or the same purpose."

"And the Nimerigar?"

Eagle Feather shrugged. "Sam suggested it after I described how fast the thing moved."

"The cave of a Nimerigar would contain bones from what the stories say."

"There are people with strong political sway in the State of Utah who seem to know about the bones. They are the people I am searching for." Eagle Feather dropped down on a stool and sat facing Shana across the narrow kitchen.

"It's not us," she insisted. "But remember, there are many tribes. Even among the Paiutes of this region there are several bands—the Cedar Band, Indian Peaks Band, Kanosh Band, Koosharem Band, and the Shivwits Band. But to be honest, even with all the bands together, I doubt we could influence the governor in this way. You have to look somewhere else."

She stood firm and straight, petite yet sturdy, unconsciously authoritative; real class, Eagle Feather thought.

"Are you thinking the governor's action and the boy's murder are related? A conspiracy?" she asked.

Eagle Feather was surprised at that, gave his head a shake. "No, not really. At least I haven't thought about it that way. I suspect the governor's action is about something else altogether. Possibly something about the bones somebody doesn't want known."

Words had run out. There was an uncomfortable pause. Shana broke through it.

"Well, Mr. Eagle Feather, I have tribal business I must attend to. Please feel free to stay and finish your coffee." When Eagle Feather grimaced, she laughed aloud. "Okay, okay, I know it's bad."

Eagle Feather rose to his feet and followed Shana out to the corridor.

She turned to him. "If there is more I can help you with, do come back."

Eagle Feather walked away. As he did, he was already planning to do exactly that.

\*   \*   \*   \*   \*

Elder Taylor waved an arm toward the apple orchard beyond the large backyard of his mansion. "Walk with me," he said.

Stan and LeRoy fell into step with their father, one on each side. The twins knitted their brows in an identical manner, wondering what he had to say. Whatever he wanted, he would be obeyed, for a contrary thought would never enter either son's head.

"I have just met with President Brown. You should know he is most appreciative of your work and support." Taylor glanced at his sons, a grimace of a smile on his habitually cold countenance. Neither twin had never seen their father actually smile. Each understood he was a man of great dignity, of high place and great power within the church. His occasional confidences, such as now, were to be treasured and revered, never questioned. None of his wives and children ever questioned him.

"The president is concerned the cave and the secrets it holds could be violated, the history of its occupation and use misinterpreted, to the detriment of the reputation of the church." Elder Taylor stopped walking and turned to the boys. He studied their faces. "He has asked me to reinforce with you the necessity to keep everyone away from the cave."

He paused, his features stiffened, grew colder. "Including Jeffrey Harlow."

Both twins showed surprise.

"Yes, even Brother Jeffrey. He has been ordered to stay away. His words to the press have already stirred controversy." Taylor gave the twins a hard look. "By every means necessary."

Both boys nodded, made no reply.

Elder Taylor turned and resumed walking. The twins followed.

"This is a critical time for the church. The US Government and their judicial system would like nothing more than to bring us down, and any misinterpretation of what has happened in that arroyo could be just the weapon they seek. We can not let that happen."

LeRoy spoke up. "Father, someone was in the cave yesterday. We chased him out."

The words stopped Elder Taylor in his tracks. He turned to LeRoy. "Who was it, son?"

Stan joined in. "We don't know, sir. He looked like an Indian."

"An Indian?"

"Yes, sir, he wore a feather. He was in the shadow of the cave so we couldn't see him clearly," said LeRoy.

"LeRoy shot at him, but he missed."

Elder Taylor stared at Stan. "You trapped him in the cave?"

Stan hung his head.

"He ran out of the cave so fast we had no chance to shoot him. He was very fast. We could not catch him," LeRoy said.

"We couldn't get a clear shot," Stan said.

"He got away," LeRoy finished. Shame covered the faces of both men.

Elder Taylor did not rage. There was no need. The cold dead look in his eyes was sufficient.

"You will find this man. Go to the Paiutes. Use our sources. Identify him, track him down, and eliminate this serpent from our bosoms. Am I clear?"

Both men nodded.

"Let me hear you say it."

"Yes, sir," they said in perfect unison.

"You must not allow anyone to enter that cave."

"What about the investigators, the scientists who are there?" LeRoy asked.

"Leave them be. We have them under control."

Then Elder Taylor's demeanor changed completely. He put his arms across the shoulders of both men and his words were cheerful and caring. "Your mother tells me there will be leg of lamb and apple pie tonight. What do you think of that?"

# CHAPTER TWENTY-FIVE

Dan Fogelberry stepped around a carelessly chained bicycle and a securely chained trashcan on the concrete sidewalk approach to the Anthropology Department at BYU. The rectangular building soared above him like the obelisk in the movie 2001: A Space Odyssey. Students limped under book bags and suited professors bustled about in the large lobby. Dan found a direction board and stared at it. He found the man he wanted listed on the fifth floor: Professor of Archaeology David Philpott, Suite A.

Dan followed the tingling bell sound to the elevators, punched a button, and stepped inside. The ride was over almost before it began, and he stepped out into a foyer, feeling the strong air conditioning. Corridors ran right, left, and straight ahead. He chose straight ahead and immediately saw the frosted glass door pane designated Suite A: Professor David Philpott - Archaeology, Quantitative Methods, Ceramic Analysis, and Archaeological Theory.

Impressed, Dan gave a courtesy knock on the door and pushed it open. He was in a waiting room with several institutional chairs and a couch. They faced a desk at the far wall, where a woman glanced up at him with an inquiring expression.

"Dan Fogelberry here to see Professor Philpott. I have an eleven o'clock appointment."

"Yes, Mr. Fogelberry. Would you have a seat, please? The professor has not yet returned from class. He should be here any time now." She gave a plastic smile and went back to her work.

Dan went to the couch, scanned the magazine table and grabbed a copy of Archaeology Magazine as he sat down. He browsed the publication from back to front, a habit from youth; bypassed Ancient Genetics at high Altitude, Decorating the Dead in Roman Egypt, Lost Kingdom of the Britons, and settled on Peru's Painted Worlds, enjoying the pictures and reading the captions. Three students joined Dan in the reception room, one an attractive co-ed who perched on the couch next to him and threw furtive glances his way.

Fifteen minutes later, Professor Philpott charged in under a load of books, nodded and smiled absently at the room before vanishing through the inner door, closing it behind him. Minutes later, the phone rang on the receptionist's desk; she mumbled and nodded.

"Mr. Fogelberry, you may go on in."

Philpott was standing next to his desk, his burden of books on the shiny surface. He was engaged in reading one of them, but glanced up as Dan entered.

"Mr. Fogelberry, please sit." Philpott read on a page or so, slammed the book shut and placed it on the stack.

"I'm sorry to appear inattentive. These books are newly arrived, it's like Christmas for me." His stern teacher expression cracked, a smile stretched and new wrinkles appeared when his eyes twinkled. Professor Philpott had bushy white hair, thinning in front and curling up away from his ears. A pair of pale blue eyes assessed Dan. "You mentioned an interest in bone dating procedures."

"Yes, Professor. I need to know how scientists can determine the age of bones they find at a site for an article I am writing."

Professor Philpott slid into his chair. For an older and somewhat plump man, he appeared quite active. "Do you mean bones found at a site with corroborating materials, or without?"

"Without. Let's say you come across a cache of bones of different ages from a wide range of time periods."

The professor stared at Dan for a moment. "In the absence of site parameters, such as geochronology, palynology or dendrochronology, for example, we are left with electromagnetic and chemical dating techniques." He raised a bushy white eyebrow. "Are you familiar with any of this?"

"I've been to Wikipedia," Dan said, grinning. "But I know little about the specific techniques."

Professor Philpott tilted his head. "I teach a yearlong course just on Archaeomagnetism and Thermoluminescence. You'd better tell me what your article is about."

Dan smiled. "I have learned of a cave with a large pile of human bones in it. Some appear recent, others very old. I wondered how accurate a scientist could be when determining a timeframe for bones."

"Don't play me for a fool, young man." A stern expression returned to the professor's face. "I believe you have come here with an ulterior purpose. It is apparent you are aware of my current project. What are you, a reporter?"

"Yes, sir, I work for the Deseret News." He put up both palms. "But before you toss me, please hear me out."

The professor stared, then nodded.

"You are aware the governor of the great state of Utah has obtained an injunction against removing bones from that cave."

Professor Philpott nodded.

"Do you know why?"

"Frankly, no." He shook his white mane. "Politics as usual, I suppose."

"I agree." Dan uncrossed his legs, sat forward in his chair. "But whose politics? I spoke with the county sheriff. He claimed to have no knowledge, but I could tell he knew something. Up to this point, as you must be aware, the position of the state toward federally controlled lands within its borders is they should all be returned to the state. Yet here is the governor backing the fed's position, saying the land and everything on it is federal property and should not be removed. Including bones. Now why would he reverse his position like that?

The professor stared, offered no response.

Fogelberry continued. "I can think of only one reason; someone brought a lot of pressure to bear on our governor. Who would do that?"

The professor shrugged, offered, "Indians?"

Dan gave an ironic grin. "That's the obvious answer, isn't it? But think about it. How does a band of Paiute Indians with little or no political power, without even a casino to wield financial influence, exert that kind of pressure? Simple answer, they don't. Who else?"

"Ranchers?"

Dan nodded. "Okay, they might have the power, but what's their motive? They don't farm up there on Canaan Mountain, they don't run cattle there; they simply don't need any resources from there. In fact, their position is the same as the state—give us back our land."

"So—"

"So who is left? The church, that's who."

Professor Philpott looked exasperated. "Why on earth would the church care so much about it?"

Dan regarded the professor with raised eyebrows. "Why, indeed?" His eyes narrowed. "And here's another question. Which church?"

The professor gaped at him. "You think the Fundamentalist Church?"

Dan shrugged. "I don't know."

"I don't think the FLDS church has that much influence with the governor. He belongs to the traditional congregation."

Dan nodded. "I agree. But it's the Fundamentalists who live directly beneath the bone pile, not the Traditionalists. Again, why would the governor care?" He leaned forward again. "What if we go back to a time, before the Fundamentalists broke away, when one Latter-day Saints Church united all of Utah, say mid to late 1860s. What if something occurred then, something every Mormon wants to keep secret, regardless of current beliefs?" He grinned at the professor. "I'm a good Mormon as I'm sure you are as well. What historic events come to mind?"

"You speak of the Fancher Wagon Train and the Mountain Meadow Massacre."

Dan nodded. "That's part of it. I think everyone knows the truth of the matter by now, despite the attempt of our forefathers to blame the massacre entirely on the Indians. We know it was the Mormons of Southern Utah exacting revenge against the Americans. We know they massacred everyone in the wagon train except several young children they then raised as their own. We know some bodies were never found, opening the possibility that certain adult members of the wagon train were captured and taken away for some purpose. What happened to them?"

The professor shook his head. "You trying to raise the possibility that their bones could be on Canaan Mountain. This is wild conjecture."

Dan sat back in his chair, crossed his legs. "Maybe. It can't be dismissed out of hand, though. And what about Dunn and the Howland Brothers?"

Professor Philpott sat up in one sudden movement, stared at Dan. "The Powell Expedition!" he said. "What do you know about it?"

"Just enough to know three men went missing."

Philpott tilted back in his chair and pulled a thick book from the shelf behind him. He flipped pages, found what he wanted, and looked at Dan. "These are notes from a research paper authored by a colleague."

The professor began to read.

* * * * *

**1869**

On August 27, 1869, Seneca Howland, Oramel Howland, and William Dunn left the Powell Expedition above what is now known as Separation Rapids on the Colorado River in the Grand Canyon. The expedition had already come over one thousand river miles in small wooden boats, meeting increasingly dangerous rapids, and seeing their food supplies dwindle. The nerve-racking suspense and anxiety grew daily; would they finally meet an impossible rapid, an impassable falls? Would they run completely out of food long before the canyon ended? Become too weak to control the boats? No one had been down the river before, no one knew what to expect.

At the lip of Separation Rapid, the three men decided they would prefer to climb thousands of feet out of the canyon and walk hundreds of miles across barren wilderness and desert to seek safety rather than run one more gut-wrenching rapid. They were last seen waving the Expedition onward after Powell's boats survived the rapid and had waited in hopes the men would change their minds and rejoin them. In fact, the three men were never seen again.

That they had succeeded in their climb up to the north rim of the canyon is certain, for Dunn's name and the year 1869 were found inscribed on a rock near the summit of Mt. Dellenbaugh, an isolated volcanic peak thirty miles to the north. From there they walked on into oblivion. In 1992, a young man searching for arrowheads on Dellenbaugh found a small brass plate with the name William Dunn in cursive. It appeared to be a nameplate, perhaps from the stock of a gun.

A dozen years prior to the disappearance of these men an event occurred destined to reside within the collective conscience of all Mormons. A wagon train of gentiles (non-Mormons) and a number of apostates (former Mormons who abandoned the faith) passing through southern Utah on the Old Spanish Road to California was attacked at a location northwest of St. George, Utah by Indians and Mormons disguised as Indians. After the company (some one hundred forty persons strong) had surrendered with a promise of safe conduct out of the country, they were massacred, sparing only small children assumed to be too young to remember clearly and therefore not to be a future threat. A political crisis was brewing at the time between the United States and the Mormons of Utah. The Mormons of Southern Utah were far removed from Salt Lake City, the core of the church, and its decisions. Of necessity, they became self-reliant and retained a radical edge that had become softened and refined in their brethren to the north. Additionally, the desires of the Prophet were frequently misunderstood due to poor communication and the sometimes wishy-washy commands revealed by God through His Prophet Brigham Young. Hence, the cause of this slaughter may be seen as a combination of circumstances spearheaded by the fear and hatred Southern Utah Mormons felt toward the members of the wagon train and what they represented. This same hostile, bitter cloud was little diminished a decade later when Dunn and the Howlands marched into the area.

When the disappearance, and likely demise of the three expedition members became known, local Mormons were quick to blame the hapless Shivwits Paiutes who lived on the plateau. Not leaving potential consequences to chance, the southern brethren composed and sent an anonymous telegram to Salt Lake City laying blame on the Indians. The fact the men were murdered, and had not expired of other causes, was thus established. Never the less the authorities of the United States and even Powel himself were strangely ready to accept the easy solution.

Yet doubts and rumors remained, and trickles of evidence emerged over the years to support the idea that once again Mormons, or a combination of coerced Indians and their Mormon masters, were responsible for the death of the explorers. Whatever the cause, the bodies of these three men were never found.

# CHAPTER TWENTY-SIX

Professor Philpott stood, came around from behind his desk and perched on the corner opposite Dan. He leaned forward with excitement. "Are you suggesting the remains of those explorers could have ended up in that cave on Canaan Mountain?"

Dan fixed steady eyes on the professor. "They were never found. And not just that. I'm suggesting the cave is in part a human refuse pile for atrocities committed and regretted by Saints past."

"Other than the Mountain Meadows Massacre?"

Dan nodded. "Possibly many more such ill-advised murders resulting from the conviction some men hold they are the sole purveyors of the will of God. Historically, we know the mood, the bitterness and vengefulness in the hearts of our predecessors in the church following their treatment at Nauvoo by Americans, and the death of our Prophet Joseph Smith at their hands. For me, believing the slaughter of a wagon train and the killing of three explorers were the only such outbursts in the desolate wilds of Southern Utah is naïve."

Philpott stared at Dan. "You said you are a member of the Faith, did you not?"

Dan gave a wicked grin. "I am. I am also a newspaper reporter and a realist. But I am not a judge. I seek the truth, I don't evaluate it."

Professor Philpott swung his leg off the desk to stand, paced across the floor and back, then turned to Dan. "You want me to tell you whose bones we found in that cave."

"In a word, yes."

Hands on hips, Philpott stared down at him. "We have several problems here. First, of course, we have strict instruction from the FBI not to reveal anything we learn in that cave. Second, we haven't learned all that much because of the conditions we have to deal with. Now, due to the injunction, we will have to do all our work in the vicinity of the cave, an awkward situation to say the least. We need a lot of equipment we do not have and the generators to run it. Some lab equipment simply can't be transported so we'll have to do without it. Third, we could make more progress if some wild creatures didn't keep stealing the bones away from us anytime we leave the site, which is nightly because, once again, we have no generators to run the lights we don't have. Finally, you are a newspaperman and as such are precisely the person I should not talk to about any of this. There's more, but why go on?"

Dan eyed him for a moment. "Yet you will, won't you, because it bothers you the Saints could be using the cave to hide evidence of wrongdoing, past and present." He leaned forward, eyes intense as if to see into Philpott's mind. "You know something, don't you? I can tell you're holding something back."

The professor resumed his perch on the desk corner and put palms up in exasperation. "Fair enough. Honestly, there is no one else I can talk to about this. I can't discuss this idea with my colleagues. They would reject it out of hand and never trust me again. I have had my suspicions, you see." He slid into the chair opposite Dan. "We can talk, but there must be rules. First, and foremost, you keep me out of this. Second, you don't publish a word of it until, and unless, I say so. Third, you tell no one else about any of this." He stared at Dan. "Unless you agree to these conditions, this little talk goes no further."

Dan grinned. "You do like to enumerate, don't you? But, yes, I agree. However, here is my amendment to your conditions. Anything I learn independently and not contingent to my conversations with you, I will publish if I so desire."

Philpott gazed back at him, thought about it. "Not contingent means not construed or surmised from anything sourced from me in any way."

Dan grinned again. "Sure."

"Okay, deal."

"So what is it you haven't told me?"

Philpott went to his chair behind his desk and sat down. His brow creased as he sorted through what he would say. His eyes swung to Dan. "We've been working on the bones up there for two days now. We have basic equipment—–microscopes, hand tools, and computers. Lacking other equipment, we are concentrating on the morphology of the skulls we've found, comparing them to data in a universal base to determine the race of the victims. We've been able to determine that at least six of the skeletal remains are European—not counting the current murder victim. Of the three most recent remains we've studied, two are European and one is Native American."

"Which tells you…"

"Nothing, other than this is more than an ancient Indian burial site." The professor studied Dan before continuing. "We've been able to roughly date four of the European skulls to the mid 1800s, the timeframe of the Mountain Meadows event and the Powell Expedition"—he gave a humorless grin—"within several decades, anyway. We can't do more without proper lab equipment."

Dan pulled out his notebook, scratched some notes. He held a palm up to Philpott. "Don't worry, these are just to help me remember, not to publish." He stopped writing, looked up. "Is there any evidence to conclude the cave is an ancient burial site?"

Professor Philpott shook his head. "We haven't gotten that far. But there are a lot of bones. It seems reasonable to assume it may have begun as a burial site and later turned into a human trash bin."

Dan nodded, smiled his appreciation, and started to rise from his chair.

"Whoa, wait a minute. There is more.

Dan, halfway up, resumed his seat and shot Philpott a quizzical glance.

"We haven't found just bones in there. We've also found leather fragments, bits of metal, even paper scraps that survived the centuries. One thing we did find, however, seems significant. It sifted down to the bottom of the pile, probably been there for a century or more."

"What's that?" Dan felt anticipatory excitement build up inside him.

"A watch. A silver watch, somewhat corroded, of course, but in remarkably good shape nonetheless." Philpott watched Dan's face.

"Did you find any markings on it, any way to identify it?"

Philpott sighed. "I wish I could tell you it was engraved, but I could find no sign of it. It's a pretty standard watch; brass gears, nickel plate, silver and metal alloy case, a production watch from the American Watch Company."

Dan leaned toward Philpott. "Does it narrow down a timeframe for us?"

"I'm not a watch expert, but I do have access to Google. The American Watch Company was formed in 1859. Beyond that, your guess is as good as mine. Although the company went out of business in 1957, an international subsidiary continues to this day. We intend to send the watch off to the company to see if their records can narrow the field."

"What are the likely years this watch might have been carried, given manufacture and design?"

Philpott shook his head. "As an educated guess, I'd say anywhere from 1860 to 1915 or so. A wide gap."

Dan was excited. "Yes, but don't you see; the Mountain Meadows Massacre happened in 1857, two years before you say the American Watch Company formed. So the watch couldn't have come with anyone on the wagon train. But one of Powell's men could have carried it."

133

Professor Philpott grimaced. "And anybody else who was victimized and left in that cave after that date could have carried it."

Dan was on his feet. "I know, I know, but the coincidence is too great. This confirms my suspicions. I believe people from the church, or maybe the FLDS Church, are trying hard to prevent that cave from being fully explored."

He went to the door, had a thought, and turned back to Philpott. "I also suspect anybody who figures it out is in danger. Be careful what you say—and watch your back."

The moment Dan was back in his car he removed his iPad from his briefcase, wrote his report, and filed it with his editor as "eyes-only."

# CHAPTER TWENTY-SEVEN

Tubs was ushered into a shiny new office on the second floor of the Robert J. DeBry building in St. George, Utah, and waved into a chair facing a woman behind a shiny metal desk. A single file folder was open on the otherwise empty surface. She wore her hair in a tight bun, a white blouse with high collar buttoned, and tiny gold earrings. Her FBI ID dangled from her neck on a silver chain like a piece of jewelry.

"I am so pleased you came to visit me, Mr. LeBaron." She had perfect teeth, which competed with the shimmer of her desk.

"Didn't seem to me as I had much choice," Tubs said.

Her face creased in concern, she placed her pen slowly and deliberately on the blotter. "Oh, my, I hope the agents were not too insistent."

"Ah guess they made their point," Tubs said. His eyes drifted to the road maps framed like artwork on the otherwise barren walls."

"Mr. LeBaron—"

"Please call me Tubs. I sometimes forget who Mr. LeBaron is."

She smiled. "Mr. Tubs, then. I consider it a great favor you came to see me. I am Agent Janice Hooper, Special Agent in Charge of the St. George Office of the FBI."

"Yes, ma'am."

Janice rose from her desk chair and walked around to another chair angled toward Tubs. She sat, legs together, trim yet athletic. Tubs watched her tight black skirt ride back from her knee. He realized Agent Hooper was an attractive woman despite her chilly presence.

"Mr. Tubs, what were you doing up on Canaan Mountain at our crime scene last Wednesday?" Janice smiled brightly as if she'd just invited him to a cocktail party.

Tubs was startled, confused for a moment. How did she know? Then he remembered—the Indian consultant he met on the mountain would have told her. "Jest curiosity, I reckon."

"What sort of curiosity, Mr. Tubs? Was it curiosity like slowing down and rubbernecking to see an accident on a highway? Or something else?"

He considered her phrasing of the question before responding. "Somethin' else. I was less curious about the murdered boy than I was about the rock slab and the cave."

"What about the slab and the cave?" Agent Hooper leaned toward him.

Tubs watched her eyes, wondered what she knew. "A few things come to mind. The slab seemed like it's been used for some sort of ceremonial purposes by an ancient people—the cave too, likely. All them bones were human, near as I could tell. Some was real old. Did human sacrifice happen there at one time?" Tubs shrugged. "Jest curious."

"So you went all the way back up there for a second look."

Tubs shrugged again. "Thet's about the size of it."

Agent Hooper leaned back in her chair and studied him, her green eyes inscrutable. "You saw something else, didn't you?"

"Ma'am?"

"You didn't go all the way back up there to satisfy your curiosity about ancient cultures. There was something else."

"No, ma'am."

She smiled, perfect teeth on full display. "Whatever it was, you saw it the first time you were there, the time you first discovered the murdered boy. But you were with someone else, weren't you? Maybe someone you didn't want to see what you saw?"

Tub's chin came up abruptly. He didn't answer, just stared back at her like a bird mesmerized by a snake.

"Randy Musser was with you, wasn't he? Why was he there?"

Tubs shrugged. "He was there for the same reason I was, to help the BLM determine the growth rate of —"

"The growth rate of the Big Horn Sheep population in the Canaan Mountain Wilderness Study Area to determine the viability of future hunting blah, blah, blah. I know all about that, Mr. Tubs. But Randy Musser isn't really a guide, is he? He's barely a hunter. He's actually a rancher in the Virgin River Watershed and an active member of Ranchers Against Federally Owned Land. He was with Bundy in 2014 in Oregon. He's an activist, Mr. Tubs, and I think you know that."

Tubs stared at her, shook his head. "No, I didn't know thet. I have hunted with him before. He's a good hunter."

The perfect teeth were gone; Janice wasn't smiling anymore. "He's an activist and he was on public land with you, Mr. Tubs, and you saw something at the crime scene you couldn't talk about in front of him and it was so significant you came all the way back up the mountain days later to check it. Was it still there?"

Tubs shook his head, like a man receiving directions in a foreign language he didn't understand. "With respect, ma'am, I don't know what you are talking about."

She stood abruptly. "Would you like a cup of coffee? We have some pastry."

Once again thrown by her rapid change of direction, Tubs said, "Frankly, ma'am, I'd as soon get back to the work you interrupted."

Janice turned and beamed at him, her expression one of sympathy. "But, of course, Mr. Tubs. So you shall. I just have one or two more questions." She returned to the chair behind her desk, stood next to it with a hand on it, her back to Tubs, staring out the window. A moment later, she turned to face him. "Mr. Tubs, I am arresting you for obstructing a murder investigation."

"What the—"

"You refuse to answer my question. You leave me no choice."

Tubs jumped to his feet. He was pissed. "I can't answer your question if I don't know the answer."

"Why did you really go back to the crime scene?"

He stared at her. "I don't know. Something about the scene didn't set right with me. It gnawed at me—I had to go back and look again."

The teeth were back. "What did you find?"

Tubs sighed, sat down again. "I'm a hunting guide. I've been a hunter pretty much all my life. I notice things. One thing I take notice of is my hunting partner's footprints, so as not to confuse them with any others." He paused. "When I went back up there later, I studied all the tracks. The area had been trampled by then, what with all the investigators and other people, but I was able to sort them out, mostly. I could still read where Randy and I had stood, where I had walked around the slab, where Randy went and lost his breakfast. I retraced my own steps hopin' I'd see what it was bothered me. And I did."

Janice came back around the desk and sat on its edge, peering closely down at him. "What did you see, Mr. Tubs?"

Tubs spoke reluctantly. "I saw one of Randy's footprints leading into the cave."

Janice gave him a quizzical look. "Why was that significant?"

"Because Randy never went into the cave that day. His prints had to have been left there from a time before we discovered the place."

Janice started, leaned back. "You're sure of that?"

"Yes, ma'am."

Agent Hooper stared at Tubs. A shaft of sunlight through the bare office window behind her turned floating particles into fairy dust. The moment stretched. "Have you asked Mr. Musser about that?"

Tubs shook his head. "No, Ma'am."

"Why not? Weren't you curious?"

Tubs raised an eyebrow. "I was mighty curious. But the way I figured it, if I asked and he was guilty of the murder, I might be his next victim, and if I asked and he wasn't guilty, he'd think I was accusing him. Sometimes it's best just to let things sort themselves out on their own."

"You would not make a good policeman."

Tubs shrugged. "Guess I'm kinda glad of that."

Janice studied him in silence. "Is there anything else you forgot to mention?"

"No, ma'am."

The perfect teeth reappeared in a sudden wide smile. "Don't plan any long trips, Mr. Tubs. I may need to speak to you again."

Tubs was confused. He couldn't figure this woman. "Does this mean I'm un-arrested?"

"Yes, Mr. Tubs."

She was back behind her desk now, opening the file before Tubs had even risen from his chair. She never looked up when he left the office.

Tubs thought about it as he walked away. It was not that he hadn't thought a lot about that footprint, its implications and possibilities. There were many. He knew Randy Musser. He was comfortable to be around, didn't intrude his thoughts; did none of the ceaseless yakking so many hunters keep up as if to steel their nerves while in fact they were scaring the game away. He wouldn't call Randy a friend, though, just a hunting companion.

But that footprint suggested something else. He couldn't see Musser in the role of a brutal cold-blooded killer. Not the way that kid was killed, lifted up and skewered on a stake like meat in a butcher shop.

Still, there was the footprint. How did it get there? Tubs had been with Randy every step of the way up that mountain and down into the arroyo. Tubs was in front as the reached the scene. Yet Randy's footprint was already there, in the soft soil up toward the cave entrance just at the end of the slab, a place Randy did not go that day. Tubs wasn't mistaken—not about that, not about footprints. Recognizing prints was his livelihood.

It meant Randy had been there before but pretended to Tubs he hadn't. Did that make him the killer? Maybe not, but it sure put him deep in the shit. There was no doubt Agent Hooper thought it made him the killer. It was hard for Tubs not to think that way too. How else to explain it?

Tubs thought of another interesting little wrinkle. No doubt that footprint was gone by now, trampled underfoot by all the investigators and anthropologists and such. Tubs had decided at the time not to mention it to anyone else, a decision that might just come back to haunt him— withholding evidence or something like that. His problem was he'd just burbled it out to an FBI agent. Why had he done that? Her good looks, perfect teeth? Or maybe she was just that good and caught him unawares. Now, it was on his word alone that the footprint had ever been there. If Agent Janice Hooper made a case against Randy, Tubs was sure to be called in to testify. And that was not something he was prepared to do.

What if Randy Musser really did have a hand in the killing? What motive could he possibly have?

Tubs pushed open the glass door and stepped out into the warmth of the morning sun. His International Scout was parked several spaces down the street. It was the early 1962 model with the fold down windshield. He liked that; when hunting out on the plateau he didn't want any obstructions to his view.

Tubs climbed into the driver's seat. The 152-horsepower four-cylinder engine started with a rusty muffler roar. He pulled out into the street.

Once on the freeway, Tubs' mind went back to Musser. What did he actually know about the man? He was a rancher, ran cattle and sheep over a large range of rocky terrain in the Virgin River Gorge area. Sure, he was an activist. But a lot of ranchers were fighting the Feds over land ownership—the question impacted their livelihood. On rock-strewn desert terrain, grazing animals required a lot of room.

Try as he might, Tubs could not imagine any credible motive for Randy Musser to kill a young kid in that barbaric, primitive way. He thought about the footprint, summoned the image up in his memory. It had appeared fresh and clear, but that meant little in a dry land. It had been a while since it last rained. And when it did, the depth of the arroyo, the cluster of pine trees, the overhang of the cliff would protect the area. Maybe the print was actually placed before the murder. Maybe Musser had nothing to do with it at all. Even so, what possible reason could he have had for being there? And why had he pretended to Tubs he'd never seen the place before?

If he knew anything about Musser, he knew he was a stubborn man. If Agent Hooper figured she could get an answer out of him, particularly with the rancher's prejudice against the feds, she was mistaken. He would deny, tell her she had got it all wrong, it wasn't his footprint, etc. Again, it all came down to his word against Randy's.

Tubs groaned. The situation was untenable. He didn't want to antagonize Musser toward him. He knew there was only one choice. He'd have to go to Randy Musser and ask the man how his print came to be there.

141

# CHAPTER TWENTY-EIGHT

Tubs got on the I-15 at St. George, Utah and headed south. A few minutes later, he took exit 27 onto Black Rock Road and on to the first of a series of unmarked turns onto unnamed roads. He didn't hesitate; he'd traveled this route several times before. The land here was arid, a sandstone tableland pocked by chaparral. He passed a large stone quarry after which the road narrowed and became rougher. Tubs saw Dinner Flat appear on his left, and soon spotted Pocket Hill a half-mile away. The land around him was less regular now, cut by arroyos and decorated with rock formations, all sloping in a gradual descent toward the river still several miles away.

A section of fence paralleled the road, leading him toward a grove of cottonwoods and several pastures shaped into large rectangles by fences. Beyond them, a small house was nestled among a grove of trees with several trailers strung out behind it. This was the Dives Ranch, named for a large rock formation in the dry riverbed a mile to the south. It was the home of Randy Musser: rancher, hunter, and apparently activist.

Tubs followed the driveway to a large metal gate festooned with barbed wire. He honked his horn twice. Five minutes later, he saw the familiar figure of Randy Musser coming toward him down the drive.

Randy unraveled several strands of barbed wire and unlatched the gate. Such precautions just to protect a few acres of red dirt in the middle of nowhere had always struck Tubs as strange, but then Randy wasn't your average guy. Tubs drove through, waited for Randy to secure the gate and climb in beside him, and they rode together back to the house.

"I wasn't expecting you today," Randy said with a curious glance at Tubs.

"I didn't expect to be here," Tubs said. "Always good to see yuh, though." Randy's eyes questioned him. Tubs waved it away, saying, "I'll tell yuh what's on my mind when we're inside."

The house was small, a one-story ranch-style structure painted white with green trim. It seemed barely large enough for the five rooms within, although large windows helped it feel more spacious. He followed Randy into the foyer and across to the kitchen counter. Tubs slipped onto a stool and Randy went behind to grab the coffee pot.

The space was open, California style, giving view from kitchen through to the living room where a large picture window framed the pastures and craggy pinyon-dotted lands beyond. Tubs enjoyed the view. In the past, he'd seen circling hawks riding the wind currents and a solitary coyote probing for ground squirrels.

While Randy poured, Tubs searched for a way to open the topic, finally gave up and simply said, "Yuh got a problem."

"You don't say."

"There's a lady FBI agent thinks yuh killed that boy up on the mountain."

Randy slopped coffee on the counter, put the pot down. "What are you talking about? How could I? We were the ones discovered him." Randy stared at Tubs with wide green eyes, then a grin slowly appeared. "You're pulling my leg."

Tubs shook his head. "Wish I was. Fact is it's my fault she's suspicious."

Randy waited.

Tubs wrapped both hands around the mug of coffee but didn't lift it. He searched for words. "Yuh never told me yuh had been to that cave before."

"Before what?"

"Before you and me found the dead boy that day."

Randy continued to stare, but said nothing.

"I saw your footprint near the cave, I jest never told yuh."

Randy rubbed spread fingers through his blond hair, turned his head away. When he looked back, he said, "I can't tell you. You are not a church member."

"What's that got tuh do with it?"

"Everything." Randy wiped up the coffee he'd spilled, then sipped from his mug before going on. "You are right, I had been up there before. But I can't talk about what I was doing." He raised his eyebrows. "But it had nothing to do with that boy, I'd never seen him before. I couldn't believe what I was seeing when you and I found him. It was sickening."

Tubs watched him. "What about them other bones?"

"I had nothing to do with them either. But that's all I can tell you." Randy grimaced. "You got to believe me, I didn't kill anyone. I wouldn't, not even for the church." A look of supplication came over his face. "Tubs, you got to drop this. Don't go asking questions. Don't get in the middle."

Tubs gave a short laugh. "Seems I already am. That FBI lady put me there."

"You saw a footprint. Did you see any other evidence I'd been there before?"

"That's all I needed."

Randy spoke with great earnestness. "Enough for you, yes. Enough for me, yes, because I know your abilities. Is it enough for everyone else? I don't think it will be. I'm not asking you to lie, just hedge a bit. Tell them you are eighty percent sure, not one hundred percent. That's all."

"Yuh don't know this FBI lady. She'll push. "

"Let her. Without you corroborating what she says, she's got nowhere to go with this." Randy paused, looked pleadingly at Tubs. "If you let this go forward, it will create a mess for a lot of people, you and me included."

Tubs regarded him. "You don't want to tell me anything to help me understand why I gotta lie? Mebbe you did no harm, but what about people who might have been there with you? I don't want to end up in the middle of some goldang conspiracy cooked up by your church."

"You won't; I promise you, you won't."

Tubs slid off the stool, walked around the counter and stood at the picture window, staring out. After a moment, he turned to Randy. "Look, I already told the FBI lady what I saw, but I'm willing to say after I discussed it with you I wasn't so sure. That work for yuh?"

Randy gave a great sigh of relief. "Thanks, Tubs, I owe you one."

Tubs gave him a long stare. "I can't believe you let me think you never seen that arroyo before. Yuh had me fooled. And here I thought I knew you."

Randy glanced away. "That's not me, not really. You can trust me. It's just that I can't reveal the secrets of the church."

Tubs shrugged, walked back to the counter. "Okay, you keep your old secrets, I don't care. Just so long as they don't come back around and bite me in the arse." He took a sip of coffee.

Randy watched him. "Really think she'll come out here?"

Tubs grinned. "The only thing I know for certain about that lady is I don't know nothin' for certain."

Tubs was unsettled in his mind as he drove away a half hour later. What part of Randy Musser's story did he believe? The man seemed sincere telling it, yet he distanced himself from the actual murder. What could he possibly be doing in support of the church involving that cave and those bones?

He glanced in the rearview mirror, a pointless action since the billowing dust coated the vinyl rear window. His driving reflexes went on automatic as he thought about his conversation with Randy. Among all the elephants in the room, there had been one particularly large one—the sense that something else was in that cave. They had both ignored it, if Randy had even noticed it. Tubs had felt it right away, something that raised the short hairs on his skin even beyond the horrific murder scene and all the bones. Randy had visited the cave on more than one occasion, yet he never mentioned such a feeling.

Tubs remembered the Navajo who appeared out of the landscape in the arroyo—what was his name? Eagle Feather, that was it. He thought Indians were more spiritual than most others. No doubt the Navajo would sense the presence at the cave. Tubs wondered idly if he should try to find the guy, feel him out and ask him about it.

He mentally shrugged. Why bother? If an entity lived in that cave it was ancient, must have always been there more or less. It wasn't going anywhere. Besides, Tubs wasn't as ready as the Indians to attribute to ghosts an ability to interact with real people. It was just a feeling, after all, despite the incredible projection of menace that came to him.

More importantly, what were the Mormons up to? Randy swore he had nothing to do with the boy's murder, but he didn't claim as much for his companions, whoever they were. He also claimed he never saw the boy. If that was true, Randy must have been there before the crime was committed, and if the Mormons were with him then, perhaps they had nothing to do with it either.

Nearing the stone quarry, the Scout bumping along the narrow-rutted track, Tubs' mind was caught up in these thoughts, and he didn't notice the huge haul truck coming toward him. When he did, it took him a while to realize how fast it was approaching. The monster truck took the entire width of the road and was barreling along so fast it seemed to bounce into the air off bumps. Tubs slowed, waited for the driver to notice him and do likewise. It didn't happen. In fact, the truck seemed to speed up. Tubs flashed his lights—the driver had to have seen him—how could he not? There was no change.

The road dropped steeply into an arroyo on one side, on the other was a three-foot-high ridge of sand and shale. The haul truck breathed down on him, its massive bumper as high as the Scout's windshield, its headlights above the roof. Tubs caught a momentary image of the driver staring down at him, intent upon his purpose.

With just seconds left, Tubs reacted and jerked the steering wheel and floored the accelerator. The Scout roared up the embankment and flew into space, leaning toward the driver's side. Tubs instinctively threw his body the opposite way to try to offset the lean, still gripping the steering wheel. It seemed to take forever for the truck to come back to earth. When it did, it landed on two wheels, teetered, started to go over, then ploughed through sand and into a stand of honey mesquite. The strong wiry branches arrested its lean and brought it to a stop. Tubs stared through the cracked windshield at the fern-like leaves framing it and breathed out slowly.

After a full minute of recovery, he pushed open the door and climbed out. Above the brush, he saw the large dust cloud of the would-be assassin disappearing off in the distance. He glanced down at the Scout. The truck's front wheels were burrowed deep into the desert sand.

Tubs walked around the vehicle, assessing his situation. He locked the hubs, climbed back in, put the vehicle in four-wheel-drive low, and muscled out of the sand. He drove through the brush and looped back to the road. The vehicle seemed to have sustained little damage other than a few more cracks in the windshield. After a glance back in the direction the haul truck had disappeared, Tubs continued on his way.

A mile or so later, he came to the wide section of road near the quarry. Clearly the haul truck had no reason to go beyond this point, and certainly no reason to continue on down that narrow track. Tubs was certain this had been a deliberate attempt on his life; but if so, how could the driver had known he was coming?

Suspicion grew in him. No one knew he would be on this road but Randy. Tubs had not told anyone he was coming to visit him. This was a deliberate attempt to kill him, and the timing of the haul truck on this track could only mean Randy had called someone to set it up.

But why would he do that? Tubs had been ready to believe Randy's story. Apparently, in the end, Randy didn't trust him, or perhaps whomever Randy had called didn't want to take chances.

Tubs glanced at his shaking hands on the steering wheel. It had been a very close call. This changed everything, to Tub's mind. He could not believe even a part of Randy's story now. The man was involved in something far more sinister than he had let on, something he and others were desperate to hide.

Once back on I-15, Tubs took the very next exit and pulled over to the side of the road. He took out his cell phone, took a shiny new business card from his shirt pocket and called Agent Hooper. He wasn't keen on siding with the FBI, but he'd rather be on the side that didn't want him dead.

# CHAPTER TWENTY-NINE

Zack held the phone to his ear with his shoulder while he poured himself a third cup of coffee. "What have you learned about the murder of the girl?"

"What girl?"

"How many murders of young girls are you investigating?"

Conley sounded put out. "None at the moment."

It was Zack's turn to feel exasperated. He put down the coffee urn and grabbed the phone with his right hand. "The girl who was killed just up the road from us in Kanab. I thought you were handling that."

"That would be the Kane County Sheriff's Department. Not us."

Zack was surprised. "You don't think it's connected to the Canaan Mountain killing? Why did you think I moved Emma and Pru out of town? Why did I ask you to watch the house? It's because the murdered girl walks home from school the same way and same time as Pru, remember? The similarity of their appearances and the location and time of the abduction and murder can't be a coincidence. But you know all that."

"Yes, I know all that, but I'm not making the decisions. The team requires actual evidence linking the two cases before they can summarily remove the girl's case from the sheriff's jurisdiction. Have you some direct evidence? If so, share it and I'll pass it on." Conley sounded miffed.

"Okay, okay. We need to contact the sheriff to get information. But I can't do that; I have no standing in this case. Either case." Zack waited.

"Yeah, I hear you, pal. I'll see what I can find out. But it's not like this case is the only thing on my desk, you know."

"I really, truly appreciate it, Pete." Zack heard a sort of mumble before the line went dead. He sighed.

Libby was upstairs packing. She had decided the FBI had their man, and that being the case, there was no longer any reason to stay in Kanab. Zack wasn't so sure; there was the wounded intruder to consider, and they had not yet learned the identity of the suspicious car but seeing the glow in Libby's eyes as she spoke of going home to Bernie caused him to keep those thoughts to himself.

He was startled when his phone buzzed. He figured Conley had some second thoughts and was calling back, but it turned out to be Eagle Feather.

"Good morning, White Man."

Zack lifted his eyebrows. "I hope so. Where are you and why do you sound so cheerful?"

He heard a quiet chuckle. "I may have just met the future Mrs. Eagle Feather."

Zack's jaw dropped. "Well, that is certainly news. Who is she, might I ask?"

"You may. She is Shana Bows, and she is the Tribal Council Chairperson of the Paiutes."

Zack glanced at the door, but Libby was still upstairs. "I can't wait to tell Libby."

"Don't get too excited, White Man. She's a cool one, and I don't think she's gonna flip over a hunting guide who is half Navajo, half Jew."

"So don't tell her."

"Too late."

Zack was stunned. Eagle Feather, who talked little, let alone about himself, had apparently revealed very intimate information in a single meeting with this woman. "What else did you talk about?"

"Well, we spoke of Nimerigars, with which she is well acquainted from the oral history of her people. She did not discard Sam's suggestion out of hand. We also spoke of the governor's injunction. She said her band of Paiutes had nothing to do with it, and she couldn't speak for all the other bands, but she doubted any of them were involved. Zack, whoever swayed the governor to act had a lot of power, much more than the Paiutes."

"I agree." Zack sighed. "I guess it's time to study up on all the state lobbyists and see where that takes us." He smiled. "What's your next move, other than looking at engagement rings?"

Eagle Feather gave a grunt. "There is someone else I'm curious about. I'd like to learn more about this Tubs character who discovered the body. I'm going to sniff around, see what I can find out about him. I'll get back to you."

Zack couldn't remember when the usually taciturn Eagle Feather had sounded so cheerful. He was filled with a strong desire to meet this young woman who seemed to have so totally turned his friend's head.

But it was time to get back to work. He went to the coffee table where he'd left his computer and did a Google search for strong lobbyists in the Utah state government. Almost immediately he was rewarded with information even more relevant, an article written by a former state senator complaining about the "secret" lobbying methods utilized by the LDS Church. In the article, the former senator also casually mentioned the fact that eighty-eight percent of the lawmakers in state government were Mormons.

Zack smacked his forehead—of course. Here was the power group. He wondered why the church even needed lobbyists. The author of the article complained that church lobbyists simply whispered into the ears of one or two senators and things magically got done their way. Well, no surprise there.

So here was an answer to his question. The power wielded by the Mormon Church was certainly enough to sway the governor, a Mormon himself. Zack's next question did not have an easy answer. Why would the church want the governor to prevent the removal of bones from a cave on Canaan Mountain? Why would they care?

A half hour of more research made it clear the second most powerful lobby in Utah government was the National Rifle Association. Here was another group that could easily sway a western state governor. But again, motive; what reason would the NRA have to stop the bone transfer? He pondered this. The NRA might well be allied with various ranchers' associations, but their concerns would be about grazing and public vs. private land, not old bones.

It was a puzzle—and a piece was missing somewhere.

Zack lifted his gaze. Libby was at the entrance to the living room, her overnight bag next to her. Her cheeks were flushed, perhaps from the exertion of packing or maybe just from the thought of seeing her child. Zack smiled at her.

"You should come with me," Libby said. "This is not your case, there's no reason to stay. They've got their man; it's just wrap-up now."

Zack kept his smile. "It does seem that way. I'll come along soon."

"How soon?" A slight pout appeared, the petulant look that had always so attracted Zack, yet worried him.

"As soon as I'm sure they do have the right man and there is no accomplice. Until then, I consider my family might still be in danger." He rose from his chair, went to Libby and enveloped her in his arms. "You go along, give Bernie my love." He leaned back to look Libby in the eye. "Keep Emma and Pru with you a while longer, have a nice visit. I'll call you when I'm completely satisfied."

Zack's day was spent researching movers and shakers in the LDS Church and the NRA. He wasn't surprised to find an overlap, just as he often found with the NRA and the Public Lands Council and other large political groups in the west. The sun had nearly set and he was thinking about some dinner, his thoughts mainly on the burger place down the street, when something rattled at the front door. He jumped up from the couch, leaving the TV on, grabbed his gun from the side table and slipped through the kitchen and around to the unlit hallway. There he melded into the shadow of the basement door and waited.

The front door opened slowly, a shadow figure slipped inside the door, paused there.

Zack's adrenaline pumped. He lifted his gun, trained it on the indistinct figure.

"Zack?"

Zack let out his breath in an explosive gasp. "Damn. Libby. What are you doing here? I almost shot you."

Libby came full into the hall, shut the door and locked it, putting the security chain in place. She left the hall light off.

Even the dim light, Zack could see she was in a panic. Her eyes were large and round, her face was white.
"Zack, someone followed me."

Zack went to her, took her hands, and led her into the living room. "Did anything happen? Did anyone approach you?"

"No. Nothing like that." Libby collapsed into a chair. "They just followed at a distance. It was pretty obvious, though, especially in the open desert." She grew angry. "They are never going to let us be, are they? They figured I was going to see Pru and followed me to find her."

"What did you do?"

"When I came to the junction with route 89, I went north to Page instead of continuing south. I pretended I'd gone on a shopping trip. I hung about in a couple of stores, then came back." She gave a sheepish smile. "There's a few charges on our credit card."

"And the tail—?"

"Stayed with me the entire way."

"Did you ever see them?"

"No, just the car following me."

Zack flicked his eyes toward the street. "So—"

"It's probably out there right now, an older sedan, dark blue."

Zack shook his head slowly. "This doesn't make sense. I need to call Conley and verify it's not his guys." He called the number as he walked to the window, took a cautious peek outside.

"Oh, yes, hi, Pete. Got a minute?" Zack glanced at Libby. "Have you got anyone watching the house or tailing anyone here? No? Well, Libby said a dark blue sedan followed her all the way to Page and back. I see it now, it's still outside, a '95 or '96 Dodge." He listened. "You will? That's great. No, I won't, I promise. Thanks, Pete."

Zack put down the phone, smiled at Libby. "Pete's sending a car out here right now. They'll try to intercept the car outside and get an identity. Then maybe we'll learn what's going on."

But it did not work out as Zack had hoped—the suspect car pulled away and disappeared, almost as if the occupant had listened in on Zack's conversation. The FBI agent came to the door and took Libby's description and promised to keep an eye out for the vehicle but he stopped short of offering to reestablish surveillance of the house. "I'll suggest it to Pete," he said, "but I wouldn't count on it. We're spread pretty thin."

After he had gone, Zack stared at Libby, frustrated. "I should've gone out there myself while I had the chance. Pete made me promise not to."

Libby's shoulders sagged. "I guess I better go unpack. I don't want to lead a killer to Pru. Either the FBI has the wrong man or something else is going on related to Pru. Which ever, we need to keep Pru safe." Libby turned and hauled her bag back up the stairs.

As Zack watched Libby go, he felt a rush of anger. This case was going nowhere. The investigating forces, FBI included, seemed mired in mud. The FBI had the wrong man, he was sure of that now. The man they held might be a pedophile, but Zack was sure he was not a part of a conspiracy to murder. And this was a conspiracy—it had to be, with the thin but distinct line of coincidences connecting the murdered boy to Pru, then the murdered girl who looked so much like Pru, the school counselor who knew their secrets, the cave full of old bones where the victim had been found. Somehow it all fit together—if only they could find the missing pieces.

But the FBI first needed to see it was all connected, which they never would unless they accepted the relationship of the girl's murder to the cave murder case. Jurisdictional politics were in the way. Well, maybe it was time that was sorted out.

Zack looked up the Kane County Administration on his smart phone, found the sheriff's number, and called.

"Kane County Sheriff's Office, Deputy Coletti speaking."

"This is Zack Tolliver. May I speak with Sheriff Rafferty, please?"

"What does this concern?"

"It concerns the investigation into the death of the high school girl."

There was a pause. "If you have information, you may share it with me. I am assisting the sheriff in this matter."

Zack groaned inwardly. "Deputy Coletti, I know it is necessary to screen calls to the sheriff. I am a former FBI agent, currently a consultant to the agency. It is of utmost importance I speak directly to the sheriff."

Another pause. "Just a minute, Mr. Tolliver, I'll see if he's available."

There was a click and music flowed from his phone, something classical, strangely enough. Zack had just identified it as a theme from Rimsky-Korsokoff's Scheherazade when there was another click and a gruff voice said, "Hello?"

"Hello, Sheriff? This is Zack Tolliver, former FBI."

"Yes?"

"You are investigating the murder of a high school girl. What you don't know is that the murder is part of a larger conspiracy. Without a liaison with the FBI you will never solve the case. Here is why." Zack launched into a synopsis of his information but was abruptly interrupted by the sheriff.

"Whoa, there—TMI. Give me ten minutes and I'll call you back."

The line went dead.

Frustrated, Zack paced the room. He was not surprised by the sheriff's response; no local law enforcement is eager to have the FBI become involved. The man's ruse of saying he would call back was irritating. He hadn't even taken Zack's number.

Yet exactly ten minutes later, his phone rang. To his surprise, it was the sheriff.

"I checked your background, Tolliver. We need to talk, just you and me. How soon can you get over here?"

# CHAPTER THIRTY

Zack left Libby to unpack and drove to meet with the county sheriff. His office was located in a brand new jail complex, an impressive building. The deputy on duty showed Zack directly to Sheriff Rafferty.

Oliver Rafferty stood and extended a hand across his desk. He was a large man with a broad fleshy face and squinched eyes, his balding head sun browned under the thin flaxen hair comb-over. His voice was strong and authoritative.

"Pull up a seat, young fellow. Since I know who you are and you know who I am, we'll skip the niceties. I'm mighty curious to hear what you were about to tell me over the phone."

It was a long time since Zack had been called a young fellow. He grinned his appreciation. "Sheriff, I believe that you and the FBI are investigating the same case, but don't know it."

"Yeah, so you said. How did that work again?"

Zack started at the beginning. "My wife's sister's child lives here in Kanab. She attends the high school, the one the murdered boy attended. She was walking home from school with the boy when he was kidnapped. She didn't see it happen because she arrived home first. But she did see a vehicle drive by slowly while they were walking."

The sheriff's eyes stayed on Zack as he spoke. "Go on."

"The girl was very upset, as you might imagine. My wife came up to help out. She picked Pru up from school, and on the way home Pru saw the vehicle again."

"Okay, I still don't see the connection to the dead girl."

"Hang on, we're almost there. Point is we were worried this killer would realize Pru was a witness and come after her. Then the other girl was found dead. My wife called me in a panic; the new victim had not been identified, she couldn't locate Pru, and the description we had of the dead girl fit Pru to a "T." Libby went down to the morgue, fully expecting to find her niece there. Instead, she finds the girl. Here's the thing—the girl has the same color and style hair, the same general figure, skin tone, and is even wearing a similar dress." Zack locked eyes with Rafferty. "I don't know about you, but after years of investigative work I stopped believing in coincidence."

The sheriff drummed thick fingers on his desk and stared at Zack. He cocked his head to one side. "So you believe one perp is responsible for both murders."

"Yes, I do."

"I need a description of that car."

"Pru is out of town, hidden away. But I can have her get in touch with you."

The sheriff nodded. He stared at Zack. "I'm guessing your compatriots in the FBI don't buy the connection?"

"Actually, I think they do, but they require solid evidence to take over jurisdiction." Zack smiled at Rafferty. "Unless you invite them, of course."

The sheriff stood.

Zack stood with him.

"First I need to talk to your niece and make up my mind what I think. When I know what I'm gonna do, I'll call you."

Zack shook his hand, slid a business card into it. "I'll have her call right away." He paused for a moment. "I do have a condition."

The sheriff raised an eyebrow.

"Someone has been following my wife Libby, watching the house. I need to know she is safe."

Rafferty eyed Zack, thinking. "Okay, fair enough. I'll have someone keep an eye on her."

Outside, the surrounding cliff faces glowed with the sinking sun and dusk shrouded the nearby trees. A gnawing in

Zack's stomach reminded him he had not eaten dinner—or lunch, come to think of it. He called Libby. "Hi, you hungry?"

Libby's voice sounded sleepy. "Really, not at all. My stomach's in a knot. I think I'll go right to bed."

"Okay. I've got my eye on a burger joint to try. Lock all the doors; I've got my key. Sleep tight. Love you."

Zack drove straight to E. 300 Street and parked behind Al's Burgers, a retro 60s joint with a drive-in type window and picnic tables inside. After he had eaten the burger, as hot and juicy as he fantasized, he called Eagle Feather.

"What is happening, White Man?" Eagle Feather sounded upbeat.

Zack smiled at that. "I was just in the local jail talking to the sheriff of Kane County. Eagle Feather, I'm beginning to think this thing goes way beyond a couple of local murders."

"You got that from the sheriff?"

"Not directly. But we both agree the two murders are connected, which ties them in some way to the injunction and all the nonsense going on about the cave."

"Big forces afoot," was Eagle Feather's comment.

"What did you learn about this Tubs character?" Zack asked.

Eagle Feather grunted. "Not a lot. The man keeps to himself. Not many people know him. Sam at the campground says Tubs guides hunters for a living, lives by himself over in Big Water. He's seen him a few times, just passing through."

"Could he be involved?"

"In the murders? It is not likely. He was one of the hunters who discovered the murdered boy, remember."

"Yeah, right." Zack thought about that. "Eagle Feather, I think it's about time I got a look at that cave."

"Whoa, White Man. That place is out of bounds. It is not just the local deputies watching it, and they are crazy men, but the entire state wants to keep everybody out. Do

you remember the injunction? We would be crazy to—"
Eagle Feather stopped talking abruptly. Zack heard him
mumble softly under his breath. In a resigned voice, the
Navajo said, "We are going up there, are we not?"

"Yes, first thing in the morning. I'll see you at your
campsite at sunrise."

The tip of the rising sun was still partially behind the
eastern escarpment darting flashes of red across a still dark
sky when Zack turned into Pipe Spring Road. The
campground was in shadow, but flames from a fire flickered
at Eagle Feather's campsite.

Zack pulled the Jeep to a stop and climbed out,
yawning. He caught the aroma of frying bacon. "Got any
extra there?"

"Always." Eagle Feather glanced up from the fire.
"About time, White Man. I thought you said sunrise." He
made the sign for Zack to sit/stay.

Zack sat and squinted at the thin line of red sun
behind the black mesa. "That's what it's doing."

"Been doing it a while now."

Zack grunted. "Pass me some of that coffee, would
you? It's too early to argue about the precise meaning of
sunrise."

They conversed as they ate. Zack told Eagle Feather
about the car tailing Libby which forced her to return to
Kanab.

"Aren't you worried about leaving her alone?"

"I always worry about her, but I know she is capable
of handling herself. Pete Conley will be chasing down the car
that tailed her, and she's got his number in case she needs
assistance. Besides, the sheriff says he'll send a man to watch
her."

Eagle Feather nodded. "We cannot hike to the cave
on trails that start from the Hildale side, it is too risky. We
must approach from behind. It will mean a much longer day."

"You know a route?"

"We will take the Eagle Crags Trail. The trailhead is off a road near Rockville, a town northwest of Canaan Mountain. We can Jeep it part way. Sam says the trail peters out, we'll need to find our own route in places." Eagle Feather looked at Zack. "Do you have hiking boots with you? It is a long way."

Zack glanced up from his plate. "Are we talking about an overnight, then?"

Eagle Feather nodded. "Do you have a sleeping bag in that Jeep?"

Zack grinned. "Always."

Eagle Feather scrubbed out the pan. "I got some jerky and trail bars. Our water bottles and filters should be enough. With luck, we'll find some good water up there."

"Let's get going, then."

# CHAPTER THIRTY-ONE

Libby woke to bright sunshine streaming through the window and across the bare wood floor near her bed. She stretched, enjoying the blanket cocoon warmth against the chill of the house. For a confused few minutes she sorted out where she was and where everyone else was; Zack had gone to the mountain cave, Bernie, sister Emma and niece Pru were all at the house in Cameron, Eagle Feather was hopefully with Zack, although she never knew for sure.

What Libby did know was that this whole extended episode needed to end—it had gone on too long. Here it was Saturday, and she had been in Kanab since Monday and nothing was resolved. Emma and Pru had been away a whole week, she was still here, and to what end? Clearly, Pru was not yet out of danger, and it seemed to Libby the FBI was no closer to solving the case. Worst of all, she hadn't seen her little boy in days.

During her call to Emma last night, she sensed her sister's impatience and growing fear for Pru. What if Libby hadn't noticed the car following her, had not changed her destination, she'd asked. Libby had no answer. When she told her sister Zack planned to go to the cave to look for clues, Emma was no more mollified. What for, she wanted to know. The place had been thoroughly searched already, to her understanding. All it meant was Zack would be out of reach for two days.

Libby slid her legs over the side of the bed and sat up. She had to agree with Emma there seemed little new Zack might discover. The upside was Zack was actively investigating this case for the first time, still unofficial, of course, but he had a way of stirring things up. The wheels might turn a bit faster with him involved.

Her phone buzzed, she picked it up. The ID said Kane County Sheriff's Office.

"Hello?"

"This is Sheriff Rafferty calling. Is this Libby Whitestone-Tolliver?"

"Speaking."

"Ms. Tolliver, I am calling because I am unable to reach your husband. More to the point, I need to speak with your niece, Prucilla. Mr. Tolliver said he would have her call me, but she has not done so. Maybe you could help with this."

"May I ask what you need from Pru?"

"I understand she may have information regarding the kidnapping of the boy Luke Wilson, leading to his demise."

"That may be so, but we are safeguarding her. Someone has attempted to get to her."

"So I understand. I have no desire to compromise her safety, but I understand from your husband she may have information critical to the case."

Libby thought about it. "Sheriff, this business has upset her greatly. I'd rather not add to that. Let me suggest an alternative; Pru told me everything that happened, including who and what she saw. Why don't we talk?"

After a pause, he said, "Uh, that's a fine offer, Ms. Tolliver, and I'm sure it would be very helpful. However, I'm told your niece actually saw the vehicle. Often a witness retains more than they know, and I might possibly help her to remember more."

"I saw the vehicle also, Sheriff. Perhaps you could help me."

"Really. Your husband didn't mention it."

"I didn't tell him."

"Well then, I accept your offer. How soon can you come down to my office?"

After a quick breakfast, Libby climbed into her car and followed the simple directions the sheriff had given her to the jail complex and his office. She searched the rearview mirror carefully during the drive but saw no sign she was followed. Too bad, she thought, I could lead him right to jail.

She found Sheriff Rafferty's manner brusque but comforting. He was a large father figure type; the sort of person who is always in control and always has an answer.

"Mrs. Tolliver, I'd like to hear what your niece saw and what you saw in the exact order it all came to you. Can you do that for me?"

Libby nodded and began. Sheriff Rafferty never interrupted, watching her with eyes almost closed, a picture of rapt attention. When she finished her narrative, he closed his eyes completely and drummed his fingers on his desk. A moment later, they flew open. "Mrs. Tolliver..."

"Please call me Libby."

"Libby, can you describe the vehicle in more detail? When you say a large SUV, do you mean tall or long or both?"

"More long than tall."

"When you say it was mud covered, was the mud splattered or smeared?"

Libby stared at him in surprise. She thought for a moment. "You know, I'd have to say smeared, particularly the lower part of the vehicle. The windows were all dark, I guess probably tinted...I don't remember noticing splatter per se."

"So the rear license plate was mud smeared."

Libby nodded. "I'd have to say yes."

"Were you able to notice the color?"

"No, just that it was a dark color, like a maroon or black."

Sheriff Rafferty opened a file on his desk. He smiled at her. "You're doing great." He lay some cardboard cutouts on his desk in a row facing Libby. "Now, Libby, these are silhouettes of SUVs." He stood, indicating she should do the same. "I'd like you to look down at these and try to remember the vehicle you saw and see if you can spot it here."

Libby studied the lineup of shadow trucks. The shape of the vehicle she had seen popped out almost immediately. She placed her finger on it. "This one."

Sheriff Rafferty raised an eyebrow. "You sound very sure."

She nodded. "It is actually quite distinctive from most of the others."

The sheriff reached for the card, flipped it over, and read the label. "International Harvester third generation 1961-1968. Five door wagon with double doors in the rear, 119" wheelbase." He smiled. "Well done, Libby. There aren't too many of these still around. We'll check registration records." He invited her back to her seat. "Now that we've got your memory humming along, can you make a guess at the color?"

Libby closed her eyes, remembering. "It was a dark color, otherwise the contrast between its color and the mud would have caught my attention." She opened her eyes. "I really can't say, but I'm inclined toward a dark maroon."

"Excellent, Libby. We'll start our search with dark maroon." He scribbled some notes, neatly stacked his SUV profiles and put them back in his file. "Can you remember the exact words Pru used to describe the driver?"

"She said the man appeared angry."

"She got that from his facial expression?"

"Yes."

"So, glaring eyes, maybe creased facial features, that sort of thing?"

"She didn't say, specifically, just that he appeared angry."

Sheriff Rafferty smiled. "He could have looked angry, he could have looked intense, or he could have looked old. From a distance, through a windshield, it would be hard to tell." He kept his gaze on Libby.

"Well, yes, I suppose you're right."

The sheriff's smile broadened. "I'm going to put my money on all three. Considering the age of the vehicle, not kept as a collector's item—I'm guessing so because of the muddy condition—I think we can begin by assuming he's a man in his fifties at least, but likely older." He gazed at Libby with kindly eyes. "This has been most helpful, Libby. But I must warn you there will likely come a time I will need to speak directly to Pru, preferably face to face. She was one of only a few students to talk to this boy at any length, I gather. I will need to know what she learned about him—did he have any concerns, worries, thoughts of impending danger, that kind of thing."

He stood, extended a hand. "But for now, I have plenty to work with, thanks to you, Libby."

# CHAPTER THIRTY-TWO

The news that the body of journalist Dan Fogelberry had been found lodged behind the wheel of his automobile at the bottom of a steep embankment on a road fifty miles south of Salt Lake City came as no more than passing interest to most readers of the Saturday morning Deseret News in Southern Utah, but not so for Jeffrey Danes Harlow. He found the story tucked near the bottom of the first page. The article was written as news as well as a tribute; the paper was mourning one of its own.

Jeffrey was shocked and sickened. He put down his coffee, picked up the paper in both hands and studied it. The impact of the news was a physical blow; his eyes filled with tears and blurred, he had to wipe them with his sleeve to continue reading.

There was little information. The preliminary conclusion was Dan died of wounds sustained when his small sedan rolled down the slope. The victim had not been wearing his seatbelt.

That it had been a car accident was not a great surprise to Jeffrey, who knew Dan had a tendency to careen along winding roads chasing stories and meeting deadlines, but the news was crushing. He had known Dan all his life, their families gathered on holidays. Dan had been his go-to friend when he needed one. And lately, he'd needed him often.

He reread the article. One statement puzzled him, that Dan wasn't wearing his seatbelt. Jeffrey knew Dan was fastidious about clicking his belt, a fact that helped ease Jeffrey's worries when Dan took off in his car like a scalded goat. Maybe Dan had lived long enough after the crash to disengage the belt in an attempt to exit the wrecked car.

But what was his friend doing near Redmond, a pokey town on a lost byway? There was no reason Jeffrey could think of for Dan to be on that stretch of road at all, with the much faster SR 89 parallel to it.

Jeffrey wanted to know more. The responding officers had come out of Salina, a few miles to the south. Jeffrey occasionally connected with a policeman there, a man named McDougal. He decided to give him a call.

* * * * *

Sheriff Oliver Rafferty would normally be home with his family on a Saturday morning, but the need to meet with Libby brought him in to the office and with an active murder case in the works it was best to be visible, so he had transferred his coffee and morning paper ritual to his office desk. He was scanning the front page of the Deseret News when his attention was caught by a name in an article near the bottom. He lowered the paper and hollered through the doorway to the deputy at the reception desk.

"Hey, Mio, what was the name of that reporter who was in here the other day?"

His deputy's voice floated back. "Uh, wait a minute, let me check the sheet. Uh, Fogelberry; Dan Fogelberry."

"Shit. The man was just killed in an auto accident. Drove off the road, apparently. Jesus!"

"Anything you need me to do?"

"No, no. Just seems weird, is all."

Rafferty sat staring at the article. Here's a reporter who was digging deep into that affair on Canaan Mountain, obviously looking for a conspiracy of some sort. Trying to connect the murder of that kid with the murder of the girl in Kanab—just like Zack Tolliver was doing. Next thing you know, the man is dead. Rafferty hadn't given the man's ideas much credence. The guy was annoying, his questions way out there—but now?

Sheriff Rafferty was an experienced policeman and not inclined to accept such circumstances at first glance. This reporter's untimely death accomplished what all his questions had failed to do; it aroused the sheriff's curiosity.

"Hey, Mio," he bellowed. "Do you know anybody in the police department up in—wait a minute—Salina?"

"Yeah, I know a guy."

"Give him a call, will you? Just on the QT. See what you can learn about that reporter's death."

* * * * *

Professor David Philpott sat up in bed, his white hair tousled, and stared at the clock radio. He was behind schedule again. The alarm was set to a news program that began half an hour ago, but it failed to awaken him. He was due in Kanab later that morning to meet the team for the trip up the mountain to the crime scene, but at this rate he'd never make it. He leapt out of bed and into the shower, toweling off as he pulled underwear from the dresser drawer and snatched a pair of pants off a hanger in the closet. All the while the radio news program was a blur of background noise until he heard the name Dan Fogelberry.

Philpott stopped to listen. Stunned, he could scarcely believe his ears. The man was dead, killed when his car went off the road. Philpott dropped to the edge of his bed, still listening. The news item was brief; there was very little detail. The announcer went on to other news.

He remembered Fogelberry's warning as he left his office yesterday: "Be careful what you say—and watch your back." And now Fogelberry was dead. Could it be it was not an accident?

Philpott's head spun. He thought over the words he had exchanged with the reporter during their meeting. After that conversation, he had felt it was a real possibility the bones in the cave might lead to the missing Powell Expedition members and maybe victims of the Mountain Meadows Massacre as well. He knew the church would go to great lengths to avoid disgrace and embarrassment. But would they actually kill someone?

Philpott wanted to believe this was an amazing, horrible coincidence, but he was a scientist. He knew the odds; he knew Fogelberry's death coming so close on the heels of their meeting was very unlikely to be pure mischance.

But it didn't necessarily mean murder. Perhaps the man's anxiety caused him to drive with fatal carelessness. Perhaps he had spotted a car behind him, become suspicious and afraid, ultimately driving too fast for the winding road. Maybe—"

Philpott cut off this train of thought. It would do him little good. He knew he must decide: did he believe the church, his church, was capable of committing murder and that his own life could be in danger—or was he experiencing neurosis brought on by a very convincing story delivered by a talented journalist?

The easiest path was to believe the latter and do nothing.

But the bones—the bones spoke for themselves. This was hard science, not theory; and the watch—how else to explain the watch? Coincidence piled upon coincidence?

David Philpott came to the realization that he was about to make perhaps the most critical decision in his life— and it needed to be the correct one: to run or not to run; that was the question.

If he ran, where would he go, what would become of his family, how would he live? Besides, he knew the reach of the church was endless; it could get to him anywhere in the world. Yet he couldn't simply sit around and wait for the hammer to fall. There must be something he could do. First, he must calm down, get hold of himself, and try to think this through.

If his suspicions were correct, and the church had sent someone to assassinate the reporter, it must have been because of the questions he was asking, like the ones he had asked Philpott yesterday. It must have been to protect the reputation of the church, to prevent the publication of facts casting doubt and shame on the Saints. But would Fogelberry's demise really kill the story? Wouldn't Fogelberry be working with an editor, maybe a colleague? How could they be so sure eliminating the reporter would eliminate the danger?

Philpott remembered Fogelberry's intensity, his stubborn persistence. The man wasn't seeking answers; he was looking for ways to substantiate what he thought he already knew. Maybe he was a loose cannon and was pursuing the story on his own, maybe even despite being told to leave it alone. He certainly seemed to have that attitude.

Philpott felt moderately relieved. If the church, or someone who thought he represented the welfare of the church, believed Fogelberry had come to Philpott for answers, they would want to know what was said before simply deciding to assassinate an esteemed college professor. They would send someone to talk to him first, wouldn't they? If he ran now, he would be admitting his fears and confirming their suspicions.

No, he wouldn't run. His decision made, Philpott felt his nerves settle. He should go about his business as planned. If someone wanted to interrogate him, they'd have to follow him up Canaan Mountain because that was where he was going now.

# CHAPTER THIRTY-THREE

Jeffrey Danes Harlow glanced at the cell phone, saw the caller's name and answered.

"Deputy Harlow here."

"Deputy, it's Kirk McDougal from Salina. I got your message. How can I help?"

"Thanks for returning my call. I was hoping to get some particulars in regard to the death of Dan Fogelberry. He was a friend of mine."

"Well, I'm sorry to hear that. There's really not much to say, though. Seems he must have been speeding, lost control, and went over the edge at a curve near the bridge and rolled over. Without his seatbelt on, he didn't stand a chance. He was DOA at the hospital."

"You're sure about the seatbelt? He was usually quite careful about that."

"No question. It was not fastened. The investigating officers checked it, but there was no malfunction."

"That's quite surprising. Was there anything out of the ordinary? Anything anyone noticed?"

"No, nothing. It was an accident, pure and simple. He must have been traveling at high speed, maybe his attention drifted, and over he went."

"How about the skid marks? When did he brake?"

"Can you hang on, Deputy? I need to check on that." Jeffrey listened to some country music until the line came live again. "Deputy? I just checked the investigative report. There were no skid marks."

Jeffrey sat upright. "None?"

"That's not unusual. We see it a lot up here. People look away for a moment, then have no time to react." There was silence for a while. "Say, Deputy, how close a friend were you? The officer hasn't contacted the family yet. Are you close enough to the deceased you might like to do that?

We've got some personal effects here you could pick up: a jacket, his wallet and phone, a journal—things like that."

A journal. Jeffrey felt new excitement. "Yes, I'd like that. Thank you. I'll drive up today."

After the call, Jeffrey sat for a moment and thought about it. The journal might hold not only notes about Dan's investigation but possibly clues to his killer. Jeffrey was very sure it had not been an accident.

Home for the Salina City Police Department was in a small square brick building on Main Street. It was insignificant looking and without obvious signs. Jeffrey drove by it twice before he noticed a truck with 'Sheriff' written in gold letters on the side. He pulled up next to it. Inside the building, he approached a counter and asked for Deputy Kirk McDougal. A man slouched at a nearby desk reading a newspaper glanced up, put down the paper. "Deputy Harlow?"

"Yes, sir."

"I'm McDougal. I know we've spoken, but I don't believe we've met."

Jeffrey shook his head. "Never had the pleasure."

Deputy McDougal unwrapped his long legs and stood, a lean six-footer with sandy hair. He stuck out a long arm. Jeffrey shook his hand.

"Let's take a stroll outside." McDougal took a cowboy hat with a badge on its headband from a coat tree and tucked it on his head. He steered Jeffrey out the door he'd just come in. "Not much room inside as you can see. Besides, it's a beautiful day." Outside, McDougal reached into a pocket and extracted a pack of cigarettes, offered one.

Jeffrey shook his head. This was the real reason McDougal wanted to go outside, he thought, to grab a smoke. He also guessed it unlikely Deputy McDougal was a Mormon. The church didn't take to smoking, as a rule.

"I've got Mr. Fogelberry's effects in a box inside. There wasn't much. You'll see." McDougal eyed Jeffrey. "You sounded on the phone as if you questioned whether this was an accident."

Jeffrey shrugged. "I just wondered about it. Dan was fastidious about fastening his seatbelt. That it wasn't fastened seemed a little strange to me."

McDougal waited. When Jeffrey didn't continue, he said, "This reporter's death has sparked a bit of interest. There've been at least three other inquiries besides yours."

Jeffrey was startled, looked up at McDougal. "Really? What kind of inquiries? Who from?"

McDougal gave a half smile. "So there is more to this than just the seatbelt thing." He gave Jeffrey a questioning glance before going on. "My boss had a call from someone in the Kane County Sheriff's Office, kind of digging around. We couldn't tell him anything either."

"The other inquiries?"

"One from the man's paper, the Deseret News. They wanted details, wanted to print an obit." McDougal nodded his head toward the small station. "I was just reading it when you came in. Good piece."

"That it?"

"Well, no. The duty officer had a call from someone who said he was a relative of the deceased, but wouldn't leave a name. Wanted to know about personal effects." McDougal blew some smoke, peered at Jeffrey through it. "I wouldn't sign off on that without a name. Maybe you know who it was?"

Jeffrey shook his head. "No idea. I was in touch with Dan's family right away. They know I was coming up to see you. His mom and dad will be coming to claim the body once you've released it. They're waiting to hear from me about that." He shook his head again. "Don't know who that caller could be."

They walked in silence for a while, heads down.

McDougal shot a glance at Jeffrey. "You got a theory about all the interest?"

"All I know is Dan was working on the story about the murdered boy on Canaan Mountain. When Dan gets going, he's mighty stubborn."

McDougal stopped walking and gave Jeffrey a long look. "You think someone tried to stop his questioning?"

Jeffrey shrugged. "It's a possibility I can't ignore. But I'm hoping I'll learn more from his personal effects."

McDougal turned on his heel. "Let's go get them, then."

Jeffrey Danes Harlow stared down at the neat pile of items, all that was left of his good friend Dan Fogelberry: a worn wallet, car keys (why? the car was totaled), a folded, dirt-marred extra shirt, his cell phone (Jeffrey figured the release of the phone meant there would be no investigation), the Stetson felt fedora he liked to wear, a Duluth Cosmetic Bag, a sports jacket and pants rolled up in a garment bag, some loose change. Dan traveled almost continually for his job; he enjoyed it. Here was a man who kept just what he needed in his car.

Tucked away, almost hidden beneath the Fedora, was a black eight-by-five inch moleskin notebook. A carry pouch with a pen was piggybacked on the outside cover. It must be the journal.

"Would you like a bag for these items, Deputy?" the property room manager asked.

"Yes, please." Jeffrey held back from immediately reaching for the journal, despite his curiosity. He watched as the man packed the items into a black plastic bag, folded over the top, and handed the packet gently through the window to him as if he held the essence of the man himself. Perhaps he did.

McDougal eyed Jeffrey. "I hope you find what you're looking for." He slid Jeffrey a business card. "If you have more questions, call me directly." His voice dropped. He jerked his head toward the inner office. "Simpler that way."

Jeffrey drove directly home to Hildale. After greeting his family, he walked into his office, closed the door, and dug out the moleskin notebook. He leafed through it. It was, indeed, a thorough record of Dan's calls, meetings, notes from interviews, and thoughts. Jeffrey's heart beat a little faster. He was about to learn what had happened to his friend. He turned back to Thursday morning, the morning Dan went to meet Sheriff Rafferty.

Jeffrey read the scrawled yet legible writing. The interview had been conducted in Dan's particular style, always keeping his subject off balance. He noted how hard the sheriff worked to learn Dan's source and how adamantly Dan refused. He saw the cleverness in Dan's approach, how he had verified his own known facts with questions the sheriff didn't answer, but didn't deny. Then there was the bit about the murdered girl. So Dan apparently felt there was a connection between the dead girl and the murdered boy on Canaan Mountain, but the sheriff wouldn't or couldn't see it. Where did Dan get that idea? Jeffrey wondered. Maybe he took a shot, just threw it at the wall to see if it would stick.

He flipped the page. The Friday entry was much more interesting. Dan had written a note about the governor's injunction. Then the word "conspiracy" followed by a large question mark. A telephone number was written beneath it and the name Professor David Philpott, BYU. Apparently, he had gone to see this man.

There was a dashed line. Notes from an interview were beneath it, Dan's record of his chat with Professor Philpott, who was apparently involved in analyzing the remains from the cave.

As Jeffrey read on, his eyes widened. Gradually, he understood these men were discussing a huge conspiracy, an attempt at a cover up of long ago murders by the Latter-day Saints. He read that the scientists who examined the bones had roughly dated some to the mid 19th century. Together, Dan and Professor Philpott had made the leap of logic the bones might be the remains of the missing Powell Expedition members, and possibly the remains of victims from the Mountain Meadow Massacre.

Jeffrey sucked in his breath. This was big stuff, the sort of thing the church leaders would rally against. More than once, Avenging Angels had visited people for embarrassing the church in a manner similar to this. He recalled how Brigham Young had sacrificed his protégée John D. Lee in 1877 to prevent church secrets from being spilled. Nothing must be allowed to impugn the name of the church.

His eyes traveled down the page, widened again. This man Philpott had evidence, a pocket watch they might actually connect to an expedition member; it fit the correct time frame.

Jeffrey read the final entry on the page. It was scrawled and underlined: "If the church learns of this, I am a dead man."

$$* \quad * \quad * \quad * \quad *$$

Mio pushed back his desk chair with a loud scrape and peered into Sheriff Rafferty's office. The sheriff glanced up and cocked an eyebrow.

"Oliver, I just got off the phone with the cop leading the investigation into that reporter's death."

"Okay, what you got?"

"As far as he's concerned, it was an accident, pure and simple. The victim went off the road at a curve and rolled down a steep slope. He did not have his seatbelt on or he might have survived, is what they think." Mio checked his notes. "Their theory is he was making a call on his cell and not paying attention; they found his phone loose in the wreckage."

"How long were the skid marks?"

"There weren't any, he says."

Sheriff Rafferty put down his pen and stared at Mio. "None at all? So they're saying he never noticed he was about to run out of road?"

Mio shrugged. "Seems so."

Rafferty's chair squeaked as he leaned back, lost in thought.

Mio waited.

"Mio, I'd like you to take a ride up there for me. Go home, change into your civvies; take your own car. I don't want to put anybody's nose out of joint up there. Go find the accident site and give it a good looking over, see what you can learn. Come back and tell me about it. That okay with you?"

Mio grinned. He was always excited to get out of the office. "Whatever you say, boss."

Mio enjoyed the trip up to Salina. His route followed the Sevier River through Circleville, a name with a familiar ring, something to do with early Mormon settlement, he remembered. It was a massacre, resulting in the annihilation of an entire band of Paiutes. Believing these peaceful Indians responsible for a series of raids on the settlement, the Circleville Saints had rounded up all thirty of them, locked them in a cellar, and cut their throats.

Mio mused on the bloody ways of the Mormons in those early days, remembering in fairness they had their own share of suffering prior to arriving in Utah. What goes around comes around, he thought, but not always to the guilty parties.

From Circleville he followed SR 89 north to I-70 and on to Salina. The scenery was spectacular, the river valley surrounded on all sides by tall mountain peaks, the valley itself lush and green. Mio breathed in the pure, cool air.

Salina had its own dubious history. Coal and salt were the attraction for early Mormon settlers. Indian troubles in the early 1860s caused them to retreat, but only until they could raise a militia and return to build a fort. The town endured its own unusual massacre during World War II. Nazis were imprisoned here, mainly Wehrmacht and Waffen-SS. On the night of July 8, 1945, a Private Clarence Bertucci from New Orleans climbed one of the guard towers and fired a light machine gun into their tents, killing six prisoners and wounding many others. That one couldn't be blamed on the Mormons.

North of Salina Mio turned off onto SR 256, the road where Fogelberry had died. It was not what he expected, not the windy mountain road where such an accident might occur. In fact, this stretch of highway might well contend for the straightest stretch of road in the state.

Mio did not have an exact location for the accident scene but remembered the officer had said it was north of Redmond just south of the Sevier River crossing. He located it by the process of elimination; there simply was no other embankment a car could have rolled down. As reported, there were no skid marks. The road continued straight across the bridge. Mio could see no reason for the car to go off the road here, even if the man behind the wheel was unconscious. His suspicions grew.

Mio couldn't understand how the Salina Police could so easily dismiss this death as accidental. Perhaps it was simply a lack of evidence leading anywhere else. Mio remembered there had been no alcohol, drugs, illness or any other specific cause, just the cell phone loose in the car leading to the belief Fogelberry had been on the phone, not paying attention. Still, he could simply have had it lying on the seat next to him. Many professionals who rely on their cell phones do just that. At the very least, the case ought to have remained open, to Mio's mind.

His job done, he made a K turn and drove back south. He didn't have a lot to tell the sheriff, and what he did have Rafferty wasn't going to like.

# CHAPTER THIRTY-FOUR

Rockville's only possible claim to fame was the ability to survive despite the sporadic rampaging floods of the Virgin River, albeit with a population of only several hundred. This location was first imagined by Brigham Young as a place to support the growth of cotton due to its Mediterranean climate, but this venture was never successful. Instead, the Saints who were sent there barely survived the river floods and rock fall. The town's greatest prosperity came in recent years from its location near the entrance to Zion National Park.

For Zack and Eagle Feather, the town's significance came from the junction with the road that led to the trailhead. They followed it across the Grafton Bridge over the Virgin River to a dirt road up the steep cliff to a parking area on the mountain shoulder. It was a difficult road.

"If this surface was wet, we'd never make it," Zack said after a particularly steep section. "I'd hate to slide off the side here."

They found the parking area deserted. Eagle Feather studied a topo map while Zack finished loading his pack.

"We will start up the trail to Eagle Crags, but turn off before we get there," Eagle Feather said.

"Lead on. " Zack shrugged into his pack.

The way was steep in places, but the views north toward Zion National Park and the East and West Temples were extraordinary. In a half hour, Eagle Feather turned off onto a narrow, less traveled trail. After several miles, it diminished even farther. Eagle Feather stopped to examine the map again.

He took a swallow from the water bottle Zack passed him. "From here on we follow game trails," he said.

Zack took a sip and tucked the bottle back in his pack. "Lead on."

A long and difficult hike followed through chaparral, up steep slick rock, and into groves of pinyon pine. Only Eagle Feather's sense of direction kept them on track. They experienced descents of several hundred feet only to regain the altitude later. It was exhausting work.

The long morning heated into afternoon. They sheltered in the shade of a rock overhang while they lunched, stripped outerwear and stuffed it into their packs. Through the afternoon they moved with the quiet of outdoorsmen, surprising the occasional mule deer, exploding flocks of Gambel's Quail, admiring a Golden Eagle.

The afternoon stretched on to dusk. An ascending ridgeline came into view. Eagle Feather said it would lead them to Canaan Mountain. They stared at it in silence.

Zack took a mouthful of water, swished it and swallowed it, and reckoned they could be there in an hour.

It took more than an hour. The game path that had assisted them died away, the brush thickened and produced thorns. The last hundred feet before the ridge the men faced steep ledge. When they at last stood on the mountain plateau, they were sweating and gasping. The sun was gone but for a sliver. Darkness encroached, the chill of night close behind.

Eagle Feather pointed. "The hidden arroyo is a half mile or so that way. We should look for a sheltered campsite."

A short time later, they came to a clearing with a rare patch of green grass edged by gnarled-limbed stunted trees. Eagle Feather raised his eyebrows at Zack, who nodded. They unloaded packs, laid out ground sheets.

"Why don't we just go on to the cave, save ourselves a hike in the morning?" Zack asked.

Eagle Feather did not look up from his task. "There are bones in the cave and so there are spirits there, good or evil. Do you wish to sleep among them?"

Zack decided he too had no desire to invite the wrath of the unknown.

Their motions for establishing a dry, primitive camp were well practiced. The weather was perfect; the sky clear but for a hint of clouds far to the west and a slight breeze. Zack inhaled the smell of pinyon and sage. With their fire down to hot embers, the men enjoyed a hot cup of cocoa and watched far away cliffs catch the last of the downing sun in a painter's pallet of radiant colors.

"Tell me about this Paiute woman who affected you so strongly," Zack said.

"Shana Bows is a very attractive woman."

"So I understand. You will admit your reaction to her was not your usual noncommittal dismissal."

Eagle Feather stirred the fire. "I will admit to an unusual number of strong feelings lately. That was one. Perhaps I am sick."

Zack grinned to himself. "Are you saying it is a passing thing?"

"In truth, I do not know. There is something to this feeling that is new to me."

Zack moved to another topic. "You said the cave caused certain feelings in you."

Eagle Feather cocked his head toward him. "Not the cave itself, White Man. There is a spirit, an entity that dwells there and has for a very long time."

"The strange creature you saw?"

"Perhaps the spirit influenced the creature living in it, or the spirit is of that being. Either way, it is a powerful thing." Eagle Feather leaned away from the fire, the details of his features now masked by darkness.

\* \* \* \* \*

Zack had just fallen into a sound sleep despite the rough ground beneath his sleeping bag when his arm was gripped hard, and he felt the warm breath of Eagle Feather's mouth against his ear.

"Something is here."

The moon lit the small clearing like daytime and created deep shadow around the small trees guarding it. The night was crisp, the air cold as Zack breathed. He kept his head still, searched with his eyes.

Eagle feather whispered, "Listen."

There were no birdcalls, no night noises. A deep hush filled the darkness. He waited, listening hard. Another sound came to his ears, very faint. It sounded like distant drums. A moment later he became aware of a scent, a smell of decay, like moldering flesh. With it was the smell of rotted leaves and dampness as of an ancient forest floor.

The friends waited, unmoving. Zack felt a prickle on his neck, felt fear rise in him. He remained still as a deer in the presence of a predator. The feeling of helpless vulnerability remained endlessly. At some point, Zack sensed the presence was gone. He felt himself begin to calm. Neither man spoke. Eventually, Zack fell asleep.

He rose with the sun. Eagle Feather was already up, boiling water for coffee over a reinvigorated fire. Zack wanted to wait until he had coffee in hand before mentioning the elephant in the room, but it was Eagle Feather who broke the silence.

"That was the creature from the cave," he said.

"Did you see it?"

"No, but I knew."

Zack sipped his coffee, thoughts whirling in his head. Eagle Feather was warming his hands around his coffee mug, gazing off through the pinyon.

"Do you think it was this creature that killed the boy?" Zack asked.

Steam from the hot coffee rose in front of Eagle Feather's face. "Could it? Perhaps. Did it? I do not think so." Eagle Feather showed a trace of a smile and tossed the remains of his coffee into the fire. "Does that answer your question, White Man?" Without waiting for an answer, he rinsed his cup and began spreading the coals wide. "Time to move out."

# CHAPTER THIRTY-FIVE

Jeffrey Danes Harlow called Professor Philpott's BYU office at eight o'clock Saturday morning. According to the answering service, the professor was gone for the weekend. He left a number his students could call if they had questions regarding their assignments.

Jeffrey called the number. He reached another recording explaining the professor had gone to do fieldwork for the weekend and students should leave a number if they needed him, and he would call when he could get a signal. To Jeffrey, this meant only one thing; the professor had gone to work a shift on Canaan Mountain. The man apparently did not understand the danger he was in.

Jeffrey knew the team of scientists used the Squirrel Canyon Trail, the only trail up the mountain that could accommodate an ATV or four-wheel drive vehicle. He knew the team usually met at the Merry Wives Cafe for coffee and Danish before heading up to the crime scene. He glanced at his watch. They might begin to gather there around ten. Jeffrey knew from the schedule presented to the Colorado City Marshal's Department by the FBI, they would set off up the trail at eleven.

He could go over to the cafe and have a private talk with Philpott after ten, maybe. The others might be curious, though, and ask difficult questions. There might even be FBI agents with them. Jeffrey had no idea how deep this conspiracy went. He needed to be very careful.

He decided on another plan. He called the student number Philpott had left. He listened to the tape, wrote down the number and dialed it, leaving a message when prompted.

"Professor Philpott, please listen carefully. I am a close friend of Dan Fogelberry. I know about your conspiracy theory regarding the bones, and I believe you are correct. I believe your life is in danger. If I am right, the danger could come from somewhere very far up in the church hierarchy.

Do not go anywhere alone; stay with the other scientists. Do not mention your theory to anyone else. I will identify myself to you when the moment is right. I repeat—be wary. You are in great danger."

After concluding the call, Jeffrey was left with a feeling of dissatisfaction. He hadn't really helped the man, just alarmed him. There must be something more he could do. He felt his anger deepen. Whoever was behind all this had eliminated his friend, as one would swat a fly.

Was the church involved? His church? Was he now distrustful of his very own foundation? Jeffrey couldn't believe it. Every organization has a few wayward members who are misguided in the way they pursue the goals of that group. It was those people, whoever they were, who were Jeffrey's enemy. He must sort them out from the whole and make them pay for their crimes.

Jeffrey was roused from his reverie by the call to the Saturday noon meal. He extricated himself from his desk chair with reluctance. Once Jeffrey sunk his teeth into an issue he became the proverbial dog with a bone. He knew this was a fault and tried to overcome it.

The cheery dining room was a pleasant change and his lovely wives and beautiful children were a tonic for his mood. When everyone was seated, he glanced around the table. His mood plummeted again. Jedediah's chair was still vacant. It was now Saturday and the old man had been away since last Monday, nearly an entire week. Jeffrey could feel Cynthia's eyes on him. He knew he would have to make it his priority to find her grandfather.

\* \* \* \* \*

Professor Philpott and three other colleagues, specialists in geology, anthropology, osteology and archaeology, left the Merry Wives Cafe at ten minutes before eleven and piled into a university SUV for the drive to the trailhead. When they

186

arrived there, they found the parking lot a scene of unusual activity. The driver parked the SUV. A man who identified himself as an FBI agent rapped on his window.

When it opened, he said, "It seems we are not working today, gentlemen. It seems the governor of the great state of Utah has convinced a judge to prohibit anyone from entering the wilderness area until the court injunction is settled. I guess you gentlemen can go home."

There was immediate unhappiness in the vehicle. These were men of prestige who had given valuable time to assist the FBI with this case, time now apparently wasted. But it was clear they were not going up to the cave today. Two Colorado City Marshal's Department SUVs blocked the trail entrance and two sheriff's deputies stood in front of them with their arms folded.

"What are our chances of going up tomorrow?" the driver asked.

The FBI agent shrugged. "Probably not very good. These things move slowly." The agent looked discouraged.

"What about the bones and materials we already have back at the lab?" Philpott asked from the back seat.

The agent peered in the window at him. "My suggestion to you is to glean everything you can from those items ASAP. Next thing, the judge will demand they be returned to the cave."

After a bit more conversation, the driver backed the SUV and drove back the way they came. Inside the vehicle, a wide-ranging discussion came down to a decision to return to the university immediately and do exactly what the FBI agent had recommended.

* * * * *

It was Saturday, but despite that, Agent in Charge Janice Hooper was at her desk at 3 p.m. when a call came through from the University Anthropology Department. It was a member of the bone study team.

Before the man could speak, Agent Hooper reassured him. "Yes, I already know your team was denied permission to access the cave. We have already begun procedures to try to reverse that order. Meanwhile, try to learn everything you can from the bones you already have."

"But that's just it," the man said. "We've only now arrived back at the lab, and they're gone."

Janice Hooper half rose out of her chair. "What do you mean, gone? What's gone?"

"The bones we were studying, our notes, everything. Someone broke in while we were gone. Left a note saying we had no right to the remains of their ancestors."

"Christ! The Paiutes? Did you call the police?"

"No. We alerted university security."

"Okay, that's fine. I'll have an agent there in fifteen minutes."

As soon as the call ended, Janice picked up the phone again. She knew the security people at the university would call the cops. She needed to get an agent there to make sure the local police understood the FBI had jurisdiction in this matter.

* * * * *

It was dusk when Mio stepped through the door into the sheriff's office ready to give his report, but before he could utter a word Sheriff Rafferty barked a question: "Do you know anyone around here owns an International Harvester Travelall, mid 1960s model?"

"Uh, no. I don't recall any."

"Well, we're looking for one. Seems that might be the model truck of the guy who kidnapped the Wilson boy. Witness says it was smeared with mud, so no license number and no color ID, except dark, so you can eliminate white or lighter color vehicles. Put out a County Wide APB, would you?"

"Sure thing." Mio hesitated. "Don't you want to hear my report?"

"Let me guess. I'm gonna say that stretch of road is as straight as a hoe handle, and this reporter fellow managed to find the only embankment on the whole road to drive off."

Mio stared at Rafferty. "If you already knew that, why'd you send me all the way up there?"

"I know most roads in these parts, but I needed you to confirm my memory and make your own judgment. What else did you get?"

Mio plopped down in the chair opposite Rafferty's desk. "Well, the only embankment is right at the river crossing, and that's where his vehicle went over. Like they said, no skid marks at all. But the funny thing is, the road goes bullet straight across the bridge. He literally had to turn the steering wheel to go off where he did."

"Did it take him into the water?"

Mio shook his head. "No, not that there was much water in the creek anyway. Judging from the crushed underbrush, the vehicle rolled one time. That tells me two things; the car wasn't going very fast, and it shouldn't have been enough to kill him, even without a seatbelt."

Sheriff Rafferty stared at Mio. "Careful what you say here because this is an official report, and you can't take it back. Are you saying you don't think that reporter's death was an accident?"

Mio squirmed in his chair. "I will say this; if the guy died as a consequence of that accident, he's pretty damn unlucky."

Sheriff Rafferty's lips twitched in a brief smile. "Okay, that'll do. Now after you put out that APB, I want you to get hold of the coroner up there and have them send us a plot of Fogelberry's injuries. If he's gone home already, leave a message telling him what you want and tell him it's urgent."

\* \* \* \* \*

When the landline phone at Emma's house rang after dinner on Saturday evening it startled Libby at first, but she knew it must be Zack calling from the mountain, or her sister Emma or niece Pru. Libby had just settled in a comfy armchair with a cup of cocoa and a copy of Real Simple magazine but set them aside and reached for the phone.

"Hi. Libby here."

There was no response, but the line was live.

"Hello, can you hear me?" Maybe Zack's signal was weak. No; now she heard breathing. "Who is this?" When there was still no response, Libby jabbed the phone back on its cradle and shuddered. It was not Zack with a weak signal because she could hear breathing on the line. It was not Emma or Pru; they would have responded. It wasn't a friend of Emma's family or a salesperson or any other legitimate call. It was the stalker; there was no doubt in her mind. He had called to frighten her—or maybe see if Pru would answer the phone.

She immediately rang Zack's number. She received a message the number she was calling was unavailable. She guessed he was out of range. She tried Eagle Feather with the same result. Finally, she called Sheriff Rafferty.

A deputy answered. "Kane County Sheriff's Department. How can I help you?"

"I need to speak with the sheriff personally on an urgent matter."

The deputy took her name and asked her to hold. Classical music filled her ear. Very classy, she thought, despite her fear. A full two minutes later, the music cut off and the deputy was back on the line.

"The sheriff says please call him on his personal number." He read off the number for her.

190

When Libby dialed that number, the sheriff answered after the first ring. "Libby? What's going on?"

Libby explained.

"Okay, okay, Libby. You don't need to worry. I told your husband I'd keep an eye on you. I have a man in the neighborhood right now. I'll call him and make sure he is close. Libby, have you got a pen? Take down this number." The sheriff dictated a phone number to Libby. "If there are any more incidents of any kind, call that number and identify yourself. It is my man's direct number. He'll know what to do."

There was a pause while Libby wrote, and the sheriff waited.

"Thank you, Sheriff."

"Libby, you'll be just fine. I'm sure you have your doors and windows locked. Don't let anyone in. If my man needs to approach you, he'll give his name. It is Andy. Okay?"

Libby felt quite reassured after the call had ended. Despite the creepy feeling just knowing this weird and possibly murderous man was somewhere out there, she felt confident in the measures the sheriff had put in place. She felt growing respect for the man. She had begun to think of him as one might a favorite uncle, as silly as that seemed.

Libby reopened Real Simple magazine and resumed her reading.

# CHAPTER THIRTY-SIX

Eagle Feather led the way across the flat mountain summit.
There was no trail to follow, but the thick brush of the prior
day had vanished and it was a simple matter to walk among
scattered pinyon, around hoodoos and avoid the gullies. The
area was a tortured landscape of geological slashes and
eruptions as if some ancient backhoe had dug here and
dumped there, and left it to harden over the eons. There were
occasional thick groves of trees, none very large, enough to
offer concealment, though, and Zack began to see how an
entire arroyo might lay hidden for a century.

The pale sky of morning had tinted toward pink when
Eagle Feather held up a hand. "We have company," he said.
"A smoker."

Zack opened his nostrils wide and tried the air but
smelled only the sweet pine aroma. He was accustomed to his
friend's uncanny senses and was not surprised. "Which way is
the smoke?"

"Seems strongest this way." Eagle Feather pointed.
"It's the direction of the arroyo."

"You think the Beastie smokes?"

"It might improve his breath."

The men moved silently. Eagle Feather brought them
unerringly to the slope at the north end of the hidden arroyo.
They stopped and listened.

After a moment, Eagle Feather nodded and they
moved on down the slope taking care to use every bit of
cover as they advanced. When they came to a small barrier of
trees, Eagle Feather motioned for Zack to wait and crept
forward. Zack settled back on his haunches. It seemed to take
a long time for Eagle Feather to reappear. Then he was there,
waving Zack in.

It was Zack's first look at the altar slab and cliff cave
he'd heard so much about. He understood now why the place
effected people as it had; he sensed an atmosphere of evil

about it. His nose caught a hint of the same musty decay scent of the prior night. There was a chill to this isolated meadow despite the unfiltered sunlight streaming in. The huge rock slab in the center of the meadow reminded him of ancient altar stones for human sacrifice he'd seen in movies, flat and wide, waist high, with the red brown color of old blood stains around the bowl-shaped hollow in the middle.

Police tape festooned nearby tree branches, some of it dislodged and trampled underfoot. Beyond the slab loomed the cave. A short slope led to a mouth that yawned open high and wide like the mouth of a huge predator. The sun's angle from above the cliff cast the entire approach to the cave in shadow.

Zack and Eagle Feather stood side by side, taking it in.

"You went in there," Zack said. He felt a strange reluctance to approach.

Eagle Feather nodded. "I didn't want to, but I did." He added, "This is not a good place."

Zack walked to the slab and moved slowly along the side, studying it. "It does appear to have fallen naturally from the cliff face, but it has been shaped by human hands over time." He paused, turned to Eagle Feather. "You know Danger Cave over in the Bonneville Flats region? They found artifacts dating back to eleven thousand years ago. This cave could have a similar heritage." He swept his eye over the slab's flat surface. "There is no evidence the Archaic hunter nomads who lived in Danger Cave and other similar sites ever made sacrifices, yet this stone seems almost to have been shaped for precisely that, with the hole in the middle to hold the victim's heart." Zack scanned the surface. "I think I see a slight depression, as if there was a channel for blood to flow off to the side. The Aztec sacrificial stones had blood channels."

"If that is what this is, the people who carved it lived a long time ago. It is almost completely eroded away."

Zack nodded. "Yes. Our modern killer simply took advantage of it." He looked toward the cave. "I see some petroglyphs."

"I found several places with petroglyphs. There are probably more. I saw pictographs inside the cave just where the western sun hits the wall.

Zack rubbed his chin. "The pictographs support the idea this cave is a sacred place for the Ancients. A popular theory suggests pictographs were done for shamans and priests on sacred cave walls while the sturdier petroglyph carvings were for communication with the common levels of society. Those tended to be on exterior surfaces."

Eagle Feather glanced at Zack. "You have unusual knowledge of these things."

Zack grinned. "Zack of all trades, master of none."

Eagle Feather rolled his eyes. "Well, Mr. Genius, here is my theory; pictographs were painted on inside walls because they would wash away on outside walls."

Zack laughed. "I can't refute that."

They stood together and studied the cave.

Eagle Feather hitched his shoulders. "Are you ready, White Man?"

Zack checked the load of his handgun, holstered it, and took a flashlight from his pack. "Okay, let's go."

Even with the flashlight it took a few moments for Zack's eyes to adjust enough to see what the beam was illuminating, but his nose sent him messages of musty old earth and decay. There was a feeling of fine gravel over a hard surface underfoot.

Zack played the beam along the interior wall nearest him, halting it on a pictograph. The image resembled an Egyptian mummy with round head and wide shoulders tapering to a narrow foot, a coffin shape. He moved the beam and found another pictograph, this one with a shorter, thicker body and similarly broad shoulders, but a head shaped as an animal with protruding ears. Similar anthropomorphic images, Zack knew, were attributed to Archaic cultures. To some researchers, such figures represented a transformation between human and animal.

What ancient culture had made these? Zack knew the location of the cave placed it in a geographic area ascribed by anthropologists to the Virgin Anasazi people, yet it was also close to the Fremont culture, just to the north. If this pictograph was Archaic in origin, it meant it was even older than Fremont or Anasazi. Whatever the case, it was clear this cave dated back thousands of years.

As he studied the images, he became aware of a palpable feeling of dread sagging over him. It seemed to leach into him from the very air of the cave. It matched Eagle Feather's description of the wave of emotions intensified by something within the cave.

He swept the beam along the floor. White glimmers told him where the scattered bones lay. His light came to rest on a heap of them, like a pile of bleached branches. The stack was not more than a foot high but it was wide and dense, all human skeletal parts. The heavier bones, like skulls, were near the bottom. Ribs, flattened but held together with leather-like sinew, contained smaller bones within them like grotesque distorted baskets. Nearby were several skulls and near them were two modern stools, evidence the scientists had been working here. He saw no tools or other sign of their presence beyond a clean space on the floor. Zack wondered if the scientists had been as effected by the moodiness of the atmosphere as he was.

Eagle Feather had disappeared toward the rear of the cave. Zack could see his light flicker here and there. Zack circled the bone pile, studied the bones. Although he had no intention of revealing he had been here, he wanted to learn as much as possible. None of the bones looked like those of animals, which surprised him. He became more and more convinced an Aztec style human sacrifice had happened here. He examined a femur protruding from the bottom of the pile.

His beam showed tiny slash-like shadows. A closer look revealed they were in fact little nicks in the bone made by a sharp tool as if someone had removed the flesh.

Zack thought again about the Aztecs, remembering how the bodies of victims would sometimes be skinned and the flesh eaten in a ritual ceremony. He was more and more convinced he was in a burial cave for victims of ritual sacrifice—but by whom?

He worked his way over to the opposite wall. There he found more pictographs, and a large painted handprint. He followed the wall toward the rear of the cave, flashing his beam side to side. There were no bones back here at all. He noticed the cave floor here was covered with a thick layer of dust. Zack felt as if the footprints he was leaving were the first in eons.

As Zack progressed farther back into the cave, he felt an uncontrolled panic begin to grow in him, a tingling of his flesh, an anxiety or apprehension he couldn't understand. He was not claustrophobic, as a rule, but the decreasing ceiling height put him in mind of a terrifying experience he'd had in a cave not so long ago. The decayed flesh smell came in waves now. A sudden touch on his arm startled him, almost caused him to panic.

"Whoa, White Man, go easy." It was Eagle Feather."

"See this?" The Navajo's flashlight beam shone at their feet.

Zack saw the area had been dug recently, the soil appeared softer, clumps of dirt were scattered about. "Yeah, I see it."

Eagle Feather came close to Zack and spoke quietly. "The victim is speared on the slab outside, eventually ends up here." He flashed his beam toward the bone pile. "Where is the middle step?"

"What do you mean?"

"Those bones are clean and dry, all the flesh removed."

"Why would they bother?" Zack asked. "I was thinking ritual cannibalism. Eating your enemy gives you his strength and virtues, that sort of thing."

"Yes."

"So the Ancients sat around a fire outside and munched until the bones were clean."

"Not such a nice picture, but, yes, something like that."

"Nothing left but the bones we see over there."

Zack could not see his friend's face. "Where are you going with this?"

Eagle Feather shown his flashlight beam at his feet, scuffed the earth. "What is down here, then? The ground is soft, it has been disturbed. Not centuries ago, recently. It smells of decayed flesh here."

Zack's mind leapt forward. "You think the murder of the boy wasn't the only killing up here, that we are in fact dealing with a serial killer—and the evidence might be here beneath our feet?"

"That is what I am saying, White Man."

"Damn." Zack thought about it. "We can't let anyone know we were here. There would be questions, miles of red tape, legal ramifications. We'd be caught up by it for years, maybe even be accused ourselves."

"What, then?"

"We leave this place undisturbed. Then we think of a way to get investigators to come back up here and dig it all up."

# CHAPTER THIRTY-SEVEN

Two FBI marksmen attached saddles to their tripods on the sloping hill west of the ranch. They triangulated their positions to a fifty-five-degree shooting angle with a clean line of fire to the house. Two FBI vehicles were parked out of sight on the roadway; the agents were now encircling the ranch on three sides, waiting for their signal.

Agent Janice Hooper pulled up to the ranch gate. She dialed a number on her phone and listened to it ring. No one picked up, and there was no message machine. She tried again with the same result. Sighing, she stepped out of the car, took a megaphone from the passenger seat and pressed the button.

"Mr. Randy Musser, this is Agent in Charge Janice Hooper with the FBI. I need to speak with you. Please come open this gate."

There was a long silence. Then a shot rang out. A bullet plunked into the wooden gatepost nearest Agent Cooper. She did not move.

"Mr. Musser, you are completely surrounded. We have no wish to harm you. Please—"

Another shot rang out. The bullet kicked up dust at her feet. With deliberate slowness, she walked behind her vehicle. She lifted the megaphone again.

"Mr. Musser, please answer your phone when it rings. We need to talk."

Agent Hooper tried the number again. After the third ring, the car's windshield exploded. She took a small walkie-talkie from her pocket and pressed the button.

"I think this will be an attempt at suicide by cop. Try to take him alive, but your priority is to keep yourselves safe. Clear?"

The radio came alive with affirming voices.

"Okay, move in."

Tension gripped the air; the silence of anticipation seemed timeless. There were no more rifle shots from the house. Agent Hooper waited for the first sign of engagement.

It came first from the rear of the house, the distant sound of a rifle. Musser had tried to escape out the back. He would now know he was trapped. Hooper tried his number again, and again he did not answer, but there was no responding rifle shot.

Now she detected movement near the north corral. The first of her men were closing in. She could not see the men to the south but knew they would be close as well. The dance would begin shortly.

She waved an arm and men rose from the brush along the fence line on either side of her and ran forward with wire cutters. Several were through before the rifle sounded from the house. A man dropped.

She spoke in her radio. "Agent, are you hurt?"

"I'm fine. The bullet missed."

Meanwhile, a volley of gunfire exploded toward the house. Agent Hooper raised binoculars to her eyes. She could see tiny dust clouds where bullets struck the siding. Taking advantage of the volley, the agents closed in on all sides. Next came the telltale burst of smoke out a broken window, a teargas grenade exploding in the house.

Hooper rushed to the fence, snipped the barbed wire and moved the heavy post. She ran back to the car, swiped glass from her seat, and drove through the gate and up the drive. She arrived at the house as the first of the men moved through the front door.

She waited there holding her breath. Another rifle shot sounded followed by a single shot from a pistol. She knew what that meant. She ran to the house. Randy Musser must not die before he could tell her what she needed to know.

Hooper put on her mask and entered the house. The short foyer brought her to an open living and kitchen area.

Glass crackled under her feet. The large sliding window over the kitchen sink was punched out in the center as if a giant rock had come through it. Randy lay on the floor near the kitchen counter.

Agents were removing their masks. Hooper did the same. Her eyebrows questioned the agent who knelt near Randy.

"He's alive, but barely."

She knelt and stared into his face. Musser's eyelids were half closed. Hooper glanced at the wound. In his attempt at suicide he'd aimed high, the bullet had passed through the upper skull and entered a section of the parietal lobe before exiting. The wound might not necessarily be life ending, but Hooper saw there was a large hole in his chest as well. A rifleman's sights had found him. This was the fatal wound.

Agent Hooper took his head in her hands. "Randy, you are a brave man. You fought well for your cause. Did you kill the boy at the cave?"

Musser attempted to respond. Despite bubbling blood at his mouth, Hooper read a negative.

"I didn't think so," she said. "Why were you in the cave?"

Randy struggled to speak. "Bones...the church..." At the last utterance, he died.

Hooper laid his head gently on the floor. "Call the team to tag him and bag him." She looked up at the team standing around her. "Anybody hurt?"

There was a chorus of negatives.

"Great. Good job, gentlemen. Go clean up and relax. I'll be in touch." She eyed two men. "Doaks and Cranford, please stay a moment."

Hooper stood and brushed off her pants. "You two held the sniper positions. Which of you fired the kill shot?"

"I did, Special Agent," Cranford said. He gazed back at her with earnest blue eyes.

"Situation?"

"An agent was in the room. I saw the perp raise a pistol. I made a judgment call."

"What was your viewpoint?"

Cranford pointed at the broken kitchen window. "I had a clear line through the window."

Hooper studied him and then nodded. "Thank you. Dismissed."

The two agents turned and walked toward the door.

"Oh, one more thing," Hooper said. "Cranford, what is your religion?"

Cranford turned, stared at her. "I am a Mormon."

"Doaks?"

"I am also a Mormon."

"LDS?"

"Yes."

The two men turned and walked out the door. Hooper was deep in thought as she walked out of the house into the front yard, more of a bare patch of dirt cleared of weed growth. She retrieved her cell from her pocket and called her office.

"Hello, this is Agent Hooper. The business with Musser is finished, no agents hurt; Musser is dead. I'll meet with Public Relations in an hour. We're starting a search of the property now. What have we learned about the break-in at the university lab?" She listened. "Just the bones?" She waited, responded, "Okay, thanks."

\* \* \* \* \*

They were almost to the cave entrance. Zack reached for Eagle Feather's shoulder. "Hold on. Hear that?"

Both men held still.

"The Keystone Cops are back," Eagle Feather said. He touched Zack's arm and led the way along the wall's shadow out the entrance, down the debris slope and along the cliff face in a doubled-over trot. In the cover of the closest trees they knelt, peered back, and waited. The deputies' voices came to them distinctly off the face of the cliff.

"LeRoy, you think you could make any more noise than that?"

"I don't get why we're creeping up on an empty cave anyway."

"Wasn't empty last time we came up here, remember?"

"Yeah, but that Indian took off like a scalded dog. He won't be back."

"We don't know that. You heard father; we got to be sure no one is up here."

"Okay, we're close now. Be quiet."

Zack heard the snapping of branches and movement of brush. Then it stopped.

"I don't see nothin'."

"He might be in the cave."

"You go see."

"Hell, no, you go see."

"Okay, okay, we'll go together. You go over on that side of the slab and I'll go on this side. Ready? Go."

More crackling and snapping and the two men emerged from the trees and advanced crouching low, their rifles at the ready. They stalked along either side of the slab. At the far end, they cautiously inched up the slope toward the cave.

Eagle Feather nudged Zack and whispered, "We can go now."

Zack had begun to rise from his crouch when a tremendous roar stunned him. He looked up. A giant bear stood at the mouth of the cave, rearing up on hind legs as it glared down at the two deputies. Froth foamed at its lips, gigantic white fangs showed as it opened its huge mouth. Its head rolled side to side as if maddened by the sight of the two men below. It roared a second time, lifting gigantic paws with claws like kitchen knives above its head

At the second roar, the two deputies, who had been frozen in place, dropped their rifles and turned and ran in terror.

Zack wasn't in much better shape. The creature was a behemoth, as fierce as a Grizzly, as large as an Alaskan brown bear. Its roar, amplified by the cliff face, was heart stopping. Its eyes glowed red as embers.

Zack didn't move, he scarcely breathed. The background noise of snapping and crackling branches as the two deputies ran hell-bent through the brush came to him while the echoes of the creature's roars died away. Rather than stare at the animal and attract its attention, he instinctively turned away, eying it peripherally. The beast slowly lowered to all fours. It stood there for several minutes, turning its head, sniffing the air. A slight breeze in his face told Zack he was downwind of the bear, and he hoped that fortunate circumstance would be sufficient to avoid being discovered.

He felt Eagle Feather behind him. They waited.

The huge bear shuffled around to reenter the cave. Zack could not comprehend what he saw next. As it moved, the mammoth creature seemed to dissolve like a soap bubble disintegrates in the air, and in its place was an old man, naked but for a breechcloth, with wrinkled, mahogany skin and long hair pulled back and secured behind his head. The man was visible for only a moment before he blended into the darkness of the cave interior.

# CHAPTER THIRTY-EIGHT

Sheriff Rafferty grabbed his radio from the pocket of his bulky canvas jacket on the back of his chair and put out a call for Chief Deputy William Brown.

"Yeah, boss."

"Will, where you at?"

"I'm just leaving for services."

"First Ward?"

"Yes, sir."

"Will, I need to know where we stand with the investigation of that murdered girl. Can you drop by after services?"

"Yes, sir. I'll be there about ten-thirty."

Rafferty contemplated the fact his deputies seemed to find time for church while their boss sat at his desk on Sunday morning. Well, that's why he made the big bucks, he supposed.

Will was true to his word. Rafferty heard the knock at his open office door. Without looking up, he gestured his chief deputy toward a chair until he'd finished his thought and scribbled a final sentence.

"How was the service?"

Brown smiled. "Good, sir." He was a tall man, appeared so even sitting down. His blue eyes contrasted with his sun-browned face.

"The girl, Elizabeth?"

Brown took out his notebook. "Elizabeth, known as Beth. Fourteen years old, goes to the same high school as the murdered boy, walks to school and home the same way. Striking resemblance to the possible witness to the boy's abduction—we think the murderer may have killed the wrong girl. We've been unable to interview the actual witness." Brown looked questioningly at Rafferty.

The sheriff waved an arm. "I know, I know, go on."

"Cause of death was a blow to the back of the head, the forensics people think it may have been a tire iron. She was not killed at the scene but at some undetermined site and transported to the scene." Brown looked up from his notes. "Here's an interesting part. Forensics found traces of chloroform around nose and mouth, suggesting she was immobilized first and struck later. There are ligature marks on her wrists suggesting she may have been bound. Our scenario is she was abducted from the street using chloroform, thrown in a vehicle, and tied up. She was then driven to an unknown location, struck with the tire iron, then transported to the roadside and left where she was found."

Brown hesitated.

"Go on."

"Well, this part is shaky. The examiner found no signs of bruising on her body—absolutely none. We think that could mean she was removed from the vehicle only one time, and that was post mortem." He eyed Rafferty. "Meaning, she was struck with the tire iron while in the vehicle."

Rafferty's mind whirred. "Meaning we find the vehicle, we find the murder site and maybe blood and tissue evidence."

"Exactly."

Sheriff Rafferty studied his chief deputy. "You made a leap back there proposing the perp killed the wrong girl. Can you back that up with evidence?"

"No, sir. But the coincidence is striking. Students and teachers at the high school commented on the resemblance even before we asked the question. And, of course, the fact the two girls used the same route to school is very suggestive."

"Good, good. Now here's what I want. I want you to find solid evidence of the link between the two murders. This girl witness may be it. If this means you have to do a little digging around on the FBI turf, so be it. Just be a little sneaky. I don't want a blowup with the feds."

Brown gave a quick grin. "Got it, boss. But the witness, how do I—"

"Don't worry about her. I'm gonna take that on. I'll keep you informed." The sheriff gave Brown a smug look. "Bye the bye, you are searching for a dark color '62 to '68 International Harvester Travelall, probably dust covered. It's likely garaged somewhere between here and Hurricane. Good luck."

\* \* \* \* \*

When David Philpott returned from Canaan Mountain Saturday afternoon, he found a break-in had occurred at the university lab. The human bones were gone from their storage space, the lab notes had disappeared, and expensive measuring instruments used to examine the bones had been damaged. He felt the same panic he experienced when he learned of the reporter Fogelberry's death. The local police had come, taken photos and notes, and gone away. Philpott was about to tell them of his concerns for his life when a thought crossed his mind. Most of the men on the Salt Lake City police force were Mormons. How many of them might be part of this conspiracy dedicated to keeping the church's dark secret?

Should he warn his colleagues on the bone examination project that they could be in danger? He realized there was a fundamental difference between him and them; he was the only one who had spoken with the dead reporter.

Once he'd made his decision not to run from possible retribution from the church, and instead go forward with the excursion up Canaan Mountain that weekend, he knew he was in a delicate situation. Consequently, when on Sunday afternoon his wife suggested she take the children for an overnight to see her mother, he encouraged the idea.

The house was dark and silent Sunday evening. Philpott puttered about the kitchen, made a grilled cheese sandwich on the Foreman grill, grabbed a soda from the fridge and went to his study in the rear of the house. It was his usual pattern to grade papers or read new books at this time, but tonight he watched a news program on TV. There was coverage of the governor's injunction regarding the Preserve, most of it supportive. None of it surprised him.

Feeling lonely and distressed, Philpott had gone to bed early with some light fiction in hopes he might take his mind off the current circumstances if only for a minute or two. It was then the neighbor's dog set up a clamor.

Most nights he would have ignored the dog's noise, assuming a skunk or raccoon had passed by. Tonight, his nerves were on edge and he thought he detected a particular urgency in the dog's barking. He switched off the light and listened. He heard footsteps on pavement. He glanced at his bedside clock. It was 9:30 p.m. He lived on a cul-de-sac. Anyone who came here did so intentionally. His neighbors on either side habitually traveled to mountain hideaways on weekends, but, of course, this weekend could be an exception. Philpott knew he was being neurotic. It was Saturday night, after all, and relatively early. Anybody in the neighborhood could be wandering around. Still, something kept him from turning the light back on.

It was then he heard a noise against the side of the house, metal on metal. Next came the distinct sound of a window being raised. He waited for the alarm to sound. He had set it before going to bed tonight and double-checked it. It did not sound. To him, this meant someone was entering his house who knew how to disarm an alarm system. It meant the person was a professional. It meant his life was in real danger.

Philpott needed an idea, and he needed it now. It came to him. He quickly made up his bed and fluffed the pillow, then found the pad and pen he kept at his bedside, took the penlight from the lamp table, and knelt beside his bed. He wrote a note to his wife on the pad, explaining to her he'd been invited to a friend's home in the country for the night and would be back late Sunday, in case she returned before he did. He put the pad with the note and the pen back on the table and crept into the hallway to the linen closet. It was larger than most, with shelves on both sides and a laundry bin in the middle. He slipped in, pulled the door shut as soundlessly as he could, hid behind the laundry bin, and turned off the penlight. He waited.

Minutes passed. The house was silent as a tomb. Waiting was difficult. When a creak sounded on the stair, it was almost a relief. Despite that, and his precaution, Philpott was terrified. He all but stopped breathing as he sensed rather than heard the intruder pass the linen closet door. Silence returned, and his heart pounding the waiting resumed.

He heard the sound of doors opening and closing in the bedroom; hurried steps passed his closet and sounded off down the hall toward the other bedrooms. As the intruder's search continued, the noise of it grew louder as the searcher apparently realized the bird had flown. Now he heard a voice, speaking as if on a phone. He could not make out the words. The voice grew louder as it neared his hiding place, opening and slamming the doors along the way. Then the linen closet door opened abruptly and the light came on. The man's words came clear now as he poked among the shelves. "Look, I don't fuckin' know. I'm tellin' you this place is empty. There's nobody here..."

Philpott felt a sudden impact from the laundry bin against his head and shoulder where he snuggled behind it; the intruder had kicked it in frustration. He held back a startled cry. The man's voice trailed off, the stairs creaked, doors opened and slammed downstairs; the killer had no more reason for stealth. When the front door slammed, bringing an end to his ordeal, Philpott collapsed on the floor, a quivering wreck. He remained there, unable to move or even think until he succumbed to exhaustion and sleep overcame him.

He awoke with the dawn, when the morning sun drew a fiery aura around the closet door. As the events of the previous night returned to him, he pulled himself together. His ruse had worked, but it was only temporary. He padded back to his bedroom, and in the morning's early light saw the room was torn apart, bureau drawers pulled open, clothing thrown about. He glanced at the notepad. It was still there, but his note was gone. Philpott sat on the edge of his bed, the only thing left undisturbed, and reached for the home phone. He started to dial 911 when a thought came to him and he stopped, put the receiver down. Who could he safely call? How could he know who might be involved in this conspiracy? Maybe the intruder bugged his phone?

Philpott trembled as the entirety of his dilemma formed in his mind. Where could he turn? He felt in his pajama pocket for his cell phone; he'd had the presence of mind to grab it before he went to hide. Had he not, the intruder might have seen it and known Philpott was somewhere in the house. He used it now to make his call.

He called his wife and told her to extend her stay and not return to the house under any circumstances until she heard from him. She'd been awakened by his call, was confused, protested, but ultimately believed him and promised to do as he asked. Next, he called the law enforcement agents least likely to be involved in the conspiracy: the FBI. It was time to show them the old watch.

# CHAPTER THIRTY-NINE

Zack and Eagle Feather didn't talk much on their hike back to the Jeep. Zack was trying to understand what he had just seen. He watched Eagle Feather's back as they walked. The Navajo appeared complacent, at least from this perspective. Eagle Feather had an ability to accept things he did not understand. Zack still did not.

He was willing to open his mind to new possibilities, thanks to the man in front of him, his mentor in things spiritual. Had his Navajo friend not been there to guide him during his first year as an FBI Agent on the great Reservation, he likely would have demanded a transfer, as had all those who preceded him. The hot sun, great distances, language barrier and cultural differences were difficult enough, but when called upon to respond to reports of skin-walkers and witches, most law enforcement agents of European descent called it quits. Such spirituality was probably much like climate change, he thought. There were those ready to accept it as reality and deal with it while others couldn't accept it and chose to ignore it, pretending it didn't exist. Zack saw himself among the former, in part from Eagle Feather's teaching. Once the sty of automatic denial was removed from his eye, Zack entered a new world of possibilities other FBI agents never could.

Now this creature, this huge bear that turned into a human, an ancient shaman by the looks of him, was a bit more difficult to wrap his mind around. Yet he could not deny the evidence of his own eyes.

They stopped for a water break at their previous night's campground. As they removed packs and dug out their water bottles, Zack shared his thoughts.

"That wasn't a Nimerigar."

Eagle Feather shook his head.

"Was that old Indian a shaman, do you think?"

Eagle Feather glanced out over the chaparral to the vista beyond. "An ancient shaman had great power. They were keepers of secrets, and are today, even though many secrets became lost when the white man and his religion changed the way our young people think. It is said the most powerful of shamans had the power to shape shift."

"As did witches."

"That is so."

"Do you think the feeling you felt in the cave come from the old shaman?"

"There is something evil living in that cave. That is what I know."

"Is the shaman we saw the evil spirit?"

Eagle Feather shrugged. "I do not know."

"Could he be responsible for all those human bones?"

"I do not know. I think the cave has a long history. Many other beings must have been there over time."

"I don't think that boy's murder was committed by an ancient witch."

Eagle Feather glanced at Zack. "Maybe not, but witches often use the help of other humans to fully utilize their powers."

"You think the murderer fell under the influence of this shaman?"

"Who can say? But our search must begin among humans, not spirits, I think."

Zack mulled it over. "I'm trying to remember the people we know who have been to the cave. Those local deputies were there. Who else?"

"That Tubs fellow was there, more than once. But we do not know how many were there before the murder."

Zack raised an eyebrow. "Wouldn't you have seen their tracks?"

Eagle Feather stood and shrugged on his pack. "Maybe. Maybe not." As he cinched the buckles, he said, "I do not have all your answers, White Man. It is now time to seek answers among the humans."

\* \* \* \* \*

Agent Janice Hooper clamped the phone to her ear as she stared at her computer. "Exactly what explosives did you find at the ranch?" She scrolled down the page on the computer screen.

"C-4. A good supply," was the response.

Janice read the paragraph on her screen. "It says here our man served in the US Army as an EOD expert." She groaned. "How did we miss that going in? We might have been blown apart by booby traps."

"There wasn't time to research thoroughly enough."

"There is always time to research thoroughly," Janice snapped. She paused. "Okay, things happen. The real question is what Musser had in mind with all that explosive power."

"The man is an activist fighting against federally owned land. He might have planned to blow up a BLM office, that kind of thing."

"Yeah, maybe. Let me know if you find anything else."

Hooper ended the call and touched another number. When a voice answered, she said, "Agent in Charge Hooper here. I need our team to research all the connections to Randy Musser, particularly any old army buddies, people he associates with in ranchers' groups like RAFOL, and the like. I need everybody he's spoken to in the last several months. Here's his cell number."

She ended the call and sat lost in thought, drumming her fingers on the desktop. After a moment or two she opened a file on her computer, found a number and called it.

"Hello, Mr. Tubs. This is Agent Hooper. We need to talk."

Tubs agreed to meet with her the next morning in Hurricane. They decided upon the McDonald's restaurant.

She went back to Musser's file. What was his part in all this? Why had he been to the cave before he "discovered" it with Tubs? What had he talked about with Tubs at his ranch? Tubs seemed sure Musser had set him up to be killed after leaving there. He was probably right. So what had they spoken about that could be so inflammatory?

The next morning as she was leaving home, her office secretary called. "A Professor David Philpott is calling. He says it's urgent. Shall I put him through?"

"Thank you, yes." She vaguely recalled a Professor Philpott among the scientists studying the bones. He would have been among those who discovered the university lab had been robbed.

"Agent Janice Hooper speaking."

"Listen." The voice was agitated. "I need protection. Someone is trying to kill me. They broke into my house last night. I hid. He went away, but he might come back. What shall I do?"

"What makes you so sure this person planned to kill you, Professor?"

"I know something. They need to keep me from talking."

"They, who? Talking about what?"

"I need to see you. I need protection."

Janice hesitated. "Why don't you call the police?"

"I can't trust them. I don't really know if I can trust you."

"Where are you right now? Are you in your home?"

"I'm just off the I-15 at Parowan headed south."

He was running! Hooper made up her mind to meet him. She glanced at her watch; time to leave for Hurricane.

"Okay, Professor. Keep coming south to Rt. 17 to Hurricane. When you get here stay on State Street through town. You'll see a McDonalds on your right. I'll be waiting for you there."

Janice scooped up her gun, car keys, and badge and headed out the door. It seemed it was going to be a very busy Monday.

* * * * *

After ending his conversation with Agent Hooper, David Philpott saw he had a message. He'd been too busy, too downright terrified to notice it before. It could be from his wife. But it wasn't. It was from a man named Jeffrey Banes Harlow. The call had come yesterday, and it warned him about a threat to his life from the same people who had killed the reporter.

The warning confirmed his worst fears.

Philpott saved the message to play it for the FBI Agent. He had something else for her as well. Yesterday, once he saw the lab had been rifled, he went straight to his desk drawer. To his relief, the watch was still there in its sample bag. He slipped it into his pocket, then into the glove compartment of his car. It was there now. The killer had not searched his car.

Philpott would have his interview with the FBI Agent. Then he would decide whether he trusted her enough to show her the watch. He believed it was the only real evidence that tied those bones to the Powell Expedition.

He drove back to the intersection with the Interstate and up the ramp headed south. Flying down I-15, he wondered why the conspirators chose to come after him. He could only imagine someone had been watching his comings and goings, spying on his office, his home. If they were watching him, likely they were watching the other members of the bone team as well.

Or maybe they had been following Dan Fogelberry, who led them to his door. Maybe they learned somehow the

214

reporter was getting close to the truth and might have shared his information with Philpott.

Either way, the conspirators had fixed on him like ticks on a dog, waiting for their moment to destroy the evidence—and him. No doubt the bones they had stolen were dust in the desert by now. But they didn't know about the watch.

Philpott had his plan. He would meet the FBI Agent and if he trusted her, tell her what he knew, what he hypothesized, and give her the watch. After that, he would climb back in his car and drive off and never return until this whole thing had blown over.

# CHAPTER FORTY

Jeffrey Danes Harlow searched everywhere for Jedediah but could not find him. He spent most of Sunday afternoon chasing down the old man's haunts, now and previous, to no avail. With evening coming on, he decided to return to the farm even though he'd already been there that day, to have a more thorough look around, hoping to find a clue to the man's whereabouts. He searched the farmhouse room by room. Only the kitchen and utility room appeared disturbed. A thin layer of dust covered all the furnishings. In the kitchen, pans lay in the sink, a plate on the counter. In the fridge he found a few eggs, a container of milk, not yet soured, half a loaf of bread, three cans of tuna, a jar of peanut butter. He found no supplies in the cabinets beyond a box of moldy oats, a box of water infused flour caked hard as a rock, and an open bag of stale potato chips. In the utility room, a sort of mudroom just off the porch and back steps, he found a stack of freshly laundered white sheets neatly folded on a shelf. There was an open box of latex gloves. The walls of the tiny room were painted bright white; the paint job seemed recent. The single window was covered in a layer of dirt and cast twisted shadows like a Rorschach inkblot test on the pristine wall opposite, a strange contrast. The room held a washing machine and drier, and a hamper filled with dirty laundry.

Jeffrey left the house by the back steps concluding little from his search other than the old man had been there recently and repeatedly, which was no surprise, and had apparently subsisted on very little food on those occasions. No wonder he ate like a ravenous wolf at the Harlow dinner table.

In the barn, two vehicles were covered with tarps as before, but he saw there had been a switch. He lifted the tarp for a better look. In the dim light he saw a dark blue sedan, an older model Dodge, well kept. Perhaps Jedediah attended antique car shows. If so, he never mentioned it. The vehicle had no plates.

Jeffrey lifted the tarp on the next vehicle. It was the same old Dodge pickup he'd seen before. It did not appear to have been moved. But the third vehicle was missing, the International Harvester SUV. In the interval since Jeffrey had been there last, Jedediah must have returned and made a switch.

That same medicinal odor came to him. Again, it smelled familiar but he still couldn't place it. It seemed to come from several spots on the greasy plank floor. Jeffrey had no flashlight, and the light cast by the dusty bulbs hanging by their electrical cords high up in the rafters was minimal. It was impossible to distinguish color or texture. He knelt and sniffed the spots. The sweet but overpowering smell stung his nose. He rocked back on his haunches, puzzled. It was somewhat like a disinfectant, but sweeter, with a touch of alcohol. Maybe the old man was using some sort of experimental cleanser.

His glance went to the workbench. Two bench seats from an automobile were pushed up against the wall. They were probably from the Travelall. Whatever the old man had in mind, it involved hauling something large; plants, perhaps or maybe fertilizer or bags of growth compound. The man was, after all, a farmer. He'd never really given up on this old farm. Somehow that thought relieved Jeffrey. He didn't want to think his wife's father was involved in wrongdoing.

The surface of the workbench held the ordinary objects one might expect: containers with fluids of various types, cans with used nuts and bolts, a box of rags. Three or four white pillowcases were stacked neatly in back. Tools cluttered the work surface including a razor knife, hammer, scissors, and pliers. A brown bottle sat in the middle of the space.

Next to the workbench was a stack of newspapers. The headline on the top paper read "Boy's Killer Still At

Large." He picked it up. Underneath another paper, the Las Vegas News-Journal featured an article about the murdered boy. Under that he found a copy of the Arizona Daily Star, also headlining an article about the murder. Apparently, Jedediah had developed a strong interest in the crime. Despite himself, Jeffrey's anxieties surged back.

He turned back to the workbench and lifted the brown bottle. The same sickly sweet odor came from it. The label read Chloroform; the distributor was The Science Company. What could this be for? Pest control? A dark suspicion swelled in Jeffrey. He wondered if chloroform had been used to subdue the Wilson boy. The FBI had jurisdiction over the case, and Jeffrey didn't know how much they had shared with his boss in the Colorado City Marshal's Department. He'd have to find out.

He walked back across the leaf littered yard to the patrol car. He would drive to the Marshal's Office; there he could access the computer and check the case file. On a Sunday evening, he should have the office to himself.

But where was Jedediah now?

\* \* \* \* \*

Agent in Charge Janice Hooper pulled into the parking lot of the McDonalds on West State Street in Hurricane. As she turned off her engine her phone sounded.

"Agent Hooper."

"Hello, Agent Hooper. My name is William Brown, chief deputy of Kane County."

"Yes, I remember you. What can I do for you, Chief Deputy Brown?"

"I was hoping we could meet. I believe our office has information relevant to the case of the murdered boy."

Janice cradled the phone to her ear as she locked her car. "Not something you could tell me over the phone?"

"Uh, I'd prefer to discuss it in person."

Janice glanced at her watch. "Where are you now, Chief Deputy?"

"I'm in Kanab."

"Can you meet me in Hurricane in two hours? I'll be in the McDonalds on West State Street."

"I'll see you there."

Janice tucked her phone away and pulled open the glass door. After the Monday morning rush the restaurant was not busy, as she had expected. She glanced around the tables and spotted the lanky form of Tubs right away. She walked over to him.

"Got you a coffee," he said. "How do you take it?"

She gave him a quick smile. "Like motor oil."

He grinned back. "You're in luck. That's what they're serving this morning."

Janice sat down on the fixed plastic chair. "I hope you don't mind the formality of our meeting place?"

"Suits me right down to the ground."

"I thought it might." She took a sip of the hot liquid, put the cup down. "Ah, yes, nasty stuff. How long have you known Randy Musser?"

Tubs blinked. He was still not ready for her abrupt style. "You don't go in for chit-chat much, do you? Well, we been huntin' together off and on for twenty years more or less."

"Did you know about his Army experience?"

"He didn't tell me no war stories if that's what you mean, but I knew he served."

"You must also know he belongs to the LDS Church?"

"Yes." He raised his eyebrows.

"But not the Fundamentalist Church."

"He never seemed that interested. He respected the mainline church, accepted all them beliefs, yuh know, just automatically." Tubs gave her a questioning look.

"Yet he was a radical."

219

"Yuh mean the land ownership fight?"

She nodded.

"That was a matter of survival to his thinking. He had to have access to the land for his cattle. He didn't trust the feds, figured they might suddenly kick him off of it." Tubs gave her a tight smile. "Kinda like the state doin' to you on Canaan Mountain."

Janice just smiled.

Tubs said, "The church always came first with him, though."

Janice went ahead without change of expression. "Why would he stockpile C-4 Explosives?"

Tubs' head jerked up. "Explosives?"

Janice scrutinized his face. "My agents found a good supply in his basement."

Tubs could only stare.

"You didn't know?"

"Uh, no. I had no idea."

Janice studied him.

"Really, I had no idea. I don't know why he would want explosives."

"You didn't know he was an explosives expert in the Army?"

Tubs shrugged. "No. What difference does that make?"

Janice took a sip of her coffee. "That's what I'm wondering. We suspect he set you up to be killed. We know he was involved with something at the cave murder scene that had to do with the church. We know he had a large store of explosives in his cellar and knew how to use them. I think it makes a difference."

Tubs nodded. "Yeah, I guess maybe you're right."

"So there's nothing more you can tell me?"

Tubs spread his palms. "I got no idea what's going on. He told me he couldn't tell me church secrets—that's all he said. He begged me to stay quiet about him being in the cave, said it could mess up the lives of a lot of people, including him."

Janice stared at him. "Whatever that secret is, it's worth killing his friend to keep."

Tubs stared back. "I guess so." After a silent moment, he asked, "Have you found out anything about that truck driver who tried to run me over?"

"You want an Egg McMuffin?" Janice asked. "I'd like one. My treat."

As Tubs watched her go to the counter, he shook his head in bewilderment.

# CHAPTER FORTY-ONE

Professor David Philpott drove much faster than he should, much faster than he felt comfortable driving, but despite frequent glances in the rearview mirror he was not convinced he wasn't being followed. The large pickup truck with its enormous grill always seemed somewhere behind him, now closer, now farther back. And the cream-colored convertible––hadn't he seen that car entering back at the Scipio onramp?

After he turned onto Rt. 17 toward Toquerville, he made a series of evasive maneuvers he'd seen done on spy television shows; first he pulled over to see if anyone stopped behind him while at the same time he scrutinized the cars passing him. No pickup truck, no cream-colored convertible. He felt a pinch of relief. Next, he reversed direction until he came to a break in the median where he performed a sudden U-turn back to his original direction. He saw no sign of pursuit.

He sped up, slowed back down to the speed limit, realizing if he were stopped he couldn't be sure of the bona fides of the officer stopping him. Philpott was dripping sweat by the time he reached Hurricane. He found the McDonalds and pulled into the lot. He spun his head, looking for an official FBI car until he realized there wouldn't be one. In fact, how would he recognize the FBI agent, or she him? He had her phone number, if worse came to worse.

Philpott entered the restaurant. His sweeping glance revealed only a few people at tables. Nowhere was there an official looking woman by herself. Now what?

He sat down at the nearest empty table and took out his phone. He was searching for the agent's number when he sensed someone standing next to him. He lifted his gaze.

"Professor Philpott?"

He saw an attractive dark-haired woman with a beautiful smile. He nodded hesitantly.

"I'm Agent Janice Hooper. I believe we are scheduled to meet."

Philpott was uncertain. "May I see some identification?"

Her smile broadened. "Certainly." She extended a folding wallet with a badge and certification.

Philpott studied it, recognized her in the picture.

"Come join us," she said. She pointed to a table where a lanky, long-haired man watched them.

"Is that another agent?"

Her smile was reassuring. "No, but he is someone you should meet. He is an innocent victim of this situation as well. Come along."

The professor followed her to the table, still unsure. The two men stared at each other.

Agent Hooper waved the professor to a seat.

"Gentlemen, I believe you are each at different ends of the same problem." She looked from one to the other. "David Philpott, please meet Tubs LeBaron."

The two men shook hands, studied each other with cautious scrutiny.

Janice spoke to Philpott. "Tubs discovered the murder victim while out hunting with another man. The other man was named Randy Musser. Tubs later discovered Randy had been to the cave at an earlier time, something he didn't tell Tubs. Tubs went to see Randy at his ranch to confront him with this information. Randy finally confessed he had been there on a special mission for the LDS Church, but he would not say what. He swore Tubs to secrecy. Subsequently, as Tubs was driving home, an attempt was made on his life that could only have been arranged by Randy. Tubs called me, and I took a team to the ranch to talk to Randy. Randy resisted, and died without revealing anything."

Philpott listened to this terrifying yet matter-of-fact account of circumstances with horror.

Janice turned to Tubs. "Professor Philpott is one of the old bones experts we called in to help us analyze the remains in the cave. The team removed three bone samples and brought them back to their lab where they have studied them. As you may have heard, the state of Utah has requested an injunction against the removal of the bones from the area, which meant the three bones in the lab at BYU were all we had. Yesterday they were stolen, along with all the research notes. That night, someone broke into Professor Philpott's home to make an attempt on his life, he believes. David hid himself and so escaped. He called me as he was getting away down I-15." She smiled from one man to the other. "So here we are." She looked at Philpott. "Would you like a coffee? It's wonderfully terrible here."

At his stunned nod, Janice began to rise.

"No, no, you stay," Tubs said to Janice. "I'll get it. You two need to talk."

As soon as Tubs strode off, Philpott turned to Janice. "Can you keep me safe and guarantee safety for my family?" His tone was desperate.

She nodded. Her manner had a calming effect. "We can and we will."

He half whispered, "Who is trying to kill me?"

"We have suspected there might be a conspiracy of some sort within the LDS Church. But just how large or small it is, or who is involved, we don't know. Tubs, there, is one of the good guys. Beyond that...?" She turned her gaze to Philpott. His expression was still anxious. "We will put you and your family in a safe house, known only to the FBI and only to those agents with a need to know."

Philpott was relieved. "My job, my career?"

Janice put her hand on top of his. "All this is just until we catch the bad guys. After that, life can go on as before."

Tubs arrived with his long fingers wrapped around three coffees. "Just in case," he said to Janice as he set them on the table.

Philpott took his cup with a glance of appreciation.

"Now what?" Tubs asked.

"I think there is someone else who has important information," Philpott said.

"Who?" Janice looked sharply at him.

"I don't know. A man left a phone message for me, warning me of an attempt on my life."

"What did he say, exactly?"

"Well, he said the reporter who died—"

"Dan Fogelberry."

"Yes, Fogelberry. The caller said the theory Fogelberry and I had discussed regarding the bones was correct, that I was in great danger, I should watch my back and stay in the company of my colleagues at all times."

"You don't know who it was left the message?" Janice asked.

"No."

"You didn't recognize the voice at all?" Tubs asked.

Philpott shook his head.

Janice gave him an encouraging smile. "Who did you tell about your theory?"

"No one but Fogelberry. We agreed to keep it quiet, at least until Dan could prove something and write his article."

"Sounds like he may have learned something but didn't get the chance to publish it," Tubs said.

"But evidently he did find time to tell someone else." Hooper fixed her gaze on Philpott. "I think it's time you shared your theory."

The professor sent a worried glance at Tubs.

"I think Tubs has slipped into the "need to know" category," Janice said.

Philpott looked at her, then nodded. He pulled the Ziploc bag containing the watch from his pocket and handed it to Janice. "Here is the evidence," he said.

For the next half hour, Professor Philpott gave a detailed account of his meeting with Dan Fogelberry and what they concluded from it.

\* \* \* \* \*

Zack climbed behind the wheel of the Jeep, the muscles in his calves twitching. Eagle Feather was already in the passenger seat, the back reclined, his feet up on the dash. The friends had pushed the pace back from the cave, driven by questions and concerns that could only be resolved by speaking to other people.

Eagle Feather wanted to see Shana to discuss bears that turned into shamans, or vise versa. Zack had in mind some research into the history of the cave area and ritual practices of ancient tribes. He also wanted to learn how the twin deputies could access the cave when everyone else was restricted by the injunction. Finally, he had some questions for his friend and fellow lecturer, anthropologist Dr. Susan Apgar, about ancient Indian shamans and their relationship to bears.

Both men had been eager to get back to civilization, but the steep and slippery road before them offered many perils and required all the attention Zack's tired brain could muster. There were near misses, despite Zack's skill. A heavy dew had moistened the road surface just enough to make the sandy mud and clay mixture treacherous, and the Jeep showed a tendency to want to continue straight ahead regardless of what that might mean. The growing darkness did not help.

Once down off the mountain and onto paved road, they made better time but it was late and they were tired and for safety's sake they decided to take a motel room in Hurricane.

At breakfast the next morning, the friends stared wearily at each other over the rims of their coffee.

"What do you intend to do now?" Zack asked.

Eagle Feather stared into the black liquid. "I want to know more about the Paiute ancestors, their First People, and learn about their powers. The Navajo Skin Walker tradition is thought by researchers to have come down from the Pueblo inhabitants who preceded us, and some suggest those early mystical beliefs were influenced by the Spanish and their Christian religion, which defames animals like wolves and snakes in their demonology. Others believe the defamation of these animals came later, from relatively modern missionaries, reasoning that The People have always used wolf pelts for hunting and adornment without derogatory meaning, and it was the white people who changed that." Eagle Feather glanced sideways at Zack. "I blame the white people for many things, but not for the creation of Skin Walkers. I believe these secrets precede the Pueblo people and reach back to the very first of our ancestors who discovered this land for my people. I believe those ancient people had real powers beyond our current willingness to accept."

Zack grinned at him. "You want to ask Shana if the Paiute hold similar beliefs about shape shifters. Let me rephrase that. You want to see Shana."

Eagle Feather cocked an eyebrow over a twinkling eye.

Before climbing into the Jeep, Zack called Libby. The phone rang, went to voicemail. He left a message explaining the circumstances.

As the Jeep roared out onto the main road, Zack glanced at Eagle Feather. "I'd like to make a stop at the Colorado City Marshal's Office. Okay with you?"

"I cannot wait."

Zack laughed. "I'm sure."

The Marshal's office was in the town office on Township Avenue. The split-level building looked more like a private residence than a public facility. He was knocking on a locked door before he noticed the office hours on a sign. He was too early.

He walked around to the rear, where he guessed the duty officers entered. A large man was climbing out of a pickup truck. The man stared at Zack, watched him approach.

"You need help?" The question sounded more accosting than inquiring.

"That depends upon who you are," Zack said. He stopped a few feet from the man, hands on hips.

The man looked Zack up and down before answering. "I guess I ought to be asking you that same question."

"My name is Zack Tolliver. I'm a consultant with the FBI."

"Well, Zack Tolliver, consultant with the FBI, I guess you don't know it's too early and all the good folk of this town are still in bed, including the Marshal."

"You're not."

The man glared at Zack. "Someone's got to look out that strangers don't run willy-nilly around the neighborhood."

Zack smiled. "I guess you must be attached to the Marshal's office?"

"I am."

"I see no reason to disturb the Marshal. You can probably answer my questions."

The big man hesitated, finally grumbled, "Yeah, okay."

"Do you hold a position of authority?"

"I'm a Deputy Marshal."

'Well, that sounds fine, Marshal—?"

"Marshall LeRoy Taylor."

"Marshal Taylor. Here's my question: why are California City Deputy Marshals able to access the Canaan Mountain crime scene when the State Courts have issued an injunction against trespass into the Preserve?"

228

LeRoy became confused. "Cuz we are the State," he said finally.

"No, you are officials of the town, not the state."

"Don't matter, the crime scene is in our jurisdiction."

"No, it's in federal jurisdiction."

LeRoy stared hard, working on it. Then came a look of suspicion. "How do you know we were up there? You must have been up there yourself."

Zack smiled. "So you admit being up there."

LeRoy's face turned red. "I don't have to talk to you. I think you need to get on out of here." He almost spluttered. "Now git!" He took a step toward Zack.

Putting palms up, Zack complied. He walked away. The deputy watched him go, hands on hips.

Zack was pleased. He'd gotten more from the visit to Colorado City than he expected, confirmation of the identity of the men who were at the cave. He didn't think LeRoy had gone there of his own volition, which suggested someone in authority in the town, either the Marshal or someone in the hierarchy of the FLDS Church, had sent the deputies. They were obviously meant to guard the site. So the question now was, what did the church want to hide?

"Get what you needed?"

Zack grinned at Eagle Feather. "More than enough." He laughed. "I wonder what Deputy Marshal LeRoy would have said to his boss about the huge bear that drove them away."

"He probably did not mention it. I imagine the deputies chose to remain quiet about that story."

Before he drove back to the highway, Zack tried Libby again.

This time she answered.

"Zack, where have you been? I expected you last night."

"We had to put up in a motel in Hurricane. I tried to call, but the line was busy. I fell asleep after that."

229

"Oh...you must have called when the heavy breather was on the line."

"The what?"

Libby described the stalker's call and her subsequent call to Sheriff Rafferty.

Zack felt a surge of anger. "We've got to put an end to this, one way or another. Has that car been outside the house recently?"

"It's not there now."

"What about the surveillance Rafferty promised you?"

"I don't know. They could be around, but I haven't seen them." Zack could hear the tension in her voice.

"Okay, I have to drop Eagle Feather off at his camp. Keep your phone near you. Call me right away if anything develops. I'll be there soon."

"I'll be able to reach you this time?"

"I promise. My phone will be on, and I'll be listening."

# CHAPTER FORTY-TWO

Eagle Feather grabbed his towel and a bar of soap and walked to the campground bathroom facility. He remained the only camper in the place and luxuriated in having the entirety of this spanking new facility all to himself. Hot water was available immediately, and after scrubbing and drying, the Navajo spent more than his usual amount of time in front of the mirror combing out his long hair and studying his image with a critical eye.

Back at his camp, he found clean pants and a freshly pressed shirt. After he'd given his moccasins a good pounding, he was ready to go.

His first stop was at a vacant field to gather a bouquet of poppies and lupine, tied with a bit of leather lace and a pendant of beaded fringe from his buckskin coat. Satisfied with the look of it, he drove on to the little Paiute town of Moccasin. He found house number 452 two blocks north of the post office. He parked his truck at the curb, gave himself a final brush-off, and knocked on the door.

A surprised Shana opened it, in her bathrobe, her hair rumpled charmingly from sleep, brown eyes wide. "Eagle Feather?"

In response, the Navajo held out the bouquet.

"Why, thank you." She did not take the flowers at first, but eyed him with curiosity. "Is it a custom among your people to visit single women you barely know at their homes?"

"No." Eagle Feather scuffed a foot. "It is important to talk to you about the cave on Canaan Mountain," he said. He thrust the flowers forward once more, his face tinged red.

Shana took the bouquet and moved aside. "It is not customary for my people to keep guests standing at the door."

Eagle Feather stepped through into a small but neat living room. Shana gestured him toward the sofa and took a seat in an armchair angled toward him. He was impressed by Shana's natural attitude toward her own appearance; not once did she so much as attempt to smooth her hair or glance at her reflection. She presented an unusual selfless confidence.

"What could be so important about the cave that you intrude upon my private life? It is not what I would expect of you." She arched her eyebrows.

Eagle Feather grimaced. "You are right. I would not, normally, yet I sensed at our last meeting your strong interest in the cave and whatever lives there. I thought it might be enough to excuse my intrusion."

Shana gave a slight smile. "Perhaps."

"I have recently returned from a visit to the cave with a friend. We both witnessed a large bear, which a moment later turned into a human, an Indian shaman, I believe."

Shana's eyes stayed riveted on Eagle Feather's face, but she showed no surprise. "Tell me about it."

Eagle Feather described the circumstances.

"The bear, when you first became aware of it, seemed focused on the deputies?" Shana asked.

"It seemed so."

"It did not see you?"

Eagle Feather hesitated. "It did not look at us, yet I sensed it knew we were there."

Shana appeared thoughtful. "I think we can assume it knew you were in its cave. As far as you know, it had come from the cave in its bear manifestation to threaten the deputies?"

Eagle Feather nodded.

"Which means it had been in the cave while you and your friend were there."

"I thought about that."

"Yet you did not see it."

Eagle Feather shook his head. "We had flashlights and searched the cave as well as we could with them. We may have missed a place where it could hide."

Shana stood and walked to a small sideboard that held an ornate coffee pot. She poured a dark liquid into a cup and brought it to Eagle Feather. "I think you will find this coffee better than the last cup I offered you."

Eagle Feather grinned. "That would not be difficult."

Shana helped herself to a cup. She glanced at Eagle Feather. "The response of this creature would suggest it felt no threat from you and your friend, but did feel threatened by the deputies. Why do you think it favored you?"

Eagle Feather looked at her curiously. "You seem to believe my story."

"Should I not believe you? My people know of such things. We are attuned to all creatures that walk the earth, physical or spiritual." She came back to her chair and sat, balancing her coffee cup on her knee. "I must confess your white friend is no stranger to me. He is a rare person—a law enforcement officer with knowledge and understanding of spiritual worlds. I attended a lecture in Las Vegas recently presented by Dr. Apgar in which Agent Tolliver supported her somewhat radical ideas about beings unknown to modern humans yet able to live near us and among us because of an extraordinary ability to adapt."

Eagle Feather raised his eyebrows in surprise. "You heard him speak?"

"Yes." She studied Eagle Feather. "I assume Agent Tolliver is the friend you mentioned."

He smiled. "Yes, he is. Yet I would be lying to say either of us could accept what we just witnessed without a struggle."

Shana nodded. "I suspect it's one thing to hear about it from the elders, quite another to see it yourself."

Eagle Feather put his empty cup on the coffee table, held up his palm to refuse another. His mind was on the cave creature. "Assuming we accept the reality of this therianthropic shaman, do you think he or it could be responsible for the death of the boy?"

233

Shana tilted her head. "You credit me with more insight than I possess."

"Just a guess, then?"

"What's your guess?" she countered.

"I'd say no."

She nodded. "I agree. Not that I believe such a creature is incapable, just that the manner of death, the symbolism of impalement on an altar stone, is more attributable to human ceremonies than mystical creatures or powerful shamans. A shaman with such powers would be unlikely to call attention to himself." She smiled. "Or herself."

"Impaling a boy on a pole on an altar stone is not the way to go unnoticed."

"Exactly." Shana waited.

After a moment of silence, Eagle Feather asked, "Were your people aware of the creature in the cave?"

"Not to my knowledge."

"You say your people have lived and worked at the very base of the mountain where this thing lives, yet no one ever saw it?"

"I'm certainly not saying that, I have no idea who might have wandered up there and seen some manifestation of this creature." Shana shifted her weight in her chair. "What I am saying is our people have no traditions, no rituals related to such a being. Remember, the Kaibab Band of the Southern Paiute has not always lived here, nor have we always been farmers. Originally, we were hunter/gatherers, as those who study such things would call us, and we traveled widely to procure what we needed. The high lands on Kaiparowits Peak, the original name for Canaan Mountain, were cold and snow covered in winter. While hunters might chase an elk to its heights, only in midsummer would conditions be reasonable to spend any time there; and even then you would be left the difficult climb back down under the weight of the fresh kill." Shana shook her head. "I have no reason to doubt the cave could have remained a secret for a very long time."

234

Eagle Feather sighed. "I will accept there is a shaman of the Old Ones who hides in the cave and has great powers. That is what I will tell Zack Tolliver. I will also tell him I do not believe this shaman murdered the boy, or anyone else." He stood, gave a slow nod. "I apologize for my intrusion. Thank you. You have helped me." He walked to the door.

Shana followed.

Eagle Feather turned to her, hesitated. "May I call on you again?"

Her eyes widened. "You mean a date?"

"I...yes."

Shana reached past him, pulled open the door. Then she smiled. "Yes, I'd like that."

# CHAPTER FORTY-THREE

Janice Hooper noticed the man entering the McDonalds as soon as he pushed through the door. Tall, blond, face darkened by the sun, he had an air of authority and the upright bearing suggesting a lawman. She watched him glance around the room, saw his gaze reach her. He appeared momentarily confused until she smiled. He smiled back and walked over to them.

"I didn't expect three people," he said, raising his eyebrows. "I assume you are Agent Hooper?"

Janice motioned to the empty seat at the table for four. "Sit down. Yes, I am Janice Hooper." She spoke to all of them. "I have had to juggle my meetings today. I apologize to you all. I've just about finished with these gentlemen."

Janice directed her attention toward Philpott, took a business card from her pocket and wrote something on it. She handed the card to him. "Please go to this address and ring the front bell. When someone answers the door, hand him this card. He'll take care of things. I'll get in touch later. Thanks for your help."

She turned to Tubs. "We need to stay in touch as well. I have your mobile number and you have mine. Feel free to call anytime."

Janice gave a broad smile of dismissal to both men.

Brown watched them leave the table.

Janice swung her eyes to him. "Now what can I do for you, Deputy Brown?"

"Chief Deputy Brown," the lawman said with a thin smile and went on without pause. "Sheriff Rafferty would like to be sure you have all the evidence you need for your investigation and asked me to share what we have."

"Well, thank you, Chief Deputy, that's very neighborly." She gave a brilliant toothy smile.

"Of course, we hope for a certain amount of reciprocity."

"Of course, you do. Let's see where this takes us." She raised eyebrows expectantly.

Brown drummed large fingers, looked thoughtful, and spoke. "I'll cut right to the chase. We believe our two investigations are connected."

"Which two?"

"The boy skewered at the cave, and the high school girl found dead on Route 89."

Janice frowned. "We prefer to think of him as impaled. Regardless, what makes you think there is a connection?"

"We came by some new evidence recently. We have learned there may have been a witness to the original abduction of the boy"—the chief deputy checked a notebook—"uh, Luke Wilson. The witness was walking home from school with him that day—"

"In Kanab?"

He nodded. "In Kanab. But she turned off at her home before the abduction occurred. She claims to have noticed an SUV pass them and return by them again before speeding away."

"But if it sped away..."

"We think the girl turned off at that moment, and the kidnapper noticed."

"And returned."

"Yes."

"Can your witness describe the SUV?" Janice felt a surge of excitement.

Brown looked grim. "We have not interviewed the witness. There has been an attempt to break into her home. The mother has the girl stashed away."

"So how—"

"There is an aunt to whom the girl relates well. The witness said nothing to her mother, but confessed all of it to the aunt in detail. The aunt gave us her story."

"I see." Janice felt a pinch of disappointment. Third or fourth hand information seldom turned out to be one hundred percent accurate.

Brown plowed on. "She described an International Harvester Travelall, a dark color like navy blue or black, 1961 to 1968 model year."

Janice lifted her eyebrows. "That's rather remarkable for a high school girl."

The corners of Brown's mouth turned up. "The aunt saw the vehicle for herself later. We have silhouette cutouts of many car and truck models for witnesses. That model Travelall is distinctive."

"Which begs the question why the perp would use it." Janice glanced at Brown. "Smacks of a novice with a vehicle of convenience."

"So we thought. In any event, we put out an APB, but no luck yet."

Janice thought about it. "How can I get hold of this witness?"

Brown shook his head. "You can't. I can't. The mother and child have disappeared. The aunt knows where, but she's not telling."

Janice took a small notebook from her purse. "Who's the aunt?"

Brown smiled. "It's getting close to reciprocity time." He beckoned for her notebook. "I'll put it down for you. Her name is Libby Whitestone Tolliver." He wrote down her cell number, handed the notebook back to Hooper.

Janice took it, looked at him. "There was an FBI Agent named Tolliver..."

Brown smiled. "His wife."

Janice felt better now. Access to the witness who was an agent's wife would be easier for her. She tucked the thought away and changed direction.

"Now what can I do for you?" she said with a bright smile.

Brown put both palms on the table. "We'd like you to commit to the idea the cases are connected and share information and resources."

"Oh, is that all?" Janice gave him a sardonic smile. "Sheriff Rafferty must understand if we perceive the cases connected, we will take over the investigation. However, I promise we will keep you informed to the extent we can and gratefully accept your help where we feel it is needed. Can you live with that?"

To her surprise, Chief Deputy Brown smiled and nodded. "Perfect."

"I will confer with my superiors to see if they agree and let you know soon."

Brown stood and extended his hand. "Thank you. We'll look forward to your call." He turned on his heel and left.

Janice stared after him. Should she smell a rat? That had been entirely too easy. She shrugged, took another sip of coffee, grimaced, and called her office. "I need any information on former Agent Zack Tolliver you can give me, including his wife Libby, their current whereabouts and contact numbers."

\* \* \* \* \*

"Is your man in the neighborhood?" the voice on the phone said. Sheriff Rafferty rolled onto his side. "Libby? Is that you?" He looked at his watch. It was 6:30 a.m.

"Cause if he's not, this could be a very bad decision."

"Libby, what's going on? What are you doing?" Rafferty swept his legs from under the blanket to the floor. His wife groaned but didn't wake up.

"If your officer is out here, send him over to E 400 S Street. He'll see me walking along the sidewalk headed west on the north side of the street. He'll also see a dark maroon sedan parked on the south side of the street a few car lengths behind me. If he hurries, he might witness an abduction."

Rafferty sprang to his feet, grabbed his pants where they were slung over the back of a chair and shoved his legs into them. "Libby, what the hell are you talking about? Why are you out of the house? Is your husband there? What abduction?" He stuck his arms into the sleeves of the nearest shirt.

"I'm tired of hanging around and waiting, Sheriff. I'm forcing this asshole to make his move. He's been parked out there in that car on and off all night."

By now Rafferty was tucked, buckled and zipped. He slipped his holster onto his belt. "The guy is after your niece. What makes you think he'd do anything to you?"

"Because I'm wearing Pru's coat and hat."

"Shit!" Rafferty grabbed his keys and ran for the door. "Keep this line open. I'm calling my deputy right now." He pushed the hold button and rang dispatch. Without preamble, he shouted, "Where's the Tolliver surveillance right now?"

"Robinson? Just a second, sir."

Rafferty was in his patrol car. It roared to life. He heard the dispatcher calling his deputy. He switched to Libby's line. "Libby, I'm contacting my man. I'm five minutes away. Don't do anything silly." There was no response. "Libby? Libby?" The line was open, no Libby. "Goddammit!" He switched lines again. "Where is he?" he yelled.

"I can't reach him, sir. He's not responding."

"Keep trying." Rafferty switched back to Libby's line. "Libby?" Still nothing. The patrol car turned north on 89A and accelerated. At the E 440 S intersection he slammed the brakes and spun the wheel and the car slid sideways, accelerating into the turn. Rafferty glanced at his watch; he'd made it in four minutes.

He slowed to a crawl, studying both sides of the street. No Libby. No maroon sedan. The dispatcher's voice came over his phone. He grabbed it from the seat.

"Yeah?"

"I can't raise Robinson. What do you want me to do?"

"Call in all deputies, alert the Highway Patrol. I want every exit from Kanab sealed. I'm looking for a maroon sedan. Stop and hold any vehicle meeting that description."

"Yes, sir."

Sheriff Rafferty pulled over and rang Libby's number. No answer. It just kept ringing—in both ears, he suddenly realized. Powering open all his windows, he listened. His eyes followed the sound to a small object on the sidewalk across the street. He jumped out and ran over just as the cell phone stopped ringing.

It was Libby's phone—but no Libby.

The sidewalk, pale, long and empty, stretched to either side. A stabbing sense of failure assailed Rafferty. Libby was such an intelligent, grounded and, well...attractive person. Why had she done this? Was she so desperate to confront her stalker? Or had she put her faith so completely in him, only to have him fail her?

His frustration turned to anger. What the hell was going on with Robinson? He had dropped the ball. Where was he? Back in the patrol car, he called dispatch. "Have you raised Robinson yet?"

"No, sir."

"Keep trying. Let me know the minute you find him."

"Yes, sir."

Rafferty started the car and drove to the Baker home. He walked up to the front door. It was locked. He knocked and rang the bell. No response. He felt his last hope disintegrate. Soon he would have a team search the house to try to find any clue to Libby's location, but he had little hope. The locked door meant to him Libby had purposefully become a target, had not wanted her stalker to enter the home in her absence. It was all about forcing the stalker's hand; a gamble she had apparently lost.

Back in the patrol car, Rafferty picked up his phone to call dispatch. It was time to call Libby's husband, and he needed the number. Before he could, his radio squawked to life.

"SD1, this is SD3. We have Mrs. Tolliver. I repeat; we have Mrs. Tolliver. Over."

Rafferty tried not to let his emotions come through in his voice. "SD3, what is her condition? Over."

"The subject seems fine, sir, except for some bruises and recovery from exposure to an unknown chemical agent. We are on our way to the emergency room now, sir."

"Where did you find her?"

"She was lying by the roadside on 89A. Looked like she was just dumped there."

Rafferty was already accelerating. "Okay, I'll be at the hospital in five minutes. Over."

# CHAPTER FOURTY-FOUR

Zack's phone did ring, but it was not Libby's ringtone. He took his eyes from the road and glanced at the lit screen. The caller ID said Federal Bureau of Investigation. He pulled over.

"Zack Tolliver."

"Mr. Tolliver, this is Special Agent Janice Hooper. I am Agent in Charge for the Luke Wilson murder case. I would like to have a word with you."

Zack glanced at his watch. "I am just returning to Kanab from an overnight camping trip. I need a shower. What's this about?"

"I have reason to believe you have information that might help us with our investigation."

"I could be available by noon."

"Fine. I'll drive to Kanab. How about lunch at the Rocking V Cafe?"

"I'll see you there."

Zack put the cell phone on the passenger seat and pulled out onto the road surface. Seconds later, the phone rang again. This time it said Kane County Sheriff's Office. Zack pulled over.

"Zack Tolliver."

"Hello, Mr. Tolliver, this is Sheriff Oliver Rafferty. Have you got a minute?"

"What is it, Sheriff? I'm in a bit of a rush."

"It's about your wife, Libby."

"Libby? I just spoke to her a little more than an hour ago."

"I'm afraid she's had a mishap."

"What sort of mishap? Is she okay?"

"She's fine, Mr. Tolliver. Just some bruises and a bit of a shock."

"What happened?"

"There was an attempted abduction. I can explain it all to you if you come to the hospital emergency room. The doctor is insisting she rest for an hour or so here. He gave her a sedative."

"I'll be there in thirty minutes."

Zack felt anger creep over him like a lava flow. This man had guaranteed Libby's safety. He had promised to have protective surveillance. How could anything have happened to Libby?

He glanced at his speedometer and saw he was approaching ninety and let up on the accelerator. He never saw the International Harvester Travelall pass the opposite way.

Zack knew the hospital was in the north end of Kanab; he went that way and followed the signs. The waiting area of the emergency reception was empty but for a sleeping man holding an arm that appeared broken; perhaps the dregs of too many Saturday night beers. He oriented himself, found the reception cubicle window and was headed there when he heard his name called.

Sheriff Rafferty stood by a door to the inner sanctum. He gestured for Zack to follow. Zack's anger flared up again, but Rafferty stayed far enough ahead to avoid conversation and then they were in a small room and Libby was there, under a sheet, smiling up at him. His anger went away at the sight of her.

"Libby, are you all right? What happened?"

Libby's response came slow and measured, the effect of the sedative. "I'm fine, Zack. A man grabbed me from the sidewalk, and I can't remember anything until I woke up in a different part of town." She added quickly, "He didn't hurt me, Zack, I'm just a bit bruised."

Zack glared at Rafferty. "Explain."

"Don't blame him, Zack. It was my fault. I was tired of this man stalking me, and I went out in Pru's hat and coat to make him show himself."

244

Zack's eyes went back and forth between Libby and Rafferty, finally settling on Rafferty. "How was she allowed to leave the house and walk down the sidewalk? Where was the surveillance you promised?"

Sheriff Rafferty hung his head. "I don't know, Zack. I just reached my man. He was at home, said he never got the order. He'll be reprimanded, but you're right, this should never have happened."

Zack turned to his wife. "Libby, why would you do something so crazy?" The echo of his words sounded harsher than he meant.

Libby stared at Zack. "No one else was getting anywhere with this. No one else can give you a description of the man."

"You saw him?" Zack asked.

Sheriff Rafferty leaned closer.

"Yes, before he had time to put me to sleep with the chloroform or whatever it was, I saw his face."

"Clear enough to describe to a sketch artist?" Rafferty asked.

"Yes. He's an old man, thick white hair, a deeply-lined face with hard expression, thin lips, hooked nose, blue eyes. I'd guess him to be in his late seventies, early eighties, but very strong. I never saw the rest of him, but he must be quite fit."

Rafferty was already on his phone calling dispatch with a request for a sketch artist.

Zack was at the bedside holding Libby's hand. "You scare me and amaze me," he said.

Libby gave a wan smile. "Even after all these years?"

"A sketch artist will be here in fifteen minutes. Do you mind?" Rafferty peered at Libby.

"That's fine," Libby said. "The sooner the better so I don't forget."

Zack turned to Rafferty. "What did he use to subdue Libby?"

Rafferty grunted. "It was chloroform. The doctor figures it was a light dose. The guy apparently knew how to use it."

Zack glanced from Rafferty to Libby. "No lingering effects or harm?"

Libby shook her head. "I'll be fine, Zack."

Zack looked at his watch. "I have a meeting scheduled for noon. I will call and postpone it."

Libby shook her head. "There's no point in that. I'm fine, and I'll be busy for a while with the sketch artist anyway. You go to your meeting."

Zack caught a whiff of his own body. "I'm gonna need a shower first." He glanced at Rafferty. "I'll be meeting with Agent Janice Hooper. Know her? She's Agent in Charge of the murdered boy case."

Rafferty smiled. "Well, well. We finally seem to be coming full circle. You'll keep me in the loop." It wasn't a question.

*  *  *  *  *

Zack stepped into the Rocking V Cafe a shade before noon. It was dim, even at midday. The glossy wood tables reflected the chandeliers' light; the carpeted floor absorbed it. It was crowded. People wended their way up the stairs to the art gallery. He scanned the tables, no one here looked like a female FBI Agent. A voice came from behind him.

"Looking for someone?"

He turned. A woman with ice blue eyes, dark hair in a tight bun, and a tidy black suit peered up at him.

He smiled. "I am, in fact. Would you be Agent Hooper?"

She gave a brilliant smile in return. "I am. Shall we find a table, Mr. Tolliver?"

Agent Hooper led the way to a waitress who grabbed two menus and took them to a center table. Hooper shook

246

her head and pointed toward a table for two along the wall. The waitress opened her mouth as if to argue, changed her mind and took them there.

Zack was impressed by Hooper's authoritative presence. He guessed she wouldn't suffer nonsense from underlings. On the other side of the coin, he bet she had a few enemies within the agency.

Hooper repeated the brilliant smile. "I'm grateful you were willing to meet me."

Zack thought he'd never seen more perfect teeth. "Thank you for driving all this way."

"Drink?"

"Just a beer."

Agent Hooper beckoned the waiter. Zack ordered a favorite session IPA. Hooper ordered a white wine. She was back with both drinks in minutes.

"The lunch is on my expenses account," she said.

The announcement left no room for polite resistance. Zack liked that.

"How can I help you?" he said.

"To be fair, Mr. Tolliver, former Supervisory Agent Tolliver, I should disclose that I have read your file."

"I would expect it at the very least."

"When you left the agency, you said it was to be with your family."

Zack nodded.

"Yet here you are involved in a murder case miles from home." Hooper lifted her glass and gently sniffed the wine.

"But just a few blocks from my wife."

Agent Hooper raised her eyebrows.

Zack sighed. "You see, I didn't volunteer for this investigation. I was drawn into it when a close relative came under threat." Zack went on to explain the circumstances.

Hooper's eyes narrowed. "So you squirreled away a witness where no one could find her and then set out to find the perp. You have no official capacity. What did you intend to do if you found the suspect?"

"I am working closely with Sheriff Rafferty," Zack said.

"I'm glad someone is," she said in a dry tone. "Ready to eat?"

"Uh, sure."

Agent Hooper turned to summon the waitress. The woman was already at her shoulder.

She's got the waitress trained already, Zack thought. "I'll have the burger platter," he told her.

Hooper gave their order, the waitress glided away, and the agent's eyes settled on Zack. "A Chief Deputy Brown from the Kane County Sheriff's Office came to see me this morning, claiming we were working different sides of the same case. Do you agree?"

Zack eyed her for a moment. "I suspect you could benefit by sharing with one another."

"Is there anyone else I should share with, do you think?"

Zack sipped his beer and thought about it. He wiped his mouth and said, "I can't think of anyone."

Hooper's eyes were intense. "You, for instance?"

Zack was taken aback. "Whoa! I just told you I was working closely with the sheriff."

A dazzling smile gleamed on Agent Hooper's face. "I've read your file, Mr. Tolliver. It seems you are a bit of a lone wolf. You keep your cards close to your chest. You and your Indian buddy, Turkey Feather."

"That's Eagle Feather."

She studied him. "Right." She leaned toward him. "What's your wife doing in the hospital?"

Zack was caught off balance by her abrupt change of topic. "How did you know about that? It just happened."

"I'll share when you share." The smile was gone.

Zack sighed. "If you know she's in the hospital, you also know why. I assume that was a rhetorical question."

"That was a test. This is a matter of trust, Mr. Tolliver. As one retired from the agency, I assume your loyalties lie with us. I'd like to hear it in your own words."

"Agent Hooper—"

"Call me Janice." The smile was back.

Zack felt like he was trudging uphill in mud, always a step behind her. Before he could say another word, the waitress arrived with their food. The conversation went on pause.

The girl laid out the plates, checked that they had everything, sent a questioning glance at Agent Hooper, who nodded. The waitress flurried off.

"Agent Hooper—Janice—I told you before, our involvement in this case is accidental and personal. I've shared everything I know with Sheriff Rafferty."

"And the cave on Canaan Mountain?"

"What about it?" Zack was startled.

"I understand your clever friend went up there to look at the crime scene. What did he learn?"

Zack chuckled. "Where do you stand on Nimerigars?"

Janice's eyes widened. "What on earth are they?"

Zack had caught up. "According to many Southwest tribes, they were vicious little people who killed without provocation and live in caves."

Janice eyed him with arched eyebrows. "You have a reputation at the agency as the real-life Agent Mulder from Xfiles. I don't buy ghosts and extra-terrestrials in crime solving. You'll have to do better than that."

Zack shrugged. "Eagle Feather told me he sensed someone or something in the cave with him, but it was dark and he had no flashlight. One of those wild deputies took a shot at him from outside the cave, pinned him down. He said someone or something ran out of the cave with amazing speed and drew the deputies away."

"Took the pressure off him," Janice said.

"Exactly."

Janice shifted in her chair. "So that's all you've got for me, a ghost story."

Zack gave another shrug.

Janice kept her eyes on him. "Tell me how you came to use unauthorized FBI resources to forensically inspect your wife's sister's house in Kanab."

Zack fell behind again. "Well, someone tried to break in while Libby was there, almost succeeded. I'd been checking in with an old FBI colleague to see what was happening with the case; I told him about it. He sent a forensics man to try to learn the identity of the intruder."

"Your colleague is Pete Conley."

"Yes."

Janice's eyes were shimmering black points. "You could get your friend in a lot of trouble that way."

Zack hung his head. "I know. It was my fault. I put him in a position he felt he couldn't refuse."

"In a desperate attempt to safeguard your wife."

Zack nodded.

"Who deliberately put herself in harm's way this morning."

Zack glanced away. "Libby isn't particularly patient."

Janice leaned forward on her elbows. "Your wife is a very courageous woman. Sometimes such a woman is required to stir things up so men will get off their bums."

Zack had no idea how to respond to that.

Janice went on. "Libby put herself on the line, now we need to follow up. The sheriff will send the artist's conception out. All law enforcement in the area will be on the lookout. We have the color and model of the car, assuming it's the same one that's been parked near the house. If this guy is still out on the roads, we'll get him."

Janice paused to regard Zack. "Now follow me here. Everyone is convinced these two cases are connected. But we have to find evidence to support that. So we are left with several questions." Janice ticked them off on her fingers. "Is the man who snatched Libby the same man who kidnapped Luke Wilson? Did the same man who kidnapped Luke Wilson also kill him? Is he acting alone or is it a conspiracy? Who killed Dan Fogelberry? Is that case related? Who broke into Professor Philpott's home apparently intending to kill him?"

Zack raised his eyebrows at the last question.

She put up a hand. "You may not be aware of that incident, but hold your question." Janice went on to the next finger. "What is the significance of the watch Philpott found in the cave and does it point to the Mormons? If so, is the injunction to keep people out of the Preserve and keep the bones in it a chessboard move by the church or perhaps some element thereof?" Janice laughed. "I'm running out of fingers. In any case, we've got a lot of work in front of us."

"We?"

"Yes, Supervisory Agent Tolliver, I am bringing you back from retirement."

# CHAPTER FORTY-FIVE

"No, that's not going to happen!" Zack's response was automatic. He thought about the implications: past fights with Libby, long times away from her and Bernie, the malefactors who in the past followed him home and endangered his family—no, no way.

"We thought that would be your response."

"We?"

She smiled expansively. "Libby and I."

Zack was really shocked this time. "When on earth did you ever see Libby?"

Janice's smile became smug. "Just before coming here. I went to the hospital first and found her. You had gone home for a shower, apparently. I passed along the thoughts of the executive assistant director of Criminal Investigations, who feels you are unique in your particular skillset and are needed."

Zack stared. "Unique in what way? Hold on; don't answer that. You're looking for an Agent Mulder."

Janice peered at him questioningly.

"You've not seen the TV series, I gather. Agent Mulder and his partner investigate the X files, those cases with elements of the supernatural that other FBI agents won't touch."

She nodded. "Pretty much. To put it another way, the higher-ups noticed in you a particular ability to deal with cases involving cultures with, uh, sensitive beliefs."

Zack was dumfounded. "Libby agreed to this?"

"Not at first. But after I went over the special benefits we are prepared to offer you, she became more enthusiastic. She also remarked how retirement hasn't exactly brought your family together."

"Benefits?"

The smile was back. "Let's just say it's a good deal in terms of money, promotion, and work from home whenever you aren't involved in an active case. I'll go over the details with you later, but right now we've got a case to solve." She slid a badge across the table. "This identifies you as the new Director of Special Cases. Take it or leave it."

Zack felt a surge of gratitude toward Libby and the FBI. He realized he really missed the job but had squelched the feeling for the sake of his family.

"I need to make one call." He called Libby.

She answered immediately. "I thought I'd hear from you."

"And?"

"I think it is a wonderful opportunity, for you and for Bernie and me. I want you to accept."

Zack stared across the table at Janice. "I accept." He told Libby goodbye, arranged to pick her up at the hospital when she checked out in a few minutes.

Janice had been watching his face.

"Now, Agent Tolliver, let's make our roles clear. I am leading this investigation. I will be allowing you a certain amount of independence, I expect you'll take it anyway"—a quick grin—"but make no mistake, you must keep me in the loop." The eyes were ice again. "All the time."

Zack gave a sincere look. "I'll do my best."

"Okay, then. Here's your assignment. You begin with Libby's kidnapper. If Sheriff Rafferty has trouble with your involvement in that case, tell him the perp's intent was to smuggle Libby across a state line, hence into FBI jurisdiction. See if you can find a thread to connect that suspect to the two high school kids' murders."

Janice stood and smoothed out her black skirt.

Zack rose with her.

"Meanwhile, I'll keep working the boy's murder and all that goes with it. Hopefully, we'll meet in the middle."

Janice grabbed her purse and strode to the door. She was waiting for Zack as he exited.

"I assume you still have your pistol."

"It's in the glove compartment."

She turned to go, stopped. "About your Indian friend."

Zack raised his eyebrows.

She kept a straight face, but her eyes sparkled. "I know nothing about an Indian friend."

As Zack drove toward the hospital, he mulled over everything that had just happened. He knew it would take a long time for the implications to sink in: the details of his new position, what the expectations were, what it would mean to his life, and mostly what it would mean to his relationship with Libby. He was still in shock. Agent Hooper had managed to keep him off balance the entire meal, and just when he thought he had caught up, she offered him the job. He shook his head in wonder as he drove north to the hospital. He wasn't sure how he would begin his investigation. But he knew one thing for sure: he could arrange for Libby to go home now.

Libby was waiting on the concrete apron of the emergency ward. She was in the mandatory wheelchair but stood as soon as she saw Zack's red Jeep. Zack started to climb out to help her, but she waved him away.

"Home, James," she said with a smile.

Zack stared at her. "I'm not going to belabor you with my feelings about the chance you took, but I'm sure you are aware."

"Nothing that you don't do ten times a day," she said and pouted.

There was a silence between them.

"So, ready to go home?"

Libby's face lit up. "I certainly am."

"We'll go back to the house so you can pack. We'll leave your car where it is. I've arranged for an agent to follow you. If our stalker is still around, which I doubt, he won't recognize the agent's car. If a car tries to intercept you, the agent will know what to do."

"Just get me home."

Zack grinned. "Yes, ma'am."

* * * * *

"You have failed! Once again, you have failed!" The voice was terrible in its condemnation. "You abducted the wrong person yet again."

"The woman tricked me."

"And you let her go. How could you let her go?"

"I didn't know what to do. I was wrong then to kill the girl. I am wrong now not to kill the woman. I am confused."

"Did the woman see you, see your vehicle?"

"I...I don't know. She might have seen my face just before...she turned her head so quickly."

"The woman tricked you. She allowed herself to be caught just to see your face. And you let her go."

Loud gulping sound.

"But you should not worry. We are merciful. We have a plan."

"Yes, yes."

"You must now do as We command. You must follow Our plan exactly."

"I will. I will follow it exactly. Just tell me what to do."

"If you stray from the plan, We will seek vengeance. If you follow the plan exactly, you will be forgiven."

"Oh, yes, yes, I want forgiveness."

"Listen to me..."

* * * * *

A weight Zack scarcely knew he carried fell away when Libby drove off, the young FBI agent close behind her. Libby had been in constant danger here. Despite his attempts to safeguard her, despite her insistence he go off in pursuit of the killer, despite the sheriff's assurances she would be protected, Zack's attention had always been divided by worry for her safety. It made his investigation that more dangerous.

Zack sighed. Their parting had been tender, much like the early days. He'd allowed his feelings to come out of hibernation. He had also been concerned about little Bernie, away from his mother for so long, despite the thorough attention the boy was no doubt experiencing from his aunt and cousin. For now, Zack's subliminal concerns seemed resolved.

He was back in control, not just returned to his position as supervisory agent, but head of his own department in the area closest to his heart. How completely things had turned around, and so quickly.

His first call had been to Pete Conley to report his meeting with Janice Hooper and the news of his return to the FBI. It was a good conversation, a promise of renewed friendship. Next, he called Eagle Feather, but his friend's phone went to voicemail. Zack grinned to himself, imagining the Navajo was with Shana. His third call was to Sheriff Rafferty.

Rafferty seemed delighted by Zack's news. Finally, I can work with the FBI, not in spite of them, he said. He also had a development to share. The vehicle involved in Libby's kidnapping had been seen by witnesses, not just once but twice. One witness had seen her pushed out of the vehicle. This witness described the 1961-1968 maroon Travelall already on the police watch list. But even better, the same vehicle had been seen on the Cliff Road northeast of Hildale. Even better than that, the road reached a dead end at a farm near the cliffs. Only two other dwellings were located along that road. Sheriff Rafferty had asked the Marshall's Department in Colorado City to secure the road to prevent escape.

"On my way," Zack said. He gunned the Jeep's engine and headed south out of town on 89A. It took just a half hour to reach Hildale, another five minutes to find Cliff Road. When he arrived, he found a Washington County Sheriff's Department vehicle blocking the narrow road. Zack passed his credentials to the deputy, who nodded and started for his car to move it. Zack told him not to bother, put the Jeep in low four-wheel-drive and pulled around it.

There was no sign of activity at either of the other two properties along the way, so Zack kept going. Ahead were flashing blue and red lights. He had reached the farm at the road's end. Another deputy intercepted him and asked for his credentials.

"Agent Tolliver, we were told to expect you. Here's what's happening; a guy in the house back up the road has seen the Travelall come and go, says it belongs to this farm. Sheriff Max Smith has taken over here. He's waiting for you up ahead."

Zack thanked the man and followed the road to a bend. Beyond it was a wide, unkempt yard and a white, derelict farmhouse surrounded by several large trees. Behind the house was a large barn. There were no vehicles in sight.

A short wiry man in uniform detached himself from the brush nearby and waved to Zack.

"Tolliver? I'm Max Smith, sheriff of Washington County." He extended his hand.

"Agent Zack Tolliver. How'd you get here from St. George so quick?"

The sheriff chuckled. "I could lie and tell you about my jet helicopter, but fact is I was already here in Colorado City when the alarm went out."

His face went serious. "Situation is this: at least one suspect somewhere on the grounds. The suspect's vehicle, the International Travelall was seen driving toward this property and has not left." Smith gestured back toward the flashing blue lights. "He must know we are here, but there's been no sign of activity. We need to be wary of a rifle until we know what's what."

Zack stared at the house, then the barn. If the SUV indeed was here, it had to be in the barn or somewhere out beyond it, hidden. As the sheriff said, there was no sign of life anywhere.

"How many men have you got?"

"Just the two deputies you saw coming in, and two more in the trees here."

Zack rubbed his chin. "That's not enough to surround or to go in with force. We don't want to send anyone across that open ground."

"If I may offer a suggestion?"

Zack nodded.

"One of my boys has a new toy." The sheriff waved an arm toward the trees. A man ran toward them at a crouching run with something in his hands.

Zack saw what he had. A drone! Perfect!

The deputy knelt near Zack and Smith and placed the drone on the ground, then looked up at the sheriff.

The sheriff looked at Zack.

"Let's get an overhead view all around the house," Zack said.

"Yes, sir." The deputy sent the drone off. He had a small screen he shared with Zack, and they watched through the camera eye as the drone flew.

The unmanned aircraft hovered high above the lawn, moved slowly toward the house. Fifty feet away, it began a slow circumnavigation just below the roofline. All was quiet.

"Can you peek in the windows?"

"We can try, but they may be too dirty or reflective."

They watched the screen as the house came close and the large windows appeared. The drone flew one to another, but as the deputy had feared, they were too dirty for the camera to penetrate.

"I'm going in," Zack told the sheriff. "Watch for me with your bird. Give me a holler if you see anything." He grabbed the deputy's radio and sprinted across the lawn and leaped up the porch steps. With his pistol drawn, he stretched an arm to the door and pushed. It creaked open.

"Hello in the house. We are federal agents. Come out where I can see you with your hands above your head."

The house was tomblike in its stillness. Zack pushed the door with his foot until he could see down a long empty hall. He waved the sheriff's men to cross the lawn as he stepped inside and moved swiftly room to room. All were empty. The deputies arrived at the door in a rush and Zack motioned them up the stairs to the second floor, all the while knowing the house was empty. Along with the dust and mildew smell there was a dead feel to the place.

He went through to the back porch and studied the big barn, a hundred feet away across a debris covered yellow lawn. The drone whirred above him. He radioed the operator to fly it toward the barn and ran there under it. He arrived shoulder to wall by the huge barn door, fully open on its sliders. His firearm poised, he called a warning. There was no response, no movement, no sound.

Zack was uncertain, for a fleeting moment thought to wait for backup, but he worried the suspect might make an escape out the back. He spun inside against the inner barn wall. The smell of hay, motor oil, roosting birds came to his nose. He crouched, his eyes adjusting. The great barn interior was dusky and silent. The far door was framed with a large square of bright light. In the center of the light was the silhouette of a tall man.

Zack aimed his pistol. "Put your hands in the air and get down on your knees," he yelled. The figure made a slow turn away, but otherwise did not respond. The man turned slowly back toward Zack. As he did there was a strange creaking sound.

"I said raise your hands. Get on your knees or I'll shoot."
Zack moved toward him. The figure twisted slowly away
again, then back with the same strange creak. The man's head
was tilted in a funny way.

Zack understood. He holstered his pistol and walked
up to the hanging man. A rope stretched from his neck up to
the doorframe. A stool lay on its side under his feet. The old
man's eyes were open, his facial expression one of sublime
resignation. Zack felt the body, it was cold. He moved an
arm. Rigor mortis had not yet set in. The old man had not
been dead very long.

Zack glanced around the barn interior. He saw the
International Harvester Travelall parked next to two other
partially covered vehicles. He could tell one of them was a
maroon sedan.

The sheriff's deputies arrived at the far barn door in a
rush. Zack waved them in.

# CHAPTER FORTY-SIX

"Hey, J.D., you better get over here to the farm. Cynthia's old man is hanging in the barn like a side of beef in a freezer."

Jeffrey listened to Deputy Stan Taylor, thanked him as calmly as he could and hung up the phone. He sat in his office chair unmoving for several minutes while he decided how to handle this with his wife. He was strangely overcome by the news; he'd grown fond of the old guy despite his shenanigans. Jeffrey had a feeling his father-in-law's death was only the beginning in a very trying period yet to come.

Quiet chatter between his two wives came to him as they washed the lunch dishes and readied the kitchen and dining room for the evening meal. The children were at school, but he'd have to help the women with a plan to disclose the news to the young ones. He was most worried about Cynthia. She loved the old man, she had done everything for him; when she married Jeffrey, she brought him with her to keep and protect him. But the old man was his own worst enemy. No one could protect him from himself.

Jeffrey sighed and rose to his feet, leaving his work file open on the desktop. He'd need help from his first wife, Patti, with this problem; but then he must go to the farm and try to understand what Jedediah had done.

FBI forensics agents were busy in the barn when Jeffrey arrived. The twin deputies and the boys from the local sheriff's department were guarding the crime scene but parted silently when they recognized Jeffrey. He walked through the barn to the far door where two men were examining his father-in-law. Jeffrey glanced around at the barn floor, the toppled stool, and the rope, a poly-manila half-inch thick type used for heavy work. Jeffrey knelt to study the knot.

"My condolences."

Jeffrey turned, glanced up to see a man of medium height in jeans with blue eyes matching his blue flannel shirt.

He wore nothing to identify him as law enforcement other than an air of authority.

"You must be Deputy Harlow."

He stood. "I am Jeffrey Harlow."

"I am Special Agent Zack Tolliver. I believe this man is your father-in-law?"

"Yes, sir, he is. Did he...?"

Tolliver shook his head. "So far we've no reason to believe anything other than suicide. We'll go over the rope and stool for prints and DNA at the lab. The boys have begun dusting the barn surfaces for prints." Zack gazed at Jeffrey. "Have you any reason to believe this wasn't a suicide?"

"No, I don't."

Agent Tolliver's eyes searched his. "Is there something else, Deputy?"

Jeffrey shook his head. He needed to think it all out before disclosing his suspicions to the Feds.

Tolliver's eyes swept the crime scene. "Have you seen that rope before?"

"No, but it could have been around and I just didn't notice, like up in the loft or somewhere."

"What about the stool?"

Jeffrey scratched his head. "Well, that's funny, actually. I'm pretty sure I last saw it in the utility room in the house."

Tolliver's gaze swung back to Jeffrey. "When were you here last, Deputy?"

Here it comes, Jeffrey thought. "I was here yesterday afternoon."

"With the deceased?"

"No, looking for him. He hadn't been showing up at my home for meals of late and my wife was growing worried."

"Did you find him?"

"No, I didn't. Nor did he show up at the house last night." Jeffrey looked at the body on the barn floor. Two men were encasing it in a body bag. He felt an involuntary shudder as it zipped. He turned to Agent Tolliver. "When do they think this happened?"

The agent had hands on hips, watching the men settle the body on a gurney. "They're guessing somewhere around late afternoon to early evening yesterday." He cocked his head toward Jeffrey. "Deputy, I'll need you to write down everything you saw yesterday when you were here, every detail you can remember. I know you'll be busy with your family tonight, but please do the best you can. We can meet here tomorrow morning and have a quiet chat."

Jeffrey nodded and backed away, then turned and walked swiftly out of the barn, past the ambulance and cruisers. He felt strangely suffocated while in the barn. He needed time to think how to help Cynthia get through these next few hours.

\* \* \* \* \*

Back in St. George, Agent in Charge Janice Hooper dispatched a forensics team to Salt Lake City to inspect the BYU lab where the bone robbery took place and another to Professor Philpott's home. She had no great expectations, but you never knew. She was still waiting for final forensic conclusions regarding the standoff at the Musser ranch, although it was all a foregone conclusion. Issuing a sigh, she turned to the grunt work—the large mover's carton residing on her desk. It was filled with files and papers taken from the Musser ranch, all enveloped in individual FBI envelopes labeled with the place of origin—study desk, kitchen, hall closet, etc.—twenty-one thick envelopes in all. Somewhere among all those papers there might be a clue. Janice would love to delegate this, but she knew she was the only one who could do the job effectively; she was the one who had all the facts of the case. She set to work.

* * * * *

Zack watched Deputy Jeffrey Danes Harlow stride away across the littered lawn. He had watched the way the man viewed his father-in-law's body, his attention to the knot that secured the noose, the look on his face when he spoke about the stool. One thing for sure—Deputy Harlow did not believe this was a suicide. Zack tended to agree.

Yet, the implications were huge. If the old man did not kill himself, it meant someone else was involved in the murder. It opened the door to the possibility of a conspiracy. To Zack's mind, such a development would change the entire nature of the crime from the irrational acts of a demented old man to a carefully choreographed, premeditated murder—but to what purpose?

Zack grunted to himself. He needed to slow down, to take one step at a time. He must wait for the science team to finish scouring the crime scene, listen to their findings, and go from there.

* * * * *

Libby breathed a huge sigh of relief when she reached the intersection of 89A and 89 and swung south. All along the lonely drive beneath the towering escarpment of the Escalante Wilderness her eyes had flicked to her rearview mirror. The only car she ever saw in it was the FBI agent's black SUV, sometimes close, sometimes farther back, but always there.

There was never a question in Libby's mind about going home to Bernie and the girls, yet she felt she'd left a job unfinished. When Agent Hooper had stopped in and explained the agency's plan for Zack, if he agreed, she'd felt no hesitancy in saying yes. She knew Zack missed the job, missed the problem solving aspect, even missed the danger, probably. Libby needed him to be a father to their son, a wife to her, a presence in their home, but at the same time felt guilt for standing between him and his life work that meant so much to him. Agent Hooper had offered the perfect compromise, and Libby immediately said yes.

There were more cars on U.S. 89; it was the direct route from Page and Lake Powell to Flagstaff and every tourist in the world found their way along it at one time or another. Her FBI escort disappeared from the mirror from time to time, caught behind a truck hauling a trailer or cars hopscotching through traffic in haste to get somewhere or other. But the black SUV always reappeared sooner or later. To Libby's mind, no one had followed her at any point along the barren stretches of 89A, and that pretty much eliminated any prospect of someone following her now. She sat back and hummed along with the radio.

* * * * *

Oliver Rafferty was irritated—no, more than that—he was pissed. After his promise to Zack Tolliver, he had nearly gone and lost the man's wife; actually, had lost the man's wife. As it turned out, it was all because of missed communication between Chief Deputy William Brown and Deputy Clay Robinson, to whom the surveillance was assigned. Brown insisted he passed the order along to Robinson—Robinson claimed he never received it.

Rafferty accepted Brown's word and reprimanded Robinson. He leaned heavily on his chief deputy and had always found his trust rewarded. Deputy Robinson also had a sterling record and had never before missed a duty assignment. Now, Rafferty couldn't find Brown. His chief deputy had gone out to Hurricane this morning to meet that FBI Agent. He'd reported back from there with the welcome

news that Agent Hooper was willing to look at the two cases
as possibly linked and keep the sheriff's office informed. He'd
then expected Brown to return directly, but that was hours
ago. Now events were piling up faster than shit from a duck,
and he couldn't reach Brown. They'd found the Travelall at a
farm in Hildale, where some old guy had hung himself. The
case was blowing wide open, he needed his chief deputy at
the scene, but the man wasn't responding to either his radio
or cell phone. What the F***!"

* * * * *

Eagle Feather had a warm feeling in the middle of his chest as
he walked to his truck, and he knew it wasn't the coffee. He
also knew he'd find an excuse to come back to see Shana.

In his truck, he settled back in the worn and torn
driver's seat and called Zack, who answered immediately.

"What's new?" Eagle Feather asked.

Zack told him about the Travelall and Jedediah and
was it suicide or murder? "I'm inclined toward the latter," he
said.

"Umm. Just the tip of the iceberg, you think?"

"What would a Navajo know about icebergs?"

"I know most of it is hidden under water."

"Yeah, so now we have to figure out who else might
have been involved in the murders and why they don't want
Jedediah around anymore."

"I guess they don't want him to talk."

"Murder is a drastic step," Zack said. "Jedediah must
have known something important." He paused. His tone
became mischievous. "So what did Shana have to say?"

Eagle Feather could almost hear his smirk. "Get over
it, White Man. And now that you ask, Shana was not
surprised at what we saw. It was as if bears turn into shamans
every day for her. I suspect I am not the first to tell her such a
story."

"Did she tell you what it means?"

"We think it means there is a shaman living in that cave who can turn into a huge bear any time he wants. That is enough for me."

"Well, all right then." He paused. "There is news on my end." Zack went on to tell Eagle Feather of his reinstatement in the FBI and the special unit he would oversee. He chuckled as he described Janice's attitude toward Eagle Feather.

"So you are now official and I do not exist," Eagle Feather said. He paused. "I think I like that," he said.

Zack laughed. "I thought you might." His tone now was solemn. "Truth be told, I do not believe this is a suicide. I think we are headed for deeper water. Watch your tail feathers, my friend."

# CHAPTER FORTY-SEVEN

Eagle Feather spent the afternoon at Pipe Springs National Monument's Southern Paiute Ethnology exhibit. It was not large, but it was specific to the Paiute people who inhabited the region when the Mormons arrived. In addition, the ranger on duty was knowledgeable and had access to materials not displayed. She was most willing to assist him, probably as an antidote for boredom. There were no other visitors.

His research confirmed Shana's words; the area had served Ancestral Puebloan and Paiute Indians for one thousand years. Yet all the people were essentially hunter/gatherers who came, raised some crops with the aid of the spring water, and eventually moved on when nearby resources were exhausted. Some tribes returned either seasonally or years later. He found no documents to support the idea any population spent time on the mountain summits other than to pursue escaping game. So who had inhabited the cave?

Eagle Feather held a master's degree in anthropology from Arizona State University. He was aware of theories suggesting a Mayan and Aztecan influence on the people who first occupied much of the desert Southwest. Along with Aztec culture might have come the practice of animal or even human sacrifice. Could the cave and the altar-like slab in the hidden arroyo have served the nefarious purposes of long ago priests and shamans?

The sun was low above the distant western mountains, still capped with snow, now glistening like tinsel far beyond the plateau. The high desert around him was cast in shades of maroon and ginger across which long black shadows probed. A sense of peace came to Eagle Feather as he stepped from the air-conditioned building into the stillness of the desert, the sand still warm from the heat of the day, with a cool breeze promising the chill of the night to come.

He drove the short distance to the campground. There he built a fire. While he waited for the flames to reduce to hot coals, he lay back on his blanket roll and let his eyelids droop, lulled by the scent of sage in his nose, the crackling of the fire in his ears.

Something caused him to open his eyes. Across from him sat Sam, cross-legged, his back ramrod straight. It was darker now. Eagle Feather realized he must have fallen asleep.

"The magic of the desert has overcome you," Sam said.

"It seems so."

Sam gave a slight smile. "You and your white friend have seen much desert magic recently. Do you wish to know more?"

Eagle Feather hesitated, studied Sam, then nodded.

"I can help you learn," Sam said. "But to do so, we must go on a journey."

"Is it far?"

"Our spirits will travel while our bodies remain, but"–– Sam put up a restraining hand— "you must want to go and you must trust."

Eagle Feather felt he should do this. He hitched himself up and sat cross-legged in a mirror image of Sam. "I am ready."

Sam reached into a carry bag on his belt and retrieved a Ziploc bag. From it he extracted round plantlike objects.

Eagle Feather was familiar with it. "Peyote," he said.

Sam nodded.

"I have taken such journeys before," Eagle Feather said.

Sam handed four Peyote buttons to Eagle Feather. "This trip will be different. I will be your guide on this journey. There is a place I wish to take you." At Eagle Feather's questioning glance, Sam smiled. "I am a shaman. It is something I do."

"You are a man of many parts," Eagle Feather said
with respect.

The men chewed the bitter fruit. They chatted quietly
on various subjects waiting for the plant to have its effect.
Once the magic began, Eagle Feather knew to let go and
allow Sam to guide him through each level. The shaman
would suggest the way yet remain in the background.
Time slowed, dwindled, and became meaningless. Colors
grew vivid, expressed first in a bright whirling kaleidoscope
before melting into vague shapes. Eagle Feather was an
observer in a new world, a tiny passenger in space surrounded
by waves of distortion. The fire before him had become a
burst of flowers of incredible variety and beauty, his hand
before his face grew large and he journeyed close to it and the
palm wrinkles became arroyos he could enter and follow to
unknown destinations. He floated in a pool of wellbeing; safe,
secure, content.

The outline of a face quivered and formed before
him, slowly grew into Sam's face. "Follow me." The mouth
on the Sam face had not moved, yet somehow the unspoken
words formed in Eagle Feather's mind. He heard singing. The
mouth moved now, the face wrinkled and cracked, the hair
turned gray and dry, the eyes sunk into dark depressions, the
mouth grew narrow and tight. Eagle Feather felt the presence
of power, of ageless wisdom. The bodiless countenance drew
him through space and he followed and came to a different
place—a dell formed among tall pine trees with lustrous
green grass underfoot. A stream bubbled nearby. Beyond it
rose a tall cliff, and in its base a large cave. Structures of mud
brick surrounded the cave. Creatures walked among the
dwellings, human beings at first glance, but with hair over
most of their bodies and naked but for waistcloths. As he
watched, a figure emerged from one of the structures,
bending low through the portal. It stood upright and stared in
Eagle Feather's direction. It was a creature like the others, but
it had Sam's face.

270

Other figures like them came from the nearby wood. They brought with them a human being. Their captive was reluctant, jabbed and poked from behind whenever he hesitated. He was smaller than his captors, his facial features finer and more distinct, his body hairless but for a thatch of black hair on his head. He, too, wore a waistcloth.

The creatures propelled the human toward the one with Sam's face. The other creatures came and gathered around. The human stood in the center of the circle, a midget among giants.

Eagle Feather felt himself float closer. He could see the human's features clearer now; saw that the man was like him, yet not, his forehead sloped with thick eyebrows on pronounced ridges and large nostrils. The man's eyes were round with fear.

One of his captors held up weapons, an atlatl and a long spear, indicating he had taken them from the human. There was discussion among the creatures. Somehow Eagle Feather understood the human had attacked one of them with the weapon. They released the human in front of the creature with Sam's face. The man went to his knees, prostrate, fawning, terrified.

The Sam creature began to change, his face dissolved into the face of the old shaman. For several moments, the shaman gazed upon the human with an expression of deep sadness. Then, abruptly, his face changed once again. It swelled, the mouth and nose pushed out to a snout, the eyes grew small and black, the ears lifted to perch high on a huge furry head, the body grew large and coarse black hair sprouted on it, nails sprung into long claws. The shaman had turned into a huge bear.

The behemoth lifted its mighty head, tilted it to one side and threw open its jaws. Foaming spittle erupted from its mouth; its long white fangs gleamed. It roared. The sound turned Eagle Feather's blood to ice water.

It lowered its head toward the human, and mercifully the scene wavered, swirled and eddied, and became an indistinct wash of color and motion. A small dot appeared in the center of the turmoil and grew and grew until it became Sam's face floating like a balloon before Eagle Feather's eyes. The face spoke.

"We were here at the beginning," he said. "When your people came, they were naked, weak, frightened, but you had fire. The fire gave you power. Despite your puniness, you prospered and multiplied. We took refuge in the deepest forest to escape your arrows and spears." Sam's face floated closer. "You tamed the plants and animals, bent them to your purpose. You cleared away the trees and built your cities. We stayed in the forests, lived among the animals and plants. We observed them and learned from them; how the caterpillar changes to a butterfly, how the bear hides away for the winter, how the tree lives on for centuries. We studied and learned their ways and gained their powers. We walk the earth and pass before you and you do not see us. Your eyes are too full of the small details of your world, a world that accomplishes nothing but your own destruction."

The balloon face of Sam bobbled and floated off and shrunk into the swirling magma of color and grew large again and now it was the face of the old shaman. The ancient one's eyes held Eagle Feather.

"I live in harmony with my world. Your people come into it and disrupt it. They bring with them deceit and destruction and killing. I have existed in peace here for many of your lifetimes and will continue for more to come." The shaman's eyes closed for a moment. When they opened again, Eagle Feather stared into the red angry eyes of the bear.

"There are those among you who would disturb my rest, who carry murder in their heads and hearts. They must be sacrificed." After speaking these words the face became the shaman wearing a countenance of deep sorrow until, bit-by-bit, he faded away.

There was a rush of air against Eagle Feather's face, and he felt a sensation of flying. The swirling miasma pulled him into a long tunnel. At the far end, bright as the moon on a dark night, an orb grew larger and larger and he was thrust into it and indistinct colors and forms began to take on shapes and become firm. His eyes opened. The fire had died to coals. The space opposite him was empty.

# CHAPTER FORTY-EIGHT

Tubs left the McDonalds parking area with a muffler roar loud enough to bring a stern look from a cop in a black and white just entering the lot. Tubs thought the cop might stop him, but he didn't. Tubs eased up on the accelerator anyway, figuring he had enough on his mind without worrying about getting a citation.

His mind was on everything he'd just learned from Agent Hooper and the Philpott guy. Tubs saw himself as a good judge of character and was pretty sure the overeducated gerbil was telling the truth about the attempt on his life. There was a conspiracy going on here, sure as shit, and he had no doubt it involved that crazy church.

Tubs thought about Musser. He'd known Randy pretty well. Sure, they never hung out together, but you can't hunt with a man and sleep in a little two-man tent with him in the bitter cold and not learn something about him. Yeah, Randy was stubborn, Randy was a bit radical, Randy liked to jump into causes hook, line and sinker. But Randy wasn't a martyr. Tubs knew his friend would never lay down his life for a cause; he wouldn't lay down his life for anything. Randy liked his life too much and feared death even more.

So why'd he fight the FBI down to the last bullet? Tubs didn't think he did. But if not, was it an accident, what with all the bullets flying around? That didn't seem likely; Randy knew how to keep his head down. But if not that, then what? Murder?

Tubs thought about the recent attempt on his life. Again, it didn't fit the Randy Musser he knew to call and order his murder the moment Tubs stepped out the door. On the contrary, Randy had seemed relieved, conciliatory, and above all, his usual ingenuous self. It just didn't fit.

Yet no one else knew he'd be on that particular stretch of road at that particular time. Randy must have called someone who in turn called the assassin. Who would Randy most likely call after Tubs left the ranch? If he had to bet, he'd say Randy called someone in his church, someone he felt compelled to tell what he'd told Tubs, maybe to say he was not going through with the plan. By doing that he'd have signed a death warrant for himself and for Tubs. Who had he called?

Randy carried a cell phone on their hunts. He once told Tubs he used it everywhere but home. Ironically, he had no reception at the ranch. The FBI would have taken his cell phone, checked it thoroughly. But had they checked the landline phone? It was a question worth asking.

Agent Hooper told him the FBI removed everything from the ranch not nailed down. She was going through it all with a fine-tooth comb back at her office. The ranch was a crime scene, off bounds to all but FBI. But with anything of interest stripped away, would they still be guarding the place? Tubs didn't think so. He also thought he'd like to take a gander to try to determine for himself how Randy died.

Tubs performed an abrupt U-turn and headed back west toward Hurricane and I-15 and Musser's house. Near the ranch, worried about the conspicuous dust cloud he was raising, he turned off onto a set of overgrown ruts toward the western pasture. He knew this route and his slower speed would cut down the dust. From the western pasture, he could loop back on the ranch house from the far side. If he saw activity at the house from there, he could go back the way he came.

It worked out. Crime scene tape fluttered in the lonely breeze, but the house was empty when he approached on foot. He creaked open the back screen door and stepped into the mudroom, which led directly into the kitchen, the scene of Randy's death. The large sliding windows above the sink were blown out by the teargas grenades. Crime scene analysts had marked the floor with red crayon; Musser's body was outlined. A large volume of blood was at the head, consistent with suicide by gun.

Tubs remembered a snatch of a statement, something Agent Hooper had mentioned, that the sniper on the hill opened fire feeling an agent in the house was in danger. Tubs studied the crayon outline. The body's angle, oblique to the window, did not seem consistent with a bullet fired from the hill.

Stepping back, Tubs worked out a scenario in his mind from the evidence before him. The attempted suicide wound was from a pistol, purportedly Randy's. The kill wound was from a rifle. Tubs wondered how far the FBI had gone with this. Had they found the bullet from Musser's head wound and compared ballistics to his pistol? Had they assumed the chest wound, the kill wound, had come from the sniper on the hill? Tubs saw something different.

The question was, which came first, the kill wound or the suspected suicide wound? To Tubs' eye, the pistol shot to the side of the head would not necessarily cause Randy to fall backward, as he had. More likely, it would cause a side or forward fall, maybe dropping him to a kneeling position. The body outline he saw showed a man flat on his back, his head turned away from the window. Blood from the head wound had pooled where the head had been. Blood splatter that could only have been from the torso exit wound spread spear-like around the body outline, some smeared where he fell, the spearhead pointing not toward the hill but toward the rear door.

Tubs shook his head, trying to work up alternate scenarios, but could not. To his mind, from his experience reading sign, Randy had been shot by a rifle through the chest from somewhere near the rear door. The impact knocked him on his back. After that, a coup de grace was administered as Randy lay on his back, dying. But there was no bullet impact on the floor near the head. To avoid that, it had to have come from a strange angle, the pistol aimed upward from the floor through the back side of the head, not from above through the brainpan. Tubs scanned the floor and walls for other evidence, found it on the kitchen wall in the form of wide spread splatter. There were many bullet holes in the wall from the fusillade of shots coming into the room from advancing agents. A hole made by the pistol bullet could hide easily among them.

Tubs left the crime scene and retreated to the Scout convinced someone in the FBI had killed Randy after he had surrendered, and made it appear like suicide. The question was what could he do about it?

He climbed back into the Scout, ground the gears, reversed direction and rolled back along the ruts. His thoughts were as dark as the shadows cast by sun. Who could he trust?

Tubs shook his head. He wanted to trust Agent Hooper, but could he? What if Randy had been murdered on her orders? How could he know?

Somehow, he needed to learn the scope of this conspiracy. Until then, he couldn't trust anybody.

# CHAPTER FORTY-NINE

The head of the FBI Scientific Response Team was a petite mouse-haired young woman with blue eyes and a pug nose wearing an expression of never-ending excitement named Lori Hyde. Zack liked her immediately. She had a lot to say.

Her team had explored everything, from identifying all the smears and stains on the barn floor to finding every foreign fiber on the automobile carpets. When she approached Zack, she had a jack handle encased in plastic in her hand.

"Hey, boss, I've got something good for you. We found this jack handle in the Travelall. It's got blood on it. We did an analysis and compared it to the blood sample on file for the high school girl killed in Kanab. It's a match. There's no doubt the Travelall was involved in that murder; we found the same blood on the floor carpet. We won't do your job for you, but there's a pretty easy connection there."

Zack nodded and smiled. "Good work, Lori. Pieces are coming together."

Lori frowned. "Not all of them. We've been studying the knot that secured the rope around the neck of the victim. It looks like an attempt was made at a hangman's knot—the correct number of wraps, all very tidy. But they screwed up. Where they should have begun with two bights, they made only one, so ultimately it was not a slipknot. Yet he was hanging with it tight around his neck and the knot tucked behind his ear."

Zack frowned. "Spell it out for me."

Lori slowed herself down. "He could not have tied it himself on his own neck. If it had been done properly, his weight would have drawn it tight when he fell. Not this knot, though. Someone had to tie it on him, it won't slip. We'll need to do further blood analysis at the lab for drugs, but we have a suspicion he was unconscious when the hanging took place." Her blue eyes twinkled. "We don't want to do your job for you, but—"

"But we have a murder, not a suicide, on our hands, right?"

She smiled, bobbed her head.

"I was coming to that conclusion also. With that in mind, please advise me of all fingerprints, blood, footprints, or other identifying markers not belonging to the victim, no matter who, along with the time frame of their appearance, as close as you can, as soon as you can. Okay?"

The smile remained. "No problem, boss."

Zack walked through the great door at the back of the barn and up the path toward the family burial site. He found a sunny spot and let his mind whir on as his eyes went absently from headstone to headstone. To decide his next step, he needed to understand the order of things. It now seemed clear old Jedediah was an instrument in someone's hand, the Avenging Angel of old time Mormonism. The eccentric, completely indoctrinated Mormon pioneer would have been easy to manipulate given the right message, one depicted as coming directly from God, no doubt. That message would have to be explicit and specific. The conspirators must prevent Jedediah from wandering off and murdering the wrong people. He would need specific directions around how to handle the victims, where to deposit the bodies. That was a lot of detail for a simple holy message from the Almighty. Zack shook his head, wondering how it had been done.

He now knew for a fact there was at least one other person involved, but his instincts told him there were more. How many more, how far or high the conspiracy went were questions to be answered. He hoped Lori's work would supply some answers. For now, he had to be patient. And, it was time to check in. He called Janice.

"Agent Hooper."

"Hi, Janice, it's Zack. We've got the man responsible for the murders of Luke Wilson and Beth Daniels." Zack's loud voice in the lonely graveyard seemed almost a sacrilege.

Zack heard a quick intake of breath. "Well, Agent Tolliver, that was quick. It seems your reputation is deserved."

"Would that I could accept the compliment, but this was all Sheriff Rafferty," Zack said. "Problem is, the perpetrator is dead and we're momentarily at a dead end."

"You have sufficient evidence to confirm the guilt?"

"Yes, we do."

"Who is it?"

"A man named Jedediah Meekes. He's old school Mormon, a confirmed fundamentalist. He'd be an easy man to steer by someone leveraging him through his faith."

"So you suspect he didn't act alone."

"We know that from the evidence. Just how much, and why, are the questions to answer."

"Well, Agent Tolliver, it's clear the investigation is in good hands. Keep me in the loop."

Zack could almost see her white teeth gleaming as she signed off. He glanced around at the gravestones again. Some looked very new, very recent. He tried to juggle the names and dates into a pattern. He thought he found the old man's wife, dead a while now, but there were several younger people, apparently the old man's children. He must indeed have felt afflicted, yet his faith never abated. He wondered where Deputy Jeffrey Danes Harlow fit in. He was related by marriage, he'd said, and obviously felt responsibility for Jedediah—was it through his wife or through some other connection? One thing was certain; the man was holding something back.

Zack turned and walked back down the slope toward the barn. It was time to pay Deputy Harlow a visit.

\* \* \* \* \*

The difference in culture between Hildale, Utah, and any other town was evident in the high walls of private compounds that made the street feel almost tunnel-like. This neighborhood was a dead zone for Zack's way-finder app, but he had a physical address with a house number and he found it painted on the curb. He drove up to the gate panel tower and pressed the talk button. Deputy Harlow's voice answered and the gate slowly swung open. By the time Zack drove up the gravel drive and pulled up in front of the house, Deputy Harlow was there to greet him at the top of the steps.

"Thank you for coming, Agent Tolliver. I've been attempting to console my wife, but she has questions I can't answer."

Zack's smile was understanding. "We all have questions, but many will have to go unanswered for a while yet."

Harlow showed him into a large foyer with tall steps ascending on either side to a second story gallery with a banister. There appeared to be halls disappearing off to either side. A large, impressive home.

He led Zack to a sitting room and went off in search of his wife. Shortly, he reappeared with an attractive young woman whose upright posture and tight chin hinted at strong character. At this moment, her eyes were moist, her grief evident.

She took a seat on the sofa, her husband next to her. Zack found a chair facing them.

Harlow placed a hand on his wife's arm. "This is my Cynthia," he said. "She has worked hard to care for her aged father, but he was not the most cooperative of subjects."

Cynthia smiled wistfully. "I think my husband means headstrong, stubborn, and arrogant about his beliefs. His faith was ever strong in him. If it directed him a certain way, there was no turning him back."

"Did you have any idea what he was up to?" Zack asked.

"I still don't know what he was up to." Cynthia shook her head in disbelief. "Jeffrey is trying to tell me he took his own life and might be responsible for murdering someone. I can not believe that is true."

Zack gave a sympathetic nod. "Why can't you believe it, Mrs. Harlow?"

"I just don't believe my father would take a life unless to survive." Her eyes were wide, intense. "If he did, it would have to be from some deep commitment, some overpowering belief. But he would never take his own life." She held up a protesting hand. "And before you suggest he might commit suicide to protect his family from scandal or police questioning or some sort of skewed publicity, my answer is no, he would not, because if he felt his act was righteous, he would stand by it."

Harlow laid a hand on her shoulder.

"Well, you've already answered most of my questions," Zack said. "You've given me insight into the way your father thinks." He hesitated, caught her eye. "Unfortunately, the evidence is compelling. It tells us your father may have committed not just one, but two murders. The first, the killing of the young high school boy was done in such a way as to suggest there was a religious motive behind his action. The second was the murder of a young girl, also from the high school. At the moment, we believe that murder was a case of mistaken identity, an attempt to kill a different girl he thought might have witnessed his first act."

"Oh, my God." Cynthia was overcome for several long moments, sobs caught in her throat. "I just can't...I just can't see him doing that."

Deputy Harlow turned to his wife. "What if someone high in the church, someone he deeply respected ordered him to do these things?"

"I still can't see it. He would have to believe it was a direct order from God to do such awful things. And even then..." The sobs broke free now, shaking her.

Zack stood. "I'm deeply sorry to have bothered you at a time like this, Mrs. Harlow. I know it is very difficult for you." As he turned to leave, he caught Deputy Harlow's eye and nodded toward the door.

Zack stepped out into the early evening light and let out a long breath. Deputy Harlow joined him a moment later.

"Was what you heard me say news to you?" Zack asked.

Harlow gave a wry smile. "News, yes. But I had my suspicions, so surprise, no."

"Where had your suspicions come from?"

Harlow scratched his head. "I hadn't really formed them until recently. You see, Jedediah found the transition to my home difficult, despite having his own little house and despite everything Cynthia tried to do to make him happy and comfortable. He would take off from time to time, sometimes for as long as forty-eight hours. We'd wait, and sure enough he'd be back seeming much more relaxed and content about things." Jeffrey crossed his arms, stared out at the compound gate. "Lately, though, he was disappearing for much longer periods of time. Cynthia was quite distraught, and I spent way too much of my official time out searching for him." Harlow paused, looked at Zack. "You may not know this, but I was the first law enforcement agent called to the scene up on Canaan Mountain. I saw the boy impaled on that stick. It was not a pretty sight. Never in a million years did it cross my mind Cynthia's dad could possibly have had anything to do with it. I still can't believe it. But this past week, while hunting for him when he absented himself for days at a time, I stumbled on some things at his farm that left me wondering."

"Such as...?"

"Such as a stack of freshly laundered sheets in the house when everything else was filthy, a box of latex gloves in the laundry room that seemed out of context, for starters. There were some strange things in the barn, too. The old man liked automobiles and machinery and was good with them. He'd had to sell most of the machinery off to make ends meet, so I was surprised to find the three vehicles in the barn were operational, and that he had driven at least two of them recently. I couldn't understand where he went in them. But I really became concerned when I saw newspapers containing the murder articles on his workbench, along with a pile of rags and a bottle of chloroform." Harlow shrugged. "I guess I pretty much knew he was involved at that point."

"I saw you react when you inspected the rope today."

"I knew he didn't tie that around his own neck. Not like that. Like Cynthia said, Jedediah is—was not the sort to take his own life. And even if he did, he wouldn't bother to fashion an intricate knot in order to do it." He shook his head. "No, he would fashion a simple slip knot and be done with it." Harlow paused. "If he did it at all."

"If he didn't?"

"Someone did it for him."

"I should think it would have to be someone who knew him well; maybe in a religious context?" Zack asked.

Harlow nodded. "Well enough to know his strong religious commitment. It would have to be someone Jedediah respected." Harlow shook his head. "There weren't many of those."

Zack pressed. "Someone in the church; maybe someone high in the church."

"Yes, it would almost have to be that."

"Any specific ideas?"

Deputy Harlow let out a long breath. "That's difficult. I can't think of anyone he sees from the church with any regularity, other than at services. He's got no close friends, no close ties to anyone other than his daughter."

Zack put a hand on his shoulder. "Thank you, Deputy. I appreciate your candidness." He let his eyes drift around the interior of the compound, appreciating the wall with its climbing roses and attractively landscaped bushes. "As we dig deeper into this matter, trust will become an issue." He looked at the deputy. "You and I are going to need each other."

Harlow returned his gaze. "You'd better start calling me Jeffrey, then."

Zack smiled. "Call me Zack."

# CHAPTER FIFTY

Jack "Tubs" LeBaron decided he needed historical and philosophical context to solve the mystery. The thought didn't come to him in so many words, but there was a lot he didn't understand and he needed guidance.

At the McDonalds meeting with Agent Hooper, Tubs had heard enough to realize only two men truly knew the grander arch of this apparent conspiracy; one was dead and the other was Professor Nerd. The only way forward, he decided, was to swallow his prejudice and see what the professor could teach him. He called Agent Hooper.

"I need tuh speak with the professor guy."

"Philpott? I'm afraid he's inaccessible."

"What do you mean, inaccessible?"

"I mean we're are keeping him out of sight for his own safety." She was silent for a moment as if thinking. "Why do you need to speak to him? Can I help you?"

Tubs felt a moment of panic. "You know, forget it. It's not that important."

There was another silence. "You don't trust me, do you?"

Tubs didn't know what to say.

He heard her sigh. "Don't worry, I understand. I'm going to do something risky, and I hope it will take us toward a more trusting relationship. I will call Professor Philpott and ask him if he would be willing to talk to you. If so, we'll set up a meeting. But you must understand even proposing such a meeting is violating procedure and increases Professor Philpott's vulnerability, not to speak of my own."

When Tubs started to protest, Hooper said, "Actually, I think some unforeseen benefits may come from this meeting. All the professor can do is say no. I'll get back to you." She rang off.

Tubs stood for a moment holding his phone. It hadn't occurred to him the FBI might have the professor in protective custody, but it made sense, especially if he knew as much as Tubs hoped he might.

On the other hand, did he really want to learn enough about this complex mess to end up in personal danger like the professor? He half hoped Hooper would call him back to say it was impossible.

But she didn't.

When her call came, it was with directions for Tubs to follow, step by step. First, he would drive to Mesquite, just across the border in Nevada. He would take the first exit, turn right, and drive into the large gas station there. He would put gas in his tank and wait for further directions.

It felt to him like instructions from kidnappers.

Tubs didn't need much gas when he arrived there but put some in anyway. A talk show burbled along on the tiny screen on the pump. He glanced around surreptitiously, watching people as he fueled. If anyone had a message for him, it wasn't obvious. The pump shut off, the screen died, he removed the handle and was replacing it when he heard his name spoken.

Tubs whirled around, searching, but saw no one.

"Mr. LeBaron."

His head spun again.

"Here—on the screen."

Tubs peered at the tiny screen. The words he had just heard were spelled on it. More words scrolled out.

"Drive west on Pioneer Boulevard to Wedgies Sports Club. Sit in a booth and put your phone on a napkin at the outside edge of the table. Someone will contact you."

That was it. The screen went blank.

Tubs paid, turned right and at the next intersection turned left and headed west on Pioneer Boulevard. He spotted Wedgies Sports Club and Grill as the grade steepened, it was on the opposite side. He parked, entered, and followed the instructions given him. It was Happy Hour, the place was crowding up, but Tubs was able to find a booth to himself. He placed his phone on the napkin and pushed both to the end of the table.

A waitress zeroed in. "Will anyone be joining you, sir?"

"Well, yes, actually. Would yuh mind returning later?"

She smiled. "Not at all. I'll leave another set of silver." She dropped the wrapped bundle on the table and flew off.

Tubs was left alone. He stared down at his reflection in the shiny mahogany table and decided he appeared too anxious. He forced a light smile, glanced around the loud bar. People in his row of high-backed booths were not visible to him except in a squirrely way on the mirrored wall opposite. Across the aisle were tall tables with high stools where an increasing number of patrons perched. The place was becoming louder as Happy Hour progressed.

A perky short-skirted professionally dressed young woman disengaged herself from a raucous group of business types with the loud explanation she was headed for the little girlies room. She slipped off her stool and swept by Tub's booth. He caught a whiff of jasmine. He caught a stronger whiff when the woman came back and sat down opposite him.

"Why, George," she said, her voice shrill. "I didn't expect to see you here!"

"What—"

"When did you get into town?" She shifted a wad of gum in her mouth. "I haven't seen you in like forever!"

Tubs felt frustrated. "Look, lady, I don't know who yuh are, but—"

She spoke under breath, just above a whisper. "Do you want to meet with the professor or not?"

Tubs stared. "Uh, yes—"

"Then act like you know me and follow my lead."

Tubs stared while his brain caught up, then let his face crack into a smile. "Hi, uh—"

"Mary," she said in a coarse whisper.

"Mary, it's nice to see yuh. How long has it been?"

Her smile widened so much, the gum almost fell out. "It's been years and years. Why did you leave? You and I were just getting, you know, close."

"Well I—"

"We can't talk here, it's too loud. C'mon, I know a quieter place."

She dragged Tubs out of the booth. As she passed her friends she waved and grinned. "Just found an old friend. I'll get myself home."

There were catcalls and knowing grins from the group.

Outside, Mary hustled Tubs into a vintage Volkswagen. It chattered to life and she drove out of the parking lot turned west on Pioneer Boulevard. Her demeanor changed completely; her voice became brisk. "Did anyone follow you out here?"

Tubs realized he had no idea. "Uh, I don't think so."

Her eyes were in the rearview mirror even as her hands turned the wheel hard, sending the little car around the center island in an abrupt U turn. She gunned it, her eyes flitting between the rearview mirror and the approaching parking lot they had just vacated. They roared on by.

She glanced at him. "You own a pretty obvious car. Hopefully, it will keep the attention of interested parties while we motor off."

He observed her. "By the way, who are you?"

She gave a slight smile. "I'm a product of your tax dollars."

He gave a grunt. "FBI."

"Something of the sort."

"Yuh have a name, though."

"You can call me Mary."

"That's not your real name, is it?"

She gave a tight grin. "We only just met, yet you want intimate information?"

289

"Oh, sorry." Tubs turned his head to stare out the window. He could see they were back on the highway headed south. He settled back, but hardly had time to relax when Mary took an off ramp into the middle of nowhere. They were now on a state road, flying along at expressway speed. It was dusk, hard to see detail at any distance. It didn't matter. They had the entire road to themselves, it seemed. The road began to climb. It was gradual, but Tubs could feel the change in altitude. Chill air found its way into the VW interior.

There had been no small talk. Now Mary turned to him with an apologetic look. "These old Volkswagens aren't known for their heaters."

"Yuh read my mind."

"Help yourself to the blanket in the back seat if you want."

Tubs reached back, found it and he pulled it forward and laid it across his lap. "Thanks."

They came to a T intersection. Mary pulled to a stop. The dirt road before them climbed steeply up the mountainside. By now the sun was low, the shadows long. Mary turned downhill, putting the low sun directly in their eyes, and accelerated.

"I hope you can see better than I can," Tubs said, and pulled down the tiny visor."

"The car knows the way."

The grade was precipitous, forcing Mary to brake frequently. To Tubs' mind, the brakes didn't seem adequate, sometimes the little car seemed to leap forward. The road made a hard turn to the right, following a cut in the steep hillside. Mary slowed the little car and Tubs released his grip on the dash. The sun was out of their eyes now, darkness was setting in. Where the road switched back the other way in a steep downward turn, Mary turned off onto a narrow track. They bumped along a few hundred yards and came to a closed gate.

"We walk from here," Mary said. "Go stretch your legs while I get my stuff."

The air was chill at this altitude and Tubs wasn't dressed for it. He looked at the gate, a metal structure with a large lock securing it. Barbed wire fence stretched away on either side. The professor and his family were in a very secure place, Tubs thought.

Tubs took a step closer to the gate. Out of habit he studied the ground around him. There was no evidence of anyone passing through it, yet if the professor was here, there should be tracks of some sort. The rusty old lock hadn't been moved recently either. Puzzled, Tubs turned back to Mary.

She stood in front of the Volkswagen, studying him as she threaded a silencer on to a pistol. She did so quickly, efficiently, her eyes emotionless and opaque. "I probably don't need the suppressor way up here," she said in a conversational tone. "Better to be safe than sorry, though."

Tubs saw it all in an instant. What a fool he'd been, to accept this woman at her word back at the sports bar. He never once thought to ask for identification. She had made him feel the urgency of the moment, never gave him the chance to question it, knew all the right responses.

She watched him. "I see you have it all worked out. Smart guy. Too bad." She took a step toward him. "Nothing personal."

It all happened in slow motion for Tubs, as it always did when his life was at stake; each time his brain had slowed to a crawl and he became calm, reviewing all possible steps to save his life, doing exactly what was needed to survive.

"No tracks," he said to her.

She nodded, bringing the pistol up.

He turned his head and shoulders away from her, gestured back toward the gate. "That lock hasn't been opened in a very long time." As he brought the arm forward again, his sheath knife was in it and he whipped it with all the inertia of his shoulders turning back toward her, with all the skill and

291

experience of long practice. As he released it, he fell forward and to the side.

There were two sounds in rapid succession like air from a tire. Tubs felt the breeze of a bullet buzz pass his ear. He hit the ground rolling, his knees tucked to thrust back to his feet, running. But even as sprang up he saw there was no need. His aim had been true. Mary lay sprawled back against the hood of the Volkswagen, his knife projecting from her throat, her eyes wide with surprise. The silenced pistol lay in the dirt in front of her.

Tubs stood, brushed the grit from his pants and walked over to Mary. She was still alive, but she would have no answers for him. She would never talk again. Tubs reached down and retrieved his knife, ending her life as he did so. He wiped the blade on her blouse and replaced it in the sheath behind his right hip.

Professional as she had been, she had never noticed it there, under the shirttail.

If Mary couldn't tell him anything, maybe her stuff could. He searched the car. There wasn't much to search, the VW was obviously obtained just for this mission. The blanket had been the only item in it. Her purse was empty, apparently meant only to convey the pistol and silencer. He turned to her body. She wore a wool jacket over a flimsy blouse and a short skirt, not much to search. In her bra, he found a small folded piece of paper. On it was a cryptic note, giving a time, the name Wedgies Sports Bar, and the name Mesquite, and under that the words "napkin with phone on top at edge of table," and "tall, skinny guy, dressed like a hick." Tubs grunted at that.

He found no identification at all. No surprise. She was a hired gun, no doubt about that, a real professional. He'd been very lucky. But who had hired her? Tubs pondered that question. He stood staring down at her. If he left her here, it would likely be days before she was found, just as she had planned to do with him. Or he could throw her in the back seat and turn the car and body in to Agent Hooper; let her deal with the problem.

Then Tubs' mind went back to the question of who hired this killer. Hooper had set up the meeting; who else could possibly have known the arrangements? That brought another thought: if Hooper had any part in this attempt, he'd never see Professor Nerd again. For that matter, the watch, the only concrete evidence of a conspiracy as far as Tubs knew, would be long gone.

Tubs realized had the assassin succeeded in killing him, there would be no one left who knew anything about a conspiracy among the Saints. No one but the mysterious caller the professor had mentioned, that is, but that person could be dead already for all he knew.

After due consideration, Tubs decided it was best to leave Mary the assassin exactly where she was.

# CHAPTER FIFTY-ONE

As Zack drove toward Kanab the low sun was like a giant orange headlight in his rearview mirror. He reviewed in his mind the meeting with Jeffrey, deciding the man was sincere and could become an important ally in the case. It was going to be tough for him, though. As they dug deeper, Zack had no doubt Jeffrey's relationship with his wife, his religion, and his job could all be impacted. He would be hard put to emerge from this the same man.

Before Zack left, Jeffrey agreed to attempt to learn whom his father-in-law had met with lately. It would not be an easy task, for the old man never talked about his business to anyone, not even his daughter. Jeffrey would need to ask around, try to find anyone who had witnessed the old man's comings and goings.

Meanwhile, Zack planned to check in with Lori Hyde of the Response Team, hoping she might have found a lead. He also had sent a photo of Jedediah to Libby on his iPhone to verify this was indeed the man who grabbed her. He'd had no reply yet, she was likely still traveling and unable to respond. He'd also sent the photo to Sheriff Rafferty so he could pass it along to his deputies in case any of them might have noticed the old man. Any clue would help at this point.

Now Zack had to find the next link in the chain. He was convinced someone had filled Jedediah with avenging fervor, playing upon his devotion and loyalty. He agreed with Cynthia it could only be someone high in the FLDS Church, someone who could represent himself to Jedediah as the personal messenger of God. Zack had scant knowledge of FLDS Church hierarchy. Jeffrey mentioned something called a Quorum, saying he would forward a list of members of the Hildale Quorum to him. Zack planned to do background checks on each of those men.

First, though, he wanted to meet Sheriff Rafferty and compare notes. The sheriff seemed to encourage a cooperative approach, a welcome change from the "cards close to chest" attitude Zack often found with local law enforcement. He believed sharing was always a win/win proposition for both parties.

His phone vibrated. He glanced at it, saw it was FBI Agent Lori Hyde. He pulled over.

"What can I do for you, Agent Hyde?"

"There is something out here at the crime scene you ought to see," she said.

"Can't you tell me about it? I'm almost to Fredonia."

A pause. "I would if I could, but this is something I really think you need to see for yourself—before the light is too low," she added.

"Okay, I'm turning around right now."

A few minutes later, Zack saw the sign for Pipe Spring National Monument. On an impulse, he turned in and drove to the Paiute Reservation and the campground. He found Eagle Feather sitting cross-legged next to the fire. The Navajo didn't seem to notice when Zack walked over to him.

"It's nice you've got nothing better to do than sit and stare into a fire all day."

Eagle Feather's eyes shifted up to Zack. "I've solved my part of the investigation. How are you doing, White Man?"

"It's all busting apart right now. I could use your help." He caught up with Eagle Feather's words. "What do you mean, you've solved your part?"

Eagle Feather climbed to his feet without responding. "I feel I am getting too old for this." He looked at Zack. "Let's go, White Man."

Zack knew his friend would tell him his story in his own time. He climbed behind the wheel of the Jeep and watched the Navajo climb aboard. As they traveled, he filled Eagle Feather in on recent developments.

"I don't know what Lori has for us," he said. "We'll just have to see."

They parked outside of the yellow tape surrounding the property. Zack led the way toward the barn. He heard Lori's voice calling him.

"I'm over here, at the house." She poked her head around the back door.

Zack altered his course toward her. "What have you got?" he said as he drew near.

"Come in." She ushered the two men into the utility room. The bright LED work lights aided the single dusty bulb. Now she turned them off. It was dusk, still light outside, yet the utility room was in shadow despite the efforts of the cobwebbed incandescent bulb. Lori pointed to the dirty window.

"Imagine yourself an older man with not great eyesight who is extremely devoted to God. You have come into this room at night for some reason. And then—"

The dirty window suddenly glowed, as with holy light, and a cross of fire appeared on the white wall opposite. Zack was stunned. Then a voice, distant yet clear, came from nowhere. "This is God's will. You will drive to the Merry Wives Cafe and buy coffee for the Forensics Team."

Zack stared at Lori. "Good God!"

"Precisely," Lori said with a grin. "Impressive, right?" She signaled, and the work lights came on again. "Let me show you how it was done." She brought them close to the dirty window. "At first glance, this appears to be any dusty, neglected window. But if you look close enough, you see this is not ordinary dirt. There is a type of resin mixed with it to give it a red-orange tint. When you shine a bright light on the outside, it really glows." She called out to someone and the holy light reappeared. She pointed to a place high up on the window glass. "Up there you can see how the dust and resin coating was scraped away just enough to create a cross so that when bright light is applied a larger cross is projected onto the very clean white wall opposite." Lori flashed Zack a pleased look. "Easy Peasey."

Zack was amazed. "But what about the voice? It didn't sound amplified."

"It isn't." She pointed to a large crack above the window frame. "It seems like an ordinary crack, but it is actually the bell of the horn, if you will. Someone placed a metal pipe section within the wall above the window. He could speak into it from the outside, probably through a simple amplifier of some sort applied to a hole drilled in the outside wall. We used a regular kitchen funnel. The effect is to distort the voice. Ed, from our team, is out there playing God. First, he used his LED flashlight to display the cross, and once he had our attention, without moving from that position held the funnel to the wall with his other hand and become a different voice, in this case the voice of God, demanding coffee."

Zack shook his head in wonderment. "How on earth did you ever discover this?"

She laughed. "It was a fluke. I was in this room, studying the very clean wall here, wondering why it was freshly painted and the others not. Ed was outside working his way along the shadowy side of the house with a flashlight searching for evidence. At some point, his beam caught the window and really lit it up. It got my attention. I yelled out to him to keep it there while I checked it out. When he answered, his voice came from two different places, sounding like two different voices." She giggled. "Really startled me. So we set to work to thoroughly examine the window, found the drilled hole outside and pried away some of the wall up there over the window and, voila!"

"The voice of God," Eagle Feather said.

She nodded.

"Someone became a voice from above in order to direct Jedediah however he wanted," Zack said, thinking out loud. "To a zealot like that old man, a direct command from God could not be ignored. If we consider the old man's actions in the light of response to direct holy orders, we begin to see what the perp wanted to have happen. We might begin to see a motive in there somewhere."

"It should not be hard to find," Eagle Feather said. "It is about the church."

"Yes, but why? Why did the church want a young boy from Kanab murdered? Why have the boy taken all the way up Canaan Mountain?"

"A place to hide the body where no one would find it?" Lori ventured.

"In that case, why not just bury the body up there— why the dramatic bit with impaling him?"

No one had an answer.

Zack gave Lori an approving nod. "Good work, Agent Hyde." He received a big smile in return.

On the way back to the Jeep, Zack took out his phone. "I'm going to bounce all this off someone who knows the church well," he said.

Jeffrey answered after three rings. Zack took him through the discovery they had made at the farmhouse.

"Well, I'll be. He was truly hornswoggled. I can see how it would work. If Jedediah is convinced God wanted something done, there'd be no turning him."

"Apparently, he'd even murder for his Faith."

Jeffrey was silent. "I have no idea how to process this with Cynthia," he said a moment later.

"I'd say let it lie for the moment. Who knows what else we may uncover?" He switched ears. "Speaking of which, I could use your thoughts on who might have pulled off this little trick and more to the point, what was the motive? Maybe you could supply some background from the Mormon point-of-view. I'm at the farm. Can we meet somewhere?"

Jeffrey gave directions for the Merry Wives Cafe and promised to meet them there in half an hour.

It was dark by the time Zack and Eagle Feather found their way to the little cafe. By the look of things, the dinner crowd was already gone. Jeffrey waved at them from a table near the rear. Zack raised his eyebrows when he saw it was a table for six. "Expecting a crowd?"

"We're in Hildale," Jeffrey explained. "They don't have many small tables. Families are large around here, and everyone very social."

"Jeffrey, this is Eagle Feather, my friend. We've worked together on many cases."

Jeffrey stood, offered his hand. "This must be one of the stranger cases."

The corners of Eagle Feather's mouth turned up. "You would be surprised."

The waitress arrived. Jeffrey greeted her and turned at Zack and Eagle Feather. "You folks had your dinner yet?"

They shook their heads. Jeffrey smiled. "Well, you're in for a treat. The staff will tell you this place is much more than burgers, but I'll tell you if you haven't had one here, it's obligatory."

They took Jeffrey's advice. Zack ordered a Big Mama and Eagle Feather a Big Papa, both with sweet potato fries. Jeffrey settled for water. "I ate at home. But save room for the Oreo Mint Pie. I'm going to have a slice of that."

The waitress brought their beverages and the men settled back.

"We need help with motive," Zack said. "These murders clearly have something to do with religion. But to what end? Why convince the old man to kill a kid in Kanab. Why tote his body all the way up the mountain? Why impale him? Do you see this as some sort of vengeance, maybe directed at someone associated with the boy? I've heard stories of Avenging Angels among the Mormons in the past. Could that be it?"

Jeffrey shook his head. "It's nothing like that." He reached into a courier pouch slung over his chair and brought out a paper bag from which he produced a black moleskin notebook. He set the notebook on the table. "This is a journal. It belonged to my close childhood friend Dan Fogelberry."

Zack stared. "The reporter who died."

"The reporter who was murdered." Jeffrey's face expressed an anger Zack had not seen there before.

The deputy took the journal, slipped it back into the bag, and slid the whole thing to Zack. "It's worth your life to possess that. No one but a certain deputy in Salina even knows it exists, and he doesn't know the significance. I went up there and claimed it along with Dan's other personal items." Jeffrey scrutinized Zack's face. "Once you've read this, you'll have your motive. Dan was a thorough investigator and never went to print until he had evidence to prove his theories. He had not yet printed this story. As you will see, he had only one piece of solid evidence—or, I should say, someone else had it. That other individual has since disappeared and so has the evidence."

Zack stared at the bag on the table. "Is this the only— —?"

"There is a copy. I photocopied and dated every page and put them in a safety deposit box. Should anything happen to me, the location of the box and a key will be forwarded to the San Francisco Chronicle and another to the FBI." He grinned. "I guess by talking to you I'm skipping a step here."

Zack took a piece of his paper napkin and scrawled a receipt for Jeffrey. "Don't lose that in case the provenance of the evidence comes into question."

Jeffrey slipped it into his pocket.

"So. Can you give us the big picture?" Zack asked.

Jeffrey shook his head. "Not here. Go read the journal, and we'll talk after that."

Zack changed the subject. "How have you done with background research of the Council members?"

Jeffrey put down his tea. "They are all devoted men, as you might imagine. One or two are quite capable of violence in the name of the church, or so I gleaned from their past histories. All are ambitious, wealthy men. All could be hurt by that." Jeffrey pointed toward the bag. "President Brown is a formidable man. His power as Leader and Prophet of the Fundamentalist Church is absolute. As the Prophet, he has minute control over the membership, including whom they may marry, what they may wear, and other intimate details. Second to Brown in the Council is Elder Taylor. He is generally seen as the heir to Brown, who leans on his advice. The others are like a dog following a kid with an ice cream cone, hoping for an opportunity."

"You do not sound as if you have much respect for your church," Eagle Feather said.

Jeffrey eyed him for a moment, considering his answer. "I imagine it is like many organizations; you can have faith and belief in the organization itself despite faulty leadership."

"What, if any, connection is there between the FLDS Church and the LDS Church in Salt Lake City?" Zack asked.

Jeffrey gave his head a slow shake. "On the surface, none. Each disapproves of the other and understands there can be no reconciliation. Yet it's no secret a back channel exists between Brown and the LDS President."

"One hand washes the other?" Eagle Feather asked.

Jeffrey nodded. "It would seem so." He looked at Zack. "What is your thinking?"

"I'm trying to get a sense of how large this conspiracy could be."

Eagle feather grunted. "It could be very large."

Jeffrey nodded. "Read the journal."

The men were silent, contemplating this.

The waitress came, cleared their plates and distributed the Oreo Mint Pie. On this particular subject, everyone was in agreement.

# CHAPTER FIFTY-TWO

Tubs thought long and hard about his next step. There was literally no one he could call, no one he could trust. He couldn't leave the Volkswagen here; his fingerprints and DNA were all over the passenger side. No matter how carefully he wiped, he would never get it all. Even one fingerprint would place him in this car and be his undoing.

He could drive the car down off the mountain, set it afire somewhere near the river and make his way back through the wilderness. He didn't know how far it was to the Sports Bar, and he didn't know the area. He'd run the risk of being seen. It would likely take many hours to get there and each additional hour meant a greater chance of being noticed. Someone would eventually see the Scout still parked in the lot after closing, questions would be asked.

He could drive the car back to the Sports Bar as if nothing happened, park it, leave it with the keys under the rug, hop in his Scout and go home. His fingerprints wouldn't matter as much now. Witnesses saw him leave with the girl, they would expect his prints to be in the car. Tubs looked down at the front of the VW, where the hired killer had sprawled against it. There was quite a lot of blood on the car's surface, probably splatter as well, it could have gone anywhere across the front. Again, he'd never find it all. If the cops did a thorough search, they'd find it, they'd have his prints, and that would be that.

He couldn't leave the car, and he couldn't take it away.

Tubs felt a chill. It was cold at this elevation and night was coming on. He didn't have warm clothing. He wished he could just climb into the little car and go home.

Wait—why couldn't he? Was that the answer? This killer was a professional and professionals do not use their own cars to drive to an assassination. It must be stolen. Here he was, near the borders of three states: Nevada, Arizona, and Utah. The VW could have been stolen in any one of them, the plates stolen somewhere else. He doubted there was a hot search for this old car, and even if there was, it was a complicated proposition to extend a search across state lines. He could drive it out of here straight to his home in Big Water, Utah. He thought he was maybe four hours away, he'd be driving at night, no one would be looking for this little car.

What about the Scout in the parking lot of Wedgies? Well, he was paying an annual fee to AAA for just such inconveniences. He pulled out his phone, saw to his surprise he had a signal, and called the emergency number. He explained the vehicle wouldn't start, he'd found a ride to his business meeting, and he needed the Scout towed back to his home in Big Water.

Tubs put his phone away and smiled for the first time in a while. By the time his Scout arrived in Big Water, he'd already be there, the little VW tucked away in his barn. He could take his time cleaning it thoroughly, decide later where to dump it, or...maybe just keep it. He'd have plenty of time to cook up a story to meet the circumstances.

The little car rattled to life. Tubs backed up carefully, letting the corpse slide gently off the bonnet until the killer's head thudded to the ground. He had never touched her; there was no way to get to him from the body. He had his knife, he'd obliterated his footprints. Hell, he'd never been here.

He reached the I-15 without incident, the little car burbling along. It had plenty of fuel; no need to stop along the way. His thoughts went to Agent Hooper. If she had conspired to have him eliminated, as seemed likely, she would not be looking for him or for the VW, or even for the killer. She'd be waiting for a phone call to tell her the job was done. Maybe not even that—maybe they'd completed the deal with one simple arrangement. Either way, he had plenty of time to figure out his next move.

What if it wasn't Hooper? Tubs had no idea who else could have arranged it. He was very hungry, and he felt a headache coming on. Once he got home he'd have a sandwich, get some sleep and put his mind to the problem in the morning.

* * * * *

Zack dropped Eagle Feather off at the campground. The Navajo doggedly refused to reveal what he meant when he claimed to have solved his part of the mystery. As Zack drove away, he thought about it. How do you "solve" a creature that could morph into a man and live invisible in a cave?

Zack shook his head, deciding not to try to figure out how Eagle Feather's mind worked. He'd never been able to before. The Navajo would tell him when he was ready to talk. Zack knew if it had an immediate bearing on the murder investigation, his friend would have told him.

Zack suddenly felt the weight of the events of the day crushing him down. He was overcome by fatigue; he'd have to get some sleep. Libby had sent a message saying she made it home safely and was happily reunited with her family. His greatest concern was alleviated.

However tired he was, Zack could not sleep until he had read Dan Fogelberry's journal. Once he was comfortably situated in the little house in Kanab, showered, fed and ready for bed, he sat down in an easy chair in the bedroom and began to read.

When he awoke the next morning, Zack was still in the chair, the journal had slid to the floor. It took him a moment to remember why he was in this room, in this chair, with sunlight streaming across the floor in front of him. It came back to him all at once, he sat up and reached for the journal. It appeared Fogelberry had uncovered a great conspiracy, a secret hidden away for more than a century, known only to a privileged few. The motive for protecting the cave from public scrutiny was clear now—it contained proof beyond doubt of Mormon transgressions over the years, wrongdoings they were desperate to keep hidden. In doing so, it appeared they had committed murder.

How many people had been killed to protect this secret? Dan Fogelberry's death was not an accident. But why hadn't they taken the journal after staging it? The answer came to him immediately. They didn't know about it.

Zack slipped the journal into a bedside drawer. As he showered and dressed, he thought about Jeffrey. The man must have been severely torn when he threw his lot in with Zack. Everything he cherished lay in the balance—his family, his church, his job. In the end, he'd chosen to do the right thing, regardless. The man had as strong a moral compass as Zack had ever witnessed.

He toweled off, shaking his head. This case was a long way from being solved. How did the death of the boy figure in? Why such a dramatic display of the victim, impaled in front of the very place the church so hoped to keep hidden? It made no sense. Had they buried the boy, the vultures would never have flocked there and led the two hunters to the cave. Had it been an act of bravado by the murderer? Intended as a warning of some sort?

Zack's brain raced. He needed coffee. He needed Eagle Feather.

An hour later the two friends were sipping coffee, waiting for their breakfasts to arrive at Nedra's Too in Kanab. The smell of salsa and Chorizo filled the air, along with the quiet hum of conversation. A film crew was in town, helping to fill this already popular restaurant.

"Where is the journal now?" Eagle Feather asked.

"Locked in the Jeep."

"From what you describe, that journal is an important piece of evidence. Is it safe enough?"

Zack shook his head. "No, it's not, truth to tell. My intention is to send it to Agent Hooper via special courier. In any case, Jeffrey Harlow has made a copy and secured it."

Eagle Feather observed Zack over the rim of his coffee cup. "Harlow is a Mormon."

Zack sighed. "I know. But he did give me the journal in the first place." He sipped his coffee. "Besides, I have a good feeling about the man."

"Your feelings have got you in trouble more than once, White Man."

Zack grinned and shrugged.

The waitress arrived with their meals, the large plates overflowing with egg and soft taco combinations. The men dug in.

After a few bites, Eagle Feather sat back. "This is very good."

"Breakfast is my favorite time of day," Zack said.

"Where will we go from here?"

Zack chewed and thought. "Conspiracies, no matter how large they appear, usually involve relatively few people. In this case, for instance, I can't believe information about the cave was shared with everyone in the administration of the LDS or even the FLDS Church. It smacks of a few powerful people quietly making decisions on their own." He paused to take a bite of his Huevos Rancheros. "If I remember my history correctly, the Fancher Wagon Train massacre was organized by John D. Lee, who thought he was acting in accordance with the desires of Brigham Young in Salt Lake City. It was a wink and a nod sort of thing, Lee being the main South Utah Mormon with direct connections to Young. No Quorum of Twelve was involved with that idea, I suspect."

"Do you think the murders to protect the cave were suggested by leaders of the church?"

Zack shook his head. "I doubt any specific orders were given. My guess is some powerful church leader made an observation about the necessity to prevent the cave's secret from being exposed. Someone else on down the chain made a literal interpretation." He wiped his mouth. "Given

306

the traditional hierarchy of the church, it's hard to imagine any individual member deciding to take such a desperate course of action without certainty of approval from above. Yet, the leaders need deniability and would be purposefully vague."

"Which church?"

"That's a good question. There's no doubt in my mind FLDS members are involved, given their location and history. But they lack the political power to influence an injunction such as the one that was levied. To my mind, the conspiracy has to reach to Salt Lake City somehow."

Eagle Feather grunted. "That might be hard to prove."

Zack nodded. "My intention is to concentrate solely on the murders. Once we solve those, we might just uncover the next link in the chain." Zack smiled. "Or not." He began to rise from the table.

"Has it occurred to you these cases might not be related after all? Or, even if related, might involve separate perpetrators?"

Zack stared at Eagle Feather, sat down again. "You mean not a conspiracy?"

Eagle Feather shook his head. "No, I believe there is a conspiracy. I mean it is possible for there to be two or even three different killers, each doing what seemed to be expected, yet not aware of the others."

Zack shook his head at Eagle Feather. "Don't you think this business is complicated enough without making it more so?"

"Just trying to help, White Man."

Zack stood, stretched, slapped two twenties on the table. "Let's go, Navajo."

Outside, both men had to pause and admire the beautiful morning, looking north where red buttes met blue sky. Reluctantly, they turned and walked up the sidewalk to the red Jeep.

"What is next?" Eagle Feather asked, settling in the passenger seat.

"I really should call Agent Hooper and fill her in on all that's happened. I'd kind of like to get her side of the picture. But first, since we're in town, let's go visit Sheriff Rafferty and see what he's up to."

Whatever the sheriff was up to, it wasn't in the vicinity of his office. Instead, they found Chief Deputy Brown ensconced in the sheriff's worn leather chair. He spun toward them when they arrived in the doorway.

"What can I do for you folks?"

Zack produced his badge, walked over and showed it to the deputy. "Not sure we've met. I'm Agent Zack Tolliver; this here is Eagle Feather."

Brown gave them a measured look before sticking out his hand. "Heard about you. Chief Deputy William Brown." He nodded toward Eagle Feather. "How can I help you?"

"We hoped to have a word with the sheriff."

Brown relaxed back into the chair. "He's not in yet, said he had some stops to make on the way. I can help you." He waved them toward the facing chairs.

Zack sat in the one closest to the desk, Eagle Feather elected to stay on his feet.

"I guess you know we're working the Wilson boy's murder case from our end. Seems clear to us the old Mormon Jedediah Meekes had a hand in that."

"Poor old guy, not quite right in the head. A shame he went and hung himself like that."

Zack's eyebrows went up, but he kept his thoughts to himself. "We think he might have had an accomplice in all this. Have you come across anything to support that idea?"

Brown appeared surprised. "No, not a thing. Appears to us the old guy just got it into his head to come to town and grab the kid, probably because of his skin color. Threw him in that big old Travelall and took him up the mountain."

Brown shook his head. "Some crazy ritual he got into his head, I'd guess."

"Strong old guy," Eagle Feather commented.

At Brown's questioning look, Zack said, "My friend is saying it seems beyond the powers of one old man to do what he did, including carrying the boy across such rough terrain and hoisting him up on a stake."

Brown grinned, put up both palms. "Amazing what people can do when the fervor of religious zeal is upon them." He glanced from Eagle Feather to Zack. "In any case, we have no indications of an accomplice."

Zack nodded.

"By the way," Brown said, "I thought Supervisory Agent Janice Hooper was running this investigation."

Zack gave a smile. "She is, and she isn't. We've decided to split the load."

"I see. Well, when I last spoke to her, we agreed to share progress." He turned his gaze on Zack. "You folks got anything new?"

Zack shook his head. "Nothing the sheriff doesn't already know." He stood, grabbed his hat. "Did the sheriff share where it was the old man got the stool he used to hang himself?"

"You mean that the old man brought it out from the house? Yeah, he told me about that. Strange the old guy would carry it all the way out there. But I figure he knew what he wanted to do from the start." Brown shook his head. "Sad."

Before Zack left the office, Brown said, "If you wait a bit, you can meet with the sheriff."

Zack dismissed the idea with a wave. "No need. You've given us all we need for now."

In the Jeep, Eagle Feather glanced at Zack's face. "That last question seemed somewhat random."

"Yeah, but it might be an important part of the puzzle. Brown is right; it does seem strange to carry that stool all the way out to the barn when there are a number of crates and barrels, any of which would have done just as well to hang himself."

"Maybe he wasn't in a mood to experiment."

Zack gave a quick glance at Eagle Feather. "I don't think he hung himself, that's the point. Someone not as familiar with the stuff in the barn might think he needed to bring that stool." After another moment of thought, he cocked an eye toward his friend. "Here's another point. I don't remember ever telling Sheriff Rafferty about that stool. I learned that from Deputy Marshal Harlow, and I'm pretty damn sure he didn't mention it to anyone else either."

Eagle Feather half turned in his seat to stare at Zack. "If you are correct, then—"

"Then it would seem Sheriff Rafferty had to have been there in person."

# CHAPTER FIFTY-THREE

The friends drove back to town to rescue Eagle Feather's old pickup outside the restaurant. As Eagle Feather climbed out of the Jeep, Zack's phone rang. He saw it was Janice Hooper.

"Hang on a minute," he called to Eagle Feather and took the call. "Hello, Janice, I was about to call you."

"Zack, there has been a disturbing development."

"Go ahead."

"Did you ever meet Jack LeBaron, usually called Tubs?"

"Well, I heard about him. The Indian who doesn't exist met him once up at the crime scene."

"The fact is the man has disappeared. That's disturbing since he is an important witness. More disturbing are the circumstances surrounding his disappearance."

"Go on."

"Tubs called me yesterday morning asking to get in touch with Professor Philpott, saying he needed to talk to him. I saw no harm; in fact, I thought the two of them might put some ideas together to benefit our investigation. As you know, we have the professor and his family in a safe house. To protect the location, I had Tubs go through a few hoops, sent him to a restaurant in Mesquite and arranged to have an agent out of Las Vegas escort him from there. This agent, name of Miller, was to call me once the meeting occurred. The appointed time came and went and no call. I waited a half hour to allow for traffic, and when he still hadn't called me, I called the safe house.

"And—?"

"Agent Mutch, who's with the family, told me they never arrived. I told her to call me the second they got there. Meanwhile, I sent Agent Holmes from my office to Mesquite to trace Miller's steps. Holmes called me from Mesquite a couple of hours later. He'd found Miller, out in the desert beyond the filling station. He'd been shot, executed."

"Shit. You've got a leak."

"Yeah, we do. It's right here in my office in St. George. We'll find it pretty damn quick, there are limited possibilities. But we've lost an agent and we've also lost a witness. I've had no word from Tubs. He's vanished. And so has his old jalopy, which should have been left in the Sports Club parking lot there."

"You think they got to him, too."

"I see no other possibility, unless he became frightened and ran. But if the killer could take down Agent Miller, a trained FBI agent, I don't give Tubs much of a chance."

Zack was feeling the sickness in the pit of his stomach he felt when things were going very wrong.

"Zack, I need you to ride up to Big Water where Tub lives, check out his place, just on the off chance." She gave him the address. She paused. "Is the Nonexistent Indian with you?"

"Yes."

"Good. Take him along just in case." She ended the call.

Zack stared at his phone for a moment. Eagle Feather was still on the sidewalk, waiting. Zack beckoned him back in. "How'd you like to take a ride?"

The trip to Big Water took them due east, right into the sun. There was a chill in the air this morning, the warm rays on Zack's hands and thighs felt good, but he needed his sunglasses on and the visor down. The drive took a bit more than an hour. They almost passed through the small town. It was spread out over the rough landscape, buildings hidden behind clumps of brush or trees, some surrounded by high chain-link fencing.

They had a street name and house number. Neither helped, none of the streets had signposts. They stopped at the High Desert Lodge for directions and found their way to a single-lane wind-scalloped road straight as an arrow toward the high cliffs to the north. They passed a couple of corrugated metal warehouses before the road ended at a fenced property.

A sign on the fence read Private Property, Keep Out. Under it was written Trespassers Will Be Shot, and under that in small letters J. LeBaron.

"That's our boy," Zack said. He drove up to the gate.

Eagle Feather jumped out and examined the lock and chain. Both were large and impressive, the hinges sturdy. The Navajo looked close, reached out and lifted that entire end of the gate upward. The pins slid out of the hinges and the Navajo walked the entire ensemble inward and back across the driveway. He held it there and saluted Zack as the Jeep drove through.

Eagle Feather climbed back in the Jeep, glanced at Zack, answered his unspoken question. "I figured Tubs would not wish to bother with that very large lock and chain every time he went through his gate."

They followed the drive past several sheds and a barn-like structure and on to where it looped in front of a trailer. A few trees scattered about offered shade. Tub's Scout was parked under one of them. Zack pulled up behind it. The two men sat and stared at it for a while.

"Who do you think we've got here?" Zack asked. "Tubs, or the killer?"

Eagle Feather shrugged. "Fifty-fifty. One way to find out." He stepped out of the Jeep.

Zack followed, his hand on his gun.

A voice behind them said, "Yuh can climb right back into thet Jeep and get on out of here."

Zack turned his head. He saw a tall man with a rifle held loosely in his hands, the barrel pointed at the ground in between them.

"Hello, Tubs," Eagle Feather said.

Tubs stared at him, nodded toward Zack. "Is thet the FBI friend yuh told me about?"

"Meet Zack Tolliver."

Tubs stayed where he was and the rifle barrel came up a bit. "Are you here to finish the job?"

"What job is that?" Zack asked.

Tubs looked at Eagle Feather. "You too, huh?"

"I do not understand."

Tubs raised the rifle a few more inches, its muzzle aimed between the two men. "Either get to doin' what you came here to do or climb back in thet Jeep and go tell your lady boss I don't plan to lie down and die for her."

Zack raised his hands. "Agent Hooper sent us to help you, if you were still alive. They found the body of Agent Miller and thought you were dead, too. Someone in Agent Hooper's office leaked the rendezvous information. Miller was the agent she sent to guide you. He ended up dead and you went missing. What happened?"

Tubs stared at Zack. Anger grew in his face. "Thet's a nice story. Too bad it ain't true."

Zack kept talking. "Agent Hooper figured whoever shot Agent Miller was planning to kill you. Yet here you are. How did you get away?" He stared at Tubs through narrowed eyes. "Or was it you killed Miller?"

"Why would I do thet? I don't even know this Miller."

Eagle Feather broke in. "What happened, Tubs? Why should we trust you?"

Tubs stared at Eagle Feather, then Zack. "Someone met me at the Sport's Bar right on time like the plan said, but it wasn't any FBI agent, it was a professional killer. She almost got the job done, too."

"And you think Agent Hooper sent this killer," Zack said.

"What else should I think? Who else knew the arrangements?"

"That's what we're trying to tell you. Someone in the FBI office leaked the plan to whoever sent the killer."

"How can I believe you two ain't involved?"

Zack brought his arms down. They were getting tired. "Well, for one thing, if Agent Hooper wanted you dead, you'd be in the crosshairs of a sniper's rifle right now."

"Maybe so, maybe not."

Eagle Feather spoke. "We accomplish nothing with talk. We do not want to kill you. If you decide not to trust us, tell us now and we will go away. If you decide to trust us, put down the rifle."

Zack added, "Whoever is out there may not give up so easily. We shouldn't be standing out here like statues in a park."

Tubs stared at them a long while, his eyes flitting from one man's face to the other. He lowered the rife. "Well, I guess it's time to shit or get off the pot. Come inside and have some coffee and let's talk about it."

Zack and Eagle Feather followed him into the trailer. He waved them to a small table. A half-filled cup was on the table, a blackened pot on a hot plate sat on a counter nearby. Tubs searched the cupboard for two more cups.

"So if the FBI's not after me, who is?" Tubs set the cups in front of them.

"Tell us about the killer; maybe we can go from there."

Tubs gave a basic description of the woman, the car she had stolen, her weapon, her professional manner, and how he had escaped.

Eagle Feather actually grinned. "You brought a knife to a gunfight."

"Didn't seem amusing at the time."

"Where is the VW?" Zack asked.

Tubs nodded over his shoulder. "Got it hidden in the shed back theh."

Zack was putting a picture together in his head. "This woman sounds like a professional killer, not an FBI resource, from what you describe. The FBI doesn't use professionals."

"Hooper could be working on her own," Eagle Feather pointed out to Zack. "Or she could be part of a larger conspiracy and just did the setup for them."

Zack's fingers drummed the table. "Whoever it was, if they think the job didn't get finished, they'll keep on coming."

"They already did thet once. This is theh second time someone tried to have me killed." Tubs went on to describe his near miss with the quarry truck. "But yuh mebbe already knew about that?" His eyes were on Zack.

Zack showed his surprise. "No, I never knew."

"The only one I ever told was Hooper."

"She didn't mention it," Zack said. "I still don't believe it's her."

"She could be a Mormon," Eagle Feather said. "They seem to take their faith real serious."

Zack shrugged. "Whoever it is, they'll be wondering what happened."

"I thought about thet," Tubs said. "On television shows, the killer gets paid half before and the other half after the job is done."

Zack nodded. "Right. So whoever hired the killer is waiting for confirmation right now. The question is, how long will they wait before guessing something went wrong and come out here looking for you?"

"Maybe she already did," Tubs muttered.

"Did you take the killer's phone by any chance?" Eagle Feather asked.

Tubs shook his head. "No, didn't want tuh leave any trace I was ever there."

Zack gave an affirming nod. "That's smart." He sat back in his chair. "Let me summarize. Here's what we know. First, we've uncovered enough evidence to confirm there is a conspiracy of some sort connected to these murders. Second, we could say the two attempts on Tubs' life were coincidental, that he's got a lot of enemies. But if we don't accept coincidence, we're saying the attempts are connected."

"Randy Musser," Tubs said.

Zack nodded. "Right. Musser almost certainly sparked the first attempt and since he was operating a secret mission for his church, one or both churches must be involved in both attempts. Therefore, the responsible party is almost certainly a member of one of the churches, and all of it seems to connect to the bones in the cave in some way. From what I just read of the dead reporter's journal, well over a century of Mormon guilt resides in those bones. The first heinous act the bone evidence will likely reveal occurred well before the fundamentalists split from the main church body over the polygamy question."

"Meaning it is in the best interests of both churches to keep the bones hidden," Eagle Feather said.

"Well, shoot!" Tubs broke in. "Yuh mean the whole state of Utah wants me dead."

Eagle Feather shook his head. "Only some of the most powerful people in the whole state want you dead."

Zack nodded. "It isn't the membership of both churches lined up against us, it's a few people acting without the knowledge of all the others. Once the actions of those few come to light, they will be the hunted ones. We have to identify them and make them known."

"How do we do thet?" Tub's expression radiated doubt.

"One step at a time," Zack said.

"The first step is to get out of here before they come for you," Eagle Feather said.

Zack nodded. "He's right. We need to smuggle you out. Pack up only what you absolutely need to have with you until this is over, and let's get you someplace safe."

Tubs spread his arms wide. "I got everything I need right here," he said. "Let's go."

# CHAPTER FIFTY-FOUR

"It has been over twelve hours and I've not heard from the contractor. I am concerned."

"Don't be. These things take time. We must wait."

"How long can we wait? What if the contractor failed? What if our bid becomes public?"

"It won't. But even if it did, there are other contractors."

"The contract becomes increasingly difficult to complete once the public is aware, no matter how strong the bid. What if—"

"Go easy. Do not get ahead of yourself. All is well so far as we know. Take no action until we learn otherwise."

"It might be too late by then."

"You must have faith. Remember, all is foretold. Even if this contractor fails, there is another ready to make a bid. Remain calm. Your faith is being tested. Do not fail."

\* \* \* \* \*

Sheriff Rafferty glanced up from his desk at the sound of a knock.

"Howdy, Sheriff. Have you got a moment?" Zack Tolliver and a man in black leather with a black reservation hat stood in the doorway.

At his nod, they advanced into the office.

Zack motioned toward his companion. "This is my friend Eagle Feather."

Rafferty grinned, stretched across the desk to reach out a hand. "Nice to finally meet you, Eagle Feather."

"Likewise, Sheriff."

Rafferty waved them to chairs. "Where do we stand?"

Zack answered question with question. "How much do you know about Jedediah's hanging?"

Rafferty gave him a quizzical look. "Very little, actually. I understand there is some question regarding whether it was suicide or murder?"

"The crime scene itself, I mean. Anyone give you details?"

Sheriff Rafferty straightened in his chair and scrutinized Zack. "What's this about, Zack? You know I wasn't there. It belongs to the Washington County Sheriff and you boys."

Zack held up an entreating palm. "Bear with me a moment, Sheriff. I know police officers talk among themselves. I wondered how much detail came your way, even as a rumor."

Rafferty spread his hands wide. "Really, none."

"Nothing about how he hanged himself?"

"I guess I heard he hanged himself in the barn. Beyond that, nothing."

Zack persisted. "How did he do it? How was the rope secured? What did he stand on?"

Rafferty began to feel annoyed. "Zack, I know nothing of that. Would you tell me what's going on?"

Zack held up a palm. "Okay, I'm sorry, Sheriff. Here's my problem. Jedediah used a stool to hang himself, or to be hanged. I learned from the only person who had this particular information that the stool had been brought to the barn from the house. My informant and I were the only people in possession of this fact."

"Okay—"

"Except your chief deputy."

Now he had Rafferty's attention. "So how did he know that?"

Zack gave a tight grin. "My question exactly."

The sheriff kept his eye on Zack, his mind rolling over this new information. "You want I should question him?"

Zack put it back to him. "What do you think?"

"Zack, I trust this guy. He's been with me several years now, never given me reason to doubt him; he's always been reliable. Maybe you'd better let me work this angle. Obviously that knowledge makes him a suspect, but I've got to believe there are mitigating circumstances."

Zack stood and shook the sheriff's hand. "That's what I hoped you would say. Try to get as much detail as you can about it. If he wasn't involved, he must have spoken to someone who was."

Eagle Feather stood with Zack. "Nice to meet you, Sheriff."

They were almost to the door when Sheriff Rafferty called after them. "Who did Brown tell you told him about the stool?"

Zack turned back, a half smile on his face. "You, Sheriff."

After Zack and Eagle Feather were gone, Rafferty sat unmoving, thinking about this new twist. His deputy had lied, without question. He had never said anything of the kind to him. He hadn't known it to tell it. So why did Brown lie? It must have been to conceal the truth, perhaps to hide the identity of the one who did tell him that detail. Maybe Brown had his own source, a window into the investigation he did not want to share with the FBI. It had to be that.

Rafferty yelled out to his dispatcher. "Hey, Mio, where is Deputy Brown this morning?"

* * * * *

Zack had hidden Tubs away in the house in Kanab, guessing it would be the least likely place their faceless enemies would search. They let themselves in after their visit with Sheriff Rafferty. Tubs appeared at the kitchen door, rifle in hand. He lowered it at the sight of them.

"What did the sheriff have to say?"

"We're pretty sure he is in the dark about all this," Zack said.

"Brown lied," Eagle Feather said.

They went into the living room, sat and stared at each other.

"It makes sense," Zack said. "As chief deputy, Brown would be able to control things here in Kanab. He'd be privy to police action regarding the abductions and murders, and could protect Jedediah from discovery."

"Why Brown?" Tubs asked. "What's his interest? Is he even a Mormon?"

Zack pulled out his mobile. "Let's see what we can learn about him."

Tub's face showed alarm. "If you ask for a background check, won't Agent Hooper learn what you're doing?"

Zack gave a comforting smile. "I have a friend who will keep the search confidential."

After Zack completed his call to Pete Conley and was assured he'd have the information shortly, his thoughts turned to Janice Hooper. He knew any doubts about her position in this affair needed to be resolved quickly. He turned to the two men.

"While we wait for Pete to call back, we need to decide whether we can trust Agent Hooper. The things she said and did with Tubs can be interpreted two ways—as friend or foe. Any thoughts?"

Tubs' lips tightened. "She told me it was against FBI rules to let me talk to the professor after she hid him away, thet nobody else could know. Then I get bushwhacked. Seems obvious tuh me."

Zack nodded. "What she said is true. The FBI seldom will allow such a visit. It makes everyone vulnerable. Did she say why she would do it for you?"

"Well, she said she thought new information might come from the professor and me chatting."

"What did you hope to learn from him?" Eagle Feather asked.

"I thought he might know what was so important about thet cave and them damn bones."

Zack looked up at Tubs. "If Agent Hooper felt she needed you killed, she must also think she needs to kill the professor, do you agree?"

Tubs nodded.

"So, if your suspicions are true, Professor Philpott must be dead by now, from some sort of accident of some kind, don't you think?"

Tubs nodded again.

"If you were assured he is still alive, would your trust be restored?"

"Mebbe, mebbe not, but I'd sure feel better."

Zack took out his phone, saying, "Let's see what we can learn." He called Pete Conley again, asked for the number at the safe house where they were keeping the professor. Conley found it, set up a direct connection with a hub at the FBI office, untraceable. After a few moments, Zack handed his cell to Tubs. He watched as Tubs spoke to Professor Philpott.

When he was done, Tubs handed Zack the phone and nodded. "You was right," he said. "The professor is fine. He told me what I needed to know."

"Well, then, I think it's time to call Agent Hooper and tell her how things stand."

Tubs still seemed skeptical. "I'm not sure about her yet. Yeah, Philpott is alive, but she's got him tucked away under her control. Mebbe she figures I'm the dangerous one now."

Zack was frustrated. "Like you said before, Tubs, it's time for you to shit or get off the pot. We can't move forward thinking everyone is in the conspiracy. We've got to start sorting it out."

Eagle Feather put a hand on Tubs' shoulder. "We'll protect you now. You're not alone anymore."

Tubs sighed, gave a slow nod.

"Everyone sit down for a moment," Zack said. "Let's talk about suspects."

Zack took the easy chair and Tubs and Eagle Feather dropped into the sofa opposite him. Zack eyed each in turn. "We know about Jedediah. We know he snatched the boy and probably the girl. We don't know where the boy was actually killed, but we know the girl was murdered in Kanab somewhere, which may point to the old man. There was the break-in here that Libby warded off. That could have been the old man, but from Libby's description, he was likely younger and more agile, but..." Zack shrugged his shoulders.

"There's Deputy Brown," Eagle Feather said.

"Yes, Brown. If, and I say if he is involved, he has the advantage of inside information and freedom of movement around the area. His little slip about the stool is suspicious. There could be a reasonable explanation for that, which hopefully Rafferty will discover. But what's Brown's motive? He came to the sheriff's office a few years ago from back in Minnesota or somewhere." Zack shrugged. "We don't know enough about him."

"There's the evil twins," Eagle Feather said.

"Yeah, twiddle-dee-dum and twiddle-dee-dumber," Tubs muttered.

"What's our evidence?" Zack asked.

"We know they were guarding that cave, even ready to shoot me on sight without even knowing who I was," Eagle Feather said.

"We can be pretty sure they had orders to keep people away from the cave. But other than presenting a real hazard in the wilderness, they were likely just following instructions. We need to know who gave them those instructions and why." Zack paused. "We know this conspiracy must go a lot farther than just Kane and

Washington Counties. There are big bucks involved." He nodded at Tubs. "That professional killer whose career you ended cost them some bucks. Fogelberry's accident suggests another professional killing. Then consider the court injunction protecting the Preserve and the cave. That took lots of money and big politics."

"It had to be the LDS Church," Eagle Feather said.

"Thet's right," Tubs said. "The Fundamentalists don't have thet kind of power."

Zack agreed. "Okay, so we have the tiny end of the stick out here in Kanab, and the big end of the stick in Salt Lake City. Now what we got to do is pull the right string to find out who's in the middle."

# CHAPTER FIFTY-FIVE

Jeffrey Danes Harlow gave a sigh he couldn't quite conceal when he left the kitchen. The women of President Brown's household flashed sympathetic smiles for they fully understood the ordeal Jeffrey had just undergone.

He had been called to meet with President Brown and Elder Taylor, the two highest-ranking members of the Council. They wanted to know everything Jeffrey knew about the hanging of Jedediah. They would not accept there was anything he did not know. Yes, they knew it was an FBI investigation, but they also knew an FBI agent had visited Jeffrey in his home. What had they talked about?

Jeffrey had nothing to tell them. He explained that Agent Tolliver had asked Cynthia a few questions, all related to her father, his health and state of mind. The agent had explained to her Jedediah was under suspicion for the murders of both the boy and the girl. Naturally, Cynthia had been devastated by all this.

The two elders finally dismissed Jeffrey, apparently satisfied they there was nothing more to learn, but sent him away with a warning to inform them if he learned of anything new.

While they were interrogating him, Jeffrey had studied the faces of the two men. He knew Jedediah would have responded as he did only to someone of high rank in the church, but these men were portly and old, and it was hard to imagine them in such a role. There had to be someone else.

Outside the Brown home, Jeffrey felt an immeasurable sadness. He would miss Jedediah, but Cynthia would miss him more. It would be hard for her to live with the shame of her father's crimes. She would never be quite the same, he knew, and neither would their relationship.

In the past, when difficulties in the family arose, he could call Dan Fogelberry and they would meet at the cafe and talk about it, but now Dan was gone too. This web of murder had touched him in a big way. He felt anger grow along with his sadness.

Jeffrey's feelings demanded action. Before starting his car, he called Zack. "I've just come from a meeting with Elder Taylor and President Brown at their request," he said. "They are most eager to know what the FBI is doing."

Zack chuckled. "I'm sure. I'm here with Eagle Feather. We were just discussing those very people. What is your read on Brown and Taylor?"

Jeffrey's frustration surfaced. "I believe they know something, but they gave nothing away. Our little talk was more of a standoff."

"Maybe it's time I spoke to them. Do you think you can arrange that?"

Jeffrey's reply was immediate. "I'll set it up."

The moment Zack hung up, he called Janice. "I've got some good news for you."

"I could use some right about now," she said.

"Tubs is alive and well and I've got him hidden away."

He heard her sigh. "Thank goodness. What happened to him?"

"I won't go into detail right now. Let's just say a professional killer underestimated him and he went into hiding. We found him."

"Is there any cleanup to be done?"

Zack glanced at Tubs. "No, he took care of it himself."

"Good. Don't tell me where you've got him. The fewer people who know, the better." Her voice became brisk. "I've been going over the papers from Randy Musser's home. I've found a sketched diagram of the cave and some figures suggesting a plan to blow it up, probably to seal it shut. I have no doubt someone hired Musser to hide the evidence in the cave. There were no dates, I don't have a timeline, but it seems likely the murdered boy and his discovery interrupted all that. It's ironic Musser was there when the murder scene was discovered. I wonder what was going through his mind?"

"He must have begun to realize his own vulnerability right about then," Zack said.

Janice sounded thoughtful. "When you put all of this together, the history Professor Philpott and his colleagues were learning from those bones, the attempts to silence them, the injunction intended to keep us all out of the preserve, and now the plan to blow up the cave, can there be any doubt of a conspiracy to preserve the good name of the LDS Church?"

Zack grunted. "That's what we just concluded."

"Maybe it's time we spoke with some church fathers."

"Funny you should say that. I'm setting up a meeting with the FLDS big boys right now. I'll let you know when and where so you can join us."

\* \* \* \* \*

Chief Deputy William Brown walked into Sheriff Rafferty's office at noon. Rafferty looked up from his papers. "Where the hell have you been?"

Brown raised his eyebrows. "I've been on traffic patrol north of town, like usual. Is there a problem? Mio sounded urgent on the radio."

Rafferty sat back, dropping his pen on the stack of papers, and stared at Brown. "Why didn't you respond to his first call? Seems like we can never get you right away."

Brown stared back. "I'm sorry, Oliver, I was out of my unit talking to a driver I'd just stopped. You seem a bit on edge."

Rafferty swallowed his frustration. "Okay, yeah, I guess. Look, I'll get right to it. Why did you tell Agent Tolliver I told you the stool was moved from the house for the old man's hanging?" He watched his deputy closely, saw his eyes widen slightly.

"Geese, I'm sorry, Boss. To tell you the truth, I

couldn't remember who told me that. He caught me by surprise, and I admit I just threw your name out there."

Rafferty kept his eye on him. "Do you remember now?"

Brown paused. "Uh, yeah, actually, I heard it from LeRoy Taylor, the deputy marshal in Colorado City during a phone call, can't remember when, exactly."

Rafferty kept eyeing him. "Hmmm."

Brown leaned forward. "Is there a problem here, Boss? Do you doubt me for some reason?"

"William, I've never had a reason to doubt you before, and I'm not saying I doubt you now. But there was that order you didn't pass along, and using my name with that FBI Agent made me look bad, and lately it seems I'm never quite sure where you are or what you're up to."

Brown put on a formal aspect. "I'm sorry if I've given you cause for concern. I don't feel as if my behavior has changed."

Rafferty sighed. "Maybe not, maybe not. It's been chaotic around here lately with these murders to clear up, and feds all over the place, things have been tough." He gave a thin smile. "Do me a favor and hang around your radio for the next few days—make me feel better."

Brown stood, gave a brief nod, and left.

I didn't make a friend right there, Sheriff Rafferty thought. He picked up his pen and leaned over the paperwork again, but soon found his mind was elsewhere. Finally, he leaned back and plucked the phone from its cradle.

"Hey, Zack, Oliver Rafferty here. I just had a talk with my chief deputy. Of course, he came across as a little offended and put out, but his excuse for using me to explain why he knew the stool had been moved didn't hold water. On top of that, I've checked over his duty slate carefully. There were many times recently he was out of radio contact, some at critical times in regard to the murders."

"What do you suggest?" Zack asked.

"I'd feel better if you arranged to have another talk with him. I'll supply you with his duty schedule and call responses over the last month if you'd like."

"Sure, I'll do that. Let me do a bit of checking on my own first, and I'll get back to you with an official request. Meanwhile, can you give me more detail about his hiring; you know, why he came, where from, all the sort of stuff you'd have in his record?"

"No problem."

Rafferty hung up, surged out of his chair and walked over to the tall filing cabinet in the corner of the office. Current employees' files were in the front, alphabetically. He plucked out Brown and carried it back to his desk. The file was thin. There were no reprimands over the four years the man had been here, in fact there were a couple of notes commending him. He turned to Brown's employment application. Nothing unusual there. His prior employment was in the town of North Branch, a bit north of Minneapolis, population around twelve thousand. According to an attached note, there were no incidents or reprimands to transfer.

Rafferty stared at the note. It was stapled to the application, written in a hand he did not recognize. He studied it, then looked up a number for the North Branch Police Department, dialed it and asked for the chief.

\* \* \* \* \*

Zack was not surprised when Jeffrey called back with the news President Brown of the FLDS Church would not be available to meet with him. He suggested they call Elder Taylor instead. Jeffrey did so, and Elder Taylor agreed. One of Taylor's businesses was Real Estate, and they could meet in his office in Hildale at nine the next morning.

Not long after that conversation, Zack had a call from Sheriff Rafferty. He'd been in touch with Chief Nicol in North Branch, Minnesota where William Brown had worked as a police officer before coming to Kanab. Although his record was squeaky clean at Kanab, there had been some minor infractions in his first several years in North Branch. He had been a bit of a malcontent, apparently, which appeared to stem not from his work environment but from issues at home. There were reports of domestic abuse involving his mother. She denied he had ever harmed her, but neighbors had reported otherwise, and when officers were sent to the home on two occasions from neighbors' calls, they noted the woman appeared to have fresh bruises. After those incidents, Officer Brown appeared to settle down and the complaints stopped. Chief Nicol noted William's request for a transfer had come the same year his mother died. He had no other relatives in the area, it seemed, so such a move made sense. Why Kanab? Chief Nicol had no idea.

Rafferty went on to say he'd left a message for Chief Deputy Brown to see him to set up a meeting with Zack, the stated purpose to assist Zack with his investigation, but Rafferty had yet to hear back from Brown.

Zack called Janice Hooper. She agreed to attend the meeting with Elder Taylor the following morning. She had been going over Randy Musser's emails but had not found a direct connection to either church. "They must have met in person to discuss the project, likely at Musser's ranch, where no one would observe them." She planned to keep searching, hoping to find something in time for the meeting.

Eagle Feather declined to join them. "It's best I keep a low profile, keep to the background," he said. "I can learn more that way." He also declined to join Zack and Tubs for takeout; he wanted to be back at camp while it was still light. "I need to see a man about a shaman," was all he would say.

# CHAPTER FIFTY-SIX

The lowering sun stretched dark shadows across the road in front of Eagle Feather's truck as he drove down Pipe Spring Road. Ahead, the stark cliff face glowed golden orange. He found the campground completely deserted, as always, and pondered again how such an enterprise could stay afloat without customers.

He kept an eye cocked for Sam, not without some foreboding. Where the groundskeeper had been pleasant company in the past, he had a new dimension now.

Eagle Feather had declined to stay and eat with Zack and Tubs for a specific reason. He understood the danger Tubs was in from very powerful religious organizations, yet Eagle Feather alone knew something even more powerful hovered on the horizon. He wanted to learn more.

His supper was a solitary one in the deepening dusk, his fire the single spot of warmth and brightness in the empty surroundings. Darkness crept in and with it a pall of silence. The Navajo sipped aguardiente from a small flask and let it warm his belly as the peace of his solitude swept over him.

The moon rose and softened the looming cliffs. Sagebrush and buckthorn, beavertail cactus and pinyon were veiled in darkness for a short time and soon renewed in the moonlight as otherworld objects. The creatures of the night gave voice; a coyote called, night insects hummed, a fox yipped. All around him the night was alive, yet unseen.

An owl hooted nearby. The fire became embers; shadows crept close. Then Sam was there, seated cross-legged across from Eagle Feather, the red glow between them.

"You have questions," Sam said.

Eagle Feather nodded.

Sam waited.

"Why did you send me to visit your cave? You showed me the way, yet later you warned me of harm."

Sam's eyes were hypnotic. "I showed you the way so you can understand. They killed the boy on my doorstep. Others came in past years and disturbed me. They had deceit and evil in their hearts. I let you see so my message will be heard by those who desecrate the sacred ground."

"Who will listen to me?"

"Most will listen. Those who do not will meet their fate."

"We hunt the killers of the boy."

Sam nodded. "You have said so."

"We do not know where our hunt will take us. It has brought us to your door before. It may bring us there again."

"This I know also."

Both men were silent. The owl hooted again.

Sam stood, studied Eagle Feather. "You understand. That is good."

He faded into the darkness.

* * * * *

It was three minutes past nine when Zack maneuvered the red Jeep into a parking space directly in front of Taylor's Real Estate Office. The business was in its own building, a two-story construction with large glass windows. Decals offered large percentage discounts on properties and enticing mortgage rates. Already the sun reflected off the sidewalk warm and bright, foretelling a hot day.

Two other cars were parked in front of the office. Zack suspected one of them belonged to Janice. He pushed open the heavy glass door, heard the bell jingle. A receptionist at a desk directly in front of him glanced up and smiled.

"Mr. Tolliver?"

"I am."

"Please step right through." She pointed toward a short hall behind her. It led Zack to a massive wooden door, paneled and ornamented to such a degree as to suggest the Gate of Heaven rather than a seller of property. He turned the huge gleaming knob and stepped inside. The carpet underfoot was thick and plush; his feet actually sank. He was surrounded by dark maroon walls hung with rich tapestries, except for the wall immediately behind the huge mahogany desk where a large painting of pioneer Mormons and stalwart Indians was hanging, apparently portraying the original real estate deal. Two straight-backed velvet armchairs, the same color as the walls, faced the large oak desk. Zack's initial impression was he had stumbled into a mausoleum of kings, the second it would take three years of his salary to furnish this room.

Councilman and Elder Jacob Taylor did not rise from behind his desk. He gestured Zack to a chair. Janice was already in the other. She sent him a brilliant smile.

"I was just remarking to your colleague on the influx of federal agents in our little town of late," Taylor said. His voice was resonant, authoritative. "We seem to attract a swarm of attention regardless of the nature of the incident or where it occurred." There was no humor in the lines of his long and narrow face, his head was topped with thinning silver hair. He sat erect and spoke with studied deliberateness, in the tone of a man not accustomed to interruption. "I assume you are Agent Tolliver."

"I am."

"I would say welcome if I did not suspect the purpose of your visit involves an accusation of some sort."

Zack didn't respond. He glanced around the room. "The Real Estate business must be booming here."

"We do not do business in the same way as most communities. We have very few customers from beyond our borders."

"Yet you do well."

"Every church member can expect to do well in his time," Taylor said.

Janice stirred deep in her chair. "We are not here to make accusations, Mr. Taylor. We hope you can help us with our investigation."

Taylor turned his head toward her. "What is your faith, may I ask?"

"I was brought up a Christian."

"That covers a lot of territory, I would say. What denomination specifically?"

"I am—was a Lutheran."

"But no longer?"

Zack was uncomfortable with the direction the conversation was taking. "We did not come here to discuss our religious preferences."

Taylor turned to Zack. "What is your Faith?"

"Federal Bureau of Investigation."

In the pause that followed, Janice said, "Are you aware of the murder of the young man whose body was impaled at the mountain summit above your exclusive community?"

His eyes went to her. "Of course."

"There have been other murders and murder attempts associated with that crime."

"And because we reside beneath the crime scene we must have more information than anyone else? Is that your logic?"

"Of course not—"

"Or is it because our religious practices and beliefs are quite different from, say, Lutherans?"

"No, of course—"

Zack cut in. "It could be that the trails leading to the cave on the summit originate here and because your community is a closed one where everyone knows the business of everyone else."

Taylor's eyes swung back to Zack. "You have specific questions?"

"Your deputy marshals were the first law enforcement on the scene. I assume they report directly to the Marshal of Colorado City, yet we've received no report from him. In fact, we do not know his whereabouts during this time."

"Unfortunately, Marshal Rubin has had a death in the family and traveled back East to attend. His assistant marshals are quite capable."

Zack smiled. "We never received an official report from them, either."

Taylor's expression did not change. "I will see that you do."

Zack nodded his thanks. "My next question is somewhat more difficult. As you know, the courts passed an injunction prohibiting entry and preventing anyone from extricating materials from the Canaan Mountain Wilderness Study Area. The injunction is part of a long line of events presenting obstacles to the FBI investigation of that crime. This sudden and coincidental court action appears intended to slow, if not prevent altogether, our investigation of the boy's murder as well as prevent close inspection of all the bones in the cave. Few organizations have the political power to cause the state to invoke this order. Your church is one of the few."

Taylor shook his head. "Not our church; not the FLDS. We do not possess such power."

"Sounds like there's a "but" coming."

Taylor shrugged. "No."

"Were you going to say, but the LDS can?"

"I was not going to say that, and here comes your "but," but it is true."

Zack smiled. "Why would they want to do that?"

Taylor smiled back. "I have no idea."

"But I think you do, Mr. Taylor. I think you know exactly why. If the LDS Church can put that kind of pressure on the state, they can certainly do so to your church."

"Why—"

"Let's stop dancing here, Mr. Taylor. We have evidence to show at least some of the bones in that cave are victims of past heinous crimes by the Latter-day Saints. Maybe your church did not exist in those early days, but you were the southern Utah membership of the Latter-day Saints. You were all guilty of crimes such as the Fancher Wagon Train Massacre."

"That is very old news."

"You were guilty of the disappearance of Powell's men."

"That was never proven. And again, very old news."

"As far as the death of young Luke Wilson is concerned, we believe members of the Fundamentalist Church are guilty, possibly with pressure from the LDS Church."

"That is a wild accusation. If you know the guilty parties, tell me so I may know."

"At least one guilty person was Jedediah Meekes. That much we can prove."

To Zack's surprise, Taylor's expression changed to one of great sorrow. "I am very sad to hear of it. Jedediah was always a hard working, pious man, even if a bit over-zealous at times."

"So I've heard. But he didn't act alone. Someone worked with him, influenced him. Can you think of who that might be?"

Taylor remained silent for several seconds. "In truth, I can not. Jedediah kept to himself. He did not respond to the force of will of others.

"Except God," Janice said.

"Of course."

Zack rose to his feet. Janice stood as well.

Taylor did not stand nor offer his hand. "The FLDS Church will always try to protect its membership from slander and shame, but not by committing a crime. I am confident you will find our membership is not involved, and I wish you luck with your investigation."

Zack noticed Janice appeared transfixed by a framed photo on Taylor's desk. She took a step toward it. "Who is that?" she asked, pointing.

"That is our Prophet, President Josiah Brown."

Janice studied it. As she did, Zack asked another question.

"How does the FLDS consider the Wilson boy; as a gentile, an Apostate, a Lamanite?"

"I personally never considered him at all."

"Do the Destroying Angels still exist?"

Taylor's face cracked into a smile for the first time. "I see you've been enjoying Saints mythology."

Zack studied him a moment, then turned and led Janice out the door.

Once outside, he turned to her. "What was it about that picture that fascinated you?"

Janice flashed one of her brilliant smiles. "Brown and Brown; I just never put it together."

Zack raised an eyebrow.

"I saw it in the photo just now. Chief Deputy William Brown is the absolute image of President Josiah Brown."

# CHAPTER FIFTY-SEVEN

When Zack opened his mouth to respond, Janice laid a finger to her lips and motioned him to follow to her car. They got in and Janice turned the ignition. "This is not a discussion we should have out on the street," she said. She drove out to the highway, found a turnoff and parked.

She turned toward Zack. "Have you met the chief deputy sheriff of Kane County yet?"

Zack nodded. "Yes. Once."

"I met with him in Hurricane Monday morning. He came at the behest of the sheriff to offer to cooperate in the investigation."

"I've found Sheriff Rafferty to be very cooperative," Zack said.

"Yes. Well, so was his chief deputy, almost too much so, I thought."

"What do you mean?"

"Something in his manner, maybe. Also the fact he spoke of cooperation but didn't ask for anything from me." She grimaced. "That never happens. He was entirely too smooth, too willing. This morning when I found myself staring at that portrait of President Brown, something about it reminded me of that meeting. I wasn't sure why until I got close enough to isolate the facial features and then boom! Chief Deputy William Brown jumped out at me."

"According to Sheriff Rafferty, Brown came to him from Minnesota."

"And before Minnesota, where was he?"

"I don't know. Rafferty is doing a thorough background check."

Janice searched his eyes. "If the chief deputy is indeed related to the FLDS president, the implications are huge. The church might have a direct pipeline into everything the Kanab County Sheriff's Department does."

The thought caused Zack to sit upright. "I've been sharing everything I know with Rafferty, in the name of good cooperation. Thank God I never told him where Emma and Pru are."

"How much does the sheriff confide in his chief deputy?"

"A lot, I think. He told me he has always relied on him implicitly. I think we have to assume as our working hypothesis that everything the sheriff knows, Brown knows." The implications continued to strike Zack with force. "Shit!"

"We need to check our back trail."

"Forget it." Zack wagged his head. "We have to assume they know everything we know, at least up to yesterday when I told Rafferty about Brown's slip with the stool." Another thought struck him. "I can't remember if I told Rafferty about Tubs." Zack grabbed his phone and called Tubs, told him he needed to get out. "We have to assume your location is compromised. I'll send an agent with a car immediately. He'll call you when he gets there. No, it doesn't matter where you go so long as no one else knows. Wait for my call." He ended the call. "Shit!"

He glanced at Janice. She was watching him in silence.

"Rafferty is arranging for me to meet with Brown about the stool thing," he said. "How shall I play it?"

"Let's string some of this together first," Janice said. "If Brown knew about the stool taken from the house, who could have told him?"

Zack shook his head. "To my knowledge, no one knew that little detail except Jedediah's son-in-law, Jeffrey Harlow. He's the one told me about it."

"Could he have told Deputy Brown?"

"It's possible, but I don't think he did."

"If he didn't tell him, there's only one way he could know."

"Yeah. Deputy Brown had to have been present at the murder."

Janice turned to him, her face grim. "So in answer to your question of how to play it with Brown—arrest him."

Zack shook his head. "There's too much we don't know yet. I need some background before the meeting. I'll find out whether Jeffrey told Brown about the stool. Can you get deeper background on Brown and his mother from Minnesota?"

Janice nodded. "When is your meeting?"

"Don't know yet. Could be anytime. We've got to hurry."

Janice started up the car and swerved into a fast U turn. "I'll get you back to your Jeep, then I'll go to St. George and get to work." She stamped down on the accelerator. "By the way, what are Destroying Angels?"

Zack glanced at her, grimaced. "A little bit of Mormon history that might yet be relevant. Bit of a long story; I'll give you a quick version. It began in the early days of the Mormons, when they were still in Illinois. Church leaders sometimes found certain people to be annoyances, but lacked justification in terms of law or religion to do anything about it. So they formed a handy little group of thugs they called "Destroying Angels," coded DAnites or Danites, to remove them. This the church has denied, but sufficient factual and stated evidence exists to support the allegation. In short, if you transgressed in light of the church's top leaders, this secret group could be set upon you, like a pack of killer hounds." Zack glanced at Janice. "I have no reason to believe this secret group doesn't still exist, and it might well be responsible for the professional killings we are investigating."

Janice dropped Zack by his Jeep and headed on to St. George.

Zack dug his keys from his pocket and walked to his vehicle. To his surprise, Elder Taylor waited there for him.

"Agent Tolliver, if I may."

Zack paused.

"I would like you to understand something that you likely already suspect. After your parting shot, I wish to make it abundantly clear that while the Fundamentalist Latter-day Saints Church is a completely separate entity from the Latter-day Saints in Salt Lake City, that organization is able to exert considerable pressure upon us, not from a relationship, but from pure wealth and political leverage. You understand?"

"In other words, you bow to their bidding."

"Not always. The LDS Church in Utah is rather like the NRA in Congress; they hold considerable political sway from buying representatives with campaign contributions and financial favors. So one must pick one's battles."

"And resisting pressure to protect the Saints dirty secrets, even if the murdering of innocents is involved, isn't one of them."

Taylor protested. "We don't know that."

"Yes, we do. And remember, Jedediah was one of yours, not one of theirs." Zack climbed into the Jeep and left Elder Taylor staring after him.

He drove directly to the Harlow compound. Jeffrey's first wife Patti opened the door. She ushered Zack into the foyer and went to find her husband.

Jeffrey came immediately, shook Zack's hand, and smiled. "My association with the FBI is becoming well known in the neighborhood."

"Hopefully, it will not put you in danger. As a police officer, people would expect us to question you."

Jeffrey laughed at Zack's worried expression. "No fears. The community here knows how I stand on most issues. How did your meeting with Elder Taylor go?"

Zack shrugged. "He did admit in a vague way attempts to keep people away from the cave to preserve the honor of both churches, but nothing else."

"That could be all there is."

"Maybe." Zack let his doubt show on his face. "However, I came to ask you a specific question."

"Go ahead."

"Did you ever talk to anyone other than me about your suspicions regarding the stool Jedediah stood on to be hanged? That it had been moved from the house?"

"No, just you." Jeffrey was firm.

"Not anyone? Not to Deputy Brown of Kane County, for instance?"

"Absolutely not. You are the only person I spoke to about that."

Zack shook his hand, turned to go. "Thank you."

"That's it?"

"That's it. I'll be in touch."

As Zack started up the Jeep, his phone buzzed. It was Lori Hyde from Evidence Response Team Unit.

"Go."

"I found a fingerprint in an interesting place."

"Where?"

"On the stool Jedediah used."

Zack was immediately attentive. He turned off the Jeep. "Go on."

"We should have found it earlier, we went over the stool first thing and found nothing. We had no doubt it had been wiped. Later I thought about it. You know how you pick up a stool by grabbing it with one hand? When you do, your fingers curl under the seat rim and push against the inside panel with a lot of pressure. Some one wiping prints might not think of that. So I went back and dusted all around the underside of the seat panel and I found one big beautiful digitus medius print. I ran it, and it turned up in two data files, criminal and law enforcement. It—"

"William Brown."

Lori went silent. "How did you know that?"

"Lori, you are a good scientist and I am a good investigator. You have confirmed my theory. Thank you." After the call, he immediately called Sheriff Rafferty. The desk officer answered, told him Rafferty had stepped out.

Zack thanked him and called Rafferty's cell. The sheriff answered immediately.

"Hi, Zack. What's up?"

"You need to bring in your chief deputy. We need him for questioning."

"I've been trying to reach him. In fact, I'm on my way to his home now. I've warned him, but he still ignores his radio."

"Listen, Sheriff, hold up, get backup. Don't go by yourself. We have solid evidence he's involved in this thing. Or better yet, wait for me. I'm on my way to Kanab right now."

"Damn. I really hoped it wouldn't come to this." There was a pause. "Okay, I'll meet you on Rt. 89 just east of town."

Zack started up the Jeep. He spun onto 389 east and cranked up his speed. Twenty-five minutes later he pulled up behind the sheriff's cruiser on the road shoulder.

Rafferty climbed out and walked back to him. He peered in, his ruddy face bleak. "Thanks for coming along. This is not the most pleasant task I've ever had to do." He waved down the road. "Brown has been staying in a cabin at an old movie set about five miles east of here. There's a dirt road on the left leads into it. It's about three miles."

"No wonder he's hard to reach," Zack said. "How do you know he's there now?"

"Well, I don't, except he isn't anywhere else I know of." The sheriff shrugged. "So we'll go find out."

"What vehicle are we looking for?"

"He's been driving one of our cruisers, like that one." Rafferty pointed to his own vehicle. He slapped the roof of the Jeep and walked back to his car.

They headed east on Rt. 89 at a much more sedate pace. In another five minutes, the sheriff's car turned off onto a dirt road that crossed a wide meadow. The sheriff's cruiser kicked up dust. Zack paced his speed to remain behind the worst of it. They entered a wood of aspen and pine and emerged onto desert tufted with sage and mesquite. Near a section of sandstone cliffs that glowed pink and white in the bright sun were several buildings in various levels of disrepair. Zack spotted a white SUV with orange letters parked near one of them.

Zack reached behind his seat with one hand as he drove and loosened the latch that held his rifle in place. He kept an eye on the rough road and the other on the building as they approached it. When the sheriff's cruiser came to a stop the cabin door opened and a man stepped out and stood watching them. He appeared to be unarmed.

The sheriff climbed slowly out of his cruiser, the very image of a reluctant man. Zack brought the Jeep to a stop behind and to one side of the sheriff's car and waited as the two men talked. After a few minutes, Rafferty waved Zack over.

"William will ride in with me," he said as Zack approached. Rafferty offered a smile and a shrug. "I think we'll find a reasonable explanation for all of this. We're gonna head back to the office and talk there."

"Your call," Zack said. He watched the two men climb into the sheriff's car. Rafferty spun it around in a cloud of dust and lurched back down the potholed road toward the highway.

Zack stood and watched for a while. He felt uneasy, it had all been too simple. The sheriff had not cuffed Brown; obviously, he still trusted him. Zack walked to the cabin and peered inside. Two dusty windows allowed little light. He let his eyes adjust and glanced around the one room interior. He understood that Brown had been with the Kanab Sheriff's Office for four years, yet the cabin had a very temporary look. There was a cot, a two-burner hot plate, a suspended dowel that served to hang uniform pants and shirts, three stacked open-ended boxes for socks, t-shirts and underclothing. There was a box with food supplies. Zack searched for weaponry. He found pegs in the wall spaced for rifles to stand side by side, but he saw none. An empty holster hung from another peg.

Zack hurried outside, ran over to Brown's SUV and tried the door. It was locked. He peered in the windows. No rifles. He put hands on hips and thought about it. Where did he keep them? Living way out here on his own, Brown wouldn't leave all his weapons five miles back at the sheriff's office in Kanab. He must have stashed them somewhere. But the empty holster—that was the real problem. Even with all he knew, Rafferty trusted his deputy; he hadn't even patted him down.

Zack ran to the Jeep, started it up, spun around, and roared out the entrance road as fast as the vehicle's suspension would allow.

# CHAPTER FIFTY-EIGHT

He found the sheriff walking along the shoulder of Rt. 89 toward town. He had no hat, no radio, and no weapon. Zack pulled alongside. Rafferty cussed a blue streak as he climbed into the Jeep. He glanced at Zack.

"I know, I know, I should have patted him down and cuffed him. He fooled me, seemed completely ready to cooperate."

Zack gunned the Jeep and glanced at him. "Are you okay?"

"Yeah, I'm okay. He didn't seem to want to harm me, just get me out of the way. Now he's got my weapon."

"He's got more than that," Zack said. He told Rafferty about the missing rifles. "He's got them hidden and ready to use somewhere." He glanced at the sheriff. "Don't feel too bad. He had this all planned, right down to you coming to find him. Where'd he have that gun, in his boot?"

The sheriff groaned. "No, he just tucked it in his belt in back with his shirt over it. He knew me pretty well, figured I wouldn't search him." Rafferty smacked his forehead. "Goddammit, I trusted him. Even after all this I still trusted him. He knew I would."

Zack nodded. "Yeah, he did. The question now is, where's he gonna go?"

"Lemme borrow your phone."

Zack passed it to him.

Rafferty called his desk duty officer. "Mio, put out an APB on Chief Deputy William Brown. He's armed and likely dangerous."

"Deputy Brown?" There was a pause. "Uh, okay. What's he driving?"

"He's driving my cruiser—and don't you say a damn word, just put out the call. I'll be there in five minutes." He handed the phone back to Zack.

"I don't think we're going to find him just driving around," Zack said. "Like I said, he's got a plan. Whatever it is, he's piled up weaponry somewhere. Either he's got some accomplices, or he's planning to make a last stand of some sort."

"Why? Where? What's he up to?"

Zack glanced at Rafferty. "We now know Brown was involved with Jedediah, probably manipulated him into murdering the boy, although we don't have a motive yet. We have solid evidence he was there when Jedediah died. We found his fingerprint on the stool Jedediah stood on when he was hanged. We think he murdered the old guy." Zack stared ahead down the road. They had just reached the outskirts of Kanab. "We will need to question him regarding the death of Luke Wilson, of the high school girl Beth Daniels, the attempted abduction of my wife, and, oh yeah, let's not forget the attempted break-in of my sister-in-law's home."

Rafferty cursed under his breath. "No wonder he hasn't been around much—he's been too busy."

They reached the intersection with 89A in town center, and Zack turned toward the county sheriff's complex and dropped him there.

"I'll leave you to follow up the search. I have to check in with my boss and decide our next move. I'll be in touch. Good luck." When Zack left, the sheriff was rushing into his office.

He drove south to Fredonia and headed west on 389. He wanted to check in on Eagle Feather at the campground, fill him in. He called Janice and put her on speaker.

"What's up, Zack?"

"Janice, I need to report. Chief Deputy William Brown is on the run in Sheriff Rafferty's cruiser and has his gun. I just picked up the sheriff along the road and dropped him at his office. He's okay, but right pissed."

"I'll bet he is! How'd that happen?"

"I'll explain it all later. Have you learned anything about Brown?"

"I certainly did, and this information may be real important right now. It seems President Josiah Brown had a wife nobody mentions much, named Pamela. She was one of his early marriages. It was not a happy situation for her, she didn't much like sharing. They had a son, but before the kid was even a year old the mother ran away, took the boy with her. Josiah was real upset, not so much about Pamela, I'm told, but about losing the boy. He sent out private detectives by the basketful but Pamela was either very shrewd or had some help because he never located her. She ended up in—"

"North Branch, Minnesota."

"Right you are. She raised the boy there on her own. She harbored a very big grudge against the boy's father, one that William apparently inherited. She's the one steered him toward the police academy figuring President Brown was less likely to try to reclaim a cop. Again, pretty shrewd. William was hired right there in North Branch and did okay after a rough start. He has a lot of trouble with authority—go figure. Smacked his mother around a little bit as a teen. But he buckled down and cared for her until she died almost six years ago from cancer. One of his colleagues there says William blames his mom's death on a lifetime of anxiety brought about by his father. Anyway, not long after his mom died, he applied for a transfer, tried several communities, looking for a spot. I bet you can guess which ones. He applied to the Washington County Sheriff's Department, the Hurricane Police Department, even over at Page and here in St. George, but he landed in the best place possible for his purposes, right there in Kane County."

"What do you mean the best place possible?"

"I'm thinking he came out here with something in mind, and he's just now playing it out. To fulfill his agenda, he needed to be near his old man."

"We thought he might be feeding inside information to the church."

"Could be, maybe to get close to his father. But I believe he means to do the man harm."

"So where does the Jedediah business fit in with your theory?"

"Well, my guess is he latched on to the old zealot because he knew he could influence the man. Maybe he wanted to prove himself, to impress certain people."

"Why Luke Wilson?"

"Just a guess, but all this started about the time the cave became an issue. Maybe the kid stumbled onto it on one of his hikes." Janice paused. "Hey, do you expect me to have all the answers?"

"Well, I guess we'll learn the answer eventually. So what's your best guess where I'll find Brown right now?"

"It looks like he's discarded all pretensions and is enacting a plan he's had in mind for a long time. We can be pretty sure it involves his father. You better start with President Brown's compound, make sure the man is protected. I'll get some agents moving up that way and come out myself."

"Janice, we don't have all the pieces to this puzzle yet. Rafferty checked Brown's duty record. He could not have done in the reporter Fogelberry, nor do I see him hiring an expensive killer to rub out Tubs. On top of that, someone should be walking around with a serious limp after my wife shot him in the butt while he was crawling out the basement window."

"I know we've got more work to do, Zack. We'll figure it out. Until I can get there, isn't there an Indian who doesn't exist who could keep an eye on you?"

Zack smiled as he ended the call. He had every intention of enlisting Eagle Feather's help in any event. He took the turnoff for Pipe Spring Road and turned into the campground but Eagle Feather's truck was gone. When Zack called him, the Navajo's phone told him it was not in service at this time. He turned the Jeep around, he'd have to go on without him.

Zack kept his phone in his hand, called Jeffrey Harlow and asked for the Brown residence address. When Jeffrey asked why, he told him.

"What are you going to do, Zack?"

"Take President Brown into protective custody, I suppose."

"What if he's in it with his son?"

"I'll still need to keep an eye on him."

Jeffrey paused. "You do realize the son might already be there. Have you got Eagle Feather with you?"

"No, he's off on his own somewhere."

"Okay." Jeffrey sounded decisive. "Stop by my house and pick me up. I'm coming with you."

"I won't argue you out of that," Zack said.

Twenty-five minutes later, he pulled up in front of Jeffrey Harlow's compound. The deputy was waiting at the gate, in uniform with his sidearm and holding a rifle.

"I'll admit it's good to see you," Zack said and gave him a smile.

Jeffrey climbed in. As they moved out he said, "However all this turns out, I'm likely to be without a job and a religion."

"But you've still got your family—and your conscience."

Jeffrey nodded, but his thoughts were hard to read.

The Brown compound was less than a mile away. Zack was taken aback by the size of it. The exterior wall was ten feet tall and seemed to extend forever.

He glanced at Jeffrey. "What the hell is in there, anyway?"

"A park, a zoo, a rifle range, you name it." He glanced at Zack. "What's your plan?"

"I guess I'll just walk up to the front door and ring the bell."

"I will say I like your style," Jeffrey said.

They turned in the drive and approached the gate. It stood wide open. They glanced at each other. Zack drove through it, on up the drive at idle speed. It was a long drive with a large, green lawn on either side. The house was a massive two-story building with pillars rising to a balcony over a veranda. Beyond the lawn in the distance were tree groves. The tops of buildings showed over them.

"The zoo," Jeffrey said, following Zack's gaze.

They advanced warily, stopped in front of the house. They climbed out and went up the steps to the marble floor of the portico. The massive front door was ajar. Zack edged it open further with his rifle barrel.

As experienced as he was, he was shocked by the scene that unfolded. A dark puddle of viscous liquid spread on the interior floor directly in front of him. A woman lay there, on her back, dressed in plain clothes and a bonnet. On her forehead, visible beneath the bonnet rim was a small round hole. Blood pooled beneath her head and shoulders. Zack watched Jeffrey kneel and check her pulse and put a cheek to her mouth. He shook his head. She was gone. Jeffrey's face was drained of blood, his hands shaking.

Filled with dread, the men crept down the foyer, rifles ready. The wood flooring was solid and made no sound as they moved along. Zack led the way through the arched parlor entry. A fireplace was on one wall with armchairs facing it, a couch and two chairs were grouped on the opposite side. Another woman lay on her side on the couch facing the men, her sightless eyes staring past the blood that pooled and dripped off the rich velvet cushion to the floor. She, too, had a small hole in her forehead.

"My God," Jeffrey mumbled.

"Who are they?" Zack's whisper was harsh.

"Those are two of Josiah Brown's wives, Judith and Constance."

"How many more does he have?"

Jeffrey looked grim. "Two more who live here, Katherine and Prudence."

Zack gestured with his rifle toward the door at the far side of the parlor. "What's in there?"

"Dining room and kitchen."

Jeffrey went to check Constance's pulse, a hopeless gesture. Zack crossed the parlor and stepped through the open door into the dining room. Another woman in plain clothes was slumped at the large wood table, her blood staining the dainty white doilies and white brocade tablecloth with red splotches. The chair in which she sat partially supported her body. In her hand was a dinner knife, her apparent desperate attempt at defense. Her wounds were not so neat; blood stained her side and there was a hole in her temple.

Jeffrey had come up behind Zack. "Katherine," he whispered.

Beyond the dining room the door to the kitchen was closed.

"Is there an exit from the kitchen?" Zack asked.

Jeffrey nodded. "It leads to a mud-room, and beyond that a lean-to for firewood."

"Any other doors?"

Jeffrey shook his head. "If he didn't go that way, he's still in there."

Zack gestured Jeffrey to stand opposite him at the side of the door. He prodded it open with his rifle barrel. They burst in. At first the room appeared to be empty. The gas stove had a burner on and a pot of porridge bubbled away. The kitchen lights gleamed bright, a fireplace on the far wall exuded warmth. A plate of toast was on the kitchen table.

Zack glanced quickly around the room, found the door to the mud-room. It was ajar. Jeffrey touched Zack's arm, gestured toward a side door, which seemed to be a pantry. Zack went there and pulled open the door. There they found Josiah's fourth wife, Prudence huddled in the closet where she had attempted to hide. She had not succeeded, a single round hole in her forehead told the story.

"Oh my God," Jeffrey said.

"Should anyone else be here?" Zack asked. "Are there servants or children?"

Jeffrey was slow to respond, overcome by shock. "There should be four children here, I think. The help comes only on certain days."

"Would they be in school now?"

"I don't know, I don't think so."

Zack scrutinized Jeffrey. "Are you going to be okay? We need to search the rest of the house."

Tears filled his eyes, his face was sallow, but he nodded. They walked back through the parlor to the stairs. Zack took his phone from his pocket and called Janice. "How close are you?"

"I'm just arriving at Hildale."

"Come directly to Josiah Brown's house." Zack gave her the address. "There's been a massacre here, four women dead, shot, executed. We've seen no sign of Brown or his children yet. We are still searching the house. We need ambulances, forensics, a full support team."

Zack put the phone away, held his rifle ready and led the way upstairs. A thorough search revealed nothing. No more bodies, but no Brown and no children.

He let Janice in when she arrived. Her face registered shock as she inspected the scene. "Do you think he has the children?"

"I do," Zack said. "Jeffrey called the school here in Hildale, they told him the children are homeschooled.

William Brown has something else in mind for them. Something that requires a small arsenal of firearms."

"Where would he take them?"

Zack shook his head, but a small kernel of an idea had begun to form in his mind. "Can you take over here? I have an idea I'd like to check out."

Doubt was written all over Janice's face. "Not alone. Where's your Indian friend?"

"Missing."

"So what good is he?" She called out to a young agent nearby. "Theodore, go with Agent Tolliver."

Theodore was tall, lanky, and very eager. "Yes, sir, ma'am." He gave a wide smile.

Janice glared at Zack. "I know your style, but you don't go off half cocked with me, understand? The second you find them, you back off and you call me."

Zack nodded. With Theodore in tow, he walked out the door.

Jeffrey followed them. "I have to stay," he said. "I'm the only Colorado City Marshal available. The chief is away, I can't raise that knucklehead LeRoy, and Stan has been out for a week now on some kind of medical leave. It's all up to me."

Zack thought about that. "You don't know what Stan's medical issue is, do you?"

Jeffrey shook his head. "No details, he just said it was a medical issue."

"It's been a week? Starting when?"

"I'm thinking Thursday might have been the first day he stayed home."

Zack nodded. Without another word, he gestured Theodore into the passenger seat of the Jeep, climbed in himself and drove away.

# CHAPTER FIFTY-NINE

The facts and possibilities raced through Zack's mind even before he climbed behind the wheel of the Jeep. He glanced at the young agent next to him.

"Fasten your seatbelt," he said in a fatherly tone. "This will be one of the wildest rides you ever experienced."

The man grinned. "You can call me Teddy, sir." He continued all in one breath. "I've heard a lot about you. You are like a legend at the academy."

Zack felt a sadness overcome him. This kid had no idea what they were up against. It should be Eagle Feather here next to him, with that habitual sardonic look on his face, a backup he could trust in any circumstance. He wondered where the Navajo had gone. He shrugged; nothing to be done.

"Where are we going, sir?"

"First stop is the Colorado City Marshal's Office." He glanced at Teddy. "You are not to leave this Jeep under any circumstance unless I say so. Understood?"

"Yes, sir."

Zack figured he knew what Stan's medical issue was. If he was correct, it meant the deputy marshal was involved with this business. He also guessed if Stan was involved, LeRoy would be also. His speculation went further. Chief Deputy Brown had weapons stashed somewhere, at least two rifles. Zack did not doubt he had kidnapped the children for hostages. He had planned the massacre of Brown's wives. It was certain the man had no expectations to survive this, so reason dictated he intended to make a stand somewhere, make a statement. Zack thought he knew where; he was driving to the Marshal's Office to test his theory.

They approached the small station at slow speed.

"Look close as we pass," Zack told Teddy. "We are looking for Sheriff Rafferty's cruiser, with 'Sheriff' in big orange letters."

They drove by slowly. It turned out Zack didn't need Teddy's help. The cruiser sat in plain sight in a parking place fronting the building.

Zack gunned the Jeep and they sped away. Teddy stared at him, confusion on his face. Zack explained in short, succinct sentences.

"William Brown is taking the hostages up the mountain, four children and President Brown. He's picked a spot he can defend and hold us off with his rifles. There is just one vehicle trail up the mountain, the Squirrel Canyon Trail. The other possible trail is the Water Canyon Trail, but it's just for hikers. If he were taking that trail, he'd have driven straight there in the cruiser, left the car and started hiking. If he were taking the Squirrel Canyon Trail, he'd have to exchange the cruiser for a four-wheel drive vehicle. That is what he has done."

Teddy seemed to follow the logic. "But how could he expect to just waltz up to the Colorado City Marshal's Office and drive away in one of their vehicles?"

"Because he's getting help from one or more of the deputy marshals."

Teddy stared. "Oh."

Zack followed the route selected by his GPS to reach the Squirrel Canyon Trailhead. Here they found a section of fence knocked down.

"He went this way," Zack said and drove the Jeep over the collapsed fence. Fresh tracks in the sand led steeply down into the wash and climbed out the other side. Now they were on a sandy road, reasonably level for a couple of miles.

When the road narrowed and began to climb more steeply, Zack glanced at Teddy. "Their ambush could be anywhere along here from now on. Stay low in your seat, and be ready to duck under the firewall."

He stole another glance at him and grinned. "You can take your seatbelt off now."

They were encountering more difficult terrain now, and the men bounced and jostled in their seats. Zack drove as fast as he dared. At divisions of the road, Zack stopped, climbed out and hunted for the fresh tire tracks. There had been no attempt to obscure them.

They came to a section so steep the Jeep momentarily spun a wheel. Zack turned off the engine, set the brake and climbed out. He motioned for Teddy to stay where he was and walked up the sandy grade. Near the top he kept low, moved slow, then dropped to his stomach. From here he could see the vegetation marking where the road leveled off and the sharp rising cliffs beyond. Zack studied the terrain, took his time, inspected every stunted pinyon tree, each clump of sage and brush. A slight metallic gleam showed behind a clump of trees and he grunted in satisfaction. He slithered back down the slope to the Jeep, reached in and unstrapped two rifles, giving one to Teddy.

"Follow me and stay low," he said. "The party is up ahead."

He moved off the track to the right and cut obliquely up the rise, keeping low. Teddy followed. After two hundred yards, they were near the crest of the rise. Zack made Teddy stay and crept on up. He used a pinyon tree for cover and peered out. The vehicle he had spotted from the other angle was a hundred feet away. He could see it clearly now, a Colorado City Marshal's SUV. Brush was piled on the side toward the trail to disguise it. Beyond the near level ground where it was parked, red slickrock rose out of the soil, climbed steeply and grew into vertical sandstone formations at the top. A defender positioned up there had an open shot at anyone trying to approach.

This sandstone crown ran the entire length of the cliff, a natural fort. Zack studied it for any weaknesses. The ATV trail looped around to the far left. Deputy Brown would be watching that trail. To the far right were cliffs, climbable, no doubt, but he'd be exposed the entire way. Beyond them, the ground fell away into a deep canyon. It was the only possible way to work behind the defenders, but it meant a long hike just to find out if he could climb the cliff from there. He decided to wait, watch for any movement, try to locate Brown and the hostages.

He wormed down the slope to Teddy.

"Their vehicle is up there, abandoned," he told him. "They've proceeded on foot. My bet is they are tucked away at the top of these cliffs, but there is no way to know for sure and no way to approach without getting shot." He glanced at the young agent. "Any ideas?"

Teddy thought. "A distraction, maybe, something to draw fire long enough to climb the cliff?"

"Are you volunteering?"

Teddy hesitated. "What should I do?"

Zack thought out loud. "I think we can assume if they're up there they heard the Jeep coming, saw some dust. Now they're wondering how close we are but likely still expect to see us on the road. So maybe we should give them what they want."

He led Teddy to the driver's side of the Jeep, climbed in it to demonstrate. "You will coast back down this slope a couple of hundred feet, in low gear with the clutch in, like this. Count to two hundred slowly to allow me to get into position, then hit the accelerator, pop the clutch, spin the wheels and make as much dust as possible. Use the handbrake to hold your position enough so the wheels spin, but you don't move forward. Think you can do that?"

"Yes, sure I can." Teddy was all eagerness.

"You need to make it sound as if we can't make it up the steep road. You'll send up lots of dust. Repeat the maneuver several times. With luck, they will think both of us are in the Jeep, struggling to get up this patch. Got it?"

"Yes, sir." Teddy climbed in, released the brake, and began to work the Jeep back down the trail.

Zack worked his way back around to the right, mentally counting, staying just under the crest of the slope. At two hundred, he peered over to check his position. He was far to the right of the SUV. A small amount of brush suitable for a bit of cover was in front of him, after that nothing but open slickrock to the base of the cliff.

He heard the roar of the Jeep now, listened to it build, grinned in satisfaction. It sounded as he'd hoped and should draw the attention of the men above. He stayed low, worked through the brush and without pause sprinted across the slickrock in a stooping run, churning hard as it sloped upward. His legs burned with the effort, he expected to hear the slap of a rifle shot, the ping of a bullet at any moment. It didn't happen. Zack came to the base of the vertical climb, his breath coming in gasps. He was momentarily out of view from above.

Next would be the climb. Everything depended upon his approach going unnoticed. If not, they could shoot him off the wall like metal ducks in a shooting gallery.

The Jeep engine grew louder. It was time to get started. Zack strapped the rifle to his back, found a high grip, then another, followed with his feet on good footholds. The climb was not difficult. The possibility of becoming a target any moment, however, was unnerving.

The Jeep noise grew from a distant sound to a percussive resonance that sounded as if it was originating in the wall itself. He glanced down in time to see the Jeep fly into sight over the crest of the trail, front wheels in the air, then slam to the ground, grinding to a halt in full view of the cliffs above. The engine died with a shudder. In horror, Zack heard immediate rifle fire and the pings of bullets slapping into the metal of his Jeep. The windshield exploded; at the same moment Teddy launched himself from the vehicle and hit the ground rolling. He scrambled behind the Jeep followed by a trail of bullets.

Zack groaned. What the hell was he doing?

Regardless of Teddy's intentions the distraction was complete and Zack used it to finish his climb unmolested. Just before he slithered over the top he saw Teddy run and launch himself back down the slope, apparently unharmed. Zack would take up the matter of the Jeep with him later.

Safe and unseen behind a small pinnacle, Zack took stock. The percussive snaps of rifle fire were hard to pin down, but definitely came from the opposite side of the slope from his current position. He also knew there were at least two riflemen. They would be behind cover, likely small pinnacles or hoodoos similar to the one protecting him now. Because of the curvature of the ground between them, it would not be difficult to work toward them. But they may have noticed Zack was not driving the Jeep, and even now be wondering where he was. They might well figure out what he was doing; even now one of the men could be working upslope to try to move above him. Zack would be defenseless against a shooter from above.

He decided to make a similar move. He slithered up the slope, keeping a careful eye on the intervening terrain for any movement. Here there was less vegetation, mostly bald rock and isolated boulders tossed here and there as if by giants. Crawling as he was, he could see little and had to stop from time to time and lift his head to see. He had to estimate distance accurately, to judge how far his opponent would likely move up the slope before working laterally himself. He reached that point in his mind, found good cover in a slight crevice in the rock, stretched out with his rifle before him, and waited.

The wait felt long, enough so he began to doubt himself. He felt an overwhelming impulse to continue moving laterally, beginning to think he had overestimated his opponents. At that moment he heard a slight clink sound, like metal on rock. It came from the direction he faced, but a little below him. He inched his rifle to point that way.

360

There was sudden rifle fire from somewhere below. He saw movement, a head came. He aimed his rifle at the head and said, "Don't move or you are a dead man."

The head, topped by a wide brimmed hat, froze. Zack stood, kept his rifle on the man and walked to him. "Lay the rifle down on the ground in front of you. Now push it away."

The man complied.

"Turn to your back, your hands above your head."

He did. Zack was not surprised to see it was LeRoy Taylor. He prodded him with his rifle. "Roll toward me and over on your stomach. Now bring your hands down and clasp them behind your back."

LeRoy never made a sound. He appeared to be in shock.

Zack knelt with a knee in the center of LeRoy's lower back, his rifle barrel against the back of his neck, and found a plastic tie in his pocket. He locked LeRoy's wrists together with it and stood.

"Feel free to make all the noise you wish. I will wait above and shoot your friend as he comes to save you."

LeRoy tried to bluff a laugh. "He won't fall for that."

Zack chuckled. "Well, you just did. There's one more of you. Thank you for answering my question." He left the man supine and confused and continued across the slope.

He studied the sandstone fragments that marked the edge of the cliffs as he moved from cover to cover, careful to make no noise, staying low for concealment. It took a long time. The midafternoon sun baked his shoulders and reflected up in his face from the slickrock. There was a shimmer from the heat, shadows under the rock fragments appeared black and cave-like, making it difficult to see if anyone was down there.

A row of boulders forming a natural wall came into view. A few steps more and Zack saw figures huddled in tight. He brought the rifle around and studied them. He counted only four. They were the children. He studied the terrain around him with a slow scan. Where was Chief Deputy William Brown? Had he set a trap for Zack? He stared up the slope; his eye explored every niche and crevice that might possibly conceal a rifleman. No good.

Zack saw he had a signal and called Theodore, told him the children were all right, huddled above the cliff. He told him to call Janice for backup, after that he could climb up and rescue the children—Zack had his back. As soon as he ended the call, Zack moved laterally uphill away from the place he had been in case Brown had his voice zeroed in. From a place commanding the best view on all sides he waited until he saw Teddy emerge above the cliff near the place the children were hidden. He did not reveal himself. Instead, he scanned the slope for any movement. There was none.

He watched as Teddy found the children and they greeted him. He saw Teddy called the rescue in to Janice. Zack decided Brown must have moved higher up the mountain. He still held a hostage, his father, Josiah Brown. Maybe this was all about William's feelings toward his father. It would end with a murder, possibly a murder suicide if Zack couldn't intervene. He began to climb the mountain parallel to the roadway.

It took time. He could not know where Brown might decide to wait in ambush. He almost certainly would expect he was being followed.

When the vertical capstone, the red Navajo sandstone impregnated with black appeared to his right, Zack knew he was near the summit. He stayed clear of the trail, out of the open, keeping a careful watch as he progressed a step at a time. He had his mental bearings, knowing he was west of the arroyo where the cave was concealed. Brown would decide soon where to take his stand, where to deal justice to his father.

If the man was above him, the relative position of each of them was similar to the first ambush, but this time

Zack had no one to create a distraction for him. The ATV trail wound around to the left, where a gash in the mountain offered easier access to the summit plateau. It was the obvious access point and would be the obvious place for Brown to wait for him. From his current position, the capstone cliff rose above a tumble of rock chunks, a steep climb for fifteen or twenty feet, not far, but for that time Zack would be helpless to defend himself.

There were three possibilities, he decided. Brown could be waiting for him above the ATV trail, Brown could be waiting for him above this cliff, or Brown could have continued on, disregarding Zack.

He decided on scenario number three. He slung the rifle onto his back and scrambled over the boulders to the foot of the wall. Here again, the climb was not as difficult as it appeared from afar, but would require his concentration. He kept his mind blank, focused on one handhold or foothold at a time, always on the wall with three hand or footholds at one time. He was a little surprised when he pulled over the top to find a rifle barrel in his face.

# CHAPTER SIXTY

"Nice of you to join us," William Brown said. Zack stared into steely blue eyes and saw no mercy. He clambered up and over the edge when beckoned and at Brown's gesture unslung his rifle and let it drop to the ground. He noticed Brown the Elder, gagged with hands tied behind him, seated against a dwarf pinyon. Solemn eyes regarded Zack. William Brown kept his rifle barrel against Zack's back and patted him down, found the handgun, and tossed it away. He also found the plastic ties.

"Sit."

Zack did as instructed, sat cross-legged on a patch of open ground.

"I'm grateful you brought these ties along. My only set of handcuffs is in use. Hands behind your back."

Zack complied, felt his arms pulled up and back in a strong grasp, then his wrists cinched tight.

Brown walked around to face Zack, regarded him coldly. "I haven't had a chance to chat with dad here, so I'm not gonna bring you along with us. I got no reason to kill you, either. I'm sure your buddies will be along to set you loose soon enough. But I don't need you yelling and making it easier for them to find us. Now what can we use—"

His eye roamed over to his father, in shirt and vest. "Such a neat dude, my dad. I'll bet he's got a handkerchief." Brown rummaged in the president's vest pocket and came away with a white embroidered handkerchief. He balled it up and stuffed it in Zack's mouth.

Zack recoiled at the strong taste of cologne infused in it.

Brown was still eyeing him. "One more thing, I think." He hauled Zack to his feet and walked him toward the cliff edge. Zack felt instant panic and adrenalin surge through his body in equal measure. But rather than push him over, William stopped him at the edge and helped him sit, his legs out in front, parallel to the precipice. He took another tie and secured Zack's feet together. With a firm hold on the back of Zack's collar, he steadied him while he pushed Zack's secured feet around and over the cliff, then let go to study his handiwork. Zack's balance was precarious.

"I can't have you watching where we go, either. The less you know, the better for you." He slipped something over Zack's eyes and secured it tight at the back of his head.

Without sight, keeping his balance was much more difficult. Zack again had a surge of panic. It felt impossible not to teeter forward and fall off the cliff top. His abdominal muscles worked constantly for balance. He willed himself to stay calm. He heard Brown walk over to his father, and the older man's grunt as he was hauled to his feet.

"Okay, Papa, let's go meet our destiny."

Zack listened to the sound of steps on dry needles and twigs, the catch and release of brush until it gradually died away. Then nothing. Zack waited a while before he began to worm his butt back from the edge with slow, careful movements, inching bit by bit until the underside of his knees touched terra firma. Despite a strong tendency to lean forward, brought about by his arms secured behind him, he felt a little more secure. With one swift, calculated movement he fell back and to the side and with the fulcrum of balance on his hip swung his legs up onto solid ground. He lay there for minute, breathing hard from the struggle.

After catching his breath, he put the side of his face against the ground and scraped up and down in an effort to work the blindfold loose. The movement of his ear along the ground almost obscured the sound of approaching footsteps.

Zack froze, listened. The steps grew louder and came and stopped behind him. Zack's heart sank. Brown had decided he could not risk leaving him alive after all, was back now to finish the job. He waited for the push, muscles tensed.

"You look like you could you use some help, White Man."

Eagle Feather! His friend was here, impossibly, right when he needed him. He felt the pressure release on his wrists as the plastic tie came apart. There was pain while blood rushed back into his arms. He ignored it and pushed away the blindfold and removed the gag and blinked at the sudden light. He felt his legs snapped free.

He sat up, pivoted around on his butt. Eagle Feather sat on his haunches watching him, his face expressionless.

"How did you get yourself into such a pickle, White Man?"

"Where did you come from?"

"With my people, in a situation like this, an expression of gratitude would come first."

Zack grinned despite the pain. "I thought our relationship had moved beyond that."

Eagle Feather shook his head in wonderment. "No wonder your marriage has been rocky."

Zack didn't respond. He glanced around and realized Brown had taken his rifle. He stood, his balance precarious at first, and stumbled to the place Brown had tossed his pistol. It was still there. Zack picked it up and holstered it. Now he eyed Eagle Feather.

"Is it just the two of us?"

Eagle feather regarded him before answering. "In a manner of speaking."

"Did you see where they went?"

Eagle feather shook his head.

"I think I can guess," Zack said. "The cave."

Eagle Feather raised an eyebrow. "Why the cave?"

"I think it has to do with making his father face all his wrongdoings, in Brown's way of thinking. The cave and all its secrets must have come to symbolize that for him."

"Then what?"

366

"Then I think he will kill him." Zack was already beginning to move that way.

Eagle Feather laid a restraining hand on his arm. "Not so fast, White Man. We have time."

Zack stared at his friend, puzzled. "What do you mean? I think he intends to kill his father. We need to stop him."

"William Brown is not the only one up here who feels wronged. I think we should let it all play out."

Zack stared at his friend. "Whatever you think you know, I have a duty to perform. I have to try to save President Brown." He started walking in the direction of the hidden arroyo.

Eagle Feather shrugged and followed.

The terrain continued to rise, but gradually. A dark cloud had formed behind the summit directly in front of them casting shadow on the mountain, a late afternoon thunderstorm. Brown's tracks were easy to find in the soft sand but would disappear for long stretches on the slickrock. There were indications the older man had slowed or stopped and had been physically dragged to his feet until he resumed walking on his own. In ten minutes, they intersected the ATV trail and walking became easier. The trail led north and east, then jogged northwest. At that point, the Browns' footprints left it and followed a well-beaten path to the east, the one used by the FBI after the cave of bones was first discovered.

As they turned that way, Zack paused, looked at Eagle Feather. "What were you doing up here anyway?"

"Let us just say I was having a religious experience."

Zack stared at him, then resumed walking. He knew that was all he would get for now.

The tracks brought them to the head of the arroyo and descended into it. They moved cautiously here, knowing they could be targeted at any moment. When they reached the spot where Eagle Feather had first met Tubs, near the bottom of the headwall, a shot sounded. It seemed to come from beyond the copse of trees. Another split the air soon after, then another and another. They stood still, listening.

"Rifle," Eagle Feather said.

There was silence after that. The stillness lasted five long seconds, prolonged by Zack's tension. The rifle shots told their own story, the percussive reports spaced at first, rapid fire following; a message of fear and panic.

A roar shredded the silence, the bestial sound of some great predator. It pulsated off the arroyo walls. Then came a scream, a sound of incalculable horror. It grew in volume and shrillness. It expressed extreme pain and terror at a level beyond understanding. After an interminable time, the scream ended in a single cry, a human sound, followed by a hush.

Zack's hair stood on end, his nerves vibrated like strings on a violin, his breathing almost stopped. He had heard this sound long ago in a different place at the moment a nightmare predator he pursued found its prey. It had turned his body to jelly then, and it did so now.

Neither man spoke for several moments, each struggling for control. They stared at each other; faces drained of blood, eyes wide. There came a sudden crashing in the brush moving toward them. Instinct took over; Zack raised his weapon with an unsteady hand, removed the safety.

Eagle Feather placed a palm over Zack's revolver. "Wait," he whispered.

They waited. The thrashing slowed. President Josiah Brown appeared out of the trees, staggered toward them, fell to his knees, hands still manacled behind his back. The man's white face was speckled with red, as if he had measles. His shirtfront was smeared and red rivulets flowed across his copious stomach and descended toward his belt. He stared at them with unseeing eyes and hissed, "Help me."

Zack went to him. "Are you hurt? Is all this your blood?"

He shook his head. "My son is dead," he said. "I ran."

Zack grasped President Brown by his shoulders. "What happened?"

Josiah's stare went through and beyond Zack. "Help me. My son is dead."

"What was it?" Zack shook him gently.

"Help me," was the only response.

Eagle Feather put his water bottle to the man's lips. He drank. The water seemed to calm him.

"We have to go," Zack said. "You will be safe here."

"My son is dead," was the whispered reply.

Eagle Feather caught Zack's eye. "You do not need to go there. It is over."

Zack eyed his friend, shook his head. "I have to go."

Eagle Feather said nothing. The two men pulled President Brown to a sitting position against a tree.

"We will be back for you," Zack said. "I will try to find the key for your cuffs."

Eagle Feather led the way this time. They had no trouble back-tracking Josiah Brown toward the cave, despite growing darkness from the storm cloud. All along the way vegetation was crushed where his knees had landed from time to time, and spots of blood were plentiful.

A horrifying sight greeted them as they emerged from the wood. The platform stone was there as before, but a newly hewn stake six feet tall, the upper end tapered to a long sharp point, had been forced into it. William Brown's body lay skewered on it face upward, the stake passing through his back and out the middle of his chest. He had been thrust upon it with such power his body was halfway down the stake, suspended there with arms and feet dangling. His face was a twisted mask of such terror it was unrecognizable. Blood splattered and dripped everywhere.

For the second time in the space of minutes, Zack felt rising panic but fought it. He saw movement at the cave mouth.

"Something is in there."

"I know."

Before Zack could say more, thunder rumbled and lightening struck somewhere beyond the rim of the arroyo with a loud crack. He felt a strange vibration underfoot, heard a rumbling sound, low and far away. The sound and shaking grew in intensity. Zack stood, rooted.

Eagle Feather grabbed his arm. "Run, man," he shouted.

Zack ran. By now the earth trembled with such force he could barely stay upright. The trees before him swayed. When he could run no more without falling, he turned and looked back.

The sandstone wall over the cave mouth rippled like a pond in the wind. Spider webs of cracks appeared, widened. Chunks of rock began to fall, and then more, until the entire upper cliff face bulged like a tumorous growth, cracked open, and slid downward. Dust rose like smoke, spread and marched toward them. Zack watched the landslide of sandstone fall across the cave mouth like a waterfall. In seconds it piled higher than the entrance and spilled toward the altar stone, slammed onto the far end and flipped the slab over like an animal trap closing. William Brown and the stake that held him smacked into the rubble like a door slamming shut, and disappeared. The thick dust reached Zack. He put his arm across his eyes, turned away, knelt, and waited.

The trembling of the earth eased, the noise diminished to a final tattoo of falling rocks, and the dust began to settle. Zack searched for Eagle Feather, found him crouched just inside the tree line.

"You saw...?"

Eagle Feather nodded.

Zack stood. He brushed the thick layer of dust from his clothes while

Eagle Feather removed his dusty hat and slapped it against his thigh.

Zack looked at the Navajo, a question in his eyes.

"There is nothing more to be done here," his friend said in reply.

# CHAPTER SIXTY-ONE

The early morning crowd had gone their way, and customers slowed to a trickle at the Merry Wives Cafe. Two tables were pulled together in a corner. A woman and a cluster of men, sober with their coffees, held conversation in low tones.

"Thank you all for coming," the woman said. "I think it is important to review our processes and results after a case that involves several law enforcement agencies."

"Janice, whatever happened to Tubs?" Sheriff Rafferty asked.

"I'd tell you, but I'd have to kill you," Zack said from his corner seat, grinning.

Janice Hooper smiled. "Zack is right. Tubs went home—to see his family he hasn't seen for five years."

Rafferty raised his eyebrows. "Okay, I'll bite. Why hasn't he seen his family?"

"This may come as a surprise, maybe even a shock to some of you. Jack "Tubs" LeBaron doesn't exist. I can't tell you his actual name because he could be in danger from some activist members of the land use rights movement he infiltrated. Tubs is a special agent for one of the many US agencies, I'm not at liberty to say which one. He went undercover five years ago with the Oath Keepers, a radical group consisting of present and past lawmen and soldiers. This came right after the Bundy cattle range standoff, where a number of radical organizations had gathered. The Oath Keepers caused hostilities within the ranchers and the other groups. While there, Tubs grew close to certain members of the Bundy faction and along the way became privy to some well-kept Mormon secrets, one of which was the cave of bones. He befriended Randy Musser, hunted with him a number of times. He eventually learned Randy had been contracted by some influential Mormons to do a job, but Tubs didn't know exactly what. His focus shifted from the Oath Keepers to an attempt to uncover what appeared to be a Mormon underground conspiracy. Randy discovered his identity somehow and set him up to be killed. There were two attempts, both of which came very close to succeeding."

"Who knew about all this?" Rafferty demanded.

Janice gave him her brilliant smile. "No one. I just learned about it."

"So when we went to find him at Big Water...?" Zack's question dangled.

Janice placed a hand on his shoulder. "We didn't know who he was at the time. We saw him purely as a witness. On the other hand, he didn't know if he could trust us. That was a very dangerous period for him."

Jeffrey shifted in his chair. "We know now William Brown was the son of Josiah Brown and his runaway wife, and that he harbored deep hostility toward his father and his other wives, probably nurtured by his mother over many years. But how did the twins get involved in all this?"

Janice paused. "It gets complicated, but here's the short version. Both the LDS and FLDS churches became concerned the bones in the cave might be discovered. In the old days, bones were bones, but with modern technology came the tools to identify each bone in that cave. Remember, a limited number of people from each church knew about the cave, and even though the FLDS had split off long ago, the secrets in the cave were toxic to both churches. Some people formed a group to protect the secret, sort of a modern-day Avenging Angels."

Greg Stone, the BLM agent, spoke for the first time. "Why such concern about massacres and murders that happened so long ago? It isn't as if everyone doesn't already know about the Fancher Wagon Train and the three Powell Expedition members."

"There were more murders than that," Zack said.

Janice nodded. "Over the years, the cave became the depository for bodies some Mormons didn't want people to know about, accidental deaths or otherwise. There were some quite recent bones in there."

"The boy, Luke Wilson? Why was he killed?" That question came from Max Smith, the Washington County Sheriff.

Janice glanced at Zack, who answered for her. "Simply, the boy stumbled upon the cave while hiking. He saw the bones, reported it to the Kane County Sheriff's office, to the man who happened to be there, Chief Deputy William Brown."

Sheriff Rafferty let out an audible groan.

Zack continued. "By now Brown had connected with the Taylor twins in an official way, and nurtured their friendship as part of his growing scheme to exact revenge on his father. He told them about the Wilson boy's discovery, and they told their father Jacob. It appears Elder Taylor was part of the newly re-formed Avenging Angels and told his sons no one was to know about the cave, no matter what. The twins took his words as marching orders, brought William Brown into their confidence, and the scheme to quiet Luke Wilson was born."

"What about Jedediah?" Rafferty asked.

Jeffrey Harlow spoke up. "Many of you know my father-in-law had dementia, which combined with his zealous faith made him an easy man to manipulate. We don't yet know whose idea it was—I'd guess Stan Taylor—to trick Jedediah into believing he was receiving a revelation and a direct order from God, but it worked. Once poor Jedediah became fixated on kidnapping the boy and delivering him as a sacrifice somewhere on Canaan Mountain, he put his entire being into the effort. Zack believes it was William Brown who came up with the idea for the disembodied voice and the glowing cross that fooled the old man."

"Premeditated murder," Max said.

Janice shrugged. "We don't know that for sure. It could have started out as an attempt to scare the boy into silence."

"We know Jedediah's hanging was murder," Jeffrey said.

Janice nodded. "Forensic evidence conclusively proves William was present at the staged hanging of Jedediah and almost certainly murdered him."

"And the murdered high school girl was peripheral damage?" Rafferty looked at Zack.

"Yes, and the attempts to locate and kidnap my niece Prudence stemmed from the belief she had seen and could identify Jedediah."

"The house break-in?"

"That turned out to be Stanley Taylor. He has two minor bullet wounds that fit the bill."

There was a contemplative silence.

Jeffrey broke it. "Who killed my friend Dan Fogelberry?"

Janice shook her head. "We still don't know. We suspect it was a professional killer hired by one of the Avenging Angels out of Salt Lake City. We're quite sure the person who kidnapped Tubs in Mesquite and almost killed him was a professional. We also believe one of our FBI agents was an Avenging Angel. He was our leak. He shot Musser to keep him from talking. We are pretty sure of his identity." Her jaw was set.

Zack glanced at Janice. "The theft of bones from the lab at BYU, and the attempted assassination of Professor Philpott in his home—pros also?"

"We don't know for sure, but likely." Janice sighed. "This conspiracy of the churches is wide ranging. Just how many are involved, how and where this Avenging Angels group came together—all of this is under investigation but it may take years, if ever, to solve."

"I was first on the scene of the boy's murder, as you know, right after Tubs and Randy Musser," Jeffrey said. "It was a horrific scene, the boy stuck on that stake and all. I watched Stan and LeRoy's eyes when they first arrived. I could tell they were shocked, even though they tried to bluster through it. I don't think they did it, not from their reactions, anyway. So my question is, who actually killed the boy?"

Janice sighed. "As you might guess, both LeRoy and Stan point the finger at William Brown. They say Jedediah was instructed to deliver Luke to the trailhead and leave him there. After he drove away, the Taylor twins and Brown picked the boy up with their ATVs and took him to the mountain summit and over to the cave. The idea, according to the twins, was to leave him there wrapped in the shroud-like sheet, so when he regained consciousness he'd see the cave and the message would be clear."

"Why would William Brown kill the boy, especially in such a violent manner?" Greg Stone asked.

"I might be able to answer that," Rafferty said. "When I investigated his background in Minnesota, I learned he had a couple of misdemeanors registered against him as a teen, both about violence, both directed toward people of color."

"You think he was a racist."

Rafferty shrugged. "Seems likely. Since there are few people of color in my county, his prejudice wouldn't have shown itself here."

"That's a hell of a lot of anger in a man," Stone observed.

"With William Brown now unable to defend himself, and the twins adamant he was the killer, this discussion, for now, is moot," Janice said. "The other thing they both insist upon is there was someone else—actually they say something else—hanging about that cave. One says it was a bear-like monster, the other says it was a huge Indian complete with feather. Whatever it was, they were frightened by it. Anyone know what that's about?"

"It's not too hard to fool those boys," Max muttered.

"It would still require someone else to be up there."

"They might simply have seen a branch moving in the wind," Max said. "I wouldn't put much credence to it."

"We believe Randy Musser was hired by one or both churches to blow up the cave and seal it forever. Perhaps he was in it on the occasion they describe," Janice said.

"I'd say this discussion is moot as well," Rafferty said with a grin.

Janice smiled back. "I'll go along with that."

"What will happen to the Taylor twins?" Max asked.

Janice glanced around the table. "Both men have been arrested for conspiracy to commit kidnapping. Their father, Jacob Taylor, is being questioned in regard to a possible connection with the Avenging Angels group." She shook her head. "I don't expect much, however."

"Dan's killer will never be brought to justice?" Jeffrey asked.

"We can only hope an ongoing investigation of the Avenging Angels will yield results."

"And President Brown?"

"Josiah Brown has no charges against him. He may have been involved in trying to conceal the existence of the cave, but that's no crime in itself." Janice glanced around the table for reaction, got none. "He's in the hospital. He has no actual injuries beyond bruises and a laceration or two, but they want to keep an eye on him. He was severely traumatized. He watched as his wives were murdered before his eyes, was manacled and dragged up that mountain. God knows what happened at the cave"— she turned to Zack— "unless perhaps you do."

Zack glanced at her. "I had not yet reached the cave when President Brown somehow escaped. I found him running away with his hands cuffed behind his back. I sat him at a tree, told him I'd try to retrieve the key to the handcuffs and went on. When I reached the cave meadow, I saw William Brown there. I felt a tremor underfoot. The entire wall above the cave began to disintegrate and collapse. Brown was in the wrong place. When I could see through the dust again, he was gone, buried under tons of rock. I guess the church finally got its wish; the cave is sealed." Zack was aware of every eye on him.

"What caused the slide?" Rafferty asked.

"A localized quake?" Stone suggested.

"I spoke to several people who were on the mountain at the same time," Max said. "No one else felt a thing."

"I saw a storm cloud gathering up there," Janice said with a shrug. "Maybe that had something to do with it. Lightening or something?" She smiled at the skepticism around the table. "Before he left, Tubs suggested an interesting theory. He wondered if Randy Musser had already set charges to seal the cave, but was interrupted. Then maybe lightening from the storm...?" She flashed a brilliant smile. "Well, it's the best of a bad lot until a better idea comes along."

There was a long period of silence.

"Well," said Rafferty, "are we done? How about some breakfast?"

* * * * *

When Zack arrived at the campground, Eagle Feather's truck was there. He found his friend seated cross-legged next to the fire pit, now cold ashes and charred wood. The Navajo appeared to be meditating. Zack sat on the nearby picnic bench and waited.

It was a beautiful morning, warm but with a cool edge to the breeze. A few puffy white clouds skimmed the top of the Vermillion Cliffs, whose abrupt sandstone precipices shone a golden red hue in affirmation of their name. The

Uinkaret Plateau vanished into the farthest haze fifty miles away, flat as a table top.

After several silent minutes, the Navajo stirred.

"Do you feel it, White Man? Do you feel the peace, the mystery, the timelessness of this place? How can people question the infinite possibilities in a land such as this? Out here"—he waved an arm in a wide sweep—"humans are but a speck of dust, a flea in a carpet. A landscape on this scale demands giants, creatures of great intelligence, of infinite power and wisdom. If one such being should emerge, shake off the cloak of time for a short while, why would we be surprised, doubt our senses? We are the ones who do not fit this environment, not them."

"Few people are able to grasp your perspective, my friend. Humans are ever self-centered," Zack said.

Eagle Feather gave one of his rare smiles. "Sometimes, White Man, I begin to think you understand."

**If you enjoyed this novel please share your thoughts with others by submitting a review on this book's page at Amazon.com.**

# ABOUT THE AUTHOR

R Lawson Gamble enjoys the Southwest, great stories, Indian lore, and scary paranormal possibilities, all of which find their way into the Zack Tolliver, FBI crime mysteries. He lives in Los Alamos among California's Golden Hills.

\* \* \* \* \*

What brought Zack Tolliver to Tuba City, Arizona and the Navajo Nation in the first place? What was it like when Zack and Eagle Feather met? Watch for a new novella this Fall 2018 with answers to those questions and more. More information available at RLawsonGamble.com.

www.ingramcontent.com/pod-product-compliance
Lightning Source LLC
Chambersburg PA
CBHW020257030726
47499CB00001B/231